Praise for R

'If you like your chick-lit with a dash of intelligent social commentary, *Just One Wish* is the perfect summer read. Rachael Johns's latest novel is sparklingly funny, quirky and totally of this moment.' —*Herald Sun*

'Johns knows how to weave the experiences of different generations of women together, with nuance and sensitivity, understanding how competing contexts shape women's choices ... Johns has a unmistakable talent for storytelling, while throwing a compelling romance in to hook us even further. Exploring themes like motherhood, the roles of women, and lost love, *Just One Wish* will make you look at the women in your own life and wonder what stories they haven't told.' —Mamamia

'Johns draws readers in with her richly complex characters.' —*The Daily Telegraph* on *Just One Wish*

'Polished writing, and great dialogue drive this story forward. The perfectly structured plot holds plenty of surprises, but it's the beautifully crafted characters that are the glue in this wonderful novel. I adored all three women, but especially Alice. There are also a whole cast of colourful, glorious minor characters, and an unusual family structure that is a delight to read ... Utterly delightful ... and predictably great.' —Better Reading on *Just One Wish*

'*Just One Wish* is a passionate and powerful family saga. It is a book that is going to have its readers talking about it ... Whether you are a fan of Rachael's or a debut reader of hers then you are going to enjoy this book.'—Book in One Hand Coffee in Another

'Rachael Johns once again provides her readers with a fabulous contemporary family drama through the life experiences and choices of three generations of women ... *Just One Wish* is most certainly a realistic portrayal of the complexity of modern day families that is sure to resonate with many readers.' —Great Reads and Tea Leaves

'*Just One Wish* is a fabulous novel of family love, sorrow, secrets, betrayal and heartbreak.' —Beauty and Lace

'The themes of infertility and pregnancy loss are movingly interwoven into a multifaceted story ... [Rachael Johns] writes wisely and naively, hopefully and cynically, and there's a character for everyone to identify with in *Lost Without You*. A gorgeously moving read.' —Mamamia

'Heart-warming and compassionate ... Any book lover interested in life's emotional complexities and in the events that define and alter us, will be engrossed in *Lost Without You*.' —Better Reading

'A delightful glimpse into the life of families and friends who come together in the most unexpected ways.' —Starts at 60 on *Lost Without You*

'Full of heartache and joy with a twist that keeps the pages turning ... *The Greatest Gift* will appeal to fans of Jojo Moyes and Monica McInerney.' —*Australian Books + Publishing*

'I really have no idea where to start because this book was an amazing gift ... Once again Johns has written a story that will appeal to different types of readers and it is clear that her talent is becoming more finely honed with every release.' —Beauty and Lace on *The Greatest Gift*

'Heartbreaking and heartwarming in equal parts, Rachael Johns' *The Greatest Gift* takes readers on a rollercoaster ride of emotions. My advice? Make sure you have tissues handy!' —Lisa Ireland, author of *The Shape of Us*

'Rachael Johns has done it again, writing a book that you want to devour in one sitting, and then turn back to the first page to savour it all over again. I loved the characters of Harper and Jasper; their stories made me laugh and cry, and ache and cheer and ultimately reflect on all the many facets of that extraordinary journey called motherhood.' —Natasha Lester, author of *A Kiss From Mr Fitzgerald,* on *The Greatest Gift*

'A beautiful story of love and loss, heartbreak and hope—this is Rachael Johns at her very finest. With achingly endearing characters and a storyline that packs a punch, *The Greatest Gift* will make your heart swell as you reach for the tissues and leave you smiling when you turn the final pages. Told with warmth, empathy and wisdom, it's a book that will appeal to everyone who has laid plans for their life and discovered that life is something that can't be controlled and that even if you think you have it all worked out, you never know what's around the corner. My favourite Rachael Johns by a country mile.' —Tess Woods, author of *Love at First Flight*

'The bond between Flick, Neve, and Emma blossomed as their sons grew up, but even best friends keep secrets from one another ... Fans of emotional, issue driven women's fiction will welcome Johns' US women's fiction debut.' —*Booklist* on *The Art of Keeping Secrets*

'... a compelling and poignant story of dark secrets and turbulent relationships ... I fell completely in love with the well-drawn characters of Flick, Emma and Neve. They were funny and flawed and filled with the kind of raw vulnerability that makes your heart ache for them.' —Nicola Moriarty, bestselling author of *The Fifth Letter,* on *The Art of Keeping Secrets*

'Written with compassion and real insight, *The Art of Keeping Secrets* peeks inside the lives of three ordinary women and the surprising secrets they live with. Utterly absorbing and wonderfully written, Johns explores what secrets can do to a relationship, and pulls apart the notion that some secrets are best kept. It is that gripping novel that, once started, will not allow you to do anything else until the final secret has been revealed.' —Sally Hepworth, bestselling author of *The Secrets of Midwives*

'A fascinating and deeply moving tale of friendship, family and of course—secrets. These characters will latch onto your heart and refuse to let it go.' —*USA Today* bestselling author Kelly Rimmer on *The Art of Keeping Secrets*

'Rachael Johns writes with warmth and heart, her easy, fluent style revealing an emotional intelligence and firm embrace of the things in life that matter, like female friendship.' —*The Age* on *Lost Without You*

Rachael Johns is an English teacher by trade, a mum 24/7, a Diet Coke addict, a cat lover and chronic arachnophobe. She is also the bestselling, ABIA-winning author of *The Patterson Girls* and a number of other romance and women's fiction books including *The Art of Keeping Secrets*, *The Greatest Gift, Lost Without You*, *Just One Wish* and the recent bestseller *Something to Talk About*. Rachael rarely sleeps, never irons and loves nothing more than sitting in bed with her laptop and imagining her own stories. She is currently Australia's leading writer of contemporary relationship stories around women's issues, a genre she has coined 'life-lit'.

Rachael lives in the Swan Valley with her hyperactive husband, three mostly gorgeous heroes-in-training, two ravenous cats, a cantankerous bird and a very badly behaved dog.

Rachael loves to hear from readers and can be contacted via her website rachaeljohns.com. She is also on Facebook and Instagram.

Also by Rachael Johns:

The Patterson Girls
The Art of Keeping Secrets
The Greatest Gift
Lost Without You
Just One Wish

The Rose Hill novels
Talk of the Town
Something to Talk About

The Bunyip Bay novels
Outback Dreams
Outback Blaze
Outback Ghost
Outback Sisters

The Hope Junction novels
Jilted
The Road to Hope
Man Drought
The Kissing Season (e-novella)
The Next Season (e-novella)
Secret Confessions Down and Dusty: Casey (e-novella)

Rachael Johns

Flying the Nest

FICTION
HQ

First Published 2020
First Australian Paperback Edition 2020
ISBN 9781489276810

This is a work of fiction. Names, characters, places, and incidents are either the product of the author's imagination or are used fictitiously, and any resemblance to actual persons, living or dead, business establishments, events, or locales is entirely coincidental.

Published by
HQ Fiction
An imprint of Harlequin Enterprises (Australia) Pty Limited (ABN 47 001 180 918), a subsidiary of HarperCollins Publishers Australia Pty Limited (ABN 36 009 913 517)
Level 13, 201 Elizabeth St
SYDNEY NSW 2000
AUSTRALIA

A catalogue record for this book is available from the National Library of Australia
www.librariesaustralia.nla.gov.au

Printed and bound in Australia by McPherson's Printing Group

MIX
Paper from responsible sources
FSC
www.fsc.org
FSC® C001695

This one's for the boy who broke my heart at seventeen, which led me to start writing. It's probably about time I thanked you!

I married beneath me. All women do.

—Nancy Astor

1

Perth

It was seven o'clock in the morning and I was cutting oranges for Payton's soccer game when Adrian casually asked if I'd heard of nest parenting.

I paused and searched my memory. It sounded vaguely familiar—like I'd read about the concept online or heard it discussed in one of the many podcasts I listened to. Although I'm almost forty, I pride myself on my memory and, sure enough, I recalled there was a mum who had a kid in the year below at Saxon's school who was nest parenting with her husband. Or rather *ex*-husband!

'Yeah, what about it?' I said, as I bent to get a large container from our Tupperware drawer.

Adrian took a sip of his coffee, then, 'I was thinking we should give it a try.'

And *that* is the exact moment the bottom fell out of my world!

2

I had to have heard wrong or at least misunderstood. Or maybe Adrian had.

How did he even know what nest parenting was? It wasn't like he usually concerned himself with the day-to-day minutiae of our kids' world, never mind other people's. Adrian's world revolved around his podiatry clinic and (currently) cycling.

So, perhaps he thought nest parenting was something else—possibly something like leaving Saxon at home to look after Payton while we had a dirty weekend away down south. It had been a while since we'd had much 'alone' time, and while I didn't really miss frequent sex, my husband was as red-blooded a male as they came. When we'd first got together, we'd had sex *every* day—sometimes two or three times—but that was over twenty years ago when we were young and childfree, before life and responsibility got in our way. And, from the way my other mum friends talked, our ritual bonk on Saturday night was quite normal.

But before I had the chance to ask him what exactly he was talking about, Payton skipped into the kitchen, proudly wearing her soccer uniform, her socks pulled up to her knees, her long, golden brown hair pulled back in a high ponytail and her usual bright smile lighting her face.

'You guys ready to go?' she asked, thankfully oblivious to the dark cloud that had descended upon the room. 'I don't want to miss pre-game training. I know summer soccer is only supposed to be for *fun*, but coach says if we work on our team communication and win this game, we have a real chance of getting in the finals this year.'

'Course we are, kiddo.' Adrian dumped his mug in the sink and reached out to ruffle her hair. She ducked just in time so as not to spoil her look. She may only be ten and what some of my friends called a tomboy, but she cared immensely about her appearance. Almost as much as she cared about her juggle record.

'Mum?' Payton whined. '*What* are you doing?'

I blinked, realising that I was frozen, still semi-bent over the Tupperware drawer, my hand tightly gripping the container. Straightening fast, I said, 'Just organising the oranges,' but my voice didn't sound like mine.

My daughter rolled her eyes and gave me a look that only teenage girls should give their mothers. Payton was definitely ten going on nineteen.

As she and Adrian started out of the kitchen towards the front door, my hands shook and my eyes prickled as I placed the oranges into the container and shut the lid. What if my husband *did* know what he was talking about? Was this his less-than-subtle way of telling me he wanted a divorce?

Impossible. I forced the thought out of my head as I grabbed the container off the kitchen counter and followed after them, pausing briefly in the hallway to check on Saxon. I opened his bedroom door as quietly as possible.

'Mum?' came his sleep-soaked voice from the bed where our dog Charlie was slumbering beside him. I had an urge to curl up with them and slide my fingers through the dog's comforting black fur.

'Hey honey, we're off to Payton's game. There's some pancakes in the microwave—' pancakes I'd made *before* Adrian's bombshell, '—for breakfast.'

'Thanks,' he mumbled as he pulled his doona back over his head. 'Love you.'

'I love you too.'

Despite the quake in my heart, I smiled as a rush of love for my son filled my whole being. Sax had only started sleeping in over the last couple of months. Before that he was an early riser like Adrian and Payton, but he'd also shot up recently so obviously needed his sleep. Although at almost fifteen he was smack bang in the middle of his teens, we hadn't had the drama that many of my friends had with their adolescent boys. Sure, he had the occasional morning grump and sometimes talked back, but he worked hard at school and I never had to nag him about practising his guitar.

The horn beeping in our driveway jolted me from my thoughts and snapped me back to reality. With a deep sigh, I retreated from the safety of my son's room and headed out to the car.

'What took you so long?' Payton asked from the back seat where she was doing some kind of skill work with her bright pink soccer ball. I didn't have the energy to tell her not to. Adrian was driving; if he found it distracting, he could reprimand her. Why did I always have to be the bad cop?

'I was just saying goodbye to Saxon.' I snapped my seatbelt in place and sank back into the passenger seat.

'Is he going to music practice this arvo?' Adrian asked as he reversed *my* wagon out of our driveway. His second-hand sports car wasn't practical when we travelled as a family.

'I don't know.' My tone was terse. Saxon and his band usually hung out every Sunday afternoon—I didn't see why today would be any different—but I wasn't in the mood for small talk.

Adrian nodded and turned his attention to the road, while Payton talked about who knows what. Probably something to do with the imminent game or soccer in general. Usually her incessant chatter drove me mad, but today I was grateful for it. It meant Adrian didn't try to make any further conversation and I didn't blurt out the question that was on repeat in my head while our daughter was in our presence.

Do you want to leave me?

I racked my mind for signs that should have alerted me to something like this, but nothing seemed to have changed between us in the last few months. Sure, life had been hectic—with the kids and the clinic—but that wasn't exactly new, and I couldn't pinpoint anything specific. Finally, we arrived at the oval and I couldn't escape the car fast enough.

'Can I get you a drink?' Adrian asked, nodding towards the coffee van parked nearby. Our daughter had already shot off towards the pitch where her teammates were gathering, their parents setting up folding chairs and no doubt making small talk about their post-game plans.

'No, thank you.' I couldn't bring myself to accept anything from him right now. 'You can tell me what the hell is going on instead. What exactly do you mean when you say *we* should give nest parenting a try? Do you even know what it is? Is this some kind of joke?'

'*Ash*,' Adrian said in the tone he used whenever he thought I was being unreasonable. 'This probably isn't the place to have this conversation.'

I glared at him. 'You were the one who dropped it on me in the kitchen five minutes before we were due to go out. Just tell me one thing, what do you think nest parenting is?'

I saw his Adam's apple slowly slide up and down before he said, 'It's when a couple separates and instead of moving the kids back and forth between their new places, they stay in the family home and the parents take turns living there with them.'

'Oh my God.' My hand rushed to my chest and my legs wobbled. It was a lovely summer morning, but ice flooded through me. 'You want us to separate?'

Before he could reply, the parents of one of Payton's teammates chorused, 'Morning Adrian, morning Ashling.'

Adrian turned and smiled. 'Hey Tonia, hey Manish.' But I was frozen.

'Lovely morning for it, isn't it?' Manish replied as they both came up beside us.

Somehow, I managed to paste a smile on my face and blink back my tears. 'Just peachy,' I said, before giving Tonia a hug.

The four of us walked to join the other parents on the sidelines and Adrian set up our chairs, as if everything was normal. Payton and her team did vigorous warm-up exercises, the other parents' conversation buzzed around me, and then the ref blew the whistle to start the game as if this was just another Sunday morning soccer game.

But nothing was normal anymore. Everything had changed.

Adrian wanted us to separate, which was one tiny step from divorce.

My chest tingled, my heart palpitating so fast I thought I was in danger of cardiac arrest. It was like I'd woken up from my worst nightmare only to discover it was real. There was not enough oxygen in the fresh morning air to fill my lungs.

'You okay, Ash?' At Tonia's question I felt her hand gently touch my arm.

Okay? I almost laughed—I was so far from okay I wasn't sure I'd ever be okay again. Swallowing, I shrugged. 'Of course. Why wouldn't I be?'

'You just seem kinda quiet.'

Usually I cheered along with the rest of the soccer mums and dads, screaming until my throat went hoarse, but we were fifteen minutes into the first half and I'd barely made a noise, unable to tell you who'd kicked goals or even if there had been any.

'I'm just tired,' I lied.

Tonia nodded, placated by my reply, and turned her attention back to the game. Let's face it, what mother of school-aged kids wasn't permanently exhausted?

Although we sat side by side, Adrian and I barely said a word to each other during the rest of the game. Was this how it was going to be in the future? The two of us attending our kids' events separately, or worse, taking turns and only speaking if we had to make arrangements about Saxon and Payton?

Oh God. I felt my battle to withhold my tears failing. How long was left in this blasted game? I needed to escape before I lost it completely, right here in front of a bunch of people who were barely more than strangers.

I shouldn't have asked him. How on earth was I supposed to get through the next hour with *this* hanging over me? And maybe if I hadn't pushed him, he'd have realised the error of his ways before we had the chance to talk properly. Now, the S-word was out there, and it couldn't be unsaid.

Somehow, I survived to the end of the game. Payton's team won, so all around us parents and kids were jumping up and down, hugging and thumping each other on the back. I tried to show enthusiasm and if I didn't manage, thankfully no one seemed to notice. Except Adrian. Our eyes met as we started to gather up our things and he mouthed 'sorry' to me.

I looked away. That was the last thing I wanted him to say.

3

I'd had some pretty bad days in my thirty-nine years—the day I found out my parents were getting a divorce, the day my grandma who was the only family member I'd ever felt close to died, the time I got my period and it soaked right through my school uniform and everybody in my maths class laughed, and the day my obstetrician told me she couldn't detect a heartbeat for my first child—but today was up there with all of them.

Today, my son went off to band practice in the afternoon, my daughter went down the road to play with her friend from school and my husband poured me a glass of wine. He came into our bedroom where I'd retreated post-soccer feigning a headache, sat down on the bed and said, 'Since the kids are both out of the house, now's probably a good time to have our chat.'

Our chat? As if I had any ownership or say in any of this. Ignoring the glass of wine, I hugged my knees to my chest and pulled the bedcovers up to my chin. 'You want a divorce?'

He put my drink down on the bedside table and sighed. 'I want us to take a break. Have a trial separation.'

I shook my head, unable to wrap my head around any of this. Suddenly the final piece of the puzzle landed. The less-frequent-than-usual sex we'd been having the last few months, Adrian's extra-long cycling sessions and new membership at a gym. 'Who is she?'

'What?' He recoiled slightly. 'I'm not having an affair. I'd never do that to you.'

Relief washed through me. If there wasn't another woman, then this was fixable. But also damn confusing. 'Then why?'

'I … I don't think I'm in love with you.' At the blank look on my face, he added, 'Ash, you can't tell me *you've* been happy with the way things have been these last couple of years?'

Years? This had been going on that long? While I'd been ironing his shirts, polishing his shoes and making his damn lunches, he'd been falling out of love.

'Don't call me Ash,' I snapped. Nicknames were a term of endearment and I felt anything but endearing towards him right now.

But I had to get over my own shock and hurt and think about our children. 'You took marriage vows. You can't just give up on me, on the kids, on us. Let's go to marriage counselling. Make more of an effort to have date nights. Spend time together. Maybe we can go to Bali, just the two of us; I'm sure Hayley would look after the kids.'

Adrian sighed deeply as he shook his head. 'I don't think there's any point. Twenty years is a good innings, considering we got married young, but we've both grown up in that time, changed. I don't want to stay with you simply because we signed a bit of paper when we were kids. Most of my friends have slept with tonnes of women—I've only ever been with you.'

Nausea whirled in my gut—would he simply erase the last twenty-two years if he could?—but I swallowed it down, not wanting this stranger to see my weakness. 'You want to fuck other women?'

'Ash.' He flinched. 'Don't use that kind of language—it doesn't suit you.'

'How do you know what suits me? You've just been telling me how we've grown apart, how we're different than we once were. Well, do you? Do you want to have sex with other women? Is *that* what this is about?'

After a long pause he nodded but wasn't man enough to meet my gaze.

His silent admission sucked the breath from my lungs. I threw back the bedcovers and fled into the ensuite, tears already barrelling down my cheeks.

Adrian hurried after me, but I locked the door before he could get in. If I no longer satisfied him, if he wouldn't even consider counselling, then I was done talking.

'Ashling, please. You'll always be important to me, you're the mother of my children. Wouldn't you rather this than have me keep pretending and go behind your back?'

Sitting on the toilet seat, I shook my head, my whole body trembling. He was making out like he was a saint for *not* having an affair? That I should be grateful, maybe even give him a medal or something for showing such restraint?

When I didn't reply, he was quiet for a few moments and I thought maybe he'd gone. Where, I didn't know. Out of the room? Or out of the house? What exactly would happen now? How was I supposed to deal with this? What would I tell my children?

Adrian only gave me five seconds' peace—if anyone could call the terrifying questions swirling round my head that—before he knocked on the door. 'Open up, we need to finish our conversation.'

'No,' I retorted, sounding stronger than I felt. 'If you don't want to be married anymore, then you no longer have the right to make decisions about what *we* need.'

'Fine.' I could hear the anger and impatience in his voice. Well, too bad—I wasn't going to make this easy for him. 'But what about what the kids need? We should discuss what we're going to tell them, before they get home.'

His mention of my babies hit me hard in the gut. This was the absolute last thing I'd ever wanted for them.

'You want to tell them *today*?' I shouted at the door.

'I don't see any point in prolonging the agony. We can tell them over dinner and then I'll go.'

If he really gave a damn about Saxon and Payton, he wouldn't be doing this. And, if he'd ever truly cared about me, the least he could do was give me a few days to get used to the idea, but he probably couldn't wait a second longer to get on Tinder. I shuddered at the thought of my husband swiping right (or was it left?) on younger women who had perkier breasts and were far more adventurous in bed than me.

Yanking toilet paper off the roll, I wiped my eyes, unlocked the door and confronted him. 'Where are you going to go?'

4

'Payton, can you be quiet for a minute?' Adrian asked when we were halfway through our evening meal of takeaway from the local Chinese restaurant. After a surprisingly civil end to our conversation this afternoon, he'd been savvy enough to know I wasn't in the mood to make dinner.

Our daughter glared at him, shocked and irritated to be interrupted during her monologue on her plans to be captain of the Matildas by the time she was twenty-one.

'Your mother and I have something important to discuss with you.' Adrian sounded more nervous than I'd ever heard him, and I couldn't help noticing he'd barely eaten any of his dinner.

Well, good—although I'd do anything not to hurt my children, I didn't want this to be easy for him.

Payton and Saxon looked to me, clearly wondering what was going on, so I took a sip of my wine—a glass I'd poured myself, thank you very much—and looked to their father. He'd wanted me to tell them, but I'd flat out refused. This was his doing; he could do the dirty work.

After a long pause, Adrian cleared his throat. 'Your mother and I know this will be hard for you both to comprehend ...'

My fingers tightened around the stem of my wineglass. His sudden frequent use of the phrase 'your mother and I' grated on my already fractious nerves.

'But the last few years haven't been satisfying for either of us. We've grown apart. And although we both love you more than anything in the world, we no longer love each other.'

'You're getting a divorce?'

I reached out to grab Saxon's hand, but he snatched it back.

Payton's mouth gaped open, but no sound came out—it appeared she was suffering a rare case of not knowing what to say. As a tear trickled down her cheek, my own anger curled in my belly like a beast ready to strike. How dare Adrian make out this was a mutual decision. I wanted to yell my objection, to tell my children that I still loved their father with all my heart and didn't want any of this any more than they did, but I'd promised Adrian we'd present a united front.

It's for the best, he'd told me earlier. And deep down, *dammit*, I agreed.

So instead I sat there, my fists clenched, biting my tongue so hard I tasted blood as he explained to the kids how this separation would work. I'd thought my heart already smashed to smithereens, but it shattered even more as I watched my children come apart. Saxon's face scrunched up—he was clearly trying not to cry but Payton sobbed like a baby.

I reached out and dragged her onto my lap. Suddenly I wasn't sure if this frank conversation with all of us together was actually any better than the way I'd discovered my parents were separating—

my mum's hairdresser's daughter delivering the news in the middle of the school playground.

Then again, was there any good way to find out your family was being ripped apart?

I'd give Adrian this though, he'd had it all worked out by the time he finally hit me with his decision. If I wasn't so shocked and broken inside, I might have actually been impressed by how much he'd thought everything through, by all the research he'd done into various custody options.

He *understood* how traumatic my parents' divorce had been for me, which was why he wanted to be open and upfront with our children.

He *understood* I probably felt angry and upset—*no kidding*—but had pleaded that I think of the children and try not to show or voice my fury around them.

He *understood* I'd hated being tossed from one parent to the other, one weekend to the next—thrown back and forth like an unwanted tennis ball—which was why *he'd* decided the nest-parenting model would be a good option for us.

'Nest parenting?' Saxon scoffed. 'What kind of crap-arse term is that?'

'Look, it doesn't matter what it's called,' Adrian said, clearly trying to keep his cool at Saxon's uncharacteristic outburst. 'What matters is that this arrangement will be the least disruptive for you and Payton.'

'And where are you and Mum going to live on your weeks off?' Saxon made it sound like we'd be going on holidays, but everything about this felt like hell not paradise to me. The thought of not seeing my son and daughter every day, of being without them for a whole week at a time, was worse than any kind of physical torture anyone could have inflicted on me.

'I'm going to be staying with Uncle Brad, and your mother ...' Adrian's voice drifted off as he looked to me.

While he planned on living it up with his eternally single younger brother—they'd probably go clubbing every night like the teenagers they wished they were—he'd suggested I go stay with my mum or dad, which only proved how little he cared about me. I had no desire to move in with either of them. Not even temporarily.

Part of the appeal of getting married young was finally being able to leave both my parents, their selfish shenanigans and their games of playing me off against each other behind. A game they still weren't above.

'I'm ... I'm ... I'm going to stay with a friend,' I said finally. *Until your father comes to his senses and begs me to take him back.*

In the hours after our discussion this afternoon, I'd calmed down enough to think logically. Adrian might like the idea of being a single man about town one week and a devoted single dad the next, but the novelty of both would quickly wear thin. He was the type of guy who liked to be looked after. He couldn't cook and barely knew how to use the washing machine. This was obviously some kind of midlife crisis.

'Which friend?' Payton asked.

'I don't know yet, honey.' I stroked her hair, making the most of having her head resting on my chest as she clung tightly to me. If Adrian had his way, this kind of two-way comfort would only be available every second week.

'Maybe you can stay with Aunty Hayley?' she suggested, her voice squeaky like a mouse.

That had been Adrian's other suggestion, but while Hayley had been my best friend since we were five years old, she was also his twin sister. Did she already know about his plans? They weren't as close as some twins, definitely not as close as she and I were, but they did talk frequently, and the thought of them discussing the problems in our marriage behind my back made me feel ill. But no, surely Hayley would have given me the heads-up if she'd had any idea.

'Maybe.' I squeezed Payton's hand. 'But I don't want you two to worry about me. I'll be fine.' Another lie; see what Adrian was turning me into.

'Anyway, do either of you have any questions?' he asked.

Saxon, still glaring into his now-empty plate, shook his head. A scowl had replaced his usually beautiful smile and the creases on his forehead only intensified my anger towards Adrian. Had he really given any thought to how this would affect our kids?

Nest parenting might in theory minimise stress on the children, but divorce was still divorce. Saxon and Payton would still have separated parents and all the agony that came with that—the birthdays and holidays with only one parent; being introduced to and expected to like new partners and sometimes their children; and worst of all, the snarky remarks from one parent about the other, which always happened despite the best intentions.

No, I couldn't let myself think that far ahead. No matter what Adrian thought, I would *not* let us get to that stage.

'Will you both still come to all my soccer games?' Payton asked, looking from her father and then back to me.

'Of course,' I said, before Adrian could say otherwise. 'We'll still be your number one cheer squad.'

Adrian tossed her a clearly forced smile and nodded. 'Well, I think that's it then.' He stood and started collecting the takeaway containers from the table. 'I'll be off to Uncle Brad's now.'

After dumping the containers in the rubbish bin, Adrian dropped a kiss on Payton's head—'Night, poppet'—and then went to hug Saxon goodbye, but he shoved back his chair and stormed off to his room. His door slammed, reverberating through the house moments later.

Adrian looked at me in shock.

I rolled my eyes. 'What did you expect?'

Without another word, he grabbed his already packed bag and left.

Payton went off to have a shower while I finished tidying up the kitchen and then I snuggled up with her in my marital bed while she cried herself to sleep.

She wasn't the only one in tears.

5

The following morning Saxon still wasn't talking to us. Well, I assumed the silent treatment he gave me as he shoved six Weet-Bix down his throat before hurrying out the door would apply to his father as well, if he were actually here. Then again, if Adrian was still here, Saxon wouldn't be in a rare strop. A fresh bout of rage engulfed me, and I wondered how long this would last—which of my men would cave first?

I zipped up Payton's lunch bag and hollered down the hallway. 'Sweetheart. Time to get up!' Usually she rose long before me but I guessed the previous evening's turmoil had exhausted her.

'Coming, Mum.'

A few minutes later she padded into the kitchen in bare feet and perched herself on a stool at the breakfast bar. I pushed a plate of Vegemite toast and a glass of milk towards her. 'Morning, gorgeous.'

She made a face at the toast. 'Can I stay home from school? I feel sick.'

Instinctively, I put my hand out to feel her forehead. 'What's wrong? Do you have a tummy ache?'

'I just feel sore, in here,' she said, pointing to her chest and confirming what I already suspected.

'Oh sweetheart.' I walked around the counter and pulled her into a hug. 'I know exactly how you feel.'

Part of me welcomed the idea of my girl staying home to keep me company—we could watch movies on the couch and drown our sorrows with ice-cream and chocolate—but would that be the best thing for her? At school, she'd be so busy she hopefully wouldn't have time to dwell on her broken family. Also, if she stayed home, I'd be forced to be strong for her, when simply dragging myself out of bed and into the shower had been difficult enough. If it wasn't for my kids, I'd probably have drunk my weight in wine last night and be nursing a severe hangover today.

This was all happening so fast. Yesterday morning I'd been a married mother of two. Now, here I was, facing divorce, single-parenthood, and all the hardships that came with it. I needed a few hours to myself to get my head straight, but what did Payton need?

Damn Adrian for putting me in this quandary.

I was about to relent when my phone beeped with a text from Hayley: *Will be at your place by 10 to bitch about my bastard brother!*

I stifled my first smile in twenty-four hours—Hayley could always make me laugh even in the most dire situations.

'How about you go to school this morning and I'll pick you up early this afternoon,' I suggested.

Thankfully she welcomed this compromise and got ready for the day without much encouragement.

Although Payton was in Year 5, I was very involved at her school and had a group of mum friends I'd known since she was in Kinder. Most days when I dropped her off or picked her up, I got out of my car and socialised with these women. I wouldn't say we'd be close if it weren't for the kids, but we'd been on oodles of committees together and enjoyed enough mums' nights out that some minor confidences had been shared.

Surface friends, I'd call them; nothing like the bond I shared with Hayley.

Today the thought of facing them terrified me. Surely they'd notice my puffy eyes and wonder what was up. That's if they hadn't already heard my news. Adrian cycled with a few of the other dads and I knew they had a WhatsApp group where they shared not only details of upcoming runs but also stupid jokes and other stuff. Stuff like marital splits? I cringed.

But while logic told me Adrian wasn't that much of a wanker that he'd have sent a group announcement, nothing felt certain anymore and I wasn't ready to answer questions about my private life, so I dropped Payton off in the Kiss and Drive and said I'd see her at lunchtime.

With over an hour till Hayley's arrival, I stopped at Woolies on the way home as I did every Monday. After a weekend with two kids at home—one of whom was a hollow-legged teenage boy—the cupboards were bare. Even if our world was falling apart, we had to eat.

Suddenly a thought struck—what on earth would my kids live on when it was Adrian's week with them? His idea of a balanced meal was a piece of steak and frozen chips with ice-cream for dessert. *Protein, carbs, veggies and dairy.* I used to find it cute when he said things like that, but now that it might be about to become my children's reality, it wasn't so funny anymore.

Just one more thing to add to my growing list of reasons to resent him.

'Ashling!' Lost in my thoughts I didn't notice Melissa Diamond (mum of Payton's school nemesis and wife of one of Adrian's lycra-wearing buddies) coming up the aisle. She wore her usual attire of expensive activewear, although I'd never seen her as much as walk a kilometre in her life.

'Hi.' I pasted on a cheesy smile and sucked in my stomach, aware of the waistband of my jeans cutting into my flesh. Was that why Adrian was chasing new skirt? I'd let myself go and he no longer found me attractive?

'How are you?' Melissa cocked her head and gave me a pitying look—*she knew!*—although the amount of genuine sympathy she was capable of would fit in her little finger.

I was going to kill Adrian.

'I'm okay,' I said, no energy to try and pretend to be anything more.

Melissa sighed. 'You poor thing. Although Mark'—her husband—'said you and Adrian are going to try the whole nest-parenting thing. Very modern of you. Between you and me, the idea of living one week as a single woman is very appealing. You won't have time to get sick of your kids and will have a whole week to indulge yourself.'

I smiled politely. 'I'm really sorry, Melissa, but I'm in a bit of a rush.'

And then I fled down the aisle and marched around the rest of the supermarket with my trolley, tossing in packets of Tim Tams, bags of chips, tubs of ice-cream and other things we absolutely, definitely, did not need.

So much for my fears of Adrian not providing the kids with nutritious diets; tonight we were going to have a junk food feast!

6

Hayley let herself into my house just after ten o'clock and found me putting away the groceries in the kitchen. She took one look at the bags of unhealthy snacks, dumped her phone, keys and a bottle of wine on the kitchen counter, and yanked me into her arms.

'Oh, Ash. I'm going to kill my fucking brother.'

My head fell against her shoulder and tears sprung from my eyes as I clung to my sister-in-law. She wasn't normally much of a hugger but I really appreciated her embrace now.

'I'm sorry,' I said, pulling back slightly. 'I'm messing up your shirt.'

'What? This old thing?' She chuckled, referring to her pristine pilot's uniform. 'Don't worry about it. I've got plenty where this came from and I'm not flying again till Wednesday, which means we can crack this open.'

I followed her gaze as she let me go and held up the bottle of expensive champagne. 'Aren't bubbles supposed to be for celebrating?'

Hayley shrugged. 'Celebrating? Commiserating? There's no occasion where bubbles aren't appropriate.'

'God, I love you,' I said, sniffing again and wiping my eyes with the back of my hand. It was true—I'd loved and admired her since my very first day of school. Even back then she was a ball-breaking go-getter who knew what she wanted in life and took no nonsense from anyone. But despite her drive, ambition, and ability to make the many men she dated weep when she inevitably dumped them, she had a heart of gold and would do anything for her friends and family.

'Of course you do.' She grinned as she reached up into the cupboard for some glasses. 'Everyone does.'

'But,' I added, finally smiling myself, 'I can't have a drink. It's not even midday and I have to pick Payton up later anyway.'

Hayley waved her hand dismissively in the air. 'It's always five o'clock somewhere in the world, and I can grab an Uber and go pick up my darling niece if need be.'

I sighed—a glass of wine sounded like exactly what the doctor ordered. Knowing I'd cave, Hayley filled two champagne flutes right to the top.

We took them into the lounge room and collapsed onto the couch. Hayley toed off her far-too-glam-for-a-pilot shoes and put her feet up on the coffee table. Following suit, I kicked off my sensible shoes—my husband the podiatrist never let me buy anything but—and did the same.

Hayley took a long sip of her drink. 'So, what the hell is going on? Has my brother totally lost the plot?'

I twisted the glass in my hand. 'Well, he's apparently lost any feelings he ever had towards me. He wants to sleep with other women.'

As Hayley reached out and squeezed my knee, I took a gulp of champagne.

'Have you discussed how you're going to handle the kids? If Ads thinks he can leave you high and dry and only see them every second weekend or something, he has another think coming. One of my colleagues is married to a very good divorce lawyer. Once she's finished with him, he'll be broke, ego-bruised and rocking in the corner, wishing he were dead.'

I was torn between laughing and crying again, not ready to even think about divorce lawyers. 'He's your brother!'

'That he is, and I love him, but that doesn't mean he can't be a selfish, arrogant prick sometimes, and this time he's excelled himself.'

'Do you think maybe he's just having some sort of midlife crisis?'

Hayley pursed her lips, thinking a moment. 'I'm not sure I believe in midlife crises, but I have noticed a difference in him since Dad died.'

'You have?' I blinked, but then realised maybe she was right. 'I guess there may have been a shift in him.' Hindsight was a wonderful thing.

'But then again, it wasn't like he was close to our father anyway.'

That was true. When their dad died of a heart attack two years ago, the only time Adrian took off work was half a day to go to the funeral.

'Maybe that's it,' I exclaimed, sitting up straight. 'Maybe he's harbouring some kind of guilt or regret about not making an effort with your father and maybe that's making him depressed and the depression is causing him to look for other ways to ease the pain, find fulfillment.'

'I'm a pilot not a shrink, but does it really matter what his reasons are? He told you he wants to shag other women.' I flinched at the reminder, but Hayley continued. 'You should be worrying less about him and more about yourself and what you and the kids are going to do moving forward.'

'Oh, Adrian's got that all worked out,' I said, still thinking about the psychology angle. Even if he wouldn't talk to someone, maybe I could? And maybe they could give me some strategies to help him. 'We're going to be nest-parenters.'

Hayley blinked. 'Aren't nest-parenters those people whose kids have moved out?'

'No, that's empty-nesters.' I went on to explain exactly what our deal was going to be.

When I'd finished, Hayley burst out laughing.

'What?'

'One second.' She went into the kitchen and returned a few moments later with the bottle, refilling both our glasses, before sinking back into the couch. 'Let me get this straight, Ads is going to be a single dad one whole week at a time? He's going to have to do the shopping, make the school lunches, cook dinner, wash and iron the uniforms, get the kids ready in the morning? *That* is the funniest thing I've ever heard.'

I grinned and took another sip of bubbles, already tasting victory, because it wasn't just about the kids. Adrian had no idea about half the things I did for him and the kids, but if I *didn't* do them, I felt certain he'd suddenly miss them and realise how much he needed me.

'Quite aside from all that,' Hayley said, 'how does he plan on getting Payton to and from school while keeping up with all his precious patients, or does he expect you to do that on *his* weeks as well?'

'Apparently one of his cycling mates has a daughter at uni who's available most afternoons, so he'll pay her to pick up Payton and be there till Saxon or Adrian gets home.'

Hayley's eyebrows rose. 'He really thinks he's got this sorted, doesn't he?'

'Yes.'

'Do you have ground rules for this arrangement?'

'Uh-huh.' Adrian had them worked out too, but I'd added a few of my own. 'We'll do the swap every Monday morning—the person at home will leave when the kids go to school and the other parent will take over that afternoon. Both of us must leave the house clean for the other. While it's our week, everything kid-related is our responsibility—shopping, washing, supervising homework, et cetera. Oh, and no drinking for the adult on duty.'

'What about if one of you meets someone?'

'We've agreed not to bring any dates back to the house.' My voice caught on the last couple of words. I didn't want to think about Adrian's possible love interests.

Hayley topped up my glass yet again. 'And so, while one of you is with the kids, where's the other one supposed to live?'

'Adrian's planning on living with Brad to start with, and ...' I sucked in a breath. 'I was hoping I could rent your spare room for a while.'

'Rent?' Hayley scoffed. 'Don't be ridiculous, you can have it as long as you need, and I won't hear of you paying me a cent. It's the least I can do since I'm the one who introduced you to Adrian the Asshole.'

She spoke with a fake American accent, which made me laugh, but the truth was, there was nothing Hayley could have done to keep me away from him. Even if we weren't friends,

Adrian was her twin so we'd have been in the same school year anyway.

'Thanks,' I said, 'but hopefully I won't have to encroach on your hospitality for too long.'

'What's the plan long-term?'

'Adrian said if the nest-parenting custody arrangement works, then we should buy a two-bedroom unit or an apartment and each keep one bedroom for our weeks without the kids.'

Hayley wrinkled her nose. 'Sharing a house with your ex-husband? I can't think of anything more unappealing.'

'Me either. But I don't plan on having an *ex*-husband. I'm hoping Adrian will soon come to his senses.'

'What?' She slammed her glass down on the coffee table and champagne splashed up over the edges. 'You'd actually take him back after he sows his wild oats all over town?'

As much as I loved her, I wished she wouldn't say things like that. 'I made vows.'

'So did Adrian, but he doesn't seem too concerned with them right now.'

Hayley would never understand my stance on this—we could argue till we were blue in the face and neither would ever be able to convince the other. She came from the home of two happily married parents and took the situation for granted. She had no idea what divorce could do to people.

'Maybe this will be a blessing in the long run,' she added. 'You've always been way too good for my brother and if he can't see how good he's got it, then he doesn't deserve you.'

'I know you're trying to make me feel better,' I said, 'and I appreciate that, I really do, but I'm not ready to give up on my marriage. On my family. Now, I'm going to get us some cheese and crackers—this alcohol is going to my head.'

Hayley followed me into the kitchen, still sipping on her drink as I organised a round of brie, some gouda and my favourite crackers onto a plate.

'You know,' she said, 'who's to say any other women will be lining up to sleep with him anyway? Not all of us *fairer* sex are as crazy as you.'

7

If I'd thought my first week at home without Adrian was bad—lying in bed alone while wondering what he was getting up to and with *whom*—my first week without the kids was a special kind of hell.

While Hayley did her best to distract me, there were long hours alone each day, and sometimes evenings as well when she was working or off having drinks with some other friend or colleague. She invited me out with her, but I wasn't in the mood and didn't want to cramp her style. Hayley frequented sophisticated bars and clubs, whereas my nights out with the school mums usually consisted of a movie and dinner at the kind of restaurant that closed by 9 pm.

During the long nights as I tossed and turned, thoughts of my children haunted me. I worried especially about Payton, who I still read to every night and often lay with until she fell asleep. I'd spoken to them on the phone of course—at least half an hour each night with Payton and a stilted thirty seconds or so with Saxon—but it wasn't the same as being *with* them. I worried about what they were eating, what they were watching, whether they were showering and brushing their teeth, wearing clean clothes, getting enough sleep, and prayed to God Adrian was making Payton do her reading and spelling homework.

During the day, I lay in bed much longer than usual. What did I have to get up for? I hoped that if I slept, the time until I could see my children again would go faster. But then I didn't sleep any better when it was light than when it was dark, so inevitably I forced myself to get up. Although I'd lost the inclination to shower and eat, I kept my daily hygiene routine and ate three basic meals a day. I couldn't afford to let myself go.

After breakfast, I'd clean Hayley's apartment, which in my opinion was in dire need of not only a spring clean, but also a summer, winter and autumn one. I had no idea how she lived like she did, but she didn't seem to notice the clutter, which in turn hid the dirt.

'I'd almost forgotten those tiles were beige,' she'd joked as she surveyed her bathroom on my first day of residence.

The next day I'd tackled the kitchen. 'You know you don't have to do that,' she'd said when she returned from a flight to Port Headland and back.

But I couldn't cook in a dirty space and that was the activity that kept me busy through the afternoons. Until today.

Today, I couldn't handle the confined walls of Hayley's apartment a moment longer and, more to the point, I couldn't handle another day without seeing my kids. As Hayley was flying and a local colleague had picked her up on his way to the airport, her Audi was in the underground car park just waiting for an outing.

Praying I wouldn't have any accidents while driving her prized possession—but figuring I'd be less likely to be noticed by other school mums than in my own car—I drove the fifteen minutes to

Payton's school. Instead of parking or even idling in the Kiss and Drive drop-off-pick-up area, I stopped across the road underneath a big gum tree, hopefully hidden from the world but with a vantage point where I'd see my girl when she walked out of the school grounds.

About thirty seconds after the siren, a faded black hatchback screeched into the car park and stopped illegally on the verge. A woman—if you could call her that, she didn't look much older than Saxon—climbed out and hurried towards the gate.

How on earth she could walk in those tight black shorts and ridiculously high heels I had no clue. From the back, I couldn't see much, aside from the fact her jet-black hair was tied up in the messiest ponytail I'd ever seen and that her also-tight top was only midriff as it exposed the bare skin of her back.

Hopefully she's wearing sunscreen, I thought as I turned up my car's air conditioning.

A few minutes later, I startled and banged my head on the sun visor as I saw Payton coming out, holding the hand of and chatting animatedly to the woman from the black car. Even from this distance I could make out the stranger's heavy black eyeliner and black lipstick and something glinted on her bare midriff, telling me she had a belly button ring.

'Oh my God.' *That's* the student Adrian hired to take care of our little girl? He'd totally taken leave of his senses.

How could I, in good conscience, let our daughter go home with this person?

My hand already on the door, I was ready to leap from the car, but came to *my* senses just in time. Looks could be deceiving, so I shouldn't judge this young woman by hers. Payton seemed happy enough to go with her. My heart ached a little—was she missing me at *all*?—but as she'd already survived three rides home with this girl, perhaps I was overreacting.

Still, it couldn't hurt to be sure.

Forcing deep breaths in and out of my lungs, I waited until the hatchback turned out onto the road and then I followed at enough of a distance to ensure neither the babysitter nor Payton would notice me. Adrian would be furious if he knew what I was doing. He'd been clear he didn't want to confuse the kids by blurring the lines of our agreement. But it was okay for him—he often went away for podiatry conferences and cycling weekends, so he was used to being without our children for days at a time.

Me? The only time we'd been apart was when one of them was at camp, and then at least I'd still had the other at home.

It was a short ride from the school to our house, so less than ten minutes later, I was idling a few houses up the street like some kind of stalker, but it was worth it for another glimpse of my daughter. As Payton climbed out of the car, I breathed a sigh of relief that she'd made it home in one piece. And although every bone in my body itched to go to her, pull her against my chest and feel her lanky body in my arms, I resisted.

As they disappeared into the house, a tear slid down my cheek and I glanced at my watch to see how long I'd have to wait to see Saxon as well. He caught a bus into the city to the selective high school and often stayed after school for music lessons, debating or chess club, but luckily Thursday was his one free afternoon. I only had to wait another half an hour until he rounded the corner, dragging his feet along the ground, his nose buried in his phone.

I drank in the sight of him, pleased to see that, despite his untucked shirt and slightly ruffled hair, he didn't look like he'd been starved of food or sleep over the past few nights. Sliding low in my seat, I tapped out a message: *Hey sweetheart. How was your day? Miss you. xox*

A few moments later I received his one-word reply: *Fine.*

I sighed. He was clearly still mad at me and this made my already aching heart cramp even more. Adrian might have issues, but if his *issues* ruined the good relationship I had with my son, I'd chop off his balls so he could never have sex, with *anyone*, ever again.

8

I awoke the next morning with a throbbing headache, a queasy stomach and a throat that could give the Sahara Desert a run for its money. So, this was how you felt when you drank a bottle of wine all by yourself and barely ate a thing.

Unable to remember the last time I'd had such an intense hangover, I groaned as I rolled over to check the time. The digital alarm clock on the bedside table flashed 11:06 am and I couldn't remember waking up even once since I'd fallen into bed late last night.

If it wasn't for this physical torture, maybe I'd take to a bottle a night to numb the pain. At this thought my stomach revolted and I fled down the corridor to the bathroom, only just making it in time to avoid throwing up all over the floor.

As I retched into the bowl, I cursed Adrian. 'Look what you've done to me, bastard.'

Of course he didn't reply, the only sounds in the apartment coming from the kitchen, along with the tastebud-melting aroma of coffee. I splashed water onto my face and rinsed my mouth. Coffee might be the only thing that would stop me crawling right back to bed and pulling the covers over my head.

'Good morning,' said a deep, gravelly voice as I entered the kitchen. It took my alcohol-addled brain a few moments to register that this was not my sister-in-law.

'You're not Hayley,' I said, feeling a little exposed in my pyjamas. Granted, they were thick flannelette ones, but I wasn't wearing a bra.

The owner of the voice, who happened to have a handsome face and a rather nice body to match, chuckled. 'No, I'm Wei.'

I didn't know where to look. His chest was bare, and he wore nothing but a pair of boxer briefs.

'I work with Hayley,' Wei elaborated as she herself appeared, wrapped in a silky dressing gown.

'Oh, I see you guys have met.' Hayley smiled as she crossed the kitchen to squeeze the man-child's bum. 'This is my best friend, Ashling, who also happens to be my sister-in-law, poor darling. And this is Wei Jiangsu. Isn't that the sexiest name you've ever heard? Wei's a first officer and we ...'

Her voice drifted off, but I didn't need an explanation.

'Can I get you a coffee?' Wei asked, gesturing to the machine.

Although I desperately needed caffeine, I did not want to be a third wheel over breakfast while these two made googly eyes at each other. 'No, thanks. I was just about to hit the shower anyway. Nice to meet you.'

I was already backing out of the kitchen when he replied, 'You too, Ashling. Hope we meet again.'

I doubted that, I thought as I made my way back to the bathroom. Hayley's relationships never lasted long—she enjoyed the thrill of the chase and usually got bored once she'd succeeded at conquest.

But she also normally kept business and pleasure separate. What was she thinking sleeping with a first officer?

Had *everyone* in my life gone bonkers?

A knock sounded on my door half an hour later.

'Big night?' Hayley smirked as she entered carrying a tray of buttered toast and steaming coffee. 'I saw the empty bottle of wine on the bench.'

'Not as big as yours. How old is Wei?'

She shrugged, put the tray on my lap and sat down on the bed beside me. 'Who cares about age when he has a body like that? Did you *see* his six-pack?'

'I was trying not to look.'

She winked. 'Well, you'll have to trust me because I did a lot more than just look.'

I picked up the coffee and took a sip.

'You're not usually such a big drinker,' she went on. 'Just a bad day or did something particular set you off?'

'I saw the kids yesterday.'

'I thought you weren't going to see them during your weeks here, except for Payton's soccer games.'

'Yes, that's the agreement, but … I'm going crazy cooped up in here—no offence to your lovely apartment.'

Hayley snorted. 'I can barely recognise my apartment and you've only been here a week. I'm guessing if you stay any longer, it'll be getting a complete revamp.'

'Sorry,' I said, not admitting that I'd already had ideas about giving her lounge room a facelift. There was little I liked better than interior design and DIY and both had always been therapeutic for me.

'Don't be silly. I'm getting used to the cleanliness. I'm glad Wei doesn't know yet what a slob I can be.'

'Yet? Does that mean we'll be seeing more of the *young* pilot?'

'He's thirty, so only nine years younger than us. If the age difference was the other way around, nobody would even blink. But enough about my sex life, how are the kids?'

'They seem fine.' I couldn't hold back a sob.

'*Seem?*'

I told her how I'd staked out the school and then my house. 'Adrian has a drug-addicted hooker taking care of our daughter.'

Hayley laughed as she shook her head, then squeezed my hand. 'Look, I know this wasn't your idea and that you're feeling lost without Adrian and the kids, but if you want him to realise what he's giving up, then maybe you need to show him how much of a life you can have without him.'

'Life?' It was my turn to laugh. 'I don't *have* a life without Adrian and the kids. I don't even know who I am without them.'

'Then maybe it's time you find out.'

'What do you mean?' I asked eventually, not at all sure I really wanted the answer.

Hayley reached across me to grab my phone off the bedside table.

'What are you doing?'

'I'm downloading some dating apps.'

'What? No!' I tried to grab my phone, but Hayley was quick and sprung from the bed.

'Relax, we can take this slow, but why should Adrian be the one having all the fun? You have seven full nights of freedom in a row now, you should—'

'No,' I said firmly, holding out my hand for my phone. 'Sex might be how you avoid dealing with emotions, but I love my husband and I don't want any other man.' I wouldn't even know what to do with one. Adrian was the only guy I'd ever slept with. 'I simply want to get him back and unless you have any ideas about how I can go about doing that, then I don't want your suggestions.'

Hayley and I eyed each other a few long moments and the hurt I saw looking back at me squeezed my heart. 'I'm sorry, that was uncalled for, but—'

'It's okay.' She shrugged. 'Maybe I do use sex to fill some kind of hole inside me and maybe that's not the best strategy for you, but can I make one less tawdry suggestion?'

'Go on.' My breath stalled as I waited for her to speak.

'Why don't you get a job?'

'What?' I didn't know whether to laugh or cry. 'I haven't had a job in fifteen years. What on earth would I do? The market is bloody tough, and I'm not qualified for anything.'

'What do you call the office work you do in the clinic?'

I shrugged. 'An unpaid labour of love?' For as long as I could remember I'd been filling in for Adrian if a receptionist was sick or on holidays.

'Don't undersell yourself, Ash. There are lots of things you could do—you could get a job in someone else's office. Or why not try a bookshop? You love books.'

'I haven't had time to read in years.'

But Hayley wasn't going to be put off. She glanced around at my rigidly organised belongings. 'You could start your own cleaning business and choose your own hours. You could even sell Tupperware or something—Lord knows you have enough.'

I poked my tongue out at her. 'I'd be hopeless at selling stuff.'

But she refused to be stymied. 'Nonsense. You're such a people person—you could hit up all the kids' friends' parents. And, direct selling could easily work on the weeks you have the kids as well as when you don't.'

I couldn't garner excitement for any of her suggestions, and the fact she talked like this separation would become permanent irritated me.

I opened my mouth to tell her to leave me be when she added, 'Have you forgotten your degree in journalism? Maybe it's finally time to put all those years of study to use.'

'It's almost two decades old.'

I'd found myself pregnant a couple of months before I'd graduated and by the time I'd realised that baby was never going to be, I'd already been playing receptionist for Adrian. I'd meant to pursue my own career once the clinic was established, but somehow life had got in the way.

'So what?' said Hayley.

'*So*, I haven't written anything except emails to teachers, committee minutes, grant applications and shopping lists for as long as I can remember. Articles are a beast of their own and the industry has completely changed in the time I've been out of it. No one would ever employ someone with so little experience.'

And 'little' was an overstatement.

'Then freelance. You could write an opinion piece about nest parenting for one of the online women's magazines. Or, you could start a blog and build a profile that way. I'm sure there are other women in your position who would relate.'

As much as I loved Hayley's optimism, right now it annoyed the hell out of me. Besides, considering a job outside of the clinic—any job—would feel like accepting the possibility that Adrian and I were never going to get back together. And that was something I wasn't willing to concede.

9

I was like a kid at Christmas. Up before dawn, I showered, dressed, threw my sheets in the washing machine and collected all my things from Hayley's guest bedroom, hoping I wouldn't be coming back.

'You look like a girl who got lucky last night.' Hayley's eyes twinkled as she entered the kitchen where I was manically cleaning again to pass the time until I could return home.

I rolled my eyes. 'I'm just excited about seeing the kids. Going back home.'

And, truth be told, I was also looking forward to finding out how Adrian had survived a week without me.

Hayley and I left at the same time—she to the airport and me to the supermarket closest to our house. Yesterday, I'd written up my usual menu plan for the week and made a shopping list accordingly.

Heavily laden with shopping bags, it was almost ten o'clock by the time I let myself into our family home. Charlie greeted me at the front door and barked excitedly, almost tripping me over as I carried the groceries into the kitchen.

'Hello, my darling boy.' I dropped to the ground and yanked him into my arms. I laughed as I rubbed the fur around his neck, and he licked my face in appreciation.

'Don't worry, I have treats here for you too,' I said when I finally pushed to my feet.

I gave Charlie a bowl of the expensive brand dog food we only gave him on Christmas Day and then unpacked the shopping to the sound of him munching happily. I was surprised to find the fridge quite full, but even more shocked there were no empty bottles of milk or cartons of eggs still in there. Or hollow packets or wrappers in the pantry. Adrian had a terrible habit of doing that and both kids seemed to have inherited it from him. I was always nagging them about it.

How am I supposed to know what we need if I don't know we've run out?

It would be just my luck that all my years of pestering him had finally paid off the moment he'd decided he didn't want to be with me anymore. Then, the next Mrs Wood would benefit from all my hard work and training.

The *next Mrs Wood*? Ignoring the way that made my stomach turn, I forced the idea out of my head—there wasn't going to be *another* Mrs Wood because I wasn't giving up the role.

But as I looked around my house, my chest tightened. I'd expected to come home to a pigsty, but it was almost eerily clean and tidy. The remotes had even been returned to their little box next to the television. The kitchen sparkled, the dining table was absent of the usual crumbs, the dishwasher was empty. In fact, there were no signs that anyone had eaten anything all week.

A thought struck and, already feeling victorious, I checked the rubbish bin, expecting to see Macca's bags or other restaurant containers, but all I found was an empty bin with a fresh liner. My suspicion growing, I stalked to the outside bins—Charlie toddling after me—and stooped to an all-time low. When there was no evidence of Adrian and the kids living on fast food, I rifled deep down into the bin, but all I was rewarded with for my efforts was gunk in my hair and dirt on my hands.

I looked down at Charlie who was looking up at me, his head cocked to one side as if wondering if I was looking for something to tighten the few screws that were obviously loose in my head. 'What's been going on around here?'

In reply, he turned back to the house and, defeated, I followed him inside to continue my inspection. Aside from a load of clothes in the dryer, the laundry looked as if someone had readied it for real estate photos.

Could that be it? *No.* I reached out to steady myself on the counter. No way Adrian would organise to sell the house without me. The nest-parenting arrangement would only work if we kept it.

Then again, he'd decided we would separate without me.

As goosebumps spread across my skin, I hurried back into the kitchen and grabbed my phone from my handbag. My fingers flew across the screen: *What the hell do you think you're playing at? Why is the house so bloody clean? You can't*

But I halted mid-sentence. I didn't want him to think I was impressed. If he *was* trying to sell the house without me, I'd enlist that lawyer person Hayley knew. Just because I still loved him, didn't mean I was going to let him totally walk all over me. This was our home. This was the kids' *home.*

However, the alternative wasn't much better—if he hadn't had a cleaner in to make the house presentable for selling, then somehow he'd managed this week without me.

Not wanting to believe this, I went into the kids' rooms next. Although Saxon's had that lingering smell of teenage boy—which, even as I gagged, almost made me cry because I'd missed it so much—it was much cleaner than usual, and in Payton's room everything was spick-and-span too. Even her cuddly toys were lined up neatly on the funky shelves I'd made out of a wooden pallet.

Finally, I braved our bedroom—the space that had always felt like a sanctuary to me. A lump welled in my throat as my gaze went to our bedside tables. Normally Adrian had a few business books on his, and I had my home renovation and decor magazines on mine, but they were both empty. And it wasn't only the bedside tables—he'd stripped the room of anything personal belonging to either of us *and* put my stuff in a large box in the wardrobe with my name on it. The side of the wardrobe where all his clothes usually hung was bare—he'd obviously taken all his stuff to Brad's.

Surprisingly, he'd left our framed wedding photo on the dresser he'd found on the side of the road for me to restore, but aside from that the whole room felt barren, like I'd just stepped into a hotel room.

Desperate to feel some kind of normality, I fell onto our bed and pulled a pillow against me. I buried my head into it, hoping to smell him, but all my nose caught was the aroma of clean sheets. Changing the sheets every Monday morning had been our agreement and usually I delighted in fresh linen, but today it only made me cry as I thought about what I'd lost.

Would Adrian and I ever sleep together in this bed again?

For months I hadn't been able to find much enthusiasm for sex, but now the possibility of it had been snatched from me, I felt bereft. If only I'd put out more maybe Adrian wouldn't have left me. But my hollow feeling was about so much more than the sex. Would we ever laugh or share a fun moment together again? My eyes prickled and soon tears were cascading down my cheeks, my sobs so loud that Charlie came into the bedroom to investigate. He dropped his head onto the bed next to mine and whined.

'It's all right, boy,' I said, reaching out to stroke him. 'I'm fine.'

A total lie—I felt anything but fine. But I needed to pull myself together before Saxon and Payton came home to find me still lying on the bed, all maudlin.

10

'Mum!' Payton squealed as she rushed out of the classroom and threw herself into my arms.

'Hey sweetheart.' I squeezed her tightly, never wanting to let her go.

We'd seen each other only yesterday when I'd gone to watch her soccer game, but she'd been training before the whistle and Adrian had whisked her away almost immediately afterwards and I'd headed back to Hayley's. Our time together hadn't been nearly long enough, and it had also been overshadowed by the awkwardness between me and her father.

But I wasn't going to think about that now. I wanted to make the most of every minute we had together.

'Can we go get a milkshake?' she asked as we walked towards the car.

'I made a carrot cake for afternoon tea. Thought you might be wanting some home cooking.'

She shrugged. 'Dad made a chocolate cake last night that I had in my lunch today. *Please* can we get a milkshake?'

I stopped dead in my tracks. 'Your father made a chocolate cake? Out of a *packet* mix, right?'

'No.' She shook her head, her blonde pigtails jiggling. 'He used the Thermomix but he made it from scratch. I watched him measure all the ingredients in and everything.'

Wonders never ceased. Obviously, I'd made a monumental error in leaving him with my most beloved kitchen appliance. Anyone could cook almost anything if they followed the instructions from the screen. Well, I wouldn't make that mistake again—if things hadn't returned to normal by next week, I'd be taking Thermie with me to Hayley's apartment. It was mine after all. I still remembered how long it had taken me to convince Adrian it was a good investment. All the other mums at school were raving about them being a godsend and a timesaver, but he'd thought it an overpriced fad.

Eventually he'd given in and gifted one to me for my thirty-sixth birthday, and he had reaped the rewards ever since.

'And did Daddy clean the house as well?' I asked as we reached the car park.

'No.' She looked at me like I was stupid. 'Some woman came around last night.'

My scalp prickled. *Some woman? At night?*

Maybe he'd lied about not having an affair. Maybe he'd already met someone else and was simply biding time until he could move her in. I should be scrutinising everything, dusting my house for clues of another woman. Why the hell did I think I could trust Adrian to keep to our no-lovers-in-the-house rule?

'So, have you met this woman before?' I asked, trying to sound nonchalant as I opened the passenger door.

'No, she was from some cleaning company, I think. Daddy gave her money when she was finished.'

While the cash part sounded legitimate and I felt smug that Adrian hadn't managed to turn our home into a showroom by himself, I didn't know any house cleaners who worked at night and I hated him for turning me into a paranoid nutcase.

I walked around the vehicle, climbed inside, clicked my seatbelt into place and turned my key in the ignition. 'And what's your babysitter like?'

'Topaz? She's not a *baby*sitter, she just drives me home from school. She's cool.'

'And have there been any other visitors to the house?'

Payton frowned. 'What kind of visitors?'

And that's when I realised the trap I was falling into. My instinct was to fire question after question at her about the past week—was Daddy happier or sadder than usual? Did he talk about me at all?—but I wasn't going to be *that* parent. I could still remember clearly my own mother bombarding me with similar questions every time I came back from a weekend at my father's. I also remembered exactly how those questions made me feel.

'Never mind.' Feeling guilty about interrogating her I decided to treat her with a milkshake after all.

'How was your day?' I asked as we drove towards our favourite cafe.

That *should* have been the question I'd asked her in the first place.

She took a moment to answer. 'It was okay. Prosecco was sick and the boys wouldn't let me play soccer with them at lunchtime.'

'Bummer. What did you do instead?'

'Joined in the stupid skipping games all the other girls play.'

I stifled a smile. 'And what about in class? Did you learn anything interesting?'

'Not really,' she said, playing with the straps of her school bag.

I fired a few more questions, but she answered mostly with only one or two words.

'Are you not feeling well?' I reached out to feel Payton's forehead as we stopped at the traffic lights.

She stared wistfully out the window. 'I'm okay.'

When we got to the cafe, I waited for her to pep up—usually we couldn't get her to stop talking—but she simply stared into her caramel milkshake as she slurped noisily through a paper straw. I resisted the urge to again ask her if she was okay. How could any of us be *okay* when our world had been turned upside down?

But I hated her silence and vowed to call Adrian later and ask him how she'd been, whether he wanted to hear from me or not.

'Are *you* okay, Mum?' Payton asked when we were finally driving home.

'Of course, sweetheart,' I gushed. Worrying about my mum after my dad walked out had taken up half my childhood and I didn't want that for my kids.

'Did you miss us this week?'

'That is the stupidest question I've ever heard.' I squeezed her knee. 'I missed you and Sax like crazy.'

'What about Dad?' Her voice was so quiet I barely heard the question.

That lump welled in my throat again. 'Yep. I missed him too.'

'Then why aren't you guys together anymore?'

I wondered if she'd grilled Adrian in this same way. I wondered what his answers had been if she had and somehow resisted the compulsion to ask.

'We're just going through a bit of a tricky time, but I'm sure we'll get through this. And whatever happens, you need to remember that this is between Daddy and me. This decision has absolutely nothing to do with you and your brother, okay?'

It sounded like a stupid platitude even to my ears, but thankfully she seemed to have perked up by the time we got home. She played with Charlie a little and then headed to the couch to watch soccer videos on YouTube.

'Only half an hour,' I reminded her—she'd watch all night if not regulated.

My reunion with Saxon wasn't much better.

'Hello, sweetheart.' I smiled at him when he arrived home, managing not to grab hold of him and gush as much as I had with Payton.

'What's for dinner?' he asked, always thinking about his stomach.

'Beef stir-fry, with lots of veggies,' I said as I chopped some runner beans. Who knew whether they'd actually had any greens this past week? 'But it won't be for another hour so there's some carrot cake if you'd like a snack?' The boy had hollow legs.

'No thanks.' He pulled his lunch box out of his school bag, dumped it on the bench, made himself a peanut butter sandwich, and then started off towards his bedroom.

I cleared my throat. 'Is that all you've got for your mother after not seeing her for a whole week?'

He turned slowly and glared at me. 'What do you expect me to say?'

I flinched, too stunned to reprimand or even answer. As Saxon stomped off to his bedroom, an angry heat rushed through my body. It wasn't a coincidence that my boy's surly attitude had arrived exactly the same time his father had decided he could live without me. Normally I'd talk to Adrian if I had any concerns about the kids, but he wasn't here, and this was *his* fault anyway.

Well, to hell with him—I wasn't going to have my son shut me out just so that my husband didn't look like the bad guy.

Abandoning the vegetables, I headed down the hallway to Saxon's bedroom. My hand hovered over the door handle as I deliberated between knocking and barging right in. At the last moment—deciding it was better to not fly at my son like an angry bull—I knocked.

My heart stilled as I waited for what seemed like hours for a reply.

'What?'

'I just want to talk to you,' I said, my jaw tense.

When there was no answer after a few moments, I went in anyway.

He was already sitting at his desk, his shoes kicked off on the floor and his laptop open in front of him.

'I missed you this last week,' I said. 'Anything exciting happen at school?'

'If you missed me, why weren't you here?'

The question brought more tears to my eyes—honestly, I could probably help ease the drought in rural Australia with the amount I'd cried this last couple of weeks. 'I *wanted* to be here. I wanted to be here more than anything, but ...' I sucked in a deep breath. 'Your father doesn't feel the same way about me as he always did.'

'He said this was a mutual decision?'

My loyalty to Adrian and my need for my son to talk to me again warred within me, but I shook my head. 'No. I love your father and the last thing I want is for the four of us to be living apart. I'm hoping he'll see sense and we can work things out, but in the meantime, I need you to talk to me, to tell me how you're feeling, and I promise I'm still here for you. Even when I'm at Aunty Hayley's you can call me anytime.'

'Do you want to get back with Dad?'

'More than anything in the world.' I pulled him into a hug and Saxon's body slumped against mine. The lump in my throat eased and a desperate love for my family took its place. 'And I love you so much.'

'Okay. I love you too.' He gave me a quick squeeze and then pulled back. 'But do you mind if I get back to my homework?'

'Sure, sweetheart.' This time his question made me smile—he'd always been conscientious. 'But don't work too hard. I'll call you for dinner soon.'

As I walked out of his bedroom, I made a silent vow—from now on I was going to be more proactive in my mission to win Adrian back.

11

As I turned into the sports ground for Payton's soccer game I shivered, and it wasn't because the aircon made the temperature in my car arctic. I scanned the car park for Adrian's Mazda MX5 and wasn't sure whether I felt disappointment or irritation when I didn't see it. He'd better not be late for the game, or worse, not even show up. Not only would Payton be devastated, but this was my only chance of him noticing my makeover. I'd almost sent him a reminder last night but had resisted. Hayley thought it was better if I didn't initiate contact.

'Give him a chance to miss you,' she'd advised.

Although she had made it clear she didn't understand or agree with my desire to fix things between us, she'd also pledged her willingness to help.

In exchange for me agreeing to start writing down my experiences—'In case an opportunity for an article comes up'—she'd joined me up to her gym, booked me in with her hairdresser, encouraged me to stop drowning my sorrow in Tim Tams and wine, and taken me shopping for a whole new look. 'Less housewife, more yummy mummy.'

After two pump classes, my muscles ached so much I could barely walk, but I had to admit my hair looked better than it had in years. I glanced in the visor mirror, almost shocked at the face looking back at me. Until this week, I couldn't remember the last time I'd been to the salon for more than a trim and I'd become so accustomed to tying my hair back that I'd been shocked when I realised how long it had grown. Hayley's hairdresser had cut in some layers but left most of the length and freshened up what she'd called my 'dull, light, mousey blonde' so it was now a 'warm blonde with a touch of whisky and honey'.

My mouth had watered at the description, but now as I ran my fingers through my tousled cut exactly the way the hairdresser had shown me—'gives the vibe of bed hair without being messy'—I wondered if Adrian would simply think I looked like mutton dressed as lamb. And would the other mums see right through me? Would they think my attempt to get my own husband's attention desperate?

Oh Lord. Did I still have a hairband in my handbag? It wasn't too late to tie it all back.

'*Mum*, come on. What are you waiting for?'

Payton leapt from the car almost before I'd switched off the engine. Since Monday, her chatter and enthusiasm for life had returned bit by bit, day by day, so that this morning while she ate her breakfast, she was her usual talkative self, waxing lyrical about recent games in the Premier League. Still, I couldn't help but worry what might happen when I switched with Adrian again on Monday morning. A ten-year-old girl needed her mum.

This thought gave me the courage to follow her, but not before I reapplied my frosty-pink lipstick. There was still no sign of Adrian, or Hayley, who'd promised to come along for moral support.

My stomach fluttering like it held a whole orchestra of insects, I approached the other parents with a forced smile.

Tonia wolf-whistled. 'Look at you, Ashling Wood. That haircut is amazing. You must give me the name of your stylist.'

I blushed as a number of other mums joined in with the compliments, but it wasn't their approval I wanted. 'Thanks. It was time for a change.'

'So we've heard.' A woman whose name I could never remember winked at me. 'Looks like life without hubby is treating you well.'

I smiled. Let them think what they liked. If word got back to Adrian, it couldn't be a bad thing, could it?

'What did you get up to on your week off?' Tonia asked, a hint of jealousy in her voice.

'Oh, this and that,' I said, resisting the urge to snap that I hadn't been on holiday. These women thought they'd love a break from their kids every second week, but they'd think very differently if they'd been given no choice in the matter.

'Have you joined any of those dating apps yet?' asked the coach's wife, then she lowered her voice and added, 'Tinder sounds so much fun. Sometimes I feel ripped off that I met Cam before the age of the internet. Even speed dating came in *after* we got together.'

The grass is always greener, I thought, but didn't get the chance to come up with a less snarky reply before Tonia hissed, 'Ooh, here comes Adrian now.'

My stomach turned inside out. Where the hell was Hayley? The other mums dispersed—so much for female solidarity—as Adrian approached. I felt like a high school girl with a crush on a boy way out of her league and racked my mind for something witty to say.

When that failed, I went with, 'Hello Adrian. How are you?'

Did he look like he'd had sex in the last week? I scrutinised his face for signs. Apparently, there were plenty of women on the internet more than happy to put out.

'Good.' He nodded and gave an awkward smile as if I were an acquaintance whose name he couldn't remember. Maybe he didn't recognise me in my fancy new clothes, stylish hair and made-up face. It had been a while since I'd worn more than foundation and lipstick, but this morning I'd gone all out. 'And how are you, Ashling?'

There went that possibility. Couldn't he have at least acknowledged that I looked nice? Was that too much to ask after twenty-two years together?

'I'm fantastic.' Hopefully he didn't notice how tight my voice sounded. 'I joined Hayley's gym this week and I've never felt better in my life.'

'That's great,' he said as if I'd told him I'd cut my toenails. 'By the way, what did you tell Saxon? He's been sending me really nasty messages. I thought we agreed not to badmouth each other in front of the kids and to keep this civil.'

'I didn't *bad*mouth you, but he was clearly hurting, and he wouldn't open up to me like he usually does. So I told him the truth—that this separation wasn't my idea and if I had my way, we'd still be together. I want that, Addy. I really miss you.'

'Ash.' He shook his head. 'Please don't make this more difficult than it already is.'

'Don't you miss us a little bit? Are you sure you won't consider counselling?'

'A counsellor,' Adrian said under his breath, 'is not going to change how I feel. I need space.'

And then to make it clear the conversation was over, he stepped away and focused his gaze on the pitch where the girls were warming up.

'You okay?' Tonia whispered, sidling up beside me, but I waved her off, not wanting to talk to anyone for fear I'd make a scene.

Thankfully, the game kicked off only a few minutes later and everyone focused their attention on the children. Hayley arrived part way through the first half.

She air-kissed my cheek. 'So sorry. I had a late one—or rather an early morning—with Wei.'

I raised an eyebrow, happy to think of something other than my own shitty life. 'How many nights have you seen him now?'

Hayley giggled like a schoolgirl. 'I've lost count.'

'Things getting serious between you two?'

'Serious?' she scoffed. 'It's only sex, but damn fine sex and I can't help but keep going back for more. Anyway, has Payton scored any goals?'

'I couldn't tell you.'

Hayley grabbed my elbow and led me away from the crowd. 'Have you spoken to Adrian?' She glanced over to where he was standing alongside the pitch, shouting tips to our daughter.

'Uh-huh.'

'*And?* What did he say about your new look?'

'Say?' It was my turn to scoff. 'I don't think he even noticed—it's like I'm invisible to him now. Nothing more than some woman who gave birth to his children.'

'Oh Ash.' Hayley squeezed my hand and I was thankful she wasn't much of a hugger, because a hug right now would be like switching on my tear ducts. Although I'd cried plenty in private, it would be mortifying if I cried here. 'Maybe he just needs a little time.'

'Maybe.' But I was rapidly losing hope. Not only did he not appear to miss 'us' even the slightest, but he'd coped better than I'd ever imagined during his week with the kids and was probably having daily one-night stands on his 'week off'. 'How much time do

I give him? I'm not sure how I'm supposed to get through another week twiddling my thumbs, wondering if my kids are okay. Maybe I should ask him to reconsider our custody arrangement. Do you think he'd agree to me having the kids during the week and him having them on weekends?'

'Don't you want to get back with him?'

'Well, yes, but—'

'Then don't make his life easier. Don't give him a free pass to spend less time with his children. Anyway, I've been thinking, and I have a better idea.'

'If you tell me I need to get a job or join Tinder or Bumble or whatever those stupid dating apps are called—'

She interrupted before I had the chance to deliver my murderous thoughts. 'No, nothing like that. I know how hard you find it being away from the kids and I know being cooped up in my apartment is driving you crazy. Also, I'm not sure there's any surface left for you to clean. So, I was thinking maybe you should get away somewhere more relaxing for the week.'

'What? Like Bali?'

A few friends and I had been talking about the possibility of a girls' trip for years now, but none of us ever seemed to be able to coordinate our schedules. Maybe Hayley could come with me? My other friends probably wouldn't be able to at such short notice and also some of them had been a little off with me the last couple of weeks. As if they thought my misfortune might rub off on them and cause their husbands to follow Adrian's example. Or worse—that I, desperate newly single woman that I was, might make a play for *their* men.

Being abandoned by your husband was a good way to find out who your *real* friends were.

'I was thinking of somewhere a little closer,' said Hayley. 'Driving distance.'

'Where? It might feel weird staying in a fancy hotel by myself.' And I could just imagine Adrian's reaction when he saw the bill.

'If you'll just shut up a moment, I'll tell you.'

'Sorry.'

Hayley's eyes sparkled. 'Wei's family used to live a couple of hours north at Ragged Point. They moved to Perth when he was just a kid, but his granddad was a fisherman and lived there until he died about a year ago. He owned a little cottage not far from the beach that he left to Wei and his sister in his will. They want to do it up to use as an Airbnb, but until they get themselves sorted, it's just sitting there vacant. Wei said you can stay there for free next week if you like.'

'Seriously?' Hayley and Wei had obviously done a lot more than sleep together if she knew this history about him, but there were more important things to think about right now.

'Yeah. He said it's nothing flash, but the plumbing should work. Just think how relaxing being able to get up in the mornings and enjoy a nice stroll along the beach will be. Wei even said you might see sea lions swimming in the ocean if you're lucky, and the Pinnacles are only a short drive away.'

'You sound like a travel agent.'

But this idea sounded far more appealing than the others she'd suggested. A week on the coast would trump another week in the city stuck in Hayley's apartment.

For the first time in the three weeks since Adrian had announced he wanted to sleep with other women, I felt a flicker of excitement. It had been a long time since I'd had any type of holiday and I loved the beach.

'That sounds amazing. Where do I sign up?'

12

Ragged Point

When I dropped Payton off at school on Monday morning, I had a car full of petrol, a suitcase in the boot, coffee in my travel mug and a stomach full of butterflies. I'd driven slower than normal and taken the long route, wanting to make the most of my last few minutes with her.

'Bye, Mum.' She leaned over to the driver's side and wrapped her arms around my neck before kissing me goodbye. 'Love you. See you next week.'

And then she flung open the car door, grabbed her backpack and skipped towards her classroom as if she hadn't a care in the world, whereas I fought the urge to run after her and take her with me. The kids appeared to have accepted this new situation much quicker than me, but I didn't *want* them to get used to it.

Divorce had long-lasting effects—I should know.

'I love you both so much,' I'd gushed over breakfast. Saxon escaped before I could get even more emotional, managing to wish me a 'good week up north'. I'd told the kids where I was going and messaged Adrian, who hadn't even bothered to reply.

I had a feeling the only 'person' who'd miss me was Charlie.

A car beeped behind me and I looked in the mirror to see there was a line-up behind me in the Kiss and Drive zone. With a fleeting glance in the direction of the buildings, I caught sight of Payton as she disappeared from view, then put my foot on the accelerator before the parent behind me got a bad case of school car park road rage.

Trust me, it was a thing. I bore witness to such episodes on a scarily regular basis.

And then I was on my way, heading towards the highway that would take me north to Ragged Point. The last time I'd been anywhere near the area had to be over ten years ago when friends of ours got married in Broome, and Adrian had the grand idea that we should drive *all* the way there, from Perth. With two kids under five. It took us two days each way and needless to say it was a disaster.

We hadn't stopped in Ragged Point on the way because it was only two hours into our journey. On the way back we'd barely been talking to each other by that stage, the kids were screaming, and we'd simply wanted to get home. But I knew people who went there every summer to camp by the beach, and they raved about the place. Camping and I had never seen eye to eye, but I did like the sound of the quaint little fishing village and the slower pace of life they spoke of.

For the first half hour of my drive, traffic was busy and I didn't have much time to think while making sure I took the right turn-offs. But once I got out of the suburbs, I left the rush hour behind in Perth and, aside from the occasional road-train whizzing past, it became a pleasant and peaceful drive. The flat rural landscape on either side of me had different shrubbery from what you saw in the city—lots of grass trees and other spikey plants.

About an hour and a half into my trip, I saw big mountains of white sand in the distance off to my right.

'What are those?' I imagined Payton asking.

If she were on this drive with me, she'd insist on stopping and traipsing through the rugged vegetation so she could play on them and she'd probably get bitten by a snake or something. Payton was a magnet for such dramas.

My grip tightened on the steering wheel. What if something happened to her while I was two hours away? What if the school had to call Adrian instead of me? What if Payton was inconsolable and only wanted me—she was used to me being the one there in an emergency, to take care of her when she wasn't well.

My breath quickening, I picked up my water bottle and chugged down a few mouthfuls. What the hell was I doing driving away from my family, from my responsibility? And how on earth was I supposed to win Adrian back if I wasn't close by?

With a quick glance in the rear-view mirror, I slammed on the brakes and was about to turn back when the radio was interrupted by a phone call coming through the bluetooth. The screen flashed up Hayley's name. Sometimes she had ESP where I was concerned—it was almost as if we were the twins, not she and Adrian.

My finger hovered on the button to reject the call, but at the last minute, I pressed accept and pulled over.

'You were about to turn around, weren't you?' she said before I had the chance to even say hello.

'Um ...' I looked at the road ahead and tried to come up with a reason she'd accept. If only she hadn't arranged this, I could say my accommodation had fallen through.

'Don't even think about it,' she roared. 'The kids will be fine. You're barely two hours away and I'm only flying at night this week, so if there's an emergency during the day Adrian, me *and* Mum will be available to deal with it until you get back.'

'But—'

'No buts. I'm putting my foot down. This is your week to relax, take some time to think about your future. Do I have to come up there myself and lock you in the cottage?'

'If you did that, then you wouldn't be in Perth if there *was* an emergency.'

'Exactly. And that would be your fault.' She sighed. 'Seriously, Ash, it's only one week. Try and enjoy yourself.'

Easy for her to say—she didn't have kids, so she didn't understand how it felt to have your heart walking around outside your body—but, as I was closer to Ragged Point now than to Perth, I may as well at least take a look. I could always drive home in the morning.

'Okay, okay,' I promised her. 'I'll keep driving.'

'That's my girl. I'll call you tonight.'

Half an hour later I turned off the highway, following the sign to 'Ragged Point: Home of the Rock Lobsters', which was only a kilometre off the highway. Almost immediately the sea appeared in front of me before the town and I opened my window to let in the fresh air. My lungs inhaled the salty aroma and some of the tension in my bones eased.

One night, that's all I needed to commit to.

I drove down into the town—if you could call a place with a population of less than five hundred people a town—and took in the lay of the land. The cluster of buildings, which made up what I guess you'd call the main street, came first. I noted a service station with a small motel behind it; a general store, which included a post office and lottery outlet; a cafe called Brewed Awakening, which made me smile; a pub that looked as if it hadn't had any TLC in years; a fishing tackle shack; and a town hall. There were a few people milling about on the path outside the general store and an elderly gentleman sat at a table outside reading a newspaper, a German Shepherd lazing at his feet.

Following Wei's directions, I continued down the main street towards the beach, passing a tiny primary school on the way. There were kids playing on the equipment in the yard, which told me that somewhere there had to be more life than I'd seen so far.

Just after the school, the main street formed a T-junction with another road. Pointing left was a sign to something called The Lobster Factory, but I was going right along a street that ran parallel to the ocean. Down here, I saw a playground, a car park, some public conveniences and an orange shack with a sign on the side that claimed to sell 'the best fish'n'chips in the southern hemisphere'.

Big claim, I thought, my mouth watering nonetheless.

It wouldn't help my mission to lose weight and reinvent myself so my husband might notice me again, but if I managed to stay longer than one night, maybe I'd treat myself. Past the playground came the white sand, covered in seaweed, which led to the most stunning aqua-blue water I'd ever seen. My toes wriggled in my sensible shoes and I could imagine the feel of the sand between them, the water splashing at my ankles. It had been a long time since I'd paddled in the ocean without having the added worry of watching my kids, and I had a sudden urge to do just that.

My sensible side reminded me, however, that my priority was getting to the shack—I could check out the beach later—and so I drove on. After less than a hundred metres or so, the road curved off the water, and houses sprouted on either side—some directly waterfront, others slightly higher across the road but still with a good view and access to the beach.

I suspected some of the larger places—with their fancy architecture and full-length windows—belonged to the city folk who came here in the summer, and that the quirkier, less grand, box-like abodes might house locals. It was the latter type that Wei's directions led me to and, as I parked my car on the patchy grass in front—there was no driveway or even garden to speak of—I wondered what I was getting myself into. Hayley had described the place as a 'cottage', which evoked images of cute, cosy dwellings with thatched roofs and flowers bursting out of window boxes—the kind of house you read about in fairy tales.

The faded blue fibro construction in front of me was about as far from that as you could get. Wind swished above me between the massive gum trees I'd parked under, and a shiver scuttled down my spine. Not a sound around me—no cars on the street, no people going about their business in any of the nearby houses. Even in broad daylight, the place had an eerie feel about it.

A wide porch stood at the front with two rooms jutting forward at each end. As I approached, I noticed the paint peeling off the gutters and awnings, but I guessed it had charm in its own way.

This reckoning didn't last long. As I stepped up onto the porch the wooden stairs wobbled beneath my feet and I almost fell, grabbing out quickly to hold on to the rail and yelping as a splinter of wood stabbed into my thumb. Pain shooting through me, I shoved it into my mouth, cringing as I thought about what germs could be festering on the rail. Maybe I needed a tetanus shot. But how close was the nearest doctor? I didn't remember seeing a medical centre on my way in. Ragged Point might only be a couple of hours from the city, but right now it felt like the ends of the earth.

An old rocking chair sat on one end of the porch, a colourful crocheted blanket scrunched up in a ball on top of it with what looked to be some kind of animal droppings adorning it. My stomach revolted and I added bin bags and plastic gloves to my mental shopping list—that blanket would be the first thing to go. Followed by the empty beer bottles and crinkled newspapers that filled various milk crates surrounding the chair.

The steps weren't the only things that wobbled. At least three of the floorboards buckled as I walked towards the glass sliding door and the rocking chair creaked, moving slowly back and forth. Although there weren't any curtains at the front, the glass was so smeared I could barely see inside.

Taking a deep breath, I slid the key Hayley had given me into the lock and pushed open the door.

13

'Oh my God!'

My stomach turned and my hand rushed to cover my nose as a horrible smell assaulted my senses. I couldn't tell if it was dead fish or just mustiness from being closed up for months. Wei hadn't been kidding when he said no one had visited since his grandfather died. I surveyed the scene in what I guessed to be the living room, if the woebegone leather couch, the leaning bookshelves and the TV in the corner were anything to go by. If it wasn't for the mess, I'd think I'd stepped into some kind of museum.

The television looked like one my mother had bought in the early eighties—we were all so excited because it was twice the size of the old one. I couldn't imagine it would work in the digital era, but there was a VCR machine beside it and a number of videos in a glass TV cabinet. A medium-sized coffee table sat in the middle of the room, covered with dishes, mugs and cutlery that now looked to be growing things on them.

Stepping through the debris on the floor—more bottles and newspapers, boating magazines that went back years, a couple of broken buckets, fishing tackle and a few rods—I crossed over to the bookshelf to check out the old man's collection.

It soon became apparent that even if I did stay—which was looking less and less likely by the second—I wouldn't be able to read any of the books. They were all written in what I assumed was Chinese. As I put a book back onto the dusty shelf, I heard a noise coming from the back of the shack and my heart hitched a beat. Frozen, I cocked an ear towards the sound, hoping I'd imagined it, but the rustling only grew louder.

Did it sound dangerous? I knew I should have brought Charlie with me—he might be a total softie, but his bark had always been perfect for scaring away unwanted visitors.

Glancing around the living room for something I could use as a weapon, my gaze landed on a stray golf club leaning up against the TV cabinet and I tiptoed to snatch it up as quietly as possible. The floor creaked and I cringed as I headed through a doorway into the kitchen. I did not want to alert the interloper to my presence before I had the chance to assess their danger factor.

But the rustling continued as I stealthily entered and I wasn't sure whether I was relieved or horrified by the sight of a possum sitting in the middle of the table, tearing up an old cereal packet with its teeth.

It froze as it saw me and had the audacity to look at me like *I* was the intruder. Good God, this reminded me of the scene in one of Payton's favourite movies where a man inherits a house in the country only to arrive and find a pig hiding under a sheet on the couch. I wondered how many other animals I might find as I explored the other rooms, and anyway, weren't possums supposed to be nocturnal?

The possum must have decided I looked more foe than friend. It sprang from the table across to the bench, climbed up the half-shredded lace curtains at the window and then disappeared into a hole in the ceiling. My eyes widened as I took in not only the cracks everywhere, but also the brownish stains above me. A leaky roof or possum urine?

I wasn't sure which was the better option.

Astonishingly, the kitchen was marginally tidier than the living room, but the surfaces were grotty. No way I'd put my beloved Thermomix in a kitchen looking like this, never mind actually cook anything here.

After the living room and the kitchen, I was prepared to find almost anything in the rest of the shack. The bathroom—although also outdated—harboured a little mould in the usual places, and I shuddered at the hair in the shower grate, but it could have been worse. A good scrub, a generous splash of bleach and a new shower curtain would do wonders.

My heart squeezed as I came to a closed door, which I guessed to be one of the two bedrooms. If I found bed bugs or it smelled like death—Wei hadn't mentioned where his grandfather died—then I was out of there. With a quick breath, I pushed the door, but it hit something on the other side. Cautiously, I peered through the gap and discovered what I hoped to be the old man's spare room. It was filled to the brim with boxes that looked to contain more tarnished bottles, newspapers and books, in addition to clothes, old shoes and all sorts of other paraphernalia.

Whatever else Wei's grandfather was, he was clearly also a hoarder.

I couldn't even see if there was a bed under all those boxes. If the other bedroom was like this one, my decision would be made.

But whether it was a blessing or a curse, the other room actually looked like a bedroom, had minimal clutter and didn't smell quite as bad as the rest of the house. Praise God for small mercies! Or maybe my nose had simply become accustomed to the stench. The doona and sheets were a lurid green and probably hadn't been changed since their owner's death, but I had my own clean set in the car anyway.

Despite this, returning to the city seemed the only sensible option—this was no holiday cottage and even Hayley couldn't expect me to stay in such a mess—but something about the state of the place called to the neat freak inside of me. Although I'd done a lot of renovation work on our house, I'd never attempted anything as raw as this, but I'd always loved watching those reality shows where the contestants took a dilapidated building and turned it into something millionaires would bid for.

A thrill shot through me as I imagined myself working similar miracles with this little piece of real estate. Of course, there was only so much I could do in a week but having a project would at least keep me busy.

A scuttle sounded in the roof and I looked up at the ceiling. 'Vacation's over, little possum. If you ain't paying rent, you ain't welcome.'

Laughing at myself for talking to an animal, I pushed up my sleeves.

First things first. I started around the shack, opening all the windows; some were stiff and many of the frames looked a little rotten, but they all came free eventually.

There wasn't much more I could do until I'd bought cleaning supplies and something to help me cover up the hole in the kitchen ceiling, but I checked all the lights were still working and turned on the fridge before driving back to the general store.

As I drove, I wondered what Wei's granddad's name was. It hadn't seemed important when Hayley had given me the key but now that

I was in his home, planning to declutter and clean it, I felt an urge to know. Maybe I could ask someone who worked at the store? Or even the cafe? Cafe people were mostly friendly, and my stomach growled reminding me I hadn't had any lunch.

Unfortunately, my plans for a quick bite to eat were derailed by the closed sign on the front door of Brewed Awakening, so I'd have to make do with something from the general store. A bell above said store's door dinged as I walked inside, immediately drawing the attention of a surly looking teenager behind the checkout.

She looked up from where she was picking at her nail cuticles and gave me a once-over. Her frosty glare reminded me of *The League of Gentlemen* and their 'local shop for local people'.

Trying not to let her bother me—despite the fact I felt her eyes boring into my back as I walked up and down the rows—I found everything I needed and filled my trolley almost to the brim. My heart pitter-pattered as I approached the checkout to see another woman—early forties I'd say—with a toddler perched on her hip, talking to the shop assistant as she handed over an armful of papers.

'I think there'll be plenty there, but you know the drill. If you run out, just tell Bobby to give me a yell.'

As she turned to leave, she gave me a broad friendly smile. She had long, dark but slightly greying hair tied up in a ponytail, big round dark eyes and lovely dark skin to match. The child had slightly paler skin, the cutest button nose and a mop of chocolate brown curls.

'Hello. Wow, looks like you've got some work ahead of you.' She shifted the little girl on her hip as she glanced into my trolley. 'I'm Jedda and this,' she indicated the toddler, 'is Bindi.'

I offered her my hand and a smile. 'I'm Ashling. Your daughter is adorable.'

'She's a cheeky ratbag, that's what she is, but I wouldn't be without her.' Jedda kissed Bindi on her forehead and the little girl giggled. 'So, what brings you to our beautiful part of the world? Doesn't look like you're planning much of a holiday.'

I hesitated a moment—something about this woman almost had me blurting out the long story, but I swallowed my confession at the last moment. I'd come here to get away from pitying looks. 'I'm staying at a friend of a friend's place for the week.'

'Oh, where?' asked the frosty girl behind the counter as if now that Jedda had spoken to me she was willing to as well.

'The old blue shack with the two big eucalypts out the front on the beach road.'

Her eyes pinged with recognition and she and Jedda exchanged looks. 'Xiang's place,' they said in unison, and I wasn't sure how to read their expressions.

So that was his name—*Shung*. I nodded.

'Are you related to him?' the girl asked. 'We thought it was a myth he had any family and you don't *look* Chinese.'

I shook my head—had she listened to *anything* I'd said so far? 'No, my friend knows his grandson.'

'Well, that explains all the cleaning equipment.' Jedda nodded towards my trolley again. 'I imagine the shack is in quite a state.'

'I'm not sure state is the word I'd use. There was a possum in the kitchen when I arrived.'

'Oh my God,' shrieked the checkout operator. 'I would've run out and never returned.'

'Trust me, I was tempted.'

'You must be a brave soul.' Jedda chuckled as her daughter began to squirm.

'Brave or crazy?' I shrugged and she grinned.

'Anyway, I'd better be getting this one home for her afternoon nap,' she said. 'Good luck with everything.'

Jedda plucked an A4 booklet off the pile she'd put on the checkout and handed it to me. I glanced down to read the words 'RAGGED POINT REPORTER' in big bold print across the top.

'It's our local paper. I'm the editor-in-chief, also the copywriter, proofreader, printer and distributer.' She chuckled. 'It's not the *New York Times* but it'll give you an idea of what happens in our little town. It's usually two dollars an issue, but this one's on me.'

'Thanks.'

'No worries. It's supposed to be fortnightly but since this little one came along ... let's just say it's printed when it's printed.'

This time *I* chuckled—it was impossible not to like Jedda and I couldn't wait to read her paper.

'Well, I'll see you round,' she said, waving Bindi's little hand as she walked out of the store. 'Bye Sam.'

'Do you want boxes for this stuff?' asked Sam as I started to load my items onto the checkout. 'Or we have recycled bags but they're three dollars each.'

'Boxes would be great,' I said, thinking of the zillion shopping bags that sat at the bottom of my pantry back home.

Sam retrieved a couple from behind the counter and started scanning my things.

'Have you lived here long?' I asked.

'All my life.' She sighed dramatically. Her enthusiasm for 'the Point' appeared to be drastically less than Jedda's. 'My parents own this dump. I finished school in Jurian last year and I'm only working here to save up for a plane ticket.'

'That's great. Where are you headed?'

'LA,' she said with an almost bored tone. 'I'm going to be an actress.'

'Wonderful.' I tried to stifle my smile.

To my surprise, Sam helped me carry my boxes out to the wagon and then wished me luck with the cleaning. 'Rather you than me,' she said as I shut my boot.

'Thanks. And good luck with your saving. I look forward to seeing you on the big screen one day,' I said, then climbed into my car and drove the short distance back to the shack.

As I carried the first box inside, I was pleasantly surprised to find no wildlife in the kitchen (aside from the cockroaches but they might take longer to banish) and the stench significantly less. I couldn't wait to start the detox.

After grabbing the last two boxes from the car, I sculled water from my drink bottle and then opened the back door and sucked in a breath. Due to the shock of the possum and mind-boggling amount of clutter, it totally slipped my mind earlier to check out the view.

'Holy wow!'

Now this is more like it, Hayley. This was what I called a holiday destination.

To my surprise and delight the back porch was almost clutter free, save for a hammock hanging between the wall of the house and one of the verandah posts. Xiang must have spent more time out here than out the front. I'd always wanted a hammock, but Adrian believed they made a place look messy. Well, stuff you, hubby-o-mine, once I had the house a little in order, I could easily imagine rewarding myself at the end of a hard day, drinking a glass of wine and watching the sun go down over the ocean, which happened to be a mere fifty metres or so from the shack. Maybe I'd even read a book! *Bliss*.

I smiled as my gaze skipped over the near-white sand and landed on the pristine blue water glistening in the sun. The view could have been printed on a postcard. It felt like the definition of peaceful and serene, if I pushed what lay behind me to the back of my mind.

In the distance, almost at the horizon, I saw a massive ship that looked as if it held cargo and, much closer to shore, a small island. It looked to have some kind of construction. I squinted, trying to see exactly what it was, but would need a pair of binoculars or a boat to get a better look.

My phone rang from inside and, with one final, lustful glance at the sea, I hurried to answer it. I was fairly certain it would be Hayley and right now I didn't know whether I wanted to thank or berate her.

14

I was going to kill my best friend and sister-in-law for her crazy scheme to send me to Ragged Point. After working late into the night ridding the shack of rubbish and cleaning the kitchen enough to make a meal, I was exhausted. But thanks to the noises in the roof—which I hoped to only be the possum—the creaking of the walls, the scuttling sounds between them and the violent wind shaking the trees and stirring the ocean outside, I hadn't managed a wink of sleep. I didn't believe in ghosts, but awake, alone, and lying in a dead man's bed with nothing but my own imagination to entertain me, I swore I heard footsteps in the living room.

So much for this break giving me a distraction from my husband woes—all I could think about last night was him. At least I knew that this week he was with the kids so wouldn't be tearing up the sheets with some random woman.

At eighteen I'd refused to live with either my mother or father anymore and had moved into a share house with Hayley and two of our friends. I'd gone straight from that house to one I shared with

Adrian, so I'd never lived alone before, and I didn't like it. I missed not only the comforting warmth of his body, the knowledge the kids were peacefully sleeping down the hallway and Charlie snoring at my feet, but also the security of knowing that should an intruder break in, I wouldn't be the one who had to deal with it; Adrian kept a cricket bat under the bed just in case. I should have brought Xiang's golf club into the bedroom but by the time I thought of this, I'd been paralysed in bed, too terrified to get up.

If I had, I doubt I'd have stopped in the living room. I'd probably be back in Perth by now, safe in Hayley's spare room, exactly where I planned to be tonight. No way could I subject myself to another night in this hell hole. And how was cleaning up some stranger's house going to help me get my husband back? So far, I'd made absolutely no inroads towards that goal and, although I wasn't exactly sure what to do, Adrian wasn't going to come knocking on my door up here.

Flinging back the covers, which were drenched in sweat from my night terrors, I headed for the shower, trying not to think about what kind of fungi may be lingering in the tiles beneath my feet. I'd worked hard yesterday, washing the moth-ridden curtains in the bedroom, changing the sheets and starting on detoxing the kitchen, but I hadn't made it even close to the bathroom. Sure, my family teased me about enjoying cleaning too much, but this did not make for a relaxing break!

As soon as I was dressed, I'd leave this horrible shack and Ragged Point behind for good.

The hot water pounded into my aching bones and I felt marginally human again by the time I got out and decided on a walk to stretch my legs before the two-hour journey. Wasn't I supposed to be getting into an exercise routine to help me shift my middle-aged spread?

I headed out to the back porch and onto the beach shoeless, despite my husband's voice in my head about the dangers that might be lurking beneath the sand. It felt blissful between my toes, the fresh salty air filled my lungs in a way Perth air never did and I yelped with delight each time the water hit my heels.

There were only a few other souls on the beach—holidaymakers having mostly returned to normal life by now—and, as I admired this beautiful ocean, I thought I could get used to such serenity. Pity I couldn't get used to the shack. When my stomach started to rumble and my parched throat could wait no longer for my morning coffee, I turned around and was almost back when I saw a man in a little boat rowing towards the shore from the direction of the island.

Did he *live* out there?

The man saw me looking and lifted his hand to wave.

Not wanting to be rude, I waved back and although I meant to continue on my way, my feet didn't cooperate. I stood still, watching as he reached the shore, jumped out of the boat and dragged it onto dry sand. He wore a dark-grey polo T-shirt, which wasn't doing a very good job of hiding his impressive upper body. I guessed if anyone rowed on a daily basis, they'd quickly develop such muscles.

Maybe I should take up rowing.

'Hi there,' he called, as he straightened and started towards me. 'You're not a local.'

I wasn't sure if this was a question or a statement. 'No. I'm just visiting.'

'Welcome.' He nodded and offered me his hand. 'I'm Dan.'

'Ashling,' I said. His grip was strong, his skin warm and slightly wet, but not in a disgusting way. He was so tall I had to tilt my neck to look up into his tanned face, which boasted three-day stubble. Judging by the shaggy, sun-kissed hair that flopped on either side of his face, he didn't worry too much about his appearance.

Don't get me wrong, he wasn't ugly; I was simply used to the men in my life being clean-shaven with short-back-and-side cuts.

'Where are you staying?' he asked.

Usually I'd advise women not to tell strange men the exact location of their whereabouts, but as I was leaving, I didn't see a problem. 'I *was* staying there,' I said, gesturing behind us towards Xiang's shack.

'Was?'

'One night was more than enough.'

Dan snorted. 'I don't blame you—that place is probably a demolition order waiting to happen—but it's a pity.'

Did he mean the state of the shack was a pity or the fact I was leaving? His expression was hard to decipher.

I shook my head. The answer didn't matter. 'Do you live out on that island?'

'No. I was just feeding the cat.'

That made no sense whatsoever, but I didn't get the chance to ask any further questions, because Dan glanced down at his wrist. 'Shit, is that the time? Better be going or the boss will have my head. See ya.'

And then he turned and jogged up the beach, sand flicking up from his bare feet.

'Bye.' I waved him off and headed back to the shack.

'No!' I shrieked as I stepped into the kitchen to find my furry adversary sitting on the counter, lapping up milk from the overturned carton. What the hell? Did possums even *like* milk?

'Shoo, shoo,' I screamed as I flapped my arms at the beast, all the while wondering how it managed to get the milk out of the fridge. What kind of gifted animal was I dealing with?

The possum had one final lap of stolen, spilt milk, glared at me and then made its way up into the roof in exactly the same way as it had done the day before. Fury burned inside me as I saw a fresh hole in the cardboard that I'd used to cover the previous one. I sighed. Not only had I obviously done a crap job of covering it, I also appeared to have been so tired I must have left the milk out after my final cup of tea last night.

If this wasn't a sign that going home was the right decision, I didn't know what was.

15

Harbouring huge resentment towards the possum because I couldn't make a coffee to go in my travel mug, I packed my car in record time, secured the house—at least from human intruders—and began my journey back to Perth. As I drove down the main street of Ragged Point, I noticed a chalkboard sign outside Brewed Awakening advertising home-baked muffins.

The aroma of freshly brewed coffee wafted towards me as I stepped out of my car.

'Good morning,' said a perky voice as I entered the cafe.

'Hello,' I replied as my eyes adjusted to the lack of sun.

'Oh, it's you. Ashling, right?' Jedda, who was taking chairs down off the tables, recognised me before I did her. 'Nice to see you again. Take a seat and I'll bring you over our breakfast menu.'

'Thanks, but I'm not staying. I was just hoping to grab a takeaway coffee for my trip back to Perth.'

'I thought you were here for a week?'

'Change of plans.'

'Say no more. Now, how do you like your coffee?'

'Skinny flat white, no sugar.' Of course, I really wanted full-cream milk and two sugars but ... adjustments needed to be made. 'And a muffin, please.' I wanted to save my calories for that!

'No worries, coming right up.' After placing the final chair onto the floor, Jedda went behind the counter and began to work the coffee machine.

'What's that island just offshore?' I asked as she grabbed a takeaway cup from a stack next to the machine.

'You mean Bill's Island?' It was a rhetorical question. 'At least that's what locals call it these days. It was uninhabitable until he decided to live there and started clearing the land, building himself a place to live. He's a bit of a local—'

Jedda's words were cut off at the sound of a loud cry. I followed the noise to see a baby monitor on the counter behind her.

'That's my girl waking up. Do you mind waiting a minute for your coffee? I'll be right back.'

'No, of course not,' I said, realising Jedda and her daughter must live behind the cafe. I noticed the playpen set up in the corner not far from the counter, filled with books and baby toys. I wondered how she managed a business, a baby and publishing the local paper. I'd flicked through the *Reporter* in bed last night and it was much more professional than I'd expected. Also, there appeared to be lots more happening in Ragged Point than I'd ever have predicted. They had sports teams that played against nearby towns, a number of other groups who'd written up their news in the 'Clubs' Column' and a regular movie night at the town hall.

Less than two minutes later, Jedda returned with a sleepy Bindi. Her dark curls were flat on one side of her head, which she rested on her mum's shoulder as she eyed me warily. She wore a cute spotted jumpsuit and sucked on a blue dummy in a way that reminded me of Maggie Simpson.

'Say good morning to Ashling,' Jedda said, shifting the toddler on her hip. Bindi buried her head into her mother's chest.

I smiled. 'It's okay. My children were the same at that age when they'd just woken up.'

'How many you got?'

'Two. A boy and a girl. They're with their dad this week.' A lump swelled in my throat. It was the first time I'd volunteered information about our new situation to anyone and the moment the words were out, I wanted to take them back.

Jedda gave me a sympathetic smile. 'Well, let's see if this little one will go in the playpen long enough for me to make you a coffee.'

However, the moment she tried to lower Bindi to the floor, the tiny girl squealed and kicked her legs. 'Sorry,' Jedda said, scooping her back up. 'I'll get her a bottle and then hopefully she'll let me go long enough to make your drink. Usually someone else is here with me at this time, but my morning shift called in sick and her replacement can't get here for another half an hour. I'm a bit short-staffed at the moment.'

'It's fine. I'm in no real rush. See to Bindi first. I'd offer to hold her but I'm not sure that would go down well.'

'Thanks.' Jedda laughed. 'She used to go to anyone, but she's been super clingy lately. I don't know what's come over her.'

'How old is she?'

'Twenty-one months.'

I nodded. 'Is she teething? My youngest was shocking when she got her molars.'

'Maybe that's it, but I sure hope it doesn't last long. I don't know how much more of this I can take.'

'Does she usually stay in the cafe while you work?' I doubted Ragged Point was big enough to have a day care centre.

'Not all day.' Jedda exhaled and shook her head. 'I shouldn't complain really. She's mostly pretty good. We're closed Mondays and I'm only here to open and close and cover the lunch rush other days. My wonderful staff hold the fort between times when I take Bindi upstairs or down to the park to play.'

It probably wasn't my place to pry, but the words just came out. 'Does her father not help you much?'

'She's a sperm donor baby,' Jedda said as she filled a bottle with milk, all the while still holding her wriggling toddler.

'Oh.' I wasn't sure I actually knew anyone who'd had a baby on their own this way.

'All I know about her father is that he was born in Ireland—I've always loved blokes with Irish accents—he was thirty-five years old, had a clean bill of health and a degree in philosophy. I like them smart as well. Folks round here thought I was crazy with a business and no family to speak of to help, but I hit forty and got tired of waiting for someone else to help me fulfil my dream of being a mother. I don't regret it, best damn thing I ever did, aren't you, darling?' She kissed Bindi on the forehead as she handed her the bottle. 'I'm sorry, Ashling, you just caught us on a bad day.'

'Don't apologise—I think you're amazing. This place is great, Bindi's adorable, and I read your paper last night and it was fabulous too. Were you ever a journalist?'

'No, I could barely spell in high school. I started the paper simply because I saw a need.'

'Ah, I see.' I nodded. 'Well, I think you're a great writer anyway. I actually did a degree in journalism myself, but I've never used it.'

'Pity you're not sticking around then. I could use a right-hand woman,' Jedda said as she attempted once again to lower Bindi into the playpen. This time, clutching her bottle tightly in her chubby little hands, the teat trapped between her lips, she settled.

The bell above the door dinged again and two men wearing big grey jackets, navy work trousers and black boots entered. 'Morning Jed,' they said in unison.

'Hey Baz, hey Tony,' Jedda said. 'The usual?'

'You know it, gorgeous,' replied the taller of the two with a wink.

Jedda rolled her eyes. 'You'll have to wait your turn. Ashling here has already been waiting for her coffee long enough.'

As the two men turned to acknowledge me, I noticed the logo on their jackets—the words 'Lobster Factory' with a cartoon image of a lobster beneath.

This time the shorter one spoke. 'Well, hello there,' he said a little flirtatiously. 'You must be new around here ... I know I'd remember if I'd met you before.'

'Don't mind these two,' Jedda said as she turned back to the coffee machine.

'It's fine.' I couldn't remember the last time anyone had flirted with me and it gave me a much-needed boost. 'I don't mind waiting a bit longer. You guys are obviously off to work.'

'That's mighty kind of you,' said the tall one. 'The boss is a stickler for punctuality.'

At the word 'boss', I thought of the man I'd met on the beach and wondered if perhaps he too worked at this Lobster Factory. He looked like the type of guy who'd enjoy toiling out on the high seas.

This thought reminded me again about the island. I really wanted to hear more about this Bill person.

'Thanks, Jedda, and thanks ...?' As the men took their coffees, the shorter one's voice trailed off in a question.

'Ashling,' I replied. 'And you're welcome.'

'Maybe we'll see you round,' said the other one with a wave as they both exited the cafe.

'So sorry about that,' Jedda said. 'You're not on Facebook, are you?'

'Yes, why?'

'Because you'll probably give me a terrible review for my terrible service, but I promise you this coffee will be worth the wait, and I'll throw in the muffin for free.'

'It's honestly fine. If I knew how to leave you a review, it would be a glowing one.'

Jedda smiled her thanks as the doorbell dinged again and this time three grey-haired women entered. They sounded slightly out of breath when they greeted Jedda and they were all dressed in active wear. Quickly on their heels came a woman dragging two kids in school uniform behind her, and only moments later, a young woman with her red hair piled up in a tight bun rushed in after them.

'Sorry, I couldn't get here earlier,' she called as she headed behind the counter, stopping only briefly to wave at Bindi in the playpen.

'No worries, Cassie.' Jedda tossed her an apron. 'Can you get the muffins out of the oven and grab one for Ashling? Hope they're not burnt.'

Jedda handed me my coffee in a takeaway cup and then I stepped aside as the active wear brigade approached the counter. 'Enjoy the muffin,' she said over the top of the coffee machine a few moments later as Cassie handed me a brown paper bag. 'It was lovely to meet you. Have a safe drive home.'

'Actually, I think I'm going to stay.'

My announcement was as much a surprise to me as it was to Jedda, but she'd inspired me. Perhaps I'd been too hasty in writing this opportunity off.

If Jedda could take care of a baby, produce a newspaper *and* run what appeared to be a reasonably busy cafe, then maybe I shouldn't let a possum and a few bumps in the night scare me away from achieving something of my own. Not that the shack was mine and not that I'd be able to do a great deal in six days, but it might be therapeutic to focus on something that had nothing to do with Adrian or the kids for once.

'Good for you.' Jedda grinned as I took a sip of my coffee and started out of the cafe.

16

By Thursday I'd formed a bit of a routine. Having not been murdered in my bed the first couple of nights, I was now sleeping much better and started each day with a walk along the beach, stopping in at Brewed Awakening for a coffee and a muffin before heading back to the shack to get stuck into the cleaning and detoxing.

Although it wasn't a huge place, the extent of the clutter and grime meant that I'd only begun to put a dent in what needed to be done. But I was beginning to see that if this shack was renovated properly, it could be a really beautiful beachside escape. And I really welcomed the physical work. Occasionally I'd get so lost in the tasks of scrubbing mould from the tiles in the bathroom or trying to eradicate the dust and stains from other surfaces that I got a few moments' peace in which I forgot about the fact Adrian had decided he'd wanted to sleep with other women.

The other good thing was that the exertion was helping to combat the effects of my morning muffin. Working on the shack gave me a workout just as good as, if not better than, any gym could, and I also found it more fun and rewarding.

On my umpteenth trip outside to deliver another big bag of rubbish to the council bin, I startled when someone called 'Yoo-hoo!'

I looked up at the sound of the sing-songy voice to see an elderly woman hurrying towards me. Her rather large bosom heaved with the effort and she took a moment to catch her breath when she joined me at the edge of the road.

'Hi.' I smiled, hoping she wasn't about to have a heart attack or anything. My first aid was rusty at best.

'I've been meaning to come over and introduce myself.' She thrust out a hand covered in paper-thin skin. 'I'm Audrey Fine, and you are?'

'Ashling Wood,' I said, wiping my hand on my jeans before shaking hers, finding myself delighted by the interruption. Aside from the few people I passed on the beach and my brief chats with Jedda in the cafe, I'd barely interacted with anyone since being here. While on one hand I enjoyed the peace and quiet, another part of me had begun to crave a conversation longer than it took to order coffee and a muffin.

'You've been busy the last few days,' Audrey said. 'Are you moving in?'

'No. A friend owns this place and I'm just staying for a few days.'

She sniffed. 'I don't blame you, why anyone would want to live there is beyond me.'

'Oh, it's not too bad. Nothing a bit of a clean and freshen up won't fix,' I said, although that *was* a bit of an understatement. A total facelift would help things enormously.

She pointed to the bin I'd just delivered to the side of the road; it was so full the lid wouldn't shut. 'If you've got any more rubbish, you're welcome to put it in mine. It's just me now Walter has gone to meet our maker, so I rarely fill it myself.'

'Thanks. That's such a kind offer and it would be very helpful.'

'Pity you're only here short term,' she said. 'I don't like to speak ill of the dead, but I have to say it would be much nicer to have a normal person living next door.'

I frowned. 'Normal?'

She leaned close enough that I could see a filling in one of her teeth. 'I'm not one to gossip, but the smells that came out of that kitchen! I wouldn't have been surprised if that man was cooking up cats and dogs in there. A few disappeared around here over the years, you know. Maybe he was even selling them to Chinese restaurants.'

I honestly didn't know how to respond, but she didn't appear to register my shock and disgust.

'I questioned him about it once, but could never understand a word he said. And at least now I don't have to be so worried about where I park my car.'

'What?' I wasn't following—what did her car have to do with his kitchen fumes?

'You know what terrible drivers Asians are. I didn't want to park too close in case he ran into me. Anyway, would you like to come over for a cup of tea? I've just made a fresh batch of scones too.'

While I liked a good scone as much as the next person, less than two minutes in her company had already told me that I didn't want to spend a moment longer with her.

'I'm really sorry but I need to run a few errands.'

Disappointment filled her face. 'Maybe another day.'

'Maybe,' I said, before making a hasty escape. I had no time for people like that.

Sensing Audrey had not much else to do but watch if I followed through on my words, I grabbed my phone and bag from inside. It was a nice afternoon, so I walked the very short distance to the main street.

Although I'd already had my daily visit to Brewed Awakening, I couldn't resist the aroma of pastry wafting from the cafe.

Jedda looked up from where she was wiping down a table as I entered. 'Well, hello again.'

'Hi,' I replied with a smile. 'I decided to treat myself to a late lunch, rather than make yet another ham and salad sandwich. What have you got left?'

She gestured to the glass display fridge by the counter. 'There's some sweet potato and spinach quiche, our famous home-baked meat pie, or I can make you a sandwich a little more gourmet than what you've been making yourself.'

'I'll have a pie.'

'Excellent. One pie coming right up.'

While Jedda went off to fill my order, I walked over to the corner where Bindi was chewing on a soggy biscuit in the playpen.

'Hello, angel.'

'She's in a right grump today and has barely slept at all,' Jedda warned.

Bindi looked up at me warily and I offered her a gentle smile. 'Do you like reading?' I asked, pointing to a well-loved copy of *Where Is the Green Sheep?* beside her.

In reply she picked up the book and thrust it at me.

I sat myself down on the floor beside the playpen and began to read. After a couple of pages, she edged closer and I felt her soft breath on my neck as she listened. A few more pages and she poked me through the rails and held out her little pudgy arms to me.

'It's a miracle,' Jedda said from where she was busy behind the counter. 'I think she wants you to pick her up.'

'Is that okay?'

'More than.'

'Would you like to sit on my lap and read a story?' I held my breath as I went to pick her up. It had been a while since I'd had much to do with babies.

Holding Bindi close, I took her to a table, sat down and opened the book again. She leaned back against me and began to suck her thumb as I read. By the time I'd read *Green Sheep* through twice, Bindi had fallen asleep and Jedda had delivered my lunch to the table.

'Where should I put her?' I asked.

'I'll get the pram.'

Jedda returned a few moments later and together we gently laid the little girl down. Bindi stirred a moment and Jedda and I looked at each other—both holding our breaths—but she didn't wake up.

'That lunch is on the house,' Jedda said. 'Do you mind if I sit a moment too? Gail is cleaning up in the kitchen and I wouldn't mind a few minutes off my feet while I can get it.'

'I'd be delighted.' I liked Jedda immensely, but she was usually too busy for extended conversation.

She grabbed some water and then sat opposite me while I began to eat.

'This is so good,' I said. 'It's better than any pie I've ever tasted. What's the secret?'

Jedda winked. 'Vegemite. And consider yourself lucky—I don't tell just anyone that, but I owe you one getting Bindi to sleep.'

As I ate, we talked a little more about Bindi's teething issues and her current aversion to sleep. I also told Jedda about meeting Mrs Fine and she rolled her eyes, not at all surprised.

'How long have you lived in Ragged Point?' I asked when there was a lull in conversation.

'Coming on for twenty years.'

'Wow. So, you're a local then.'

She chuckled. 'You can't claim to be a local until you've lived here for thirty-seven years, but I'm well on my way.'

'*Thirty-seven years?*' My eyebrows rose as did the inflection in my voice. 'Do you have family here?'

'Nah. My mum's from up north somewhere. Who knows about my dad?'

Her vague reply intrigued me, but I silently told myself not to pry—I didn't want to come across as nosy. However, she continued unprompted.

'My mum was part of the Stolen Generation,' she explained. 'She was taken from her family when she was very little and never remembered anything about them or their culture. Stuffed her up pretty badly—although she was raised in a really loving family, she never felt like she fit in. She got pregnant at sixteen, had me and then did a runner.'

'Oh my goodness, what happened to you then?' Jedda seemed so together, I'd never have imagined anything like this in her past.

'Her adopted family took me in. They were good people and made sure I got a good education, but the moment I turned eighteen I left to backpack around Australia. I wanted to explore outside the city. I worked wherever I could—pubs, draft camps as a cook, picking fruit. You name it, I did it. Met some great people, but at twenty-two I got tired of being a gypsy. I decided to head back to Perth and get a proper job, but I stopped in the Point for one night and met the love of my life. One night turned to two, then to a week and before I knew it, I was pulling beers in the pub and shacked up with a rock lobster fisherman.'

I smiled at the way Jedda's eyes lit up at this last bit. The nostalgia of young love made me think of Adrian.

'Did you guys break up?' I asked.

'No.' Jedda's smile turned sad. 'Jack drowned in an accident at sea.'

'Oh my God. I'm so sorry.' The words didn't feel adequate at all. 'How long ago was that?'

She took a deep breath and I could tell talking about him still hurt. 'Seventeen years. We'd been together for three and had just got hitched. We were saving for a house and going to start a family.'

'And you never left?'

'Oh, I tried—but this place gets under your skin.'

I nodded, already understanding. I'd been here less than a week but, despite the anguish I carried about my marriage, it was like the Point had medicinal qualities. I couldn't help but feel relaxed and slightly more hopeful when I looked out of the shack and saw the ocean.

'I moved away a couple of times,' Jedda continued, 'but Jack's family is still here, and they treat me as their own. And it sounds stupid, but he's buried in the local cemetery and when I'm here, I can still feel his presence.'

'That doesn't sound stupid at all.' I paused a moment. 'So how long have you had this place?'

'About ten years. I worked for the previous owner before that—did shifts here and at the pub. When Jack was killed, I got a good payout. Would rather have him, but I knew he'd want me to use it wisely. I put a lot in savings and invested some, but when the cafe came on the market, I bought it too.'

We talked for a little while longer but just before the cafe was due to close, there was an afternoon rush and Jedda had to get up and serve.

I took that as my cue to get back to my cleaning, waving as I left and promising to see her in the morning.

'I'll have your coffee waiting,' she promised.

17

Early Sunday evening—my final full day in the Point—I had my first visitors.

'Hello!' Jedda called as she approached the shack and I hurried to the door to help her lift Bindi, pram and all, up onto the porch.

'Hi, sweet pea.' I dropped down to eye level with the little girl and tickled her toes. She squealed in delight. Since the *Green Sheep* day, she no longer clung to her mother when I dropped into Brewed Awakening for my morning coffee, and yesterday she'd even let me take her for a walk to the park when Jedda couldn't take a break. Spending time with Bindi reminded me of when Saxon and Payton were little and had gone a tiny way towards easing the pain of not being with them.

Jedda pulled me into a quick hug. 'I can't wait to see what you've done with the place.' It felt like we'd known each other much longer than six days, which was weird considering we'd only chatted when I visited the cafe.

'Don't get too excited. I'm not a miracle worker.'

She held out a bottle of white wine. 'I don't really care what it looks like as long as you've got glasses.'

I winced. 'I've got mugs, but I don't think old Xiang was a big fan of anything except tea and beer.'

'Mugs will have to do then because I'm not walking back home, and old Mrs Fine believes drinking alcohol is a mortal sin, so we can't ask her.'

I chuckled; that sounded *exactly* like the woman I'd met.

'Let's go sit out the back,' I suggested. 'The view's better there, or would it be easier with Bindi inside? Thankfully she'll no longer catch a disease if she crawls over the living room floor, but she might catch a cockroach.'

Jedda raised an eyebrow.

I held up my hands. 'I've done my best. Sadly, the cockroaches and I are still in combat, but at least I've come to an agreement with the possum.'

'Oh?'

I told her how I'd risked my life climbing up an old ladder to see if there was a way my furry nemesis could get out before I sealed up the hole properly. 'I found a possum-sized hole rusted in the tin roof. Thank God. I didn't want to board up the ceiling and then trap the thing there.'

Jedda found this hilarious.

'Hey, I might not want it drinking my milk or depositing little presents on the carpet, but I don't want its death on my conscience. Anyway, as you'll see, I've nailed a wooden board to the roof this time. The possum will need a hacksaw to get through that, so now every afternoon I cut up fruit and leave it in a bowl on the front porch. I always wake up to an empty bowl.'

'You're a real softie, aren't you, Ashling? But who's gunna cut up fruit for the little pest when you leave tomorrow?'

I opened my mouth and closed it again. 'I hadn't thought about that.'

Jedda cackled and shook her head. 'Never mind, it survived before you arrived and I'm sure it'll survive again after you go. Let's see what you've done here.'

I waited until Jedda had pushed the pram into the living room and then closed the sliding door.

'Is that dead fish I can smell?' she asked.

'Dammit.' I actually stamped a foot. I'd thought after a week of airing out the shack and going through almost a dozen bottles of bleach that the smell was gone, but I must have got used to it.

'Never mind.' She held up the wine bottle. 'Once we've had a few of these I'm sure I won't notice it either. Now where are these mugs?'

We traipsed into the kitchen at exactly the same moment as a pesky cockroach scuttled across the floor.

Jedda watched as it disappeared under the fridge. 'You must be looking forward to getting home.'

'Yes, I can't wait to see my kids—both human and fur variety,' I said.

But truthfully, I wasn't as itchy to head back to Perth as I thought I'd be. In the end, once I'd become accustomed to the unfamiliar nocturnal sounds and even the roaches, I'd enjoyed my week in Ragged Point. I was in my element tidying up the shack and I knew I'd miss my morning walks along the beach, my coffee, muffin and morning chat with Jedda. Not to mention the treat of watching the sun set every evening over the ocean. My accommodation may not be flash but its surrounds made up for that tenfold. I hadn't felt this relaxed in years and now I was energised to return to Perth and work on my marriage. I had an appointment with a therapist on Wednesday and hoped she'd give me some tips on getting through to Adrian.

'Do you want the grand tour?' I asked, pushing thoughts of my husband aside.

'Sure. Why not?' She scooped Bindi out of the pram and carried her as we went from room to room.

I soon established that Jedda had never actually been inside Xiang's shack and once I'd shown her the before photos I'd taken for Wei, she was almost gushing in her praise. 'Do you have a PhD in sterilisation or something?'

'Don't be too impressed, I enjoy this kind of stuff. When we got married, my husband and I bought a fairly run-down house and over the years I've renovated it almost single-handedly. There's still a lot that needs to be done if Xiang's family wants to turn this place into an Airbnb, but it's a start.'

'They definitely owe you one.'

I shook my head. 'They did me a favour letting me stay here. I needed to get away for a bit, clear my head.'

'And has it worked?'

'I'm not sure to be honest. I still don't have any idea what went wrong with my marriage.'

'You know what the answer always is?' Jedda's eyes twinkled. 'Wine! But I think you're right about sitting out the back. I've just given Bindi an early dinner and hopefully with the fresh air and the relaxing sound of the water, she'll be asleep in no time.'

Tour over, we went back into the kitchen and, as Jedda laid Bindi into her pram with a bottle of milk, I poured two rather large mugs full of wine and put the bottle back in the fridge. Outside, Jedda sat in the rocking chair that I'd moved from the front and gently rocked the pram with her foot. I carried a chair out from the kitchen and sat beside them. Within minutes Bindi was asleep.

'So, what's the deal with you and your ex?' Jedda asked after taking her first sip of wine.

'He's not actually my ex, well, not legally.' I sighed and told her the whole sorry story.

'Jesus. No wonder you looked like a broken butterfly the first time I saw you.'

Adrian was—*is*—my best friend's twin brother. We all went to school together, so I've pretty much known him forever. I was always at his house playing with Hayley and I had a crush on him most of high school, but he barely noticed me as anything but his sister's geeky friend. He was pretty popular at school and Hayley and I didn't hang in the in-crowd with him. I never thought anything would happen between us, so I couldn't believe it when he kissed me on the night of their sixteenth birthday. He never officially asked me out but after that we were just together. And everyone thought we were perfect. We were no longer referred to in the singular—we were always Adrian-and-Ash this or Ash-and-Adrian that.'

'And how long have you been married?'

'Eighteen years in December.' A lump swelled in my throat at the thought.

'Long time.'

I nodded and swallowed.

'Do you think this is really it then?'

I gulped some wine, my stomach twisting. 'I hope not. I want my husband and my family. Nothing is more important to me than providing a secure, loving home for my kids. But …'

'But he's broken your trust and you don't know if you can get it back?'

I shook my head. 'He didn't have an affair.'

Jedda raised an eyebrow. 'He told you he wants to sleep with other people. For all you know he's done that already.'

I took another gulp of wine. 'And you think I'd be stupid to let him back into my heart and my bed after that?' It was what everyone was thinking—even my best friend, *his* sister.

Jedda held up a hand as if I were holding a gun. 'Hey, I don't judge anyone. Life's nothing if not complicated. But if you do want to get back together with him, how do you plan on doing it?'

'That's the million-dollar question. I have no effing idea.' I slumped in the seat and stared into the mug. 'My sister-in-law tried to help me with a makeover but when Adrian saw me all dressed up … well, that didn't work at all. He spent more time gazing at the young female umpire.'

'Naked selfies.'

'What?' I spluttered, almost spilling my drink.

'When was the last time you sent naughty photos to your husband?'

I blushed. 'Never! We dated before smartphones were invented.'

'Then maybe you should give it a try. Surprise him with a sexy text. All the kids are doing it. Or so I hear. Why should they be having all the fun and getting in all the trouble?'

'I'm not doing that. I'm too fat—I'd probably scare him away even more.'

'You're *not* fat.'

'I'm fatter than I used to be. I'm sure Adrian thinks I've let myself go.'

'If he does, then I'm not sure why you'd want to get back with him, but my guess is your issues have nothing to do with the way you look. You're gorgeous, darling. My bet is this is more to do with Adrian than you. Maybe he's forgotten how much fun you guys can have together? Maybe a photo would help.'

I couldn't believe we were even talking about this, never mind that I was actually considering it. 'Knowing my luck, I'd accidentally send it to the wrong person. My brother-in-law or one of the kids' teachers.'

Jedda howled with laughter.

'Do you have any other great ideas?'

She tapped the side of her nose. 'I'll think about it.'

'Thanks.' I smiled. 'But I've talked enough about me. What about you? Have you dated anyone else since Jack?'

'Nah.' Jedda peered inside the pram to make sure Bindi was fully asleep, then grinned at me. 'I've had a few offers of course, but none of them have come close to my Jack. Although of course I'd rather he was still here, I'm not unhappy on my own. There are a lot of advantages to being a single woman you know—no man hogging the TV remote; I can watch as many girly movies as I like without anyone complaining or mocking my choices; the toilet seat is always down; no snoring bed buddy; and I never have someone tapping me on the shoulder at night wanting a bit when all I want is to go to sleep.'

I had to admit, that did sound appealing—particularly the lack of snoring, Adrian was a shocker—but I'd been thinking about sex more than ever since he'd left. Granted, I'd never wanted it as much as he had, but the thought of never having *any* intimacy again depressed me something chronic. 'You don't miss sex?'

'I said I hadn't *dated*. A girl has needs and I find ways to see to them when necessary. Although it's been a tad more difficult since this one'—she nodded towards the pram—'came along.'

I thought of Hayley and her string of one-night stands, but that wasn't the only reason why I believed she and Jedda would get along well—they also shared a similar no-nonsense, fun-loving attitude. I admired their gusto and zest for life, even though I could never imagine having even half of it myself.

Jedda went inside to fetch the wine and returned to refill our mugs. 'I'd like to make a toast. To new friends.'

'To new friends,' I echoed, and we clinked mugs.

'I hope even though you're going tomorrow you won't be a stranger. I'd love to keep in touch and catch up next time I'm in Perth.'

At her words I teared up a little—I was really going to miss Jedda and her gorgeous little girl. It had been a long while since I'd clicked with someone in such a short period of time. 'I feel the same. And I hope your trip to Perth will be sooner rather than later.'

'You'll have to call or message me to let me know how things are going with your husband,' she said.

'I will,' I promised, but I didn't want to think about Adrian tonight. Looking out to the ocean, I smiled as the last of the sun dropped down to the horizon, leaving a fiery orange belt above the water and a stunning purple sky that was getting darker by the second. On Bill's Island the palm trees were swaying gently in the evening breeze.

'Have you been out to the island?' I asked.

'Me? Yeah, but not for a long time. I'm terrified of water these days.' Jedda took a big swig of wine and visibly shuddered. 'This is about as close as I get. Haven't been swimming in seventeen years.'

I didn't need to ask her if the arrival of her fear coincided with Jack's drowning—the melancholic expression on her face gave me the answer. I could only imagine how hard it must be to live this close to the ocean, how conflicted she must feel inside, because while the sea had taken her love, Ragged Point held all her beautiful memories as well.

'So, does Bill still live out there?'

'Nah, he passed away a few years back; caused a bit of a stir actually.'

'Oh?'

'The media were all over the Point, but it died down pretty quickly. You don't remember hearing anything on the news?'

I frowned, trying to rack my mind. 'What should I remember?'

'Bill was a John Doe—the authorities were called in when he died because any death not relating to long-term illness has to be investigated. They declared his death a simple heart attack, but there was absolutely no identification on him or the island to say who he was, so they couldn't contact any next of kin.'

'Hang on ... that does sound vaguely familiar.' My mouth gaped open—I'd known there was something intriguing about the island from the moment I first laid eyes on it.

'It dropped out of the news pretty quickly when no leads came forward.'

'Wow. Does anyone live there now?'

'No,' she said, looking out to the island. 'Well, aside from Lion and the other wildlife.'

'There's a *lion* out there?'

Jedda chuckled. 'Bill's cat—a stray he found as a kitten—is called Lion. The poor thing must be getting on in years now. The cat's almost as famous as the castle is round here.'

'The *castle*?'

'Yeah. Well, it's a shelter Bill made of shells and other debris, but it certainly looks like a castle; it has turrets and everything.' She shrugged. 'Or so I've heard.'

I took another sip of wine—it was very good. 'Do you know Dan?'

'Emerson?'

'I'm not sure of his last name, but I met him on the beach my first morning.' Although I hadn't been close enough to talk to him again, I'd seen him every morning—sometimes in the early evenings as well—rowing to and from the island. 'He was coming back from the island.'

'Yep, that'll be Daniel Emerson. He and Bill were mates and I hear he's become Lion's unofficial guardian. Most people would move the cat to their place, but apparently Dan didn't want to unsettle the animal.'

'That's sweet of him.'

'Sweet?' Jedda snorted. 'Now there's a word I wouldn't associate with the Emersons.'

'What do you mean?'

'You've heard of The Lobster Factory, right?'

I nodded. It hadn't taken me long to discover that many of the townsfolk worked at the local icon—either in the factory, the shop, the restaurant, as tour guides or as cray fishermen out on the boats. It sounded like a multimillion dollar business and, in addition to crayfishing, The Lobster Factory also offered fishing charters and a sea lion tour, but I'd been so busy cleaning up the shack and enjoying just chilling on the beach, I hadn't visited the reason most people came to Ragged Point. Truth be told, it didn't hold much appeal as I wasn't big on seafood. Plain fish was about as much as I could stomach.

'The Emersons own The Lobster Factory and they invest a lot in the local infrastructure. Dan is Stephen Emerson's youngest son and runs the family business with his domineering father, his arrogant brother and his stuck-up sister.'

'They sound like a nice bunch,' I said, unable to reconcile Jedda's description with the man I'd met on the beach. He'd seemed friendly enough, and I remembered the slight anxiety in his voice as he'd mentioned his boss and not wanting to be late for work. Had he been talking about his own father?

'Do you want a refill?' Jedda asked, nodding towards my mug.

I downed the last couple of dregs and nodded. 'But it's my turn to do the honours.'

I went inside and emptied the last of the bottle into our mugs. Our conversation flowed easily for the next hour or so as we finished the wine, then Jedda decided that she'd better take Bindi home.

'Thanks for a wonderful night,' I said, giving her a quick hug after helping her lift the pram off the porch.

'No, thank *you*,' she replied. 'Now that I have this one, I don't get out much. You'll stop by in the morning on your way out of town, won't you?'

I promised I would—'I'll need my coffee for the drive'—and then waved her and Bindi off into the night.

18

Perth

After giving Jedda and Bindi quick hugs goodbye, I hurried to my car. I'd dawdled on my morning walk—wanting to soak up my last bit of serenity—which meant by the time I'd packed the car and locked up the shack, it was midmorning. And then I'd lost over an hour sharing coffee and cake with Jedda, reluctant to say farewell to this beautiful town. Don't get me wrong, I was excited about seeing the kids, but as I drove out of Ragged Point, I found myself a little despondent. In the end, my week's escape had been both relaxing and invigorating. It had almost been like I was living someone else's life. Hayley would be delighted and smug when I told her.

But did that mean she might be right about other things? Like me trying to get a job or signing up for Tinder?

No. I shuddered at the thought of the latter. Quite aside from the fact that the thought of hooking up with another man—and wasn't that what Tinder was all about?—made my skin go all clammy, it would also mean admitting defeat on my marriage.

And, while I wasn't ready to do any such thing, I had to concede Hayley might have a point about the job.

When the kids were little, Adrian and I had been on the same page about me staying at home. We'd agreed I'd get work when they got older, but the time had gone so quickly and there'd never been any urgent need until now. I'd always assumed Adrian and the podiatry clinic would support us and me being at home had been convenient because it meant I could help out there whenever needed, but now I could clearly see how naive I'd been.

It was time to stop relying on Adrian—even if I did manage to win him back—and think about looking for work.

Although the prospect was a little terrifying, I tried not to focus on the reason why I needed to get a job and instead started thinking about the kind of work I might get while mentally rewriting my resume. It would be severely lacking in paid work, but hopefully my involvement on school committees, my relief days at the clinic and the wisdom of age would have some credence.

By the time I got to Perth, I actually felt energised at the thought of entering the workforce again. I whipped around the supermarket in record time, buying enough for tonight's dinner and tomorrow's school lunches, and pulled into Payton's school just as the siren was going.

'How was your holiday?' she asked as I met her outside her classroom.

'It wasn't a holiday—just someplace to stay while Dad was with you guys,' I told her, pulling her in for a quick hug. 'But it was quite good. The shack I stayed in was horrific, but you'd have loved my furry intruder.'

'What intruder?'

Heading for the car, I told her about the possum and relished the sound of her laughter when I got to the bits about it eating on the table and spilling the milk. It was so good to be with my girl again and this feeling made me more determined to make progress with the counsellor this week. The four of us being apart had to end. Soon.

'Can you take me to Ragged Point?' Payton asked.

'Well, I don't know when I'll go back again but maybe we can visit Jedda next summer,' I suggested.

'Sounds good,' she said as we pulled up at the house.

The moment I stepped inside, Charlie jumped up at me, making me drop two shopping bags on the floor, and didn't even calm down after his usual minute of craziness.

'Did anyone walk Charlie while I was away?' I asked as Payton yanked open the pantry. The dog was still leaping up at me, almost managing to lick my face.

'Nope. I told Dad we need to walk him, but he wouldn't let me go by myself. He said Charlie's too old to need daily walking anymore.'

Is that right? My jaw twitched. 'Didn't Saxon take him?' This task was part of his requirements to get his allowance.

'Saxon hasn't left his bedroom the whole time you've been away.'

No wonder Charlie was acting like a lunatic. 'Down boy!'

He recoiled slightly and I stooped to give him a proper welcome. It wasn't his fault that his basic needs had been ignored. And I didn't care if Adrian was having some kind of midlife crisis, he couldn't forget his responsibilities, which meant reminding Saxon of his! Not even waiting to unpack my shopping, I grabbed my phone and started a message to my husband. So much for sending naked selfies; right now, I wanted to make a voodoo doll of him and stick it with needles.

Part of our bargain was that you would make sure—

'Um, what are you doing?' I asked, pausing my typing as I watched Payton scoop ice-cream into a large glass and then pour Fanta from a can over the top of it.

Since when did we have soft drinks in the house?

'What does it look like I'm doing?'

Payton loved spiders—the drink, not the eight-legged variety—but they were a special treat, not an everyday after-school snack. 'You know you're not allowed soft drink except on special occasions.'

Sticking a pink straw in the top of her drink, she said, 'Dad lets me have whatever I want after school.'

I raised my eyebrows—almost backing down because I didn't want her to like Adrian better than me. At the last moment, common sense prevailed. I wasn't here to be liked, I was here to raise healthy, well-balanced children. 'Well, I'm back now and when it's my week, it's my rules.'

I held out my hand for the ice-cream and soft-drink concoction. 'You can have some fruit and cheese and crackers if you're hungry.'

'I don't want stupid fruit. Daddy's so much nicer than you,' Payton cried, all but throwing the glass at me as she ran off. Her bedroom door slammed a few moments later and I stood there wondering what the hell had happened to my sunny-natured girl.

She'd always been a little precocious, but she'd never been so blatantly awful to me. If she or Saxon had even come close to such disrespect, Adrian had always pulled them up—'Don't speak to your mother like that!'

I squeezed my eyes tight, trying to ward off more tears. I couldn't blame Payton for acting up—as much as it broke my heart, her behaviour was normal for a child who felt unsettled by her home situation. Why couldn't Adrian see what his selfish actions had done?

At this thought, my despair once again gave way to anger—these days my emotions were constantly jumping back and forth between the two states—and I returned to my message. I hadn't been home two minutes and already I had two major complaints to lodge with my husband. But as I stabbed my fingers on the phone screen, I wondered if pointing out Adrian's shortcomings was really the best way to win him back.

No man liked a nag.

Swallowing my frustration, I deleted the message, finished unpacking the groceries and then took Charlie outside for a run around the garden. Once Sax was home, I'd get him to take the dog for a proper walk, but I didn't want to leave Little Miss Disrespectful home alone. After throwing a ball so Charlie could fetch it about twenty times, the back door opened and Payton emerged, no longer wearing her school uniform but a Tottenham T-shirt, shorts and her soccer boots.

'I'm just gunna kick the ball around for a bit before I do my spelling homework, okay?' She looked contrite and I knew this was as good an apology as I was going to get.

'Good idea. Do you want me to kick around with you for a bit?'

Her eyes lit up. 'Really?' Any kind of physical exertion was generally Adrian's domain, but I wanted to make the effort.

'Yep. Just let me go and change into my sneakers.'

Half an hour later, by the time I looked through the kitchen window to see Saxon raiding the pantry, I'd worked up quite a sweat. 'I'm just going to talk to your brother,' I told Payton. 'How about you get your spelling done soon and then you can help me make a chocolate pudding'—her favourite—'for dessert.' I might not approve of sugary after-school snacks, but I wasn't an ogre—I didn't mind a treat after a healthy dinner!

Saxon had already disappeared, presumably to his bedroom, by the time I got to the kitchen. A bottle of orange juice left on the bench and his lunchbox dumped by the sink were the only pieces of evidence that he'd ever been there at all. Sax generally left his door open unless he was playing music too loudly, but today I found it closed. Not wanting to invade his privacy, I knocked.

'Hang on, Mum.' I heard a zip, the scuffling of papers and then he called, 'Come in.'

'Hey sweetheart.' I crossed to his desk and bent down to wrap my arms around him. 'So good to see you. How was your day at school?'

He barely met my gaze. 'Okay, but I've got lots of homework.'

I glanced at all the folders and textbooks on his desk. 'Don't you have time for a bit of a break first to chat to your old mum?'

He sighed. 'Not really. Year 9 is a lot more work and if I want to get into the good classes next year, I can't stuff around.'

Most parents would kill for a kid like Sax. We'd never had to nag him about homework or music practice, but I didn't want him killing himself working too hard.

'Have you had anything to eat?' I asked.

'I had a muesli bar on the way home from school. Look, Mum, I'm fine, but I really need to get on with this. Can we talk later?'

'Of course, honey.' He sounded so stressed, I decided not to berate him about Charlie but take the dog for a walk myself. 'Can you listen out for your sister while I take Charlie out? Then I'll start on dinner.'

'Sure.' He opened his laptop.

'Don't work too hard,' I said as I left his bedroom.

19

The words 'Megan McGuinness—Couples Counsellor' were printed in capital letters on a gold plaque next to a bright yellow front door. My insides wobbled as I approached. I still couldn't believe I was in a position to need this kind of therapy. Especially since turning up at 'couples counselling' on my own made me feel like a failure even before I'd begun.

How was I supposed to fix our marriage when Adrian refused to come to the party?

Hoping Megan could work miracles, I rang the old-fashioned bell. The door pulled back mere moments later to reveal a woman with a coltish figure, a heart-shaped face and bright red, curly hair. Her skin was luminous and wrinkle-free. She was so *young*!

'Hello.' She thrust out her hand and smiled. 'You must be Ashling? I'm Megan.'

I nodded, my mouth suddenly too dry to speak.

'Such a beautiful name. Do come inside.'

I followed her into a room off the hallway and she gestured for me to sit on a white leather couch opposite a matching armchair, a black square coffee table in between with a fancy candle and a box of tissues on top of it.

'Can I get you a coffee or tea before we start?' she asked.

'How old are you?' I blurted, before realising how rude I sounded. *Damn nerves.* But seriously, what could she possibly know about mending marital rifts when she didn't even look old enough to be legally married herself?

'I'm thirty-two,' she said with a knowing grin, 'and I'm also married.' She lifted her hand to show me her wedding ring. 'But even if I wasn't, I promise you, I'm qualified to do what I do, and I think I do it well.'

I nodded, feeling suitably chastised. 'Sorry. I'd love a coffee. White with no sugar, please.'

She disappeared to make the drinks and I took the opportunity to scrutinise the room. A tall lamp stood in one corner, a couple of indoor pot plants in another, a clock I recognised from Ikea hung on the wall and the couch held two bright red cushions, a similar colour to Megan's hair. That was the extent of the decoration—she was obviously a minimalist—but weirdly the room felt warm and comfortable.

'Here you go,' she said, returning a few minutes later with a tray that held two steaming mugs and a small plate of melting moment biscuits.

I tried to take a sip of my drink, but my hands were shaking too much. Did she want me to talk first? This felt like some kind of test and I had no idea of the answers. I put my coffee back down on the table before I spilled it.

Megan did the same, then—thank the Lord—finally spoke. 'Now, I know we chatted a little about your situation on the phone.

You're currently separated from your husband? You're giving nest parenting a try in terms of custody?'

Although she was merely repeating the facts I'd given her, she made them sound like questions, so I nodded at each one.

'And you're unhappy with this situation?'

Unhappy? 'Of course I'm unhappy. I don't want to see my children only part-time. I don't want to lose my husband. Splitting up was the last thing I wanted. It came completely out of the blue.'

'Did it?' That sounded like a trick question.

'What do you mean?'

'Prior to Adrian telling you he wanted to trial a separation, how did *you* feel about your marriage, Ashling?'

'I felt fine. I've never wanted anyone else. Adrian has always been a good husband and I tried to be a good wife. I thought we had a good life. We own our own home, we've got a successful podiatry business, our kids are happy, healthy and doing well at school.'

Megan nodded. 'And what things do you do together?'

'We always eat together as a family and we're both very involved in our daughter's soccer—we take turns taking her to training, but Sunday mornings are family time when we go to the games and cheer Payton on. Saxon used to come but he stays at home most of the time now as he's growing up and not interested in sport in the slightest. Between you and me, I'm not either but I make an effort for Adrian and Payton.'

'Family time is wonderful.' Megan smiled in a way that made me feel like she didn't actually mean it. 'But what about couple time?' When I didn't reply immediately, she added, 'What things do you both enjoy doing together—without your kids. What interests do you both have in common?'

Her question stumped me. 'Well, life's busy with a business and two children in different schools, so we don't have a lot of opportunity.'

She stared at me intensely.

'I guess maybe we haven't been spending as much time together as we once did, but I assumed it was just a stage of life thing. We're getting older, relationships change and grow.'

'This is true. Some couples grow closer as time passes by and others simply grow apart. I know you've said you're busy, but if you were to make the time … what things do you both enjoy doing? What interests do you have in common?'

'We …' I felt my cheeks redden.

'What brought you together in the first place?' Megan prodded.

'Hormones.' I laughed nervously. 'I didn't have this extra tyre around my middle back then and Adrian's hairline hadn't started receding.'

Megan didn't seem amused.

'We got together when we were at school and we both liked all the usual stuff teenagers do,' I said, trying to make her understand. 'We listened to music, watched movies, hung out with our friends. Discovered sex. Had a lot of it. Adrian played footy and I went along to watch. Then when we went to uni, we got more freedom—being able to drive and stay out later—and we went to the beach lots and to concerts. Life consisted of studying, part-time jobs and lots of parties with our friends.'

She held up a finger. 'Did you do the same course at university?'

'No. I did journalism and Adrian podiatry.'

'Okay,' she continued, 'what things do *you* like to do in your spare time?'

'Spare time?' This time I did laugh. How many conversations had I had with other mums about how little time we had for ourselves since having kids? I suspected Megan didn't have children. 'I don't really have time for hobbies.'

'Does Adrian help you much in the home?'

I swallowed. 'I guess we have a quite traditional division of tasks—I'm the homemaker and do most of the kid stuff because I don't have a permanent job, but Adrian mows the lawn and keeps the garden under control.'

She nodded again. 'Okay, let's pretend you have a week free of your normal obligations. What would you do with your time?'

I took a moment, thinking of the week I'd just spent in Ragged Point. 'Well, I'd probably take our dog for long nature walks. I'd get back to reading. Maybe I'd restore some old furniture or redecorate something—I love that kind of stuff. Oh, and I used to like sewing as well—I made all the kids' clothes when they were little. Is that enough?'

Megan almost smiled. 'That's a good start. Now, does Adrian have any hobbies?'

I nodded. 'His current passion is cycling, but he's a serial hobbyist. He rides to work most days and goes out at least once a weekend with a group of other cyclists. Before that he was obsessed with golf, and he has an Austin Healey that he's been slowly doing up.' *Very slowly*, if you asked me.

'Seems like Adrian has plenty of time to himself.'

Once again, I wasn't sure what to say. As much as I hated our current situation, I didn't hate Adrian—he wasn't a *bad* person.

Megan filled the silence. 'Do you ever go riding or play golf with Adrian?'

I laughed. 'No, I don't even own a bike and if I gatecrashed his rides or his golf games he'd be horrified.'

'Hmm.'

I saw what she was saying, but it seemed very simplistic. 'Just because we don't have hobbies in common, doesn't mean our relationship is doomed. We used to love watching TV or movies together. We've been through so much and supported each other through highs and lows. We have a similar sense of humour.' Although when I thought about it, there hadn't been a whole lot of laughs in our lives lately. 'And when I was pregnant, we used to lie in bed together and Adrian would read to me.'

'So you both like reading?'

My shoulders sagged. 'We used to, but I read mostly magazines lately and I can't remember the last time Adrian read anything besides podiatry journals. His iPad gets most of his attention these days.'

'Do you resent that?'

I half-laughed. 'Are you asking if I'm jealous of his iPad?' The truth was, lots of times I found it a blessing. If he was playing games on his iPad when I came to bed, it meant *I* didn't have to entertain him when I was tired.

Megan answered my question with one of her own. 'You mentioned sex earlier. Do you still have a healthy sex life?'

I squirmed a little. 'What do you define as healthy? Is there a specific number of times a week married couples are supposed to make love?'

'That's like asking me how long a piece of string is, but a sexless marriage is defined as one in which the partners have sex less than once a month or less than ten times a year.'

Again, her tone made this statement sound like a question. I tried to recall the last time Adrian and I had slept together before we separated. Was it the night we'd come home late from his mum's seventieth birthday after having quite a lot to drink? That was about six weeks ago. Now that I thought about it, I think we both might have just fallen into bed and passed out. Shit.

Did we have a sexless marriage?

At the shock on my face, Megan said, 'You're not alone. A recent survey estimated that fifteen to twenty per cent of marriages are in the same boat as you, but only five to seven per cent of the people in those marriages are happy with that. More often than not the partners are not on the same page.'

My eyelids felt scratchy and I leaned forward and snatched a tissue from the box. 'Adrian left me because he wants to have sex with other people. Do you think I could have avoided all this if we'd just had more sex?'

How hard would it have been to lie back and think of England for the wellbeing of my husband, and thus my family, once in a while?

'I can't pretend to know what Adrian's reasons were without talking to him, but you need to try and work out *why* the sex dried up in the first place. Usually a lack of intimacy is a symptom of something deeper. Was it you or him that stopped initiating sex? Or both of you?'

I tried to think but came up blank and shrugged.

'Do you think you stopped having sex because you weren't feeling particularly amorous anymore or because you were no longer attracted to him?'

'No. Adrian is still the sexiest man I know.'

'Okay then, but how about you? Do you still feel sexy? Attractive? Does he make you feel wanted? Desirable?'

Again, I took some time, trying to remember the last time Adrian had told me I looked good or cuddled me when it wasn't going to lead to sex. 'Not really, I guess, if I'm being honest. When we first got together, he constantly told me how hot I looked, and he'd been unable to keep his hands off me, but … maybe I haven't been as gushy or affectionate as I should have been either?'

'So somewhere along the line, perhaps you've both stopped feeding your relationship. A marriage is like a well-oiled machine, each member represents a vital part and each part needs to be serviced and fine-tuned.' Megan paused. 'What was your childhood like?'

Her question gave me whiplash. Weren't we just talking about sex? 'My childhood?'

'Yes. Was it happy? Did you have siblings?'

She asked so many questions when all I wanted was answers. But I swallowed my frustration and told her. 'I guess the best way to describe my childhood would be tumultuous. No brothers or sisters. My parents got divorced when I was nine, but I think they had problems long before that—maybe that's why they never had any more children. For as long as I can remember they fought a lot. Until I started school and went over to other people's houses, I think I thought parents who screamed more than talked to each other was normal. I actually remember being happy when they said they were breaking up, but it didn't really get much better. They still argued—only they did it from different houses and often got me to be the messenger.'

'And how did all that tension and drama make you feel?'

'Crap. I just wished I could have a normal, happy home life. They'd be constantly berating each other to me and trying to make me like them better, so I spent as little time with either of them as possible, staying with friends at every opportunity. I was so happy when I was old enough not to have to live with either of them.'

'And what's your relationship with your mother and father like now?'

'It's functional, but I'm not close to either of them,' I said, then sighed. 'But I'm not worried about my relationship with them, it's the one with my husband that I want to fix.'

'I understand that, but the relationships we witness as children have a massive effect on those we have as adults.'

Well, duh. I didn't need to be a psychologist to work that out. 'I get that, but I'd really rather focus on me and Adrian right now.'

Megan twisted the pen she was holding between her fingers. 'Okay then, let's look at the end goal—what do you want to happen with you and Adrian, moving forward?'

Finally, a question I could easily answer. 'I want to get back together and give our children the happy, secure family home they deserve.'

'What about what you deserve?'

'I deserve to have my husband back!'

Megan linked her fingers and placed her hands in her lap. 'In that case, how do you plan on working towards that goal?'

Tired of her never-ending questions—if this was all it took to be a marriage therapist, maybe I could be one—I threw my hands up in the air. 'I don't know. Adrian will barely talk to me at the moment, that's why I'm here. I want to fix my marriage and I need *you* to tell me how to do that!'

'I can't tell you how to fix your marriage,' Megan said calmly. 'I can only help you try to work out what the issues are so you can work on them together.'

'But how am I supposed to do that if Adrian will barely talk to me?'

'He definitely won't come to counselling?'

I snorted. 'No way. No offence but he thinks therapy is a scam.'

Truth be told, I was starting to wonder if he might be right.

'That's a pity. I can only help those who want to be helped, so if Adrian refuses to even consider couples counselling, then dragging him here may well be a waste of time anyway.' Megan's gaze drifted to the clock on the wall. 'I'm sorry, Ashling, but I'm afraid we've run out of time so we're going to have to wrap things up. However, I think it would be good if we see each other again while you're going through this trying time. Next time we can talk about some of those highs and lows you mentioned.'

As I walked out of Megan's office, I felt like throwing something at her, but I started to calm down on the way home. She may not have provided me with solutions but she'd certainly given me a lot to think about. It was clear that Adrian and I hadn't been prioritising 'us' and that if we had any hope of saving our marriage, we needed to spend more time together.

The question was, how was I going to get him to commit to that?

20

Friday night, the doorbell rang as I was making dinner. My heart leapt with the prospect it was Adrian. Following my counselling session, I'd tried to call him and when I got his voicemail, I'd left a message that I wanted to catch up asap. My plan was to talk to him about some of the issues Megan had brought to my attention and ask him for the chance to work on them.

He'd replied via text message a couple of hours later: *Is it about the kids?*

What kind of question was that? Whatever happened between Adrian and me affected the kids, but I knew that wasn't what he meant. I'd ummed and aahed about saying yes, because he'd make time if he thought it was for Saxon or Payton, but in the end, I couldn't lie. I didn't want to meet him under false pretences.

I went to see a marriage counsellor today and she's given me lots of things to think about. I'm not sure how long you had to get your head around all this, but it was a shock to me, and I'd really like us to have a chat so I can understand more.

I'd resisted the urge to put my usual kiss on the end of the message, pushed send and held my breath waiting for a reply.

Once again, he'd taken his sweet time and the reply came when I was brushing my teeth later that night: *Pretty busy the next few days but will let you know.*

My heart sank—I'd been torn between sadness and all-out rage. We'd been together over twenty years and he couldn't even make time to fit me into his busy schedule. I hadn't heard from him since, but it wouldn't be unlike Adrian to show up out of the blue, expecting that I'd just fit in with *his* timetable.

Taking a deep breath, not wanting to appear too eager, I headed for the front door, quickly checking my appearance in the hallway mirror as I passed. A swipe of lipstick would have helped, but I didn't want to leave Adrian waiting.

'Oh, it's you,' I said, unable to hide my disappointment as I opened the door to find Hayley and Wei.

'And it's a delight to see you as well,' she said, leaning forward and kissing my cheek.

'Sorry … I just …'

Hayley waved her hand at me. 'Never mind. Wei wanted to give you these.'

He grinned, thrust a massive bouquet of colourful flowers at me and kissed me on the cheek. 'To say thanks for all the work you did at the shack. Hayley showed me the photos and I was blown away. Thanks for the heads-up on the roof. I'm so sorry—I wouldn't have suggested you stay there if I'd known how bad it was.'

'Don't worry about it. I'm one of those weird people who actually like cleaning. It was cathartic. And Ragged Point is just beautiful.'

'That's great. I haven't been there since I was a kid. Mum fell out with her dad and we stopped going, but I have fond memories of fishing on the beach and collecting shells with him before that. I meant to go visit the old guy when Mum died a few years back but then … well, life got in the way.'

Hayley squeezed Wei's hand.

'Would you like to come in for a drink?' I asked.

They exchanged a look, then Hayley glanced at her watch. 'That would be lovely, but we've only got half an hour as we're off to a concert tonight.'

A concert? That sounded like a proper date. I couldn't remember the last time Hayley had dated someone after she'd slept with them.

'Sounds wonderful,' I said as I stepped back to let them into the house.

While I put the flowers in a vase, Hayley made herself at home, grabbing a bottle of white wine from the fridge. 'Where are the kids?' she asked as she poured. 'I haven't seen Saxy in ages.'

'You and me both. Payton has a friend over for a sleepover so they're in her bedroom playing with makeup. And Saxon is where he always is these days—in his bedroom.'

'Typical teenager,' muttered Hayley.

'But is he?' I asked as we all sat down at the dining room table with our drinks. 'I've barely seen him this week. He retreats into his room to do his homework the moment he comes home, emerges for about ten minutes for dinner and then disappears again. I'm worried he's putting too much pressure on himself to achieve, or else he's avoiding me because he's angry at us. But of course when I try to talk to him about it, he tells me he's fine.'

Wei chuckled. 'If he's doing homework, you should count yourself lucky. My parents had to bribe me to do anything school-related. Sadly, our home computer was in full view of everyone so I couldn't look at porn.'

I shuddered, my hand freezing with the glass halfway to my mouth. The fact porn was even available on the internet when Wei was in high school showed just how young he was, but that wasn't what worried me. 'Oh my God. Do you think Saxon is spending so much time in his room because he's looking at porn?'

At least when I was at school, the only porn the boys could access were copies of *Playboy* or *Penthouse* stolen from their dads. Now even worse porn was readily available at the click of their fingers, and I'd been to plenty of parenting talks preaching the dangers of such exposure.

Hayley laughed. 'Don't stress. This is Sax we're talking about. The golden child. And even if he is looking at a bit of porn, it's not the end of the world. There are worse things he could be doing. Let the poor boy be a teenager and tell me how you went at the counsellor the other day.'

I noticed Wei shifting in his seat—he probably didn't want to be talking about either of these things and I didn't blame him.

'It was pretty useless,' I confessed. 'She thinks Adrian and I have drifted apart and that we need to reconnect emotionally so we can come together again on all levels, but the problem is Adrian is refusing to talk to me and the therapist didn't give me any practical ideas for how to get him to listen.'

'Hmm.' Hayley took a sip of her wine. 'Maybe you just need to give him more time. How's he going with the kids when you aren't here?'

'Fine,' I said bitterly. 'The house has been immaculate each week and I haven't found any evidence of takeaway containers or anything else that tells me he's broken our rules. Oh, except that he's letting the kids run free on sugary drinks and after-school snacks.'

'He's probably just feeling guilty and trying to bribe them, so they don't blame him for deserting you all.'

'Well, so far it's working,' I pouted, explaining about the spider.

'Payton's not stupid and neither is Saxon. The novelty will wear off soon. For *all* of them.'

'I hope you're right. Have you spoken to him much? Do you know …' I shut my mouth before I asked the question I both wanted the answer to and didn't, but Hayley knew me so well she could read my mind.

'I dropped around when you were away last week. He didn't mention any women, but … well, he probably wouldn't tell me, considering our friendship. Brad told me Adrian is on Tinder though.'

I closed my eyes and slumped in my seat. I knew all about Tinder from the single mums at school. If my husband was on it, he'd almost certainly bonked somebody else by now and wine curdled in my stomach at the thought. Had he enjoyed it? Was it better than our sex had ever been?

Hayley tossed me a sympathetic smile. 'It's only been a few weeks. Being a single man about town is still a novelty; give him a bit more time and he'll remember how much he loves you. He'll probably be begging you to take him back.'

Despite what she said, I knew she thought I'd be an idiot to do any such thing, but I couldn't just throw away over two decades of my life because my husband lost the plot for a while, could I? After all, we were only human. Everyone made mistakes.

'Well, I don't think I should hold my breath,' I said, feeling as if my marriage was slipping between my fingers. I wanted to do something to fix it but didn't know what. Pity there wasn't an app for *that* like there seemed to be for everything else these days.

'I guess this means you'll be staying with me next week?'

'If you don't mind,' I replied, not wanting to cramp Hayley and Wei's style.

'Of course I don't mind. You're my best friend *and* you're family. You're welcome as long as you need.'

'Thanks.' But my voice broke on that one word because that was the thing—I didn't want to need another place to stay. I wanted to stay here with my husband, our two gorgeous kids and our adorable dog.

A tear slid down my cheek and I blinked and swallowed in an aim to try to stop more following. As much as I didn't want my kids to see me crying, it would be even worse and embarrassing for both Hayley and me if her friend witnessed my meltdown.

'Oh honey.' She put down her wineglass, edged her chair closer to mine and wrapped her arm around my shoulder. Her effort to comfort me ruined my attempt to hold it together.

'Get the tissues, Wei,' she barked. 'On the bench.'

His chair scraped on the tiles as he pushed back and hurried to obey. He returned moments later and thrust the whole box towards me.

'Thanks.' I smiled up at him through my sobs as I grabbed one and tried to pull myself together.

'There is another option, you know?' Wei said tentatively.

Hayley and I both looked at him in confusion. 'Another option for what?' she snapped. 'If you're going to suggest Ash murder Adrian and bury him in the backyard, you're too late, I already thought of that but she's far more pure and generous-hearted than we are.'

Wei looked at me uncertainly as if he didn't know whether it was safe to laugh or not.

When I smirked and elbowed my sister-in-law, he let out a deep chuckle, then cleared his throat. 'Anyway, as I was saying ... I might be way out of line suggesting this and feel free to say no. You've done such a great job with my granddad's shack so far but there's lots of work still to do, so I've got a proposition for you.'

'I'm listening,' I said, twisting a soggy tissue between my fingers.

He sat back down in the chair opposite. 'Hayley told me how you renovated this place and that you're pretty handy at fixing things up, which as you saw for yourself is exactly what the shack needs. How would you feel about staying there on your non-home weeks and doing a bit more work for us?'

'What exactly do you want me to do?'

'Well, thanks to you I've arranged for the ceilings to be replaced, but what else do you think needs doing?'

I didn't need to think long—I'd spent plenty of time last week imagining what I'd do to the shack if it were mine.

'At the bare minimum, it needs a new coat of paint throughout and new carpets in the bedrooms. Unless you decide you'd rather some other type of flooring—I think there might be floorboards under the bedroom carpets that might be salvageable. The kitchen and bathroom cabinets could both do with replacing, the tiles really date the place and there's lots more you could work towards.'

'Is that the kind of thing you know how to do?'

'Most of it. Although there's a few months' work there at least.'

Wei nodded. 'I can see that. Look, I've run this by Meili, my sister, and we wouldn't expect you to do all of that yourself, but how would you feel about coordinating the renovations for us, being there to get quotes, let in tradesmen, et cetera? You could stay in the shack while you did, and we'd also pay you a fair wage for whatever you can do yourself.'

'Wow. That's a generous offer.' A place to stay for no rent and I'd even get paid for the honour. The shack was worse than anything I'd ever attempted to 'refresh' before, but I'd never been afraid of hard work and it would help pass the time.

Wei chuckled. 'It's a selfish offer—you've done more in one week than we'd have done in a year. We should probably just sell the shack but Meili likes the idea of an Airbnb because she says we'll have a place to stay whenever we want that also makes money for us. My sister is a little ... how should I put it? Pretentious. She likes the idea of being able to say she has a holiday home by the beach.'

Hayley laughed. 'I can't wait to meet your sister.'

But I was too busy turning over the logistics in my head for small talk. 'What if Adrian and I get back together and the work's still not done?'

Wei shrugged. 'You stay as long as you can and do as much as you can, but of course your family and your marriage come first.'

I nodded, but Adrian and I getting back together wasn't my only concern. What happened when Hayley inevitably dumped Wei? He seemed rather besotted with her and if she left him broken-hearted, would that be the end of our arrangement? Then again, even if I only got another week in beautiful Ragged Point, it would be one less week of driving myself insane in Perth. And the thought of seeing Jedda again and a few more morning walks along that pristine beach was hard to resist.

'It sounds perfect, but I've got canteen duty next week—'

'So, cancel or swap with someone else. It's only volunteer work,' interrupted Hayley. 'Or better yet, tell Adrian as it's his week with the kids, it's his turn to don the school apron and hand out sausage rolls and ice-creams.'

I smiled at that image. 'There's no sausage rolls or ice-creams anymore. Our school's canteen is green—we have veggie sticks with hummus, fruit, plain air-popped popcorn, lentil burgers and stuff like that.'

Hayley and Wei exchanged a look of horror. 'They've taken all the fun out of school,' Wei said with a shake of his head.

'It's okay, they've added iPads to practically every lesson from kindy,' I said. 'But jokes aside, even if I can get out of canteen, I'll have to come back early as Payton will kill me if I miss another soccer game.'

'Then drive back first thing Sunday morning. That'll still give you six days there. But only if you want to,' Hayley added, squeezing my hand. 'My apartment and my mess are also available if you'd rather stay with me.'

I laughed. 'You really should get a cleaner, because I'm going back to Ragged Point.'

21

Ragged Point

This time as I drove into Ragged Point, the car was jam-packed with supplies—more cleaning equipment, cockroach baits, oil for the creaky doors, strong-scented candles and lots of other purification paraphernalia. Charlie sat on the seat behind me. I obviously couldn't rely on Adrian or Saxon to take care of him properly, so I'd dognapped him for the week.

'We're almost there, boy,' I said, reaching over to ruffle his fur.

I pulled over in front of Brewed Awakening and waved to Sam who was heading into the general store. Typical teenager, she didn't seem at all surprised to see me again, but Jedda's response more than made up for her lacklustre one.

'Oh my God. What are you doing here?' she shrieked when she opened the back door—as it was Monday, the cafe was closed—to find Charlie and me standing there.

'Surprise!' I smiled, holding the leash firmly as he tried to jump up at her.

'Who is this gorgeous thing?' She dropped down onto her haunches.

'This is Charlie. He's nine years old but still acts like a puppy when he's around new people. He'll calm down in a moment.'

'Ooh, you're perfect just as you are, aren't you, baby?' Jedda held Charlie's face between her hands and nuzzled his wet nose with her own. 'What kind of dog is he?'

'A standard schnauzer.'

'Gorgeous.' She straightened and looked back to me. 'So, why are you and this divine creature here? Not that I'm complaining.'

I gave her the short version of the progress I'd made in my marriage. Or lack thereof.

'Did you try the naked selfies?' she asked.

'I couldn't bring myself to do it.'

Truthfully, I wasn't sure an image of me in my birthday suit would actually entice Adrian home. I'd had two kids, I liked eating cake and drinking wine, and until recently exercise and I weren't on first name terms. How could I compete with the young things he'd likely find online?

I told her about Wei's proposition and how I didn't think I had much to lose. 'It's not like I have a job or anything in Perth yet. This way I'll be occupied and hopefully the times when I'm not with the kids will go faster.'

'Well, I'm sorry things aren't any better with your husband,' Jedda said, reaching out and squeezing my arm, 'but I'm so happy to have you back for a little bit. Ooh, if you're here the week after next you'll have to come to our Aussie Icon Trivia Night.'

I wasn't sure whether that sounded exciting or terrifying. 'We'll see.'

'Yes, we will.' Jedda gave me a conspiratorial wink. 'Do you want to come in for a cuppa? I've just had lunch but if you're hungry I can rustle something up.'

As tempting as that sounded, I really wanted to get to the shack, unload the car, take Charlie for a walk on the beach and start making a plan for the week ahead.

'Can I take a raincheck? This one,' I said, gesturing to Charlie who had finally calmed down a little, 'has been cooped up in the car for two hours, so I want to give him a bit of a run on the beach.'

'Of course. Bindi's having a nap but she's gunna be so excited to see you. She's spent all week pointing at the cafe door and saying, "Ashy?"'

I beamed. 'I can't wait to see her either.'

'Hey, why don't you come over for dinner later?'

'I'd love to.'

'Bring Charlie as well. I have a feeling Bindi might fall in love with him even more than she has with you.'

I pouted and pressed a hand against my chest, feigning hurt, and then gave Jedda a cheek-kiss goodbye. 'The wine's on me tonight.'

'Awesome,' she said as she waved us off.

Charlie objected about getting into the car—no doubt terrified we were about to embark on another long journey—but I was firm; when he saw the beach, he'd be beside himself.

Sure enough, a few minutes later when I stopped the car, he looked up in surprise from where he'd been sulking on the passenger seat and all was forgiven.

'Welcome to your home for the next week,' I said as I led him towards the house. His tail wagged furiously, and his nose twitched as he sniffed the sea air.

'Soon,' I promised.

This time as I stepped into the shack, I didn't feel dread but potential.

I let Charlie off his leash so he could explore his new surrounds and gazed around myself, imagining how cosy and relaxing it would be once I'd finished. I was going to have to work fast because I didn't like leaving a job half done—and surely Adrian would come to his senses soon—but the shack would be perfect no matter the season. In summer guests could relax in the hammock out on the back verandah after a swim on the beach, and in winter they could read or play board games in front of the roaring fire as the rain pelted down outside. Pity I'd be long gone by the time winter came—I kinda liked the idea of passing time in front of the fire myself.

Maybe once Adrian and I were back together again, we could book the Airbnb from Wei and Meili and bring the kids up for a week of family bonding. Or better still, we could come alone and work on rekindling some of that spark we'd somehow lost over the last few years.

My thoughts were interrupted by Charlie barking. I followed the sound towards the kitchen to find his paws up against a cupboard as he snarled at the ceiling. Guess my resident possum was still around. Hopefully the dog would get used to the noises in the roof because his barking would certainly grate before too long.

'Come on. Walkies.'

At my announcement, Charlie slid down the cupboard, dropping his paws to the floor. He glanced at me then back to the ceiling. Usually the word 'walkies' had him spinning circles in excitement, crashing into furniture as he headed for the front door, but today he was torn.

I picked up his leash, still trailing behind him, and yanked him towards the back door. The moment he spied the sea, all thoughts of the noise in the roof were abandoned. The sand kicked up behind us as we jogged to the water and within seconds my socks and sneakers were soaking wet.

Cursing my lack of forethought to take them off before we left the shack, I glanced up and down the beach and, not seeing anyone in the near distance, risked letting Charlie free. While he frolicked in the gentle waves, I plopped down on the dry sand, slipping off my soggy sneakers and grimacing as I peeled the wet socks off my feet.

A shadow appeared as if from nowhere as I was wringing out my socks. 'I thought you'd left.'

I startled at the sound of the deep voice and looked up to see Island Dan now standing beside me. He wore blue shorts, a black short-sleeved shirt and a scruffy cap with The Lobster Factory logo on the front. His legs, which were right in front of my eyes, were tanned and rather hairy, and he wasn't wearing any shoes. 'Excuse me?'

He lowered himself down onto the sand. 'Last time we met, you said you were leaving—sounded like you couldn't get out of here fast enough.'

His close proximity flummoxed me a little so I focused on rolling up the wet bottoms of my black yoga pants. 'I changed my mind.'

'You know,' he said, nodding at my discarded shoes and socks, 'most people go barefoot on the beach or at least wear thongs.'

'I don't have any thongs. Their thin unstructured soles offer no support and can lead to injuries such as sprains, tendonitis, bunions and even stress fractures, to name just a few.'

His eyebrows rolled towards each other. 'Are you a podiatrist or something?'

'No.' I laughed. Adrian had been waxing lyrical for years about the dangers of flimsy footwear and his doctrine had been ingrained in me. 'My husband is.'

'Your husband. I see.' He pulled his knees up to his chest and wrapped his arms around them. 'Is he here with you?'

My stomach clenched. Dan seemed pleasant enough but if I said no, would he get the wrong idea? Maybe see me as an easy target? Almost immediately, I mentally cringed at this thought. If Adrian didn't want me, why on earth did I think this guy would be interested?

He was obviously just being friendly, which was nice considering I didn't really know anyone but Jedda.

'No, we're …' My voice drifted off. 'He's otherwise occupied at the moment, so I'm helping out a friend doing up his grandfather's shack when I can get away for a few days.'

'Lucky friend. I imagine that might be quite a big job.'

I nodded.

'Well, if you ever need any help … or even if you just need someone to lift heavy things, I live a few houses up—just where the coast curves round—so we're neighbours.'

'That big modern house with all the glass windows?' He couldn't live there all by himself.

He chuckled. 'Yep, that's the one.'

I surreptitiously checked his hand for a wedding ring—he probably had a wife and a dozen kids—but his fingers were bare.

'Actually, do you know how I could hire a skip bin? There's a lot of junk in the shack that I need to get rid of before I can do much more.'

'Sure. Give the shire a call and they'll have one delivered for you or you could have a garage sale? One man's junk is another's treasure and all that.'

'Trust me,' I said. 'Pretty much all of this is junk.'

'Fair enough.' Dan nodded towards the ocean where Charlie was still splashing about. 'Is that your dog?'

'Yes. I brought him up from Perth to keep me company.'

'He's gorgeous,' he said, and then silence fell between us.

It wasn't exactly awkward, but it wasn't comfortable either and after a few moments, I felt compelled to fill it. 'You're not usually here this time of day.'

He turned his head to look at me. 'You've been tracking my coming and going?'

'No,' I blurted, my cheeks heating rapidly. 'Of course not. But the shack is—'

'It's okay. I'm just teasing. I go out there once or twice a day to feed my old friend's cat.'

'You mean Bill?'

He raised an eyebrow. 'Yeah. You've heard of him?'

'A little.' And I'd also done a bit of online snooping during my week back in Perth; not that I'd found much more than the fact he was a drifter who'd turned up in the Point about forty-five years ago, worked as a cray fisherman and never moved on. 'He sounds like an interesting man.'

'Yeah, he was.' Dan paused a moment and his eyes grew serious. 'Anyway, this morning when I went to feed Lion, he didn't seem quite himself. Thought I'd go out on my lunch break and check on him. See if I should take him to the vet.'

'Does the cat like going in the canoe?'

'How many cats do you know who like water? Lion might be surrounded by the stuff, but he stays firmly on land. He's only been off once in his life when he got bitten by a snake. Bill tried to take him out in the boat a few times, but, not surprisingly, he wasn't a fan.' Dan pushed to his feet and lifted a hand to wave. 'Anyway, see you round.'

I nodded as he jogged a few metres away to where the canoe was tied to a post in the sand.

'Hey,' he called as he started pushing it towards the sea. 'Don't suppose you'd like to come out for a look? If Lion's still sick, I might need some help bringing him back.'

Super curious about the island and also this so-called castle, part of me desperately wanted to go with him, but my heart raced at the thought. Making polite conversation on the sand was one thing but what would we talk about on the boat ride to the island and back? I had no idea how to be alone with a man that wasn't my husband, nor did I want to learn.

'Thanks,' I said, trying to smile nonchalantly at him, 'but I'd better not. I've got lots to do.'

Dan shrugged. 'No worries.'

'But if Lion is sick,' I called as he started to walk away, 'come back and get me and I'll help.' I wouldn't turn my back on an ill animal.

'Thanks.' He turned his attention to the boat. As he pushed it into the water, Charlie ran over to him and he paused to give him a pat. He spoke but I couldn't decipher the words over the wind and the waves.

When Dan jumped into the canoe and started rowing, Charlie pined.

'Come,' I shouted. As usual, the dog took his sweet time obeying, and then shook himself the second he got to me so water splashed all over my clothes.

Cursing, I clipped the leash back on his collar and then walked him up the beach a few hundred metres in an aim to dry him a bit. When we got back to the shack, I still needed to towel him and within seconds of us entering, he'd curled up in front of the TV and was snoring peacefully. I was tempted to have a cup of tea myself and read for a while, but I still had to unload the car and the shack would feel much more homely once I had.

It took almost half an hour for me to carry everything inside and then another hour or so to unpack and arrange it all. I dumped the extra cleaning supplies I'd brought in the laundry and put my clothes into the wardrobe, which I'd cleaned and fumigated on my first visit. Next I set up scented candles all around the shack to help further eradicate the musty/fishy smell, then threw some cushions and a snuggly blanket on the couch and put a rug down next to Charlie on the horrible old carpet. It really needed to be professionally cleaned or, better still, ripped up and replaced completely, but at least the rug meant we'd have somewhere clean to rest our feet on in the meantime. Charlie immediately woke, transferred himself to the rug and then promptly fell back asleep. I laughed as I set up my music docking station and a DVD player, which we never used anymore because of Stan and Netflix. I'd brought some old movies from home, although I wasn't sure I'd be able to get the player to work with Xiang's ancient TV. Pity I didn't have Sax with me; he and his friends seemed to be experts in all things technology.

I spruced up the dining-slash-kitchen area with a tablecloth and a vase of artificial flowers in the middle. Fresh would be better of course, but I didn't think they'd have travelled well. After placing framed photos of my family on various surfaces—many of which I needed to re-dust—I packed Xiang's books up into the cardboard boxes I'd brought. Wei said he had a friend who taught Chinese at TAFE and knowing we were going to donate rather than toss them made me feel much better about putting a few of my own novels on the shelves. The one good thing about this hiatus in my marriage was that I now had so much more time to read and I'd treated myself at the local bookshop before I left Perth.

Thank God I was going to Jedda's for dinner because by the time I'd finished unloading and arranging everything I was knackered.

I hadn't seen Dan return from the island, but the canoe was once again resting on the shore.

Time for a cup of tea, but ... I had just one more thing to do first.

Charlie, awake again, followed me outside, peeing against one of the gum trees and sniffing at smells in the dirt as I unloaded the final box from where I'd wedged it safely in the boot.

I whistled to him as I headed back to the shack and miraculously, albeit reluctantly, he schlepped after me inside and into the kitchen. I put the box on the table, lifted out my Thermomix and placed it on the kitchen bench. It looked completely out of place in the 1970s décor—faded orange countertops and warped wooden cupboards—and I might not even use it this week, but I couldn't help grinning at the sight.

Take that, Adrian!

22

Perth

My second week in Ragged Point flew by. I'd barely had time to breathe and hadn't managed to finish even one novel, but by the time I drove to Perth early Sunday morning, I felt invigorated, despite the calluses on my hands and the ache between my shoulder blades.

I couldn't say the shack looked a whole lot better yet, but I'd made good progress. The shire had provided me a bin almost immediately, so I spent most of the first couple of days carrying rubbish to it. Clearing the house as best I could, I uncovered more areas in dire need of cleaning or repairing. The paint was more peel than colour and some of the walls were growing mould along the bottom, indicating there might be a damp issue, but at least I could see what I was up against now. Wei and Meili had told me they wanted a complete overhaul—not a beach shack stuck in the last century but a comfortable holiday retreat. So I had permission to redecorate, totally renovate the kitchen, bathroom and laundry *and* give both the front and back porches a facelift. They'd pretty much given me free rein and, although the budget was limited, my imagination was buzzing with ideas and possibilities.

Wednesday, I took a break from cleaning to make an inventory of everything that needed to be done. Some of the tasks I felt confident I could do myself:

- Fix creaky doors and windows.
- Rip up old carpets and polish the floorboards beneath them, if they weren't rotten and the owners preferred wood to tiling.
- Strip back the walls and eventually paint them—only the bedrooms to start with as every other room would likely need significant work.
- Choose and install new light fittings once the ceiling had been replaced and I'd had an electrician check the vintage wiring.
- Sew new curtains—although perhaps those lovely white, wooden plantation shutters would suit better once the rest of the shack had been updated.

This list went on and after exhausting the possibilities of everything I could handle myself, I'd made another list of local tradespeople to give me quotes for the bigger tasks and started making phone calls to arrange on-site meetings. Wei and Meili were trusting me with a lot and I didn't want to let them down, but it was like being on *The Block* or *Renovation Rescue* without the TV cameras, bossy partner and annoying contestants.

On Thursday morning, I'd driven twenty minutes north to a hardware store and loaded my car with all the supplies I'd need to prep the bedroom walls for painting. I bought canvas drop cloths, buckets, sponges, scrapers and blades, sandpaper, filler, sealant and masking tape, keeping all the receipts for Wei so he could reimburse me. I'd checked with him and Meili regarding the colour scheme before starting the actual painting.

That afternoon and Friday I worked my butt off prepping the walls for paint, removing picture hooks, light switch covers and the odd patch of mould from the walls using a bleach solution that aggravated my nose a little, but I refused to let anything deter me. Next I sanded back places where the old layers of paint had peeled and patched all the dents and holes with filler.

I think Charlie thought I'd gone mad, but I was glad of his company and at least I wasn't worrying about his welfare in the way I worried about the kids. Payton chatted as much as usual on our daily phone calls and sounded like she was coping well, but phone calls weren't any way to gauge Saxon's wellbeing. With every question I asked, I got a one-word answer. I couldn't work out if he was still angry with me or if it was just a teenage thing.

I'd only spoken to Adrian once. Not that the conversation was anything to get excited about. A text message on Wednesday morning from the dentist reminding me of Payton's Friday appointment—which I'll admit had slipped my mind—had given me the perfect excuse to hear my husband's voice. But after leaving multiple messages with his receptionist and many more on his voicemail, I'd almost lost my patience by the time he finally returned my call late Wednesday afternoon.

'What is it, Ashling?'

'And it's delightful to talk to you as well, Adrian. Yes, I'm doing okay, thanks for asking.'

A deep sigh travelled down the phone line. 'I don't have time for games. I've still got three more appointments and then I have to go home, organise dinner and take Payton to soccer training.'

I rolled my eyes. He made it sound like he had to run an outback marathon while simultaneously achieving world peace.

'Tough being the primary parent, isn't it?' I replied, not sympathetic in the slightest. This was *his* choice.

'It's not that bad,' he said, backtracking. 'Now, what is it?'

'I'm just letting you know that Payton has a dentist appointment Friday morning at eleven that you need to take her to.'

'Not possible. I've got back-to-back appointments. Why didn't you schedule this for when you'd be here?'

I half laughed, unable to believe his audacity. 'Because medical appointments as you'd well know are scheduled well in advance and when I booked this one my husband hadn't yet informed me of his plans to destroy our family, so I didn't *know* I wouldn't be available.'

'Ashling, be reasonable, can't you reschedule whatever you've got planned? You know it's not good business to cancel or reschedule a patient at this short notice.'

Reasonable? Like he'd been reasonable when he told me he wanted to sleep with other people?

Still, thinking of the nameless person who needed work on their bunions or ingrown toenails and my poor daughter's teeth, I almost caved. I'd never been the type to go out of my way to make life difficult for others.

But you don't want to make things easy for him either, Hayley's voice came from somewhere deep inside my head.

'I'm sorry, but that won't be possible. I'm two hours away and not coming back till Sunday morning. You'll have to make it work.'

My heart palpitated as I disconnected the call, half proud of myself for standing my ground, half wondering if I'd just hammered another nail into the coffin waiting to bury my marriage. I didn't want to make Adrian angry, but he needed to realise he couldn't walk all over me.

Thankfully, between all the manual labour and helping Jedda on the *Reporter*, I didn't have too much time to dwell on it. Bindi's teething had got a lot worse—I suspected she was getting her two-year-old molars early—and this was making Jedda's life rather difficult. I could hear the stress in her voice when we had dinner together on Monday night and immediately wanted to help if I could. 'Is there something I can do to give you a break?'

'Are you any good at typing?'

'Yes. I sometimes do reception work for Adrian and I'm the secretary for the school fundraising committee. Why?'

'I'm way behind on typing up all the handwritten articles the oldies have sent in and people are starting to ask when the next issue of the *Reporter* is out. The one I delivered to the general store the day we met is the last edition I've managed, and that's bad even for me.'

'I'd love to type up the articles for you.'

So that's how I ended up spending most nights at Jedda's. While she struggled to get Bindi to sleep, Charlie and I would sit in her office and I'd type up reports from the bowling club, the CWA and the Men's Shed, to name but a few. Although I wasn't supposed to, I couldn't help rewriting some of the awkward sentences, which amused Jedda. I didn't mind typing but the unofficial editing gave me a real thrill. It was almost as if I'd written some of the articles myself.

Once Bindi had finally settled, Jedda would bring me in a slice of cake or a glass of wine, or both. Then, while she worked on the layout of the paper ready to print, I'd keep her company late into the night. I enjoyed learning more about the production of the *Reporter* and also hearing stories about Ragged Point and the people who lived there.

As much as I loved Payton, I felt semi-resentful about having to leave the Point early simply so I could stand on the sidelines and watch her bazillionth soccer game. It wasn't even the proper season yet.

Geez, what kind of mother was I to be more excited over prepping walls and sandpapering doorframes than I was about seeing my daughter?

Perhaps if I knew I wasn't also about to see Adrian, I'd be more enthused. But my stomach churned at the thought of more awkwardness between us. I'd seen him a grand total of three times since that fateful day and each time I hoped for a sign that he'd started to miss me. Instead, each time he became more and more of a stranger and I felt the chasm between us growing, and my hope of mending my family slipping away.

Said stranger's car was already parked at the soccer grounds when I arrived, and I could see Payton in the distance kicking a ball around as she warmed up with her team. Adrian—his phone in front of his face like a teenager—stood on the sidelines with the other parents.

Was he checking out the options on Tinder? Setting up dates, or rather hook-ups, for his upcoming week of freedom? My heart squeezed at the possibility.

Charlie whined in the passenger seat. I hadn't had time to drop him back at the house so I'd brought him with me, which might be a blessing in disguise. Instead of having to make small talk with my estranged husband or the other parents, who I no longer felt like I had much in common with at all, I could use Charlie as an excuse to walk around the outskirts of the pitch.

With a deep breath, I climbed out of the car. Charlie jumped over the seat after me, tugging on the lead as he spotted Adrian. Payton ran towards us, threw her arms around me, squeezed tight and then let go to kiss Charlie on the nose.

'You're here!' She sounded surprised.

'Of course I am,' I said. 'Wild horses wouldn't have kept me away.'

Adrian stashed his phone in his pocket when he saw us. 'Morning, Ashling.'

'Hi,' I managed and then spoke to Payton. 'How was your dentist appointment?'

'Great. Grandma took me. The dentist said I had near-perfect teeth, so she bought me a lollipop on the way home to celebrate.'

A lollipop? *Good Lord.* But that wasn't what bothered me.

I waited until Payton skipped back to join her teammates and then I turned to look at Adrian.

'You got your *mum* to take her?' I said almost under my breath as I didn't want eavesdroppers to hear the argument we were about to have.

'Yes.'

'She's *your* daughter and your responsibility during *your* weeks.'

'Don't be so antagonistic, Ash.' He sighed heavily. 'She went and that's the important thing. I'm not a stay-at-home parent like you, but I'm doing the best I can.'

I didn't like the way he made 'stay-at-home parent' sound like a dirty word. Where was the appreciation for everything I'd always willingly, lovingly done for him and the kids?

And what was with his self-pitying, hard-done-by tone?

'Maybe you should give yourself a medal,' I spat. 'But when it gets hard, remember, this was your choice, not mine!'

I crossed my arms and turned my back on him, but not before I saw genuine hurt in his eyes. *Way to go, Ashling.* Acting like a surly bitch was really going to win his favour. Of course, if he hadn't lost the plot first, then we wouldn't have even been having this conversation.

23

'Can you go and get your brother for dinner, please?' I asked Payton as I pulled a lasagne out of the oven.

She slumped against the kitchen bench. 'But I just laid the table.'

'Because it was your turn. I'm asking you to get Saxon as a favour to me.'

With a dramatic sigh, she wandered off towards the bedrooms and I began to dish up dinner.

'His door's closed and I don't have a death wish so I'm not going in there,' Payton announced when she returned a few moments later.

'Did you call through the door?'

'*Yes*, but he's probably got his headphones on and can't hear me. He never takes those bloody things off these days.'

'Mind your language, young lady. And can you get the salad dressing out of the fridge and put it on the table?'

'When did your last slave die?'

Her rudeness and back-chatting were becoming an issue. Did she talk to her father like this? Maintaining our close relationship was harder when I only saw her every second week, but that didn't mean I should let her get away with murder.

'You just lost your screen time on the weekend, missy,' I called over my shoulder as I went to get Saxon myself.

I raised my hand to knock on his door, but before my knuckles met the wood, he shouted, 'Fuck!'

I blinked. 'What on earth is going on in there?' I demanded as I flung open the door to see Saxon sitting at his desk, bent over his laptop, glowering at the screen as his fingers flew across the keyboard. He looked up, clearly surprised to see me, and then snapped the computer shut before I could get a look at what was on the screen.

The swearing was forgotten as Wei's comments from a week ago haunted me. 'Oh my God. Were you looking at porn?'

'What? *Mum!* No.' He grimaced, his cheeks turning red as he yanked out his headphones so they curled around his neck.

'Show me,' I demanded, nodding towards his laptop.

'Fine.' He opened it up and I recoiled as the screen came to life with graphic images of blood and gore against a soundtrack of gunshots and explosions. 'It's a video game,' he said as if I was stupid. 'It's called *The Tournament*.'

I didn't know whether to be relieved or not. What was worse—sex or violence?

'You know you're not allowed to play games on school nights.'

Since the kids were young, Adrian and I had always had strict screen rules—we limited TV on weeknights, and gaming and movies were only allowed on weekends—and our draconian stance had paid off. Or so I'd thought.

Saxon opened his mouth to argue, but I rode right over the top of him.

'You told me you were doing your homework. And if playing that awful game makes you use such foul language and get so pent up, then I don't think you should be playing it at all. From now on, I want you to do all your computer work at the kitchen table. No more computers or phones in your bedroom.'

'Mum, I'm sorry about swearing but can you just calm down and listen to me for a moment.' He sighed and ran a hand through black curls that were almost identical to his father's. 'This is for a school assignment.'

I narrowed my eyes at him. 'Are you having me on? I was a kid once too, you know.' Although things were a lot simpler back then—our parents never had to worry about online games, social media and too much screen time.

'No. I promise,' he pleaded. 'It's part of my media class. We're studying computer games—we have to choose a game and analyse it.'

'Seriously?' I put my hands on my hips. 'What exactly do you have to analyse?'

'Plot, graphics, target audience and key-binds, that kind of stuff.'

I had no idea what he was talking about but I guess I didn't have any reason not to believe him. Saxon had never been able to lie well, whereas Payton had been an expert almost as soon as she could talk—but I couldn't believe the school was encouraging kids to play video games. What happened to analysing adverts and newspaper articles?

'Okay, but don't let it get you so worked up. No game *or* homework requires swearing.'

'Sorry, Mum.'

'No, I'm sorry,' I said, giving him a hug. 'Sorry for doubting you. It's just ... things are hard at the moment. I ...' My mouth went dry and I couldn't get the rest of my sentence out.

'It's all right, Mum.' His warm breath tickled the side of my face. 'I know you don't like being apart from us, but Payton and I are doing okay. Dad makes us eat veggies, even if they are frozen ones. You need to take care of yourself. Work out what you're going to do with the rest of *your* life.'

I tensed, not sure how to respond to the insinuation in his statement—did even my son think my marriage was a lost cause? Did he think I was pathetic hoping otherwise?

In the end, I forced a laugh. 'What are you, a life counsellor or something?'

'No.' He laughed.

'Come on, let's go have dinner,' I said. I wanted to spend some quality time with my children on our first night back together and show them some photos of Ragged Point and the 'before' photos of the shack. At least this would be proof that even if I was sad, I wasn't spending my weeks alone wallowing, but doing something productive.

However, as we pulled apart, I caught a stronger than usual whiff of teenage boy smell (what I affectionately called TBO). 'When was the last time you had a shower?'

He hesitated a moment. 'Last night … I think. Why?'

I leaned in again to sniff him, trying to work out if it was him, the room or his clothes. I spied at least five single socks scattered around the bedroom that were no doubt adding to the stench. How often was Adrian doing the laundry?

'*Mum*. Stop.' Sax took a step away from me. 'I ran out of deodorant. I've been borrowing Dad's, but I guess he took it with him this morning.'

'Did you tell him you needed more?'

'Yeah, I wrote it on the shopping list on the fridge, but he always forgets to take it with him.'

I sighed, trying not to show my aggravation. 'I'll buy you some tomorrow.'

'Thanks.' Leaving the game open on his screen, Sax started out of the room.

The optimist inside me wanted to believe that Adrian would see sense and our lives would return to normal soon, but the way things were going I feared that might take a little longer. So, before I left next Monday, I'd have to make sure the house was stocked with all the little things he wouldn't think of. I bet it wasn't only Sax's deodorant he'd omitted. Had he checked we had enough toilet paper? Toothpaste? Washing powder? Dog food? Or perhaps he thought those things simply restocked themselves when they ran out.

No! I wasn't going to let him off the hook. This nest-parenting thing wasn't going to work if we didn't both keep up our side of the agreement, and maybe now we'd been doing it for over a month, I needed to remind him of the rules *he'd* laid on me. He would continue to pay the household bills, I'd still reply to all school communication, but we would *share* the cleaning and the shopping. Adrian might have hired someone to take care of the housework, he might even be managing to feed the kids veggies, but there was a lot more to running a household than just that. It was all the invisible things I did that kept things from falling apart.

I was going to have to talk to him.

The joy that I had a valid excuse to call my own husband again was short-lived. However I put it, I'd sound like a nag and that would merely give Adrian another reason not to want to be with me. I didn't want to only talk to him when I had things to whinge or complain about, but he'd given me no choice. I had to take care of my children and if he insisted on this ridiculous custody arrangement, then I wasn't going to pick up the slack for him. He needed to do his bit.

But first, dinner.

'Finally,' Payton said when we entered the kitchen. She was sitting at the table, one arm draped across it and her head resting on her arm. 'I thought I was going to die of starvation.'

'Thanks for waiting for us.'

'Like I had any choice,' she retorted, referring to my rule that we always sat down to dinner as a family. It wasn't something I ever remembered happening at home when I was a child, but friends' family dinners were some of my favourite memories of growing up. The food was usually much better than what Mum would cook and when I went to Dad's house, we mostly got takeaway from Maccas. But even hot dogs at my friend Jane's place—they were the only things her mum could cook—were had round the table with her whole family, everyone chatting about their days, laughing and sometimes commiserating as they ate.

I longed to one day have a family like that.

It wasn't until I was about sixteen and I slept over at Hayley's house and she complained about us not being allowed to take our dinner into the TV room to eat by ourselves that I heard her mum—now my mother-in-law—say, 'Families that eat together stay together.' It was the first time I'd ever heard that sentiment and it made so much sense. Maybe if my own parents had placed similar importance on sharing a meal together, my home life wouldn't have been such a shambles.

Until recently, I'd naively believed this to be one of the many secrets of a happy family, but sadly, the theory hadn't worked out so well for us.

24

After numerous failed attempts to contact Adrian the previous evening, I packed the kids' lunches, took Payton to school and then called the clinic.

'Wood's Podiatry,' sang our lovely young receptionist, Kristen. 'How may I help you?'

'Hello. I'm calling to make an appointment,' I said, trying to alter my voice so she wouldn't recognise it.

'Wonderful. And have you seen any of our podiatrists before?'

'No. But my good friend Davy Edwards'—one of Adrian's most frequent patients who'd been seeing him for years—'recommended Dr Wood.'

'Oh yes, Mr Edwards is right, you won't find a better podiatrist than Dr Wood. What exactly is your appointment for?'

I cleared my throat. 'I have some awful bunions that are super painful when I walk.'

'Ouch,' Kristen sympathised. I'd trained her well. 'When were you hoping to come in?'

'As soon as possible; I'm in a lot of pain and don't want it to deter from the enjoyment of my holiday.'

'Of course not. Hmm. Dr Wood is generally pretty booked up but let's see what I can do for you.' I heard tapping on her keyboard. 'Or perhaps I could slot you in with one of our other podiatrists?'

'No, thank you. After Davy's recommendation, I'd be disappointed if I didn't see Dr Wood.' And, I added silently, I'm sure he'd be horrified if I talked to any of his employees about my true complaint.

'Ooh, you're in luck,' Kristen exclaimed. 'We've just had a cancellation. Could you be here by midday?'

'Today?'

'Yes.'

I gulped. That was sooner than I'd expected. But maybe that was a good thing—I'd have less time to chicken out.

'Of course,' I said, knowing this was Adrian's last appointment before he took his lunch break and so we'd have plenty of time to talk. 'Thank you.'

When I strolled into the clinic a couple of hours later, Kristen smiled from behind the reception desk. 'Ashling, long time no see. How are you?'

I held a shaky finger to my lips as I glanced towards the closed door of Adrian's consulting room. 'I'm Louise Murphy today.'

It took her a couple of seconds to connect the dots. '*Oh*. Right.'

I smiled at the twinkle in her eyes. Just how much did she know about what was going on between Adrian and me? Or rather *not* going on? 'Is Dr Wood running on time?'

She nodded.

'Thank you.'

I retreated to one of the comfy leather chairs we'd invested in for the waiting room. Although I flicked through a magazine from the coffee table, none of the articles registered. I couldn't think properly over the noise of my heart thumping in my ears—how could I possibly be so nervous about talking to my husband? The seconds seemed to take minutes and the minutes hours, but finally, Adrian's door opened and he emerged with an elderly gentleman.

He looked so familiar in his black work trousers and pale blue striped Oxford shirt that I'd ironed numerous times, but it was the hot pink flamingo tie that Payton had given him for his last birthday that almost unravelled me. I remembered the horrified look on his face when he'd unwrapped it, but despite the fact it was something he'd never choose himself and there were plenty of men who wouldn't be seen dead in it, he wore it proudly because his beloved daughter had given it to him.

Whatever was going on with him right now, I still believed he was a good man, and I missed him so much.

Adrian didn't even spare a glance to the waiting room as he crossed to the reception to pick up the folder for his next patient. My heart froze when he looked down at the page, but he merely lifted his head and called 'Louise Murphy' as he would any other patient.

His gaze flitted over the people in the waiting room and came to rest on me. 'Ashling?'

I jumped up, lifted the picnic basket that was at my feet and started towards him.

'What are you doing here?' It was clear from the expression on his face he couldn't believe my chutzpah—him and me both—but he wouldn't want to make a scene in the waiting room.

My nostalgia vanished as self-preservation kicked in.

'It's all right, I'll pay my bill,' I told him as I stalked past, although we both knew that would be futile as we hadn't even spoken about dividing our finances yet. The fact Adrian hadn't actually insisted on this gave me hope that this 'phase' would indeed pass, but the way he looked at me with such irritation did not.

I was already sitting in the chair opposite his desk when he closed the door behind us.

'What are you playing at booking an appointment using a fake name?' he asked as he sat down in his chair and crossed his arms over his chest.

'Louise *is* my middle name, and Murphy my maiden name, so it's not really fake, and considering you're refusing to answer my calls, I had to be creative.' I gestured to the basket I'd put on his desk in a hope to defuse his anger. 'Do you want some lunch while we talk? I bought orange juice and made BLTs. There's also some caramel slice in there.'

Adrian stared at the basket as if he were stuck between a rock and a hard place—BLTs and caramel slice were his favourites—and I noticed dark bags under his eyes. My stomach dropped as I wondered if they were down to tiredness—too many late nights out with other women.

My intervention had clearly come not a moment too soon.

'I don't know what we've got to talk about,' he said, dragging his eyes from the basket.

I sighed, lifting the lid of the basket and laying a sandwich wrapped in wax paper in front of him. 'I think we need to set up some kind of regular communication so we can discuss any issues with the kids. And if one of them tells you they need something, you need to follow through.'

'What are you talking about? What haven't I done? They've eaten, Payton's done her spelling, Saxon's still a stellar student and I've kept the house clean!'

I refrained from mentioning the cleaner. If I knew one thing about marriage it was that it paid to pick your battles. Right now, my primary concern was looking out for the kids and hopefully not alienating Adrian even more in the process.

'I'll admit you're doing well with the big picture, but it's the little things I'm talking about. Saxon's room is a pigsty; there were dirty clothes all over the floor—'

'His room is his domain,' Adrian interjected. 'When it gets too bad, he'll clean it. You've mollycoddled the kids too much, Ashling. They need to learn a bit of independence and that's what I'm teaching them.'

Mollycoddled? I was about to tell him exactly what I thought of that but managed to swallow the words at the last moment. I wasn't here to fight.

'Maybe,' I said instead, 'but Sax asked you to buy him deodorant and you haven't, so it's not just his room that stinks, but also him! Do you want him to get teased because he's walking around with bad BO?'

Adrian leaned back in his chair and gestured at the spread I'd laid out on his desk. 'This is about deodorant? You're really clutching at straws.'

'It's not just about deodorant and toilet paper,' I said, not wanting him to think I was *that* desperate to see him.

'Toilet paper?'

'Yes, toilet paper, and all the other things you haven't kept stocked up.' Last night I'd checked all the cupboards and made a list of all the things we'd almost run out of. 'But that's not important right now; I'm worried about the kids. I'll admit they seem to be coping emotionally better than I expected, but deep down they're probably confused about what's going on.' Lord knew I was confused enough myself. 'The marriage counsellor I saw a couple of weeks ago—'

Adrian shook his head. 'I still don't understand why you saw a marriage counsellor on your own.'

'I'm trying to make sense of what's going on. You won't talk to me about us, so I reached out to a professional. Anyway, she reminded me that communication is the key in marriages and in families. You might want out of our *relationship*,' my voice cracked a little, 'but we're still a family. We still have children together and we need to make sure we're on the same page about them.'

'Aren't we?'

'I hope so, but Payton has been acting a little too big for her boots around me. Not sure if she's backchatting and making snarky remarks to you as well, but we really need to nip this sort of behaviour in the bud. I've banned her from screens this weekend because of a few things she said to me last night, and I'd like you to make sure she doesn't get away with rudeness as well.'

'I have noticed her being a little more defiant than usual,' said Adrian. 'She pushed back on bedtime a few nights last week and I caught her playing a game on her iPad on a school night. When I asked her what she was doing, she told me you let her play games if she's finished all her homework.'

'And that there is a total lie and you know it.' I dug my nails into my palms, fighting the impulse to rage at Adrian that this was all his fault. Our children were fine until *he* left! 'But it's not unusual behaviour for kids of separated parents; they soon learn to play one off against the other—I should know. So we need to be aware, but also stand together where they're concerned. Payton says you let her eat whatever she wants after school. One thing can't be acceptable for one of us and not the other.'

'Okay.' His shoulders slackened as he uncrossed his arms. 'I'm sorry.'

'If you've ever got any doubts or questions, just call me,' I said, hoping he'd take me up on this. Somehow, we needed to get talking again.

He nodded, picked up half a BLT and took a bite. *Progress*—he'd actually apologised and at least we weren't staring daggers at each other now.

'This is good,' he said a few moments later when he'd finished his mouthful. 'Thank you.'

I merely smiled, but inside my heart swelled at the compliment.

'Are you going to have any?'

'I had a big breakfast,' I lied. No way I could stomach food right now. 'While we're talking about the kids, have you noticed Saxon behaving any differently?'

He finished his mouthful. 'What do you mean?'

'Well …' I swallowed. 'He seems to be spending an awful lot of time in his room and last night he barely touched any of his dinner. I'm worried he'll burn out.'

'He's always been a hard worker.'

'Yes, but all that time alone isn't healthy. I think we need to try and get him to relax and spend a little more time out of his room.'

'At least he's got his band,' Adrian said through another mouthful. 'That gets him out of the house and hanging with other kids a few hours on the weekend. Most parents are worried about their children not doing enough homework and here we are worried ours is doing too much.'

'I don't know ...' I shook my head. 'The type of assignments the schools are handing out these days, I reckon lots of kids might be a little more dedicated.'

When he quirked an eyebrow, I explained about the game assignment.

'Geez. School's a lot different now from when we went, hey?'

'You can say that again.'

We both chuckled, and the sound of our laughter mingling gave me a buzz inside. I glanced at the clock on the wall, willing the hands to slow down.

'I miss this,' I said. 'Just you and me, talking, eating and laughing together.'

When that merely made him look uncomfortable, I decided to torture myself as well. 'So, have you ... ah ... been successful in your mission yet?'

We both knew what I was talking about, even if I couldn't bring myself to spell it out.

Adrian put the rest of his sandwich back down on the desk. 'Do you really want me to answer that, Ash? I don't want to hurt you.'

It was the first time he'd used my nickname since we'd separated, and I had no idea how to answer his question. He'd *already* hurt me.

At my silence, he sighed. 'I've had a few dates with some really nice women. I'm having fun, but I'm not rushing into anything.'

Nice? *Nice?* I had to bite my lip to stop from grinning. I knew him well enough to read between the lines. He hadn't slept with any of these 'nice' women yet—of this I was ninety-nine per cent certain.

Warmth radiated from my heart. If he hadn't found anyone he wanted to sleep with, maybe we weren't a lost cause. And maybe I *should* send him a naked photo.

'What about you?' he asked.

'Huh?'

'Hayley tells me you've been fixing up the house you're staying in?'

'Oh. Yes.' I told him about the renovations I'd begun on the shack that belonged to Wei's grandfather. 'I spent the morning at showrooms looking at paint schemes, light fixtures, kitchen and bathroom cabinets.'

'You sound like you're in your element.'

Was that sadness, maybe even a little jealousy, I heard in his voice? Trying not to show my glee, I nodded. 'I'm having so much fun.'

'Good for you. Speaking of this Wei, do you think he's more than just a lover? Hayley brought him round to Mum's place last Tuesday for Brad's birthday dinner. I don't remember the last time she brought a plus-one anywhere.'

My heart ached at the mention of the family dinner. I wouldn't have been able to go as I'd been in Ragged Point, but it would have been nice to have been invited. It also hurt a little that Hayley hadn't mentioned it. I had a vision of what the future might entail if our separation morphed into divorce—I wouldn't simply lose Adrian, but also the large and loving clan that had welcomed me not only when I was their neighbour and Hayley's best friend, but even more so when Adrian and I had started going out. I even called his parents 'Mum and Dad' and was closer to them than I was to either of my folks.

What would my father-in-law have made of all this if he was still alive?

'Um ...' Trying to form a sentence while my tear ducts welled wasn't easy. 'Yes, I think maybe this one will stick.'

Adrian laughed; thankfully he seemed unaware of my imminent meltdown. 'Miracles do happen, I guess.'

Let's hope so, because I certainly needed one.

Willing my tears to hold off a little longer, I said, 'I'm sorry for tricking you into seeing me today but thank you for taking the time to listen.'

'It's all right.' He reached into the basket for a piece of caramel slice. 'You made it worth my while.'

My insides turned over and suddenly I knew I couldn't let this opportunity pass. While I hadn't gone there with the intention of begging him to reconsider his decision—to reconsider *us*—who knew when I'd have his captive attention again.

'Listen,' I began, 'seeing the marriage counsellor forced me to take a good look at our marriage and also at myself. I'm willing to admit that there were cracks I might have been burying my head in the sand about. I was perhaps too focused on the kids and didn't put enough effort into us.'

He raised an eyebrow as he popped the last of the slice into his mouth.

'I'd really love it if you'd come to a few sessions with me so we can discuss where we went wrong. Even if the goal isn't to get back together but simply because I need some closure.'

My heart quivered as I waited for his reply. It wasn't true—I wasn't looking for closure. I was looking for one of those miracles he'd mentioned and I hoped that if I managed to get him to visit Megan with me, maybe she'd be able to help me convince him that we had a future together after all.

Adrian took his time replying, then, 'Let me think about it, okay?'

I nodded. 'Thank you.' That was a huge leap from the past few weeks of not answering my calls and barely even looking at me when our paths crossed at soccer.

Not wanting to overstay my welcome, I gathered the leftovers back into my basket.

Adrian beat me to the door and opened it for me, clearing his throat as we stepped into the waiting area. 'See you soon, Ms Murphy. And, if you keep wearing good shoes like those,' he said, glancing down at my sensible hidden support shoes, 'you'll never have serious foot problems.'

I gave him a look. Foot problems were the least of my worries!

25

Ragged Point

'I can't believe I'm doing this.' I cringed at my reflection in the bathroom mirror as I tugged on my short denim skirt. Thank God I had black leggings underneath.

'You look fantastic,' Jedda said as she adjusted a platinum blonde afro wig on her head. 'And I say if you've got it, flaunt it.'

'That's the problem. I'm not sure I do have it.'

'Oh, you do, trust me. Now hold still so I can finish your makeup.'

I puckered my lips so she could paint them with a bold, frosty pink. Like Jedda, I was also wearing a wig, although mine was brown and halfway down my back with a thick fringe that was already irritating my eyes.

'Are you sure this T-shirt isn't too tight?' I asked.

She smiled at my black top with the word 'Sexy' scrawled in hot pink across my chest. 'It's supposed to be tight. But don't forget you'll also be wearing this, which should make you feel a little less self-conscious.'

The 'this' she held out to me was a magenta-coloured tracksuit jacket—the kind of thing Barbie had worn in the eighties.

Where on earth Jedda had got our outfits I had no idea, but somehow along with my monstrosities, she'd managed to find herself a pale blue parachute tracksuit, which she now wore proudly. We were going as Kath and Kim to the Aussie Icon Trivia Night and it'd be a tough call to decide which one of us looked more ridiculous.

'I must have been drunk when I agreed to this,' I said with a sigh.

Jedda winked. 'Then let's get you drunk again.'

I followed her into the kitchen. Sam was babysitting Bindi tonight because 'stupid dress-ups' and 'boring trivia' were not her thing, which was why Jedda had come here to 'have some fun' while we got ready.

'Relax,' she ordered as she pulled a bottle of Bundy Rum out of a calico shopping bag, unscrewed the lid and took a swig. 'Everyone will be dressing up. That's half the fun of trivia nights. Just be grateful you missed our pimps and hoes casino night.'

My eyes gaped—I was beginning to understand Sam's sentiment. 'Do you want a glass?'

'Nah. I'm getting in character.'

'I'm pretty sure Kath would have used a cup, but it might have been plastic.'

'You know what your problem is?' Jedda didn't wait for me to reply. 'You get too hung up on details. Now, here. Drink.'

I don't think I'd ever had rum in my life—I was definitely more a white wine kind of girl—but Ragged Point had already given me lots of new experiences, so I took the bottle and gasped as the liquid hit my throat.

Jedda smirked. 'Don't worry, I've got Coke in the car for when we get there. We should take a quick selfie before we leave. Moments like these need to be documented.'

Again, I knew there'd be no point arguing, so, like a couple of teenage girls about to go out on the town with fake IDs, we snapped photos on our phones. I sent one to Saxon and Payton to give them a laugh and then decided to shoot it to Adrian as well. It was important that all our communication wasn't negative and/or about the kids.

I'm going to a themed trivia night! I think I've lost my mind.

'You ready?' Jedda said.

'Ready as I'll ever be.' I'd just slipped my phone into my handbag when it beeped. 'Oh my God!'

'What is it?'

Everything inside me buzzed. 'Adrian replied to my text.'

'What did he say?'

'*LOL. And have a good night.*'

'Right.' Jedda didn't sound impressed.

'It might not seem much, but if I'd sent this text a couple of weeks ago, he wouldn't have even bothered to reply.'

She gave me two thumbs up. 'Good idea to show him that you can have fun without him. Now, let's go.'

'Be a good boy, Charlie,' I said and then locked the front door. He and the possum would no doubt have a fun-filled night tormenting each other.

I tried to calm my nerves as I climbed into the front seat of Jedda's car, once again tugging down my skirt. I'd met a few of the locals so far during my weeks in Ragged Point. I frequently saw Sam and her parents at the general store, knew my neighbours, some of the regulars that came into the cafe, and Dan, of course—but I wasn't sure meeting the rest of them dressed like this was the best way to make a good first impression.

As we walked towards the building and joined the others heading for the hall, my nerves subsided a little. Everyone else was also dressed in goofy costumes—many much more outrageous than ours. Even before we'd stepped inside, I'd seen a couple of Dame Ednas, a bottle of Emu Export, a shark with a surfer's arm in its mouth, a couple of koala onesies and even someone dressed as Jeanne Little in her famous garbage bag dress! Jedda seemed to know everyone and took it upon herself to introduce me.

'This is Ashling; she's new to the Point and she's been a lifesaver for me these past few weeks. If it wasn't for Ash, I'm not sure when I'd have managed to get the *Reporter* out again.'

Everyone was extremely friendly, but now I had a new panic. How the hell was I going to remember all their names? If only we were all wearing badges.

Aussie classics blared from speakers on either side of the stage, where two people dressed as B1 and B2 were bent over a clipboard in deep conversation. There had to be about twenty tables set up, all rapidly filling with people. Drinks were BYO but you could buy snacks through a hatch off the main hall that opened into the kitchen.

Jedda led us to a table near the front where two of her Brewed Awakening employees were already sitting. I said hi to Cassie and Gail, who I already knew, and was introduced to Gail's husband Jim. Cassie had come dressed as Mr Squiggle and Gail and Jim were wearing handmade costumes—she a koala and Jim a tree.

I laughed as she clung to him. 'Very creative.'

After we'd gushed over each other's outfits, we discussed our trivia strategy. Jim apparently had the music covered, Gail the sport, Jedda the history and geography, and Cassie announced herself as a 'walking pop culture encyclopedia'.

'What's your area of expertise?' Gail asked me.

'Um …' I racked my brain for something useful but was thankfully saved from answering by Terri Irwin (or at least someone dressed like her) bumping into my chair.

'Oh, I'm so sorry,' she said, not sounding as if she meant it in the slightest; she'd already continued on before I could reply.

Jedda leaned forward and whispered in my ear. 'That's Gemma Emerson-Dobson,' she explained as the tall woman—who didn't need a wig as she had long, straight blonde hair anyway—continued on to a table in front of us along with a weedy kind of man who didn't look anything like Steve Irwin, despite the fact he was dressed in the iconic khaki shirt and shorts. 'And her husband Wayne.'

'The Emersons always get that table because they're the major sponsor of trivia night,' Gail told me.

'They're the major sponsors of anything and everything that happens in the Point,' Cassie added.

A broad-shouldered man, who took up a lot of space and looked to be in his late sixties, and a gorgeous but much younger woman joined the couple at the table. They both wore elaborate, expensive-looking lobster costumes. The others informed me this was Stephen Emerson—owner and CEO of The Lobster Factory, which had been in his family for generations—and his Thai wife, Apinya, who was only a year older than his daughter.

'What happened to his first wife?' I asked.

Gail shook her head. 'Such a tragedy—Bonnie died when the kids were only young. She was a gorgeous soul—we were great friends and I miss her dearly.'

'That's awful.' My heart went out to Dan and his siblings.

'My parents have a picture that she painted of them hanging in our hallway,' Cassie said. 'It's a masterpiece. It's almost like she knew things about them they didn't even know about themselves. It's hard to explain.'

'Oh, yes.' Gail nodded and her eyes grew a little misty. 'Bonnie had such talent. I've never seen anyone paint the way she did. It was like with each brushstroke she peeled back a layer of the person.'

As they discussed this tragedy, I learnt more about the Emerson empire. Stephen still had a big hand in the business, but his oldest son now managed the export of live lobsters around the world and Gemma their fleet of fishing vessels and crew. Meanwhile, another couple and two teenage children appeared at their table. Cassie informed me this was Benjamin Emerson (the eldest son) and the teenagers belonged to him and his wife, Heaven. Ben had come as Crocodile Dundee and Heaven was clearly dressed as the ditsy journalist from the movie.

'Heaven!' Gail sniggered. 'Apparently her parents were hippies.' She was very straitlaced and clearly didn't approve.

'Why isn't Dan sitting with them?' I asked, realising there weren't any spare seats at the table.

'He got pushed aside when Apinya arrived and Heaven started making the teenagers tag along. They're home-schooled but she doesn't trust them home alone and they reckon they're too old for a babysitter,' Jedda said, then nodded towards a table much nearer the back. 'Dan's over there with his mates from the Island Progress Association.'

I followed her gaze to the back but couldn't make him out among the sea of colourful characters.

'Poor Dan,' Gail said, 'first his wife leaves him, then his family can't even find space for him to sit with them.'

'Poor Dan?' Cassie rolled her eyes and reached for her drink. 'I heard Tessa left him because he beat her.'

Gail blew air through her lips. 'Those rumours are absolute piffle. I don't know why she left, but Dan worshipped the ground she walked on. No way he would have ever laid a finger on her.'

'You never know what's happening in someone's relationship and Dan does seem the odd one out in his family,' said Cassie. 'My mum always said it was the quiet ones you had to watch out for.'

I desperately wanted to hear more about these rumours and also about this island group, but B1 boomed into the mic and the conversation died. 'Good evening everyone. Are you ready for some good Aussie fun?'

The crowd roared various versions of 'yes'.

In reply, B1 and B2 introduced themselves as Sharon and Garry from the pub and explained how the evening would progress—eight rounds of trivia with some other fun games in between. 'Remember, tables can win good points for the games so it's a way to stay afloat if your general knowledge isn't up to par,' Garry advised.

While B1 (Sharon) went through a few housekeeping items, B2 (Garry) made sure that every table had a notepad and pens, then the first round of questions kicked off. 'How ocker are you?' was about decoding Aussie slang and Gail and Jim were both very good at it.

'What is a bushman's clock?' Sharon asked.

Jim leaned over towards Jedda who'd been given the task of scribe. 'It's a Kookaburra laughing.'

'Question two,' Sharon said. 'What does it mean if someone is driving a Toorak tractor?'

'A fancy four-wheel drive that's never been off road,' Gail said smugly, before taking a sip of her rum and Coke.

I laughed—I knew a fair few women in the city who drove such cars, Melissa Diamond being one of them.

After a couple more rounds of questions—Aussie politics and famous Australians—Garry pressed a button and Cold Chisel's 'Khe Sanh' blasted from the speakers and carnage erupted as people exploded from their seats, shoving others out of the way in a mad dash to get to the front.

'What's going on?' I whispered to Jedda.

'You'll see.'

There were four blow-up electric guitars in front of the stage, and these appeared to have inspired the hysteria. They were snatched up on a first come, first served basis, and two people embarked on a tug of war to claim the fourth. The loser reluctantly returned to her seat and those remaining entered into an air guitar contest—the prize twenty points for their table.

These guys were actually pretty good, but you couldn't pay me enough to get up there and do anything like that myself. The contest was close—judged by who received the loudest cheer from the crowd—and then we continued with the next trivia round.

By the time Garry announced it was the half-time break, the rum and Coke had gone right through me and I made a mad dash to the bathrooms. Jedda hurried behind me but a queue had already formed and was poking its way out the door of the ladies' bathroom. Of course, the men had no such wait.

'If this line doesn't start moving much faster, I'm going in there,' Jedda announced, almost knocking out a passer-by as she pointed.

'Shit, I'm so sorry,' she gushed.

'It's fine,' he said and then looked to me. 'Well hello there, neighbour.'

'My goodness. Dan?' My hand rushed to my mouth at the sight of him in cut-off denim shorts and a red flannelette shirt covering the biggest fake beer gut I'd ever seen. 'Who are you dressed as?'

He feigned hurt. 'Thought that was clear—I'm a classic bogan.'

'You look even more outrageous than us. That wig!'

'Hey!' He frowned and stroked his hand over his hair, letting his fingers glide through his impressive orange mullet. 'I kinda like it. I'm thinking of getting my hair cut like this.'

As I laughed the line shuffled forward a little and Dan glanced down, taking in my outfit. 'And I think *you* taking the piss out of *me* is the pot calling the kettle black.'

'Ah yes, maybe,' I replied, 'but Jedda organised it, so I can't take the blame.'

He chuckled. 'You have good taste,' he said to Jedda, then looked back at me. 'I'm not sure those shoes quite fit the look though.'

'They're pretty much all she has,' Jedda added, turning up her nose at my podiatry brand flats.

'Is that right?' Dan replied.

I glanced down and saw he was wearing the kind of thongs you bought in a $2 shop, and he had the most enormous feet I'd ever seen. The Emersons obviously had big genes—even Dan's sister looked over six foot tall.

'Anyway, I'll see you ladies later,' he said, forcing my eyes back up. 'Enjoy the rest of the night.'

'Did you see the size of those feet?' Jedda whispered as he disappeared into the men's room. 'You know what they say about the size of a man's feet?'

'That's just a myth,' I told her, quoting an article I'd read in the 'fun' section of one of Adrian's podiatry journals. 'A research study proved absolutely no correlation between the two.'

The line shuffled forward a little more—we were almost, *finally*, into the bathroom.

'I think he likes you,' Jedda said.

'He does not.'

'And you were totally flirting with him.'

'I was not! Don't be silly. We're just friends.' I wasn't even sure you could call it that as the longest conversation we'd ever had was about five minutes. 'We're neighbours.'

Jedda wriggled her dark eyebrows at me. 'Methinks the lady doth protest too much.'

'Stop it,' I said, feeling my cheeks heat at her ridiculous insinuation. 'You know I'm married.'

'Uh-huh.' She glanced down at my wedding ring. 'But I thought that was on hiatus. If your hubby's having a bit of fun, why shouldn't you?'

'I'm not having this conversation with you.'

Jedda chuckled. 'So, if you weren't married, you'd go there?'

'I am married so that's a moot point,' I hissed. 'If you like him so much why don't *you* go there?'

'Me?' She snorted. 'No way. I could never get with an Emerson, even if Dan is the best of the lot.'

She backed down after that, and by the time we bought some raffle tickets and returned to our table, the break was almost over. Thankfully, Gail had bought a cheese platter for us to share. I feared I may have imbibed too much rum and should not only eat something but drink less for the rest of the night, or I wouldn't be any use for answering questions.

The next round of trivia was all about Aussie TV and I surprised myself by getting almost as many answers as Cassie did.

'Who is the longest serving presenter on *Play School*?' Garry asked.

'I think that's Benita,' I said.

'Who's Benita?' Cassie asked, too young to remember her.

There was brief discussion of other possibilities—'What about Noni?' Gail said—but in the end we stuck with Benita and we were right.

Although we weren't too bad on the trivia, no one at our table won any of the raffles or the games between rounds, but I had to admit it had been a very fun night. Probably the most fun I'd had in ages.

'All right,' Sharon called, 'we're almost done but ... we still have one important task. We have to crown the costume winners!'

Once the cheer died down, she said, 'Each table nominate who you think is your best and send them up for the fashion parade.'

To my utmost dismay, everyone at our table pointed at me and Jedda.

'But you guys have much better costumes than us,' I argued.

Surely Gail and Jim were onto a winner and no way I wanted to get up there and parade about in front of a hall of strangers.

'Don't be a spoilsport,' Jedda said, grabbing my hand and pulling me to my feet.

We headed to the front, my heart hammering all the way. As well as us, there were four women contenders and seven men, Sam's mum Michelle and Dan among them. All looked far more confident than I felt, but somehow when Garry called Jedda and me forward, I forgot all my inhibitions—maybe the rum helped—and sashayed along the imaginary catwalk beside her, pouting to the audience and swishing my long fake hair from side to side.

Gail, Jim and Cassie shrieked from our table, giving us a standing ovation, and there were even a few wolf-whistles from other members of the audience. I rushed to the side, unable to believe what I'd just done as the next woman took her turn.

'You're a natural,' Dan whispered to me as I passed him.

I bit my lip as an unfamiliar heat washed through me.

I was sure Michelle, who had made the most amazing Australia Post Box costume, would win so couldn't believe it when they awarded me and Jedda the prize. We won a bottle of Jack Daniels and a plastic crown between us and I told Jedda she could keep both. 'Give the crown to Bindi—I'm sure she'll have more use for it than I do.'

'Thanks,' Jedda said and plopped the crown on her head. 'Dear God, I hope Sam managed to get her to sleep as I'm not at all up to the task tonight.'

'Fingers crossed.'

'Come on, I'll drive you home.'

'I can walk,' I protested, silently thinking it might be more of a stagger. Although I'd slowed down, I'd still had way more to drink than I usually would, but I was lucid enough to know Jedda shouldn't be driving anyone *anywhere*. 'And I think you should leave your car here and walk too.' It was even closer for her anyway.

'I have to agree with Ashling,' came a deep voice from behind us. 'And I'm walking in the same direction so we can walk together.'

'Oh, good job, Daniel Emerson.' Jedda leaned past me and rested her hand on his chest.

He smirked. 'Hardly a job.'

She blinked and then narrowed her eyes at him, his words seeming to remind her of her misgivings. 'You look after her, you hear me,' she said, jabbing her finger into his chest. 'Because if anything happens to her, I'll kill you.'

He grinned, clearly amused. 'I promise I'll see she gets home safely.'

'I can look after myself,' I told Jedda, leaning forward to give her a kiss goodnight before Dan and I headed to the door and joined the mass exodus from the hall.

26

'Beautiful night,' I said as we set off along the beach road, leaving crowds of people piling into cars and the lights of the town centre behind. Thankfully the moon shone brightly, giving us enough light to see the road ahead.

'Mmm ...' Dan took a deep breath, inhaling the fresh evening air. 'I love this time of year. It's still beautiful most days but the chill's starting to creep in at night, giving us a taste of what's to come.'

I wasn't cold at all but put that down to all the rum. With any luck the fresh air would help me sober up a bit. And maybe the soft sounds of the waves lapping the shore might calm the dull roar in my head.

'We've had really good weather recently, but there's talk of a couple of tropical lows forming up north near Darwin and if one of them becomes a cyclone, we could be in for some stormy weather over the next few weeks.'

'Have you been in many cyclones?' I asked.

'Nothing too bad down here in my lifetime; if we get anything it's the tail end of what the north gets and by the time it reaches us, it's usually been downgraded to a category one. All the Point ever really experiences is strong winds.'

'Well, that's good,' I said, but it also kind of killed the conversation. I'd been hoping Dan's tales of battling Mother Nature would get us all the way to the shack, avoiding any opportunity for awkward silence.

But while I couldn't wait to get home, guzzle a huge glass of ice-cold water and fall into a deep slumber, my companion didn't appear to be in a hurry at all. For a guy, he walked rather slow—maybe it was the thongs not supporting his feet properly or maybe he was dilly-dallying for my benefit. Even in my comfy, practical, medically sound shoes, I wasn't completely steady on my feet. I was never drinking rum with Jedda again.

I was never drinking rum with anyone again.

Hell, maybe I'd never drink *anything* again.

'You okay?' Dan gently touched my arm.

'Not really.' I flinched and placed a steadying hand on my stomach. The last thing I wanted to do was throw up in front of a stranger. 'I'm feeling a bit queasy. Guess I'm not a teenager anymore and not used to late nights out drinking.'

'It's only eleven o'clock. You can hardly call yourself a hedonist.'

Eleven o'clock? It felt like the middle of the night. 'A *hedonist*?'

He chuckled. 'Sorry, English was my favourite subject at school. I like variety in my words.'

'Really? Me too.'

'That doesn't surprise me. I noticed your influence on the last *Reporter*. Don't get me wrong, Jedda does a great job, but you edited all the community columns, didn't you?'

'Yes.' I was impressed he could tell the difference. 'If you like English so much, have you ever thought about helping with the *Reporter*? I'm sure Jedda wouldn't knock you back.'

'Nah, I'm too busy with the Island Progress Association right now.'

'What exactly is that?' I asked.

'We're working on turning Bill's island into a tourist attraction, but it's a time-consuming process. We've got the shire doing a risk assessment with their insurer to see what needs to be done for us to get public liability coverage approved, and then we've got to petition local government to allow public access. There's also the ongoing maintenance of the building and the grounds and other issues we need to work out.'

'Wow, sounds complicated. Is it really that amazing out there?'

'It's like nothing you've ever seen. When Bill started going to the island on a makeshift raft, it was deserted and overrun. Not many people went over there because they were scared of snakes, but Bill saw its potential. He started spending all his free time out there, making a clearing and then eventually beachcombing for anything he could use to make a shelter. Over time he created a true island paradise for himself. A bunch of us even built him a throne a few years before he died. We joked that he should secede from the rest of the country and create his own kingdom, like that bloke up near Northampton who declared his farm to be a country.'

I laughed. 'I remember hearing about that when I was a kid. So Bill wasn't a hermit?'

'No, not really. He didn't leave the island much in his last few years, but he was happy to have visitors, as long as they rang the bell on his little jetty to signal their arrival. He let the primary school visit once and the kids couldn't get enough of his castle. They felt like they were in a fairy tale.'

'When you say castle ...'

'You really have to see it to believe it,' Dan said. 'My offer to take you over still stands. You could come tomorrow when I feed Lion, if you like. If we're lucky, we'll see some sea lions. They're often frolicking in the water on the other side of the island.'

Despite Cassie's rumours about him still ringing in my ears, his invitation was even more tempting now. I liked making up my own mind about people, and so far Dan hadn't been anything but gentlemanlike towards me. I also still hadn't seen any of Wei's promised sea lions.

'I'd love to, but my daughter has an early soccer game tomorrow morning, so I'm heading back to Perth first thing.'

'Ah, never mind,' he said as some kind of birdsong sounded above us in a tree. 'Maybe next time?'

I wanted to say yes, but would there even be a next time? I'd only come here to take refuge from the breakdown of my marriage and for the first time in weeks I actually held some hope that Adrian might be coming around to reconciliation. The thought of not returning to the Point, of not getting a lot further along in the renovation, put a dampener on the evening.

But then again, Adrian and I wouldn't solve our issues overnight. He had put doubt in my heart, and we'd need to work towards a new normal. That would mean several sessions with Megan, so perhaps I might be able to sneak away to the Point a few more times. Maybe even finish what I'd started.

'I'd really like that,' I said. 'I'll be back next Monday.'

'Monday it is then.' Although I couldn't see his face in the dim light, I swore I heard a smile in his voice.

'So, what do you do at The Lobster Factory?' I asked, breathing a sigh of relief as the shack came into view. Thank God our conversation had distracted my body from evicting the contents of my stomach.

'That's the million-dollar question,' Dan replied with a chuckle.

'What do you mean? You don't know what your job is?'

'Last census I was seriously tempted to write general shit-kicker in the occupation box. Basically, I'm a jack of all trades. Sometimes I'm out on the boats catching lobsters, other times you'll find me in the processing facility helping prep them for local sale and export. I also take tourists out on our day trips and have even been known to don an apron and serve tables in the restaurant.'

This visual made me laugh. 'What do you like doing best?'

He replied without a second's thought. 'Taking visitors out on fishing charters to catch lobsters or look for sea lions—it's magic when someone sees one for the first time. I love showing off the coast and folks get a kick out of catching their own dinner.'

Our steps slowed even more as we arrived at the shack. The fresh air had done me good—I almost felt normal again.

'Well, thanks for walking me,' I said.

'Not a problem—you're on my way.'

Charlie barked at the sound of our voices and Dan's eyes widened.

'His bark's a lot worse than his bite,' I promised.

'Having seen him, that's not too hard to believe. That big goofy face doesn't look like it would hurt a fly.'

I smiled. 'Anyway, thanks again. Goodnight, Dan.'

He nodded. 'Goodnight, Ashling. I'll see you next Monday.'

27

Perth

When my phone crooned early in the morning, I had a moment of disorientation as I blinked open my eyes. Where was the sun that usually fell across my face at this time? And why couldn't I hear the sea birds and the ocean? I sat up in a panic, then shook my head at my stupidity as I looked around the bedroom I'd shared with my husband for over half our married life.

Of course. It was Tuesday morning of my week with the kids and I was home. In Perth.

I picked up the phone, surprised by the name on the screen.

What could Adrian possibly want at this time of the morning? Maybe something had happened to his mum? Or Brad or Hayley? Although I knew all the statistics about planes being safer than cars, I'd always worried about Hayley's occupation. If something did go wrong with a plane, I didn't like her chances of survival.

Stop being such a prophet of doom.

Maybe Adrian was calling to ask if I'd made the appointment for couples counselling yet. My optimism evaporated as another possibility struck. He was probably calling to tell me he'd forgotten to take the washing out of the machine. Too late—I'd discovered this when I'd done my grand tour of the house upon arrival yesterday.

While I stared at the phone it went silent again; Hayley would call this karma for all the times Adrian had let my calls go to voicemail in the last month or so. Although I badly wanted to call him back immediately, a little voice in my head told me not to be so fast. He'd call again if it was truly something important.

So, instead I put the phone down and listened for sounds of activity in the house—hoping the kids were already up and getting ready for school—but all was quiet. As comfortable as my bed was—the ancient one in Ragged Point creaked whenever I rolled over—I dragged myself out of it and shoved my feet into my slippers.

Charlie roused and followed me down the hallway to the kids' bedrooms.

I rapped on Saxon's door first. 'Morning, honey. You getting ready?'

'Yeah, Mum, be out in a minute,' came his reply.

Payton's door was open—she was still scared of the dark. I smiled at her curled up in a ball, the doona wrapped around her like a cocoon, in the corner of her bed. As I crossed the room and opened the curtains, she groaned.

'Good morning, princess. Time to rise and shine.'

'I'm not a princess,' she objected from under the covers. 'And close my curtains or I'm not getting up.'

I laughed, closed them, switched on the light instead and sat beside her. 'You've got that excursion at the zoo today. You don't want to miss that.'

At this reminder, she slowly peeled back the corner of her doona and poked out her head. 'You're still coming, aren't you?'

'Of course.' I reached out and stroked her hair. I'd only maybe missed one or two excursions since my kids started school. 'Hopefully we get to see the elephants pooing like we did last time.'

Payton made a face but giggled nonetheless and I tapped her lightly on the bum. 'Right, missy. Up you get. I'm going to make brekkie.'

Today that consisted of bacon, scrambled eggs, fried tomatoes and wholegrain toast as I had a suspicion that the most they ate when Adrian was in charge was toast or cereal. One look at Saxon as he walked into the kitchen ten minutes after me confirmed my decision was a good one.

He looked as if he'd bypassed the brush and used his fingers to groom his hair, his clothes were crumpled despite the fact I'd ironed his uniform last night, but it was his bloodshot eyes and the dark bags beneath them that worried me.

'Are you feeling okay, sweetheart?' I asked as I put a full plate of food in front of him.

'Yeah. Why wouldn't I be?' Saxon grunted as he picked up his cutlery. He looked as if he hadn't slept a wink. Had he been up late doing homework? I dared not ask him for fear he'd snap at me again. I thought we'd sorted things out when I'd laid my heart on the line to him about wanting to get our family back together, but he still spoke in bare syllables to me, his tone generally pissed off when he did. Perhaps he needed an iron supplement.

I grabbed a pen to write that down on my shopping list as Payton skipped into the room dressed in her school uniform and holding my phone in her hand.

'Mum, couldn't you hear this?' She thrust it towards me. 'It's Dad.'

No time to be nervous, I lifted the phone to my ear. 'Good morning, Adrian.'

'Ash, thank God.'

My heart leapt to my throat. 'What is it?'

'Kristen's caught the blasted flu.'

Who? It took me a second to work out he was talking about our head receptionist. Of course, *now* his phone call made sense. 'Oh, that's awful. Poor Kristen.'

'Yes, I hope she recovers quickly, but in the meantime, I need you to do me a favour.'

I could guess what it was, and it irked me that he'd demanded rather than asked.

'Laura is good, but she can't handle everything on her own and the doctor's given Kristen a whole week, possibly two, of sick leave. Can you come and fill in for her until she gets back?'

That was *almost* a question.

I glanced at Payton happily munching her breakfast and lowered my voice. I *could* tell him to call a temp agency. 'What time do you need me?'

'As soon as possible. We've got a full day of back-to-back appointments.'

Saying no wasn't my forte—I hated letting anyone down—but I had little choice right now. Whatever I did, either Payton or Adrian was going to be angry with me.

'I'm going on a school excursion with Payton's class today.' I wanted him to know I'd not only be sacrificing spending quality time with our daughter but also letting down the school if I helped him. Let him beg a little.

Payton looked up as I mentioned her name.

'So, cancel it,' Adrian said, oozing frustration. 'She'll understand.'

I wasn't so sure about that, but it would likely be easier for the school to find another parent than it would for him to find another receptionist at such short notice. Our school was in an area where most of the mums didn't work and they always had an overabundance of parents scrambling to volunteer.

'Please, Ash. I need you.'

And *there* was the begging I'd secretly wanted.

I turned away so Payton couldn't see my face as I grinned. Adrian may be pleading over the phone and it may be a work thing, but it still felt good to hear those words in his deep, attractive voice.

'Okay.' I let out a long sigh, so he didn't register my glee. 'I'll drop Payton at school and be there as soon as I can.'

'Thank you,' he breathed.

I'd barely ended the call when Payton threw her fork on the table. 'You promised me you'd come on the excursion. You're such a liar. You always say we need to keep our promises, but you never keep yours.'

I raised my eyebrows. That was a touch unfair—I couldn't remember the last time I'd broken any promises, unlike her father—but I understood her anger.

'Payton, please listen,' I said as she shoved back her chair and ran from the kitchen. Seconds later I heard her door slam and I slumped back against the kitchen counter.

So much for a lovely breakfast reuniting with my children.

I didn't have time to go after her now—I needed to find something to wear for a day in the clinic—and she wouldn't be ready to listen to reason yet anyway, so I quickly collected up the dishes instead.

I frowned as I scraped Saxon's plate into the rubbish bin; he'd maybe eaten half a rasher of bacon and a few mouthfuls of scrambled eggs. He'd sneaked off when I was on the phone, but I'd assumed he'd finished as teenage boys ate like it was an Olympic event.

What was going on with him? I didn't really have time to waste but decided Adrian could hold the fort a little longer. I went down the corridor to tell Sax I thought he should stay home and rest. I was prepared for a battle—there wasn't one class the boy would be prepared to miss—but when I pushed open the door to his bedroom, I found it empty.

Dammit. I screwed up my nose and started picking up the dirty clothes scattered across the floor. On his desk, I found a bowl of Nutri-Grain growing mould, a couple of empty cans of energy drinks—banned in this house—and dozens of lolly and chocolate wrappers. If this was an indication of his current diet, no wonder Saxon looked terrible.

Had Adrian been paying *any* attention to our children?

'Are we going or what?'

I turned to find Payton standing in the doorway.

'Saxon's gunna kill you for going in his bedroom. Can't you read?' She pointed to the door where a sign read, 'WARNING: NO TRESSPASSING. VIOLATORS WILL BE PROSECUTED.'

'I think that's meant for you,' I said, crossing the room, my arms laden with dirty clothes. I'd deal with the other mess later—or rather I'd make Saxon deal with it. 'I'll be five minutes.'

Payton groaned as I rushed past her, hurled the clothes into the laundry and hurried into my bedroom.

Six minutes later, after a one-minute shower, another minute trying to select an outfit that looked professional but womanly, and the rest of the time spent doing my makeup and pulling on my boots, we were in the car.

I tried to explain why I needed to help Adrian, that me spending time with her father would ultimately be a good thing for all of us, but Payton wasn't in the mood to listen to reason. She was uncharacteristically silent and didn't even look at me but gazed out the window the entire time instead. I thought she might deign to open her mouth to complain when I dropped her off in the Kiss and Drive rather than walking her in, but she got out, slammed the door and headed into school without even a backward glance.

Just fabulous.

Nothing I liked less than my daughter being angry at me, but sometimes the ends justified the means. Payton would get over her disappointment eventually, and Adrian and I working alongside each other would give me the chance to remind him how good we were together.

28

On Friday when the phone rang, I glanced at the bottom of my computer screen to check the time before picking it up.

'Good afternoon, Wood's Podiatry, Ashling speaking. How may I help you?'

'Oh, hi Ash, it's Kristen.'

My heart sank at the sound of the cheerful, *healthy* voice on the end of the phone line. 'Hey. How are you feeling?'

'Much better.'

We small-talked for a few moments about how much TV she'd been binge-watching during her enforced bed rest and how she'd almost drowned in tissues.

'Anyway, I just wanted to let you know I'll be back to work on Monday,' she said eventually.

'Are you sure? You don't want to rush back to work. I don't mind covering a little longer—we don't want you to overdo it or risk passing on your flu to the clients.'

'Oh, no, I'm fine,' Kristen said, and I resisted the urge to beg her to pretend not to be. 'The doctor said I'm definitely no longer contagious and if I'm stuck in my unit any longer, I'll be homicidal.'

My grip tightened around the phone. While I couldn't begrudge Kristen feeling better, I'd loved my week working full-time in the clinic.

I drove Payton to school in the mornings and Adrian arranged for his babysitter to pick her up in the afternoons so I could do a full day, which I'd not done in the past. Payton had started talking to me again Tuesday night—she'd never win a silence competition. I'd thought she might be annoyed at the fact I wasn't going to be there in the afternoons, but she barely batted an eyelid.

She liked hanging out with Topaz and when I'd met the girl myself, I could easily see why. Although the terms 'emo' and 'goth' came to mind whenever I saw her, she was much more than her appearance. I discovered she was studying child psychology at university and also played chess professionally. Every day Topaz encouraged Payton to do her spelling, maths and reading homework and then she'd kick the ball outside with her or try and teach her a few chess moves.

I'd be lying if I said that seeing my husband on a daily basis wasn't a big part of the appeal of working right now. It reminded me of the old days when we were young and broke and doing everything we could to build the business together. Best of all, it had helped eradicate the tension that had festered between us since we'd embarked on nest parenting. We'd even shared lunch a couple of times, discussing crazy clients, the kids, and all sorts of other things while we ate. Nothing gave me a bigger buzz than when Adrian smiled or laughed at something I said.

So many times I'd almost invited him to come over for dinner, but as much as I desperately yearned to have my family together again at the table, I didn't want to push him too far too fast. For this reason, I'd been counting on another week in the clinic. We were getting along so well that I hoped Adrian might actually make the first move towards proper reconciliation if we spent just a little longer together.

But one phone call from Kristen sent all my hopes plummeting and put a certain pressure on the next couple of hours. I had to make the most of them because once they were over, we'd be back to seeing each other once a week at Payton's soccer game.

By the time Adrian's last patient left, Lauren and the other podiatrists were long gone. I ran my hands through my hair and checked my reflection in a little mirror Kristen kept in her desk as I waited for him to emerge from his consulting room.

'You're still here?' he said when he finally came out about ten minutes later, quickly shoving his phone into his pocket. My heart hitched a beat as I wondered what he'd been doing on it. Even after our pleasant week working together, I still felt anxious every time I saw him busy on his phone. Especially if he was smiling or laughing quietly.

'Just tidying up a few things,' I lied. 'Making sure everything is in order for Kristen's return next week.'

He nodded. 'Excellent. Thank you.'

I picked up my handbag and went to the door where he held it open for me.

'I owe you one, Ash. Don't know what I'd have done without you this week.'

Warmth flushed through me and it took all my self-control not to beam like a crazy person. 'It's been my pleasure,' I said as we walked towards our cars. 'I always enjoy working here and I'm actually thinking of looking for a more permanent job.'

He frowned. 'What kind of job?'

'I don't know. Maybe some kind of reception work. Or something in a shop. Anything really to get me back in the workforce.'

'What about the kids?'

'They're growing up. As you say, you've managed to work and take care of them. We always planned on me going back to work eventually. Maybe we could throw some more after-school work to Topaz to make it happen?'

'Maybe. But what about all your committees?'

'I think I might be done with them anyway.' Payton only had a couple of years left of primary school and high school required a lot less parent involvement. 'It's time for me to bring some money into our household.'

Possibly money for Adrian and I to spend on couples therapy or that holiday that was *long* overdue.

'It's probably not a bad idea,' he agreed, glancing quickly at his smart watch as we paused alongside our cars. 'Well, I guess ...'

This was my chance. 'I was thinking it was time to book that couples therapy we discussed,' I blurted. 'When's a good time for you?'

When he blinked, I added, 'I know your schedule is pretty busy next week, but you have a few free spaces the week after. And my counsellor said she can do evenings or weekends if stretched.'

'Um.' Adrian cleared his throat and for one brief moment I thought he was going to renege on his promise and that I'd been wrong about us making progress this past week. But then he said, 'Okay, week after next sounds good. Let me know the time and day and I'll get Kristen to reshuffle my appointments if necessary.'

'Thank you,' I breathed. He wouldn't lock in an appointment if he wasn't serious about us getting back on track, would he?

Adrian merely nodded. 'See you Sunday at soccer. I'll bring you a coffee.'

And if that wasn't even more confirmation that we still had a future together, I didn't know what was!

29

Ragged Point

On my fourth trip to Ragged Point, I didn't feel any of the anxiety I had on my first visit. More optimism filled my heart than it had in months. Adrian and I were talking to each other again, and I looked forward to seeing Jedda, continuing my work on the shack and also going out to see the island. Yet, within seconds of driving into the tiny town, I could tell something was amiss.

Cars lined the main street, locals were streaming in and out of the general store pushing trolley-loads of goods, and in the few other businesses, people were dragging in signs and taping up windows. Outside the post office, Don the postmaster was lowering the Australian flag. I slowed as I passed Brewed Awakening to see Jedda struggling to carry in the outdoor umbrellas.

What on earth was going on?

It wasn't easy, but I managed to find somewhere to park about a hundred metres down the road and my door almost flew off its hinges as I opened it.

'Stay here,' I barked to Charlie, my hair flapping about my face in the gusty wind. It was then I noticed the massive pine trees down by the seafront swaying madly from side to side and the waves beyond them larger and more fearsome than I'd ever seen.

It had been a little blowy when I'd left Perth a couple of hours ago but, eager to get on the road, I hadn't thought much about it. Early April was often like this—one beautiful sunny day followed by a cold cloudy one, giving a hint of what was to come. But Perth's weather had nothing on this.

I staggered up the road, fighting the gale as it tried to blow up my light jumper. Locals nodded distractedly to me as they loaded packs of plastic water bottles into their cars.

'What's going on?' I exclaimed as I stepped inside the cafe a few minutes later.

'Haven't you heard? There's a cyclone coming!'

'What? But Dan told me that a cyclone only makes it this far once in a blue moon.'

'Guess tonight's gunna be a blue moon then.' Jedda hurried outside to grab the last umbrella.

Holy shit. My head spun as her words registered.

'Is there anything I can do to help?' I asked, glancing around. 'Where's Bindi? Can I look after her for you?'

Jedda shook her head. 'She's napping.'

I raised my eyebrows. How could anyone possibly sleep through all this pandemonium?

'We're almost done here anyway,' Jedda said, reaching for a couple of rolls of electrical tape. 'Here, take these—I've got plenty. Tape up your windows, but leave one at the front and one at the back of the house ajar to relieve air pressure. Then bring anything that's not tied down in from outside and get the hell back to Perth.'

'Perth?'

We looked at each other like we were both insane. I'd only just arrived.

'You may as well go back home,' Jedda said. 'I doubt you'll get a chance to do any work on the shack over the next few days—that's if there's even a shack to come back to.'

'Is it really going to be that bad?' I asked, ignoring her reference to 'home'—I didn't exactly *have* one this week anyway.

'They're predicting the worst we've had in forty odd years. Usually they hit far north or south of us.'

'Oh my God. I had no idea.' Clutching the rolls of tape, I suddenly berated myself for not paying more attention to the weather reports. 'But I'm not going back to Perth.'

I'd seen the chaos outside and heard the fear in Jedda's voice. I may only be a newcomer, albeit a temporary one, but this already felt like my town. Dressing up like a whacko for trivia night along with everyone else had cemented this feeling and I wasn't about to do a runner and abandon my friends in their hour of need. If things hit as bad as predicted, then I imagined tomorrow, or the next day, or however long these things lasted, they'd need all hands on deck to help put the town back together.

Jedda shrugged. 'Suit yourself. Then go and get cyclone ready and come back here and stay with me and Bindi tonight.'

'Okay, thanks. I'll see you soon.'

'Have you got any candles?' she asked as I reached the door.

I turned back. 'Only some scented, decorative ones.'

'They'll do. Bring all you have.'

Charlie was whining loudly, his paws scraping the windscreen, when I arrived back at the car and he didn't stop as I drove more slowly than usual to the shack. I wasn't sure I'd ever driven in such strong winds. My car wasn't tiny, but it felt like it could blow right off the road at any moment. The two gum trees out the front of Xiang's place were swaying so much I thought they might rip themselves out of the ground.

I hoped my possum would survive the storm. No doubt it would take refuge in the roof, because the trees certainly didn't look safe anymore.

Leaving Charlie in the car again, I gave him a treat chew stick and then hurried inside with only the electrical tape Jedda had given me. Following her instructions, I carried all the loose items off the front porch, then I did the same out the back. I was in the middle of untying the hammock when I glanced out to sea and gasped at the sight of Dan in the canoe, jerking back and forth, struggling against the swell in his efforts to get back to the shore.

What the hell was he doing? Maybe I should try to help?

I immediately scoffed at the idea; my swimming skills were no match for the wild ocean right now. A few minutes later, I let out a sigh of relief as he jumped out and tugged the boat ashore. It was only when he picked up a box that I twigged. He'd been out to rescue Bill's cat.

Catching me looking, Dan started up the sand towards the shack. Towards me. I lifted a hand to wave, even though he couldn't wave back, and although I called out 'Hi', my words were carried away on the wind. He opened his mouth, but I didn't hear a word he said either until he got much closer.

Stopping just before the porch steps, he held the shuddering box against his chest. It sounded like he carried a pack of wild animals inside. 'I think we'll have to take another raincheck—no pun intended—on our island visit.'

I nodded. No way in hell I was getting in that tiny canoe in this crazy weather.

'Did you just arrive back?'

'Yep. And this—' I shouted above the noise of the wind, 'was a bit of a shock. Somebody led me to believe cyclones rarely made it to the Point.'

Dan smiled sheepishly. 'I swear I spoke the truth at the time. This is either climate change or Mother Nature making me look bad.'

'Trust a male to blame a female when things don't go his way.'

He laughed as another ear-piercing yowl sounded from the box. 'Anyway, do you need any help?'

I winced. 'Sounds like you've got your hands full as it is.'

'Hmm.' He glanced down at the box as if it were a bomb about to explode. 'Perhaps you're right. I'm going to take Lion and get him settled at my place, but I'm happy to come back and help you.'

'What about your own house?' I suspected Dan had rescued the cat before thinking of anything else, and even though the island wasn't huge, that could have taken some time.

'It's insured. And it was only built six years ago to cyclone-level specifications. Whereas Xiang's shack ...' He glanced up at the patchy tin roof and grimaced. 'Was sadly not.'

This I could not dispute but, thanks to the decluttering over the past few weeks, there also wasn't much to move inside or tie down. 'I think I'll be fine. I've only got the windows left to tape and there's not that many.'

'Okay then, if you're sure.' He tightened his hold on the box. 'I don't really feel good about the idea of you staying here on your own in this weather though. I've got plenty of beds if you and Charlie want to ride out the storm with me?'

'Thanks for the offer,' I said, 'but I'm heading to Jedda's to stay with her as soon as I'm done here.'

'Ah right. No worries. You'll be safe there. I'd better be getting this beast inside then.' He shifted the box in his arms. 'I guess I'll see you on the other side then. Stay safe.'

'Thanks. You too.' I waved as he walked off towards his big glass abode. Would he be all alone there during the long hours ahead? The idea didn't sit right with me, but it wasn't my place to invite him to come hang at Jedda's and surely, as a local, Dan would have plenty of people to keep him company if he wanted.

30

I went back inside and taped up the windows, turned off the water, electricity and gas, and did a final check that there were no loose items lingering outside before locking up.

By the time I got back to Jedda's, rain had come out to play with the wind, so I parked as close to Brewed Awakening as I could and then Charlie and I made a mad dash to the back door, pausing only for him to cock his leg against a tree on the way. I delivered him to Jedda and then made a couple of trips back and forth to get the candles and other supplies.

I was drenched through by the time I'd finished and Jedda handed me a towel, followed quickly by a cup of tea, which we drank sitting at the kitchen table. Bindi, blissfully unaware of the trepidation in the air, played with Charlie on the floor.

'He's so good with her,' Jedda said, smiling wistfully at the two of them as Bindi climbed all over him. 'He doesn't even flinch when she pulls his fur.'

I smiled too—watching Bindi and Charlie play reminded me of when Payton was small and our dog just a pup. It seemed like another lifetime. 'He had good training. My daughter terrorised him as a toddler and he never once snapped at her.'

'Tell me more about Payton and Saxon,' Jedda said.

As we chatted, the wind grew louder, the rain heavier and the sky darker, despite the fact it was now only midafternoon. Having turned off the electricity due to possible power surges, we lit some candles and threw on an extra layer of clothing as the temperature inside dropped rapidly. While at first Charlie had been distracted by Bindi, he started to whine more as the hours went on, his fur standing up at the commotion coming from outside. He'd always hated storms, hiding under our bed whenever thunder struck. I was glad I'd taken up Jedda's offer to stay; she and Bindi were good company, but I hoped Charlie wasn't going to be too much of a nuisance.

'Don't be silly,' Jedda said when I voiced this concern. 'I doubt any of us are going to get much sleep anyway.'

While we waited for the cyclone to hit, we guzzled tea, ate the endless snacks Jedda had prepared, entertained Bindi with songs and picture books, and listened to weather updates on the portable radio. Although a cyclone hadn't hit Ragged Point in decades, Jedda had experienced a few during her travels in the northern part of Australia, so I felt in safe hands.

In addition to the taped windows, outside preparations, the radio and its never-ending supply of batteries, she'd filled a number of buckets and the bathtub with water, as mains water sometimes got contaminated during a cyclone, and set up a little gas camping stove so we wouldn't be without a hot drink. She'd dragged her mattress into the living room, which was the most central and thus the safest room in her house, and set up a travel cot for Bindi. Her couch was a fold-out, which I'd use, and she'd even found an old doona and laid it out for Charlie.

At about 6 pm, the radio announcer informed us the cyclone was fast approaching and would hit Ragged Point in the next half an hour. While Jedda fed Bindi her dinner, I heated more water on the camping stove to warm the water already in the bath, so Bindi's evening routine could stay as close to normal as possible. I'd thought it loud outside already, but as she splashed about in the tub, the decibel level rose beyond anything I'd ever heard before.

Rain lashed against the windows like buckets of water being thrown at us by a giant. The wind screamed as if said giant was right outside whining in a high-pitched voice. When Bindi started to cry, Jedda scooped her out of the bath, wrapped her in a fluffy yellow towel and brought her to join Charlie and me in the living room, where she dressed her in soft flannelette PJs. But while Charlie had distracted Bindi earlier, neither of them were able to be distracted by anything else now.

While Jedda rocked Bindi in her arms, singing her favourite nursery rhymes, which were barely audible over the cacophony, I tried to calm Charlie, who was also beside himself. Eventually the little girl cried herself to sleep but we had no such luck with the dog. It was going to be a *long* night and I silently berated Adrian for not taking care of Charlie properly in that first week. If he had, then the dog would be safe in Perth now, rather than terrorised here with me.

This thought had barely left my head when a light sparked from within my handbag, which I'd discarded on the coffee table hours ago. I reached inside for my phone and was both surprised and happy to see a message from Adrian.

Are you okay? It's pretty hairy down here but I hear it's worse where you are.

I felt chastised that he was worried about me when I hadn't even thought to call him or the kids to let them know what was going on. And also overjoyed that he still *cared* enough to worry.

Due to the noise, I'd also missed three calls from Hayley.

There was barely any charge left on my phone, but I tapped out a quick message.

I'm okay and safe. Staying with a friend tonight. Phone about to die but will make contact as soon as I can. Give my love to the kids and keep them safe too. xx

I second-guessed the kisses and deleted them right before I pressed send. Then I sent a quick message to Hayley, almost identical to the one to Adrian, but adding that I'd safe-proofed the shack as much as possible and would assess any damage as soon as I could and let Wei know.

'Want to play Uno?' Jedda asked as she risked taking her hand off Bindi's back. The little girl had screamed blue murder when her mum had tried to put her in the travel cot and now slept fitfully on the mattress next to Jedda.

'Sure,' I said, placing my phone on the coffee table.

Jedda went to get the cards and returned a few minutes later, also carrying a bottle of wine and two glasses.

We sat on the floor alongside the mattress, so as not to go far from Bindi and also to try and comfort Charlie, who kept trying to burrow under the couch. I covered him with a blanket, which miraculously calmed him a fraction, and we drank and talked as the storm roared around us. It was like having a surround sound stereo playing the very opposite of a relaxation CD and I prayed that everyone was safe inside somewhere like we were.

While Jedda's place felt solid, I couldn't help thinking about the stumps that held up the shack, hoping the wind wouldn't lift it right off them just like it had done to poor Dorothy in *The Wizard of Oz*.

Aside from the screaming wind and rain, the only other constant was the voice of the woman on the ABC—our only connection to the outside world—as she gave updates on the cyclone's intensity and predicted duration. What had begun as a category five up north near Dampier had thankfully been downgraded to a category three now it had hit us. Apparently there was the possibility of a storm tide, which sounded terrifying considering our proximity to the beach. We'd be safe here at Jedda's, but once again my thoughts drifted to the shack. Would there be anything to return to?

I suppose it could have been worse—I could have finished the renovations. Seeing all my hard work destroyed would have been so disheartening.

When Jedda and I grew tired of Uno, we played a couple of rounds of Pass the Pig and then moved on to a jigsaw puzzle.

'My friend told me this would come in handy one day,' Jedda said as she peeled the plastic off a present she'd been given five Christmases ago. Entitled 'Crocodile Tale' and painted by a Yindjibarndi artist, the image made my heart simultaneously sing and palpitate. While the thousands of tiny, brown, yellow, black, red and orange dots made a captivating picture, piecing them together felt near on impossible.

Luckily, we had all night. Possibly even longer.

Although Jedda said she couldn't remember the last time she'd done a jigsaw, she turned out to be a pro. We put the border together quickly and then started to fill in the middle. As we worked, our conversation grew more personal. Jedda told me about how the depression following Jack's death had almost killed her and I spoke about my childhood, being tossed between my mum and dad like a tennis ball and longing for parents who didn't have a love/hate relationship with each other. We talked about our hopes, dreams and fears for our children, growing up in a world that seemed to get scarier and more dangerous by the minute.

But it wasn't all deep and meaningful, serious talk. Jedda's stories of backpacking around Australia and the guys she'd met in various jobs and hostels made me laugh so hard I got a stomach-ache.

I couldn't help thinking how a situation like this could be good for Adrian and me. Confined inside with nothing to do but talk would surely give us the perfect opportunity to reconnect, the chance to discuss something other than house or kid stuff and remind ourselves what it was we'd loved about each other in the first place. I guessed this would be the goal when we saw Megan, but I couldn't help worrying that such an artificial scenario would make us clam up rather than relax.

However, I couldn't exactly summon a cyclone to fix my marriage, so couples counselling it would have to be.

A few hours later, the puzzle started to take shape, but my eyes were drooping and exhaustion was seeping into my bones when suddenly everything went still and quiet outside, as if the giant had got bored and left. After hour upon hour of unrelenting racket, it felt a little eerie.

Charlie twitched beneath the blanket and finally poked his head out from under it. I reached out to stroke him.

'Is that it? Is it over?' I asked, letting out a long slow breath, feeling as if I'd just run some kind of marathon.

Jedda shook her head. 'No. This is the eye of the cyclone.'

'The what?'

'I'm no weather expert but it's basically the calmest part. If it was daytime, the sky might clear up now and it would feel safe as the wind seems to have stopped, but it's actually only the middle of the storm. It'd still be dangerous to go out now because it will start up again, but we may as well try and get some rest while it's quiet.'

Despite having now been awake for twenty hours, I wasn't sure I'd be able to sleep after all the excitement, but rest sounded like a good idea. Jedda curled around Bindi on the mattress and I snuggled under a couple of thick blankets on the couch with Charlie finally slumbering on the floor beside me.

Sometime in the early hours of the morning, I must have fallen asleep because I woke just after six to the sounds of wind howling again and rain lashing against the windows. Bindi was awake and playing with Charlie who appeared to have got used to the squalling soundtrack.

Jedda was boiling water on the camp stove. 'Morning, sleeping beauty,' she said.

I glanced out the window—not that I could see much as it was still quite dark. 'So yesterday wasn't a dream?'

Jedda chuckled. 'Nope. But our friend on the ABC tells us the worst is over and things should settle again in the next few hours.'

'Good.' I reached for my phone, but of course it was completely dead.

31

As predicted, the power went out during the storm and didn't come back on until late Tuesday evening, but we were safe to go outside by noon. Jedda and I popped Bindi in the pram, put Charlie on his leash and took a slow walk to assess the destruction. He was in his element, excited by all the people and sniffing all the various odours that had been drawn out by the squall.

I couldn't believe I'd actually been caught in the middle of a cyclone. Now that it was over, it almost felt surreal, except for the fact its effects were visible everywhere. The normally tidy streets were dirty with mud and debris as if someone had flown over the town and emptied a massive rubbish bin. People from the shire and the SES were clearing tree branches and other mess off the main street with ropes and chainsaws.

Although many trees had been ripped apart, the buildings appeared to have been relatively unscathed—thank God—apart from a couple of broken windows. Jedda's house was fine and the cafe had only suffered a few leaks. As we did our tour of the town,

Jedda took photos and spoke to locals for an article in the next edition of the *Reporter*.

Closer to the beach, the impact on properties was significantly greater—a number of houses had sheets of corrugated iron or gutters torn off and one house appeared to have lost its roof completely. Falling trees had landed on cars, almost splitting them in two; windows were broken, the tape seeming to have had little effect at all. At least one trampoline had ended up on the beach.

My heart went out to the residents; according to Jedda, the damage could take weeks, even months, to repair. My sensible shoes were among the casualties, turning from white to a muddy brown as we trudged along the road.

I held my breath as we approached the shack and Jedda took my hand and squeezed it, but I let out a sigh of relief as it came into view. The roof was still pinned to its awnings and although debris littered the yard, it wouldn't be too difficult to clean up.

Sadly, inside told another story.

The front door stuck as I tried to open it and, after slamming my body against it like they did in the cop shows, it budged with a loud groan.

'Oh my God,' I gasped. The ceiling in the tiny entrance and living room had completely fallen in. The carpet was no longer visible, but mixed in with the broken ceiling, rainwater and the odd dead cockroach were hundreds of little black dots. My stomach revolted. *Possum droppings!* 'Ew.'

'Lucky you stayed with me last night,' Jedda said as she stepped inside behind me, Bindi on her hip.

I let out a manic laugh and tugged on Charlie's leash to stop him going any further.

'Maybe we should go around the back way and see if this little ceiling disaster is throughout?'

'*Little* disaster?'

She smirked as we backed out and went around the side of the house. The beach no longer looked like a postcard image; there were branches, bits of driftwood, seaweed and other rubbish strewn across the sand.

'Bill's canoe,' I said, halting as I stared out at the ocean.

'Huh?' Jedda asked, hitching Bindi up her hip.

'The one Dan uses to get out to the island … it's not there.'

'It could be halfway to Africa by now, but don't worry, the Emersons aren't exactly short of sea transport.'

The rail on the steps leading to the back porch had snapped off, one of the steps had disappeared and the wood was drenched through. We stepped gingerly across to the door and this time I held my breath as I pushed against it.

But blessedly the door opened easily. The small dining area between the kitchen and living room had soggy carpet, but thankfully the water hadn't made it into the kitchen or the bedrooms, and I'd been planning to rip up all the floor coverings anyway.

I bent to lift a corner of the carpet to see how bad it looked underneath but Jedda shrieked, 'Don't touch anything until the insurance assessors have been out. They'll want to see the damage for themselves.'

I shuddered. 'I don't even know if Wei and Meili have insurance for this place. Or if Xiang did. Do insurance policies continue after someone dies?'

Jedda shrugged. 'How the hell should I know?'

'I guess it's a good thing the ceiling hadn't been replaced yet,' I said, glancing around.

'What's more of a good thing,' she replied, 'is that you've already got a tradie booked to come fix it. It'll be near on impossible to get anyone now.'

I sighed. 'Then again maybe if it had already been fixed this wouldn't have happened.'

'Who knows. Anyway, I'm going to head back to the cafe to make up some sandwiches and see what else I can cobble together for the SES.'

'I'll come help.' It wasn't like I could do anything at the shack until I'd spoken to Wei, but I wanted to do my bit for the community I'd grown to love.

'That'd be great. Thanks.'

'Is there any way I can contact my family and let them know I'm okay?' I asked as we walked back towards the main street.

'I'll try to find someone with a satellite phone for you.'

One of the kind men from the SES let me borrow his phone and even though it was during business hours, Adrian picked up on the second ring.

'Hey Adrian.'

'Ashling? Thank God. Are you okay? I could barely get the kids off to school this morning. They wanted us to drive up there and check on you.'

'I'm fine,' I said, feeling touched that he clearly still cared. 'The night was a little scary—Charlie was terrified, but we made it through. Good thing I stayed at my friend Jedda's place because—'

'Who's Jedda?'

'Remember I told you about her?' I'd mentioned the shack and Ragged Point more than once—had he actually listened to anything I'd said? 'Jedda owns the cafe here. We've become good friends.'

'Well, I'm glad you had someone to take care of you.'

I bristled at his words—I could take care of myself, thank you very much—but phone calls with my husband were few and far between and I didn't want to ruin this one by getting into a futile argument. 'Sadly, the shack I've been renovating got hit pretty hard in the storm. Half the ceiling has fallen in.'

'Geez. What are you still doing there?'

'I'm helping Jedda feed the volunteers at the moment—they're all working so hard to clear up all the mess.'

'Why don't you come back and stay at Hayley's?'

If he'd asked me to come home and stay with them, I'd probably have left in a heartbeat. Instead I told him I wasn't going anywhere. 'I get bored at Hayley's. At least here I can be of some use. Anyway, I've got to go—this isn't my phone. Tell the kids I love them, and I'll call again as soon as I can.'

I returned the satellite phone to the man who was taking a break in the cafe and went into the kitchen to help Jedda. As we served food and drinks throughout the afternoon, locals wandered in and out, offering us reports about various places around town. Thankfully no one had been hurt, but some houses had been hit pretty badly and apparently Bill's island had copped the brunt of it.

My ears pricked up.

'Dan went out there this morning,' said one man who was part of the Island Progress Association. 'Trees have been uprooted and flotsam and jetsam is everywhere. Some of the castle walls have crumbled and water inundated Bill's hut, soaking everything. It's a mess.'

'Guess that's gunna hold up your plans to open the place to the public,' said Jedda.

He nodded glumly. 'We'll have to rebuild or throw in the towel. None of us want to give up, but ...' He let out a long heavy sigh. 'Money's going to be the issue. We've been struggling enough to cobble together the fees for shire applications, insurance and everything else we needed.'

'You'd think the Emersons would throw in some funds,' mused another volunteer who was sipping a coffee nearby.

'Yes, I guess Dan might ask his dad,' replied the man, then downed the last of his drink. 'Anyway, thanks for the cuppa, I'd better be getting back to it.'

'That's super sad,' I said to Jedda as we went back to buttering bread for sandwiches. 'And I didn't even get to go out and take a look.'

'Hmmm ...'

'Are you okay?' I asked.

'I'm just thinking. Bill's castle is a big part of this community, so everyone will be expecting an article about the damage, or at least a few lines and photos.'

'I suppose so.'

'And there's no way in hell I'll be the one going out there, so ... How about you take this one?'

'What?' I blinked.

'Didn't you say you had a journalism degree?'

'Yes, but—'

'And haven't you been curious about the island since you arrived?'

'Yes, but—'

'So how about you go across, take some photos for the *Reporter*, ask Dan a few questions about what will happen now and then write it up for me? I can't pay you, but I'm happy to give you free coffees for the rest of your time in the Point.'

My head spun. 'You already give me free coffees.' It had been a point of contention ever since my second week here, but Jedda hadn't listened to my objections.

'Is that a yes?'

I let out a weird strangled sound as my stomach squeezed and my mouth went dry.

'Okay, free coffees and free muffins but that's my final offer,' Jedda said as Bindi stirred in the pram.

While she tended to her daughter, I took a moment to contemplate her proposition. What was the worst that could happen? She wasn't asking me to write for *The New York Times* or *The Washington Post*, not even *The West Australian*.

'Okay, I'll do it,' I said, my insides pulsing as she turned back to face me. It might only be a small paper, but this could be my chance to flex my writing muscles again, to see if I had the chops to pursue a career in journalism after all. 'But how will I get there?'

Before Jedda could reply the little bell above the door jangled.

I glanced up to see Dan, dressed in the same bright orange SES uniform as all the other volunteers. As our eyes met, the expression on his face not only confirmed the rumours about the island, but also put a dampener on my excitement.

While my long-lost ambition might about to be reignited, Dan's dreams for the island had been crushed in less than twenty-four hours by a freak storm.

'Hey there,' I said as he approached the counter. 'Is that offer to take me out to the island still valid?'

32

'Morning!' Dan waved as I walked along the beach towards him the following day.

'Hi.' Noticing he hadn't said *good* morning, I waved back and pulled my waterproof jacket tighter around me. 'It's a bit cooler than usual.'

A shadow of a smile appeared on his lips. 'At least it's not raining. You ready?'

'Yep.' I gestured to my backpack, which held Jedda's camera and a pen and notebook so I could jot down my observations and Dan's answers to the questions I'd been awake half the night coming up with. It felt wrong to be excited considering, but I couldn't help it.

'Excellent.'

'New boat?' I asked, indicating the shiny red and white beast moored in the water. It was at least triple the size of the canoe and from what I'd heard about the Emersons, much more their style.

'Yes. Sadly, Bill's canoe got washed away in the storm. I should have tied it down but I was more focused on Lion. This one has less character, but it'll do the trick. Come on.' He held out his hand to help me into the boat.

I took a few steps, and as my hand slipped into his, my breath caught in my throat. I almost pulled back as the warmth of his skin seeped into mine.

'Thank you,' I managed and then shrieked as he scooped me up into his arms like a baby. 'What are you doing?!'

'Putting you in the boat. Don't want you getting wet.'

My heart was thumping too loudly for me to reply, but I couldn't remember the last time anyone had picked me up. Not long before we separated, I'd jokingly asked Adrian to give me a piggyback. His response—'Are you kidding? You'd break my back.'

But Dan didn't seem to work up even a small sweat; I guess working on cray boats meant he could probably handle a heavier weight than Adrian could. His chest, which I was now awkwardly pressed against, certainly felt harder than my husband's. I willed my cheeks to cool as Dan lowered me onto one of the luxurious leather seats.

'These are not the circumstances I'd hoped to be bringing you out to the island under. It's a mess out there,' he said, his tone solemn as he handed me a life jacket. 'Here. Put this on. I know it's only a short distance but better to be safe than sorry.'

I shoved my arms into the bright yellow safety vest as Dan did the same with his, then he sat in the seat beside me and started the engine.

The island was so close, I couldn't imagine it would take more than a couple of minutes to get to, but I planned to throw myself straight into the interview to alleviate the possibility of any awkward silences. However, Dan got in first.

'How'd the shack shape up in the storm?' he asked, shouting slightly over the noise of the engine.

'Could have been worse—the only real damage seems to have been the ceiling falling in at the front part of the house.'

'Shit. Thank God you weren't there. Guess the rain must have got into the roof somehow.'

I nodded. 'The ceilings weren't looking so flash before the cyclone. When I first arrived there was a massive hole above the kitchen, and a possum had taken up residence and was helping itself to whatever it could find.'

Dan chuckled. 'Possums can be cheeky buggers. Is it still giving you grief?'

'Could be worse. I patched up the hole and now I'm leaving fruit outside on the porch for it. It's weird that the part with the hole didn't cave in. Anyway, I'd already spoken to Xiang's grandson Wei about getting the ceiling replaced and he'd booked a tradesman in for next week. I talked to him last night about insurance and he's contacting them today, but hopefully we can still go ahead with the original team.'

'Geez, that was lucky.'

'Well, maybe I was due for a bit of good luck.'

'If you need any help cleaning up ready for the roof guys let me know.'

'Thanks.' It was a lovely offer, but I wasn't sure I'd accept it as I didn't want to feel in his debt. 'Did your place suffer any damage?'

He shook his head. 'Survived without even a scratch. Are you staying at Brewed Awakening?'

'Yep. I could stay in the shack—the bedrooms, bathroom and kitchen are fine—but Jedda wouldn't hear of it, at least until the rubble is removed. She says she likes the adult company but I'm also glad I can repay her generosity by writing this article.'

'So, what's the deal with you and your husband?' he asked, surprising me with not only the swift change of topic but also his blatant nosiness. Who was interviewing who here?

'What do you mean?'

'Well,' he glanced quickly at me, 'although you mentioned you were married, aside from your ring and your aversion to thongs, I haven't seen any evidence of such. Your husband doesn't mind you coming up here every other week?'

I twisted said ring on my finger. 'My husband and I are ... complicated,' I said after a long pause.

'Like the Facebook status?'

I opened my mouth to say 'no' but it was as close to the truth as anything. 'I suppose so. We're kind of on a break.'

'I see. Like Rachel and Ross?' The corners of his lips lifted a little.

'I wouldn't have picked you as a *Friends* fan,' I said, trying to distract him, but also myself from thinking about Adrian sleeping with another woman like Ross had.

He scoffed. 'Who isn't a *Friends* fan? Nothing fixes a gloomy mood better than a few episodes of the famous six.'

I laughed. 'Maybe I should try that on my fourteen-year-old. He seems to be in a constant grumpy mood of late.'

Dan smiled properly now as he caressed the steering wheel—was that what it was called on a boat? 'How many kids do you have?'

'Two.'

'Are they with your husband then?'

'At the moment, yes,' I said with a sigh. 'We're currently nest parenting.' At the blank look on his face I explained the concept and the ideology behind it.

'I guess that makes sense for the kids, but you must miss them.'

'I do.' A lump formed in my heart and bubbled up to my throat. I didn't want to cry but talking so openly about my kids with someone I barely knew made me emotional.

'Shit, I'm sorry,' Dan said. 'I didn't mean to upset you. I was just curious—pretty girl like you comes to the Point alone, there's usually a story.'

'No one has called me a girl for quite some time.' *Or pretty*. I pushed that thought aside. 'Do you have kids?'

'Nope. Always wanted them but …' He shrugged. 'My swimmers are duds.'

His honesty shocked me and although he made light of it, I thought I detected a wobble in his voice. Was *this* the real reason his wife had skipped town?

'Anyway, enough chit-chat.' He killed the engine. 'We're here.'

He dropped the anchor, mooring us just offshore. 'There used to be a jetty; it all but disintegrated in the storm. Just another thing we'll need to rebuild.'

When Dan shrugged out of his life jacket, I did the same, and when he jumped out of the boat, I made to follow.

'Oh no, you don't.' He scooped me into his arms again. 'I didn't keep you dry back there only to have you get wet over here.'

Feeling more relaxed the second time, I didn't protest, instead glancing ahead onto the island to take in the view. Although I hadn't seen it pre-cyclone, the destruction was obvious. With even more debris on the sand here than there'd been back on the mainland, it looked like a war zone, or what I imagined a war zone to look like.

Dan lowered me to the ground. 'Told you it was a mess. Bill turned an almost barren island into a tropical paradise and now this is all that's left.' He paused as if to collect himself. 'I'm kind of glad the old bloke isn't around anymore. Seeing all his hard work destroyed would have broken his heart.'

It sounded like it was breaking Dan's as well and I really didn't know what to say at his choked-up words. I put my hand on his upper arm and squeezed lightly. The muscle beneath my fingers twitched and was even harder than his chest. I pulled back my hand and focused on getting down to business.

'Shall we take a look around?' I asked.

Over the next half hour, I took notes and lots of photos while Dan gave me a sombre tour of the island. The palm trees Bill had planted had either been displaced or torn apart by the wind and their branches were now scattered over everything.

'This was his castle,' Dan said, explaining that the mammoth structure had been built with rocks, wooden sleepers and planks scoured from the ocean and nearby junkyards. Apparently once locals knew what he was up to, they also started to bring him useful building materials as an excuse to take a look.

'Wow.' I admired the circular design with its battlements, turrets and large ornamental shells that decorated the perimeter at the top. It truly was a work of art. 'Did he build this all by himself?'

'Yeah, pretty much, over a period of about ten years. He chipped away at it whenever he wasn't working on the boats.'

'It's very detailed. Almost reminds me of something from the Mediterranean. Was Bill from Europe?'

Dan shrugged. 'Who knows? He never spoke about his time before he came to the Point.'

I frowned, remembering what Jedda had said about what happened when he died. 'Did nobody ever question him?'

'I guess they probably did, but long before my time. He proved himself to be a hard worker, a good guy, and everyone accepted him as a little eccentric but not a threat. I did ask him once, but he told me he'd rather not talk about it. Still, I was as surprised as anyone when he died and we discovered he was living identity-less.'

'How did he survive without an identity? Surely he needed a bank account to buy things? A Medicare card for when he got sick? What about a licence?'

'He always paid for everything in cash—from money he made working the boats. Happened lots years ago. Fishermen didn't mind because they didn't have to worry about all the stuff that comes along with employing someone. He hitched into the Point and I guess that's how he was getting around before then, while also doing odd jobs. After that he never really left, or he got lifts with friends if he needed to go further afield. He didn't need much though; most of what he ate he grew here in his veggie patch or caught in the sea. And as for visiting a doctor—I don't remember him ever getting sick. If he did, he probably self-medicated.'

Dan chuckled fondly. 'I know it all sounds bizarre when I say it now, but it's just how it was. He was that kinda guy and he never hurt anyone, so people just let him be.'

'What about the island though? Squatting is one thing, but what he did here … didn't he need some kind of permission?'

'You'd think, but for most of his time here, he somehow managed to stay under the radar of authorities. By the time he started building, he was known and accepted by other locals. No way you'd get away with it these days, but I guess he wasn't doing any harm, so no one questioned him. There was talk of some kind of gentlemen's agreement a few years ago when a new cop started asking questions, but Bill died before anything came of it. Maybe it was the stress that killed him.'

Although Bill's story fascinated me, I remembered I was actually here to document the destruction and ask Dan about the Island Progress Association's plans for the future.

'Be careful,' he warned as we stepped up to the 'official entrance'—an archway of rock that led into the interior of the building. 'Parts of the walls have come down, other bits are wobblier than they were, so I'm not sure of any invisible structural damage.'

'Did the storm take off the roof?' I asked, glancing up into the now clear blue sky.

'No. There was never a roof. Bill's castle was more a work of art and a place where he sat out when the weather was good. Underneath all this rubble, there's a fire pit. He'd often get it going in the evenings on the weekends and have friends over—those who'd helped with building or supplies. They'd camp on the island and then head back to the Point the next day.'

'Bill sounds like quite a character.' And obviously he had most of the town on side, which went some way to explaining how he'd got away with all he did.

Dan gestured to the walls surrounding us. 'He stored all his collectibles here. Sadly, a lot of them have been blown away, but I plan to scour the place and find as many as I can.'

'What did he collect?'

'Mostly stuff other people no longer wanted—sculptures, forgotten artworks, old glass bottles, shells he found, gifts his visitors brought out to him, vintage signs. Anything really. He was interested in lots of things.'

I snapped some photos inside the castle and then we moved on to Bill's actual living quarters—or rather what was left of them. A tree had fallen on top of his outside dunny, so there was no longer any door. And the rest of the building, made from what looked like old wooden pallets, looked as if it could crumble at any moment.

Only a couple of metres away stood another hut-like structure. I'd thought Xiang's place a little rustic, but his shack was practically a palace compared to Bill's place and I didn't think the cyclone was entirely to blame. It had been built from more pallets and what looked to be odd pieces of scrap metal and corrugated iron and painted almost the same aqua blue as the ocean.

Dan held the door, which hung from one hinge, open for me and I was surprised at what I saw as I stepped in. Aside from the fact everything had been soaked due to half the roof completely lifting off, it was quite well-appointed. The open plan living space held a large rectangular table and a few plastic chairs, a couple of couches with a card table, bookshelves and cupboards, and a bed and a couple of chests of drawers at the back. None of the furniture matched and looked as if it may have been found on the side of the road, but the place had a cosy vibe.

Bright paint and a few framed photos covered the walls. The rest had been ripped off by the wind, Dan said, and he'd collected what he could of them and placed them on the table.

I took a look. One man, who Dan confirmed to be Bill, featured in most of them, usually with his arm around another person, always with an enormous smile on his face. For someone who lived such a simple existence, he sure looked like a happy guy. He was tall too and incredibly thin, with tanned leathery skin that grew more wrinkled in the more recent photos.

'Who are all the other people in the photos?' I asked.

'Mostly locals from the Point. People would take photos when they came to visit—one person gave him a framed one for a gift and then it kinda became tradition. Bill joked this was his wall of fame.'

I smiled at that.

There was also a kitchen of sorts with a camping stove similar to the one Jedda had used the night of the cyclone, loads of old pots and pans, a couple of gas lanterns and an ancient radio on a shelf. All of it was dirty—the rain had mixed with dust to create a layer of sludge on everything.

No wonder Dan looked so despondent.

He went across to one of the bookshelves and shook his head as he picked a soggy edition of a World Book Encyclopedia—I hadn't seen a set of those in decades. 'All ruined.'

Once again, I remembered my article. 'What do you and the Progress Association plan on doing now?'

Dan put the book back on the shelf with a squelchy thump. 'We'll salvage what we can and clean up the mess but I think this cyclone might have killed our plans to open the island to the public. There were enough hoops we were working through before, but now ...'

He let out a long sigh. 'We'll have to get structural engineers out to check the integrity of the castle. This hut shouldn't be too hard to rebuild—or maybe we'll just demolish it as the castle is what people will hopefully come to see. Either way, it'll cost us a lot of time and money when we're short of both.'

Dan's despondence broke my heart and I desperately wished there was something I could say, or, better still, do to help.

'Are most of the community behind your plans for the island?'

'Yeah. As I said, Bill was a local legend, but even putting that aside, most of us were in awe of his craftmanship. We'd like to preserve his legacy and show it off, use it to draw more tourists to the Point outside of the usual summer season.'

I loved the passion Dan had for the island and this community.

'What about getting some kind of benefactor or corporate sponsorship?' I said, recalling the discussion in the cafe yesterday about his family having the funds.

'There's only one company round here that might have that kind of money and ...'

When his voice trailed, I prompted. 'The Lobster Factory?'

He nodded. 'And unfortunately Dad isn't too keen to invest in something that might lure tourists away from *his* business. Which is bullshit—we won't have a cafe or anything here and people go to the Factory to learn about the local lobster industry or buy a sea experience. Here, the most anyone will be able to do is bring a picnic to enjoy the island while admiring the castle. If they're lucky, they'll see some sea lions, but with our tours, they're almost guaranteed.'

'Can't you explain this to your father?'

'Believe me, I've tried. But Stephen Emerson is a stubborn man, and this is something he won't budge on.'

So much for the community spirit I'd heard people mention when talking about the Emersons; it sounded like the head of the family only cared about *his* hip pocket.

'What about the shire?' I asked after a few moments' deliberation. 'Surely they're interested in bringing more tourists to the region?'

Dan chuckled. 'Maybe some of the council, but my father is the president and they all kowtow to him.'

'Oh.' My heart sank, but there had to be something that could be done. Now that I'd seen the castle myself, I too believed it deserved to be made a landmark. Then an idea struck. 'I know, why don't you organise a big busy bee and get more locals involved in the clean-up than just the IPA? That will take care of the mess, which will make it easier to assess how bad the actual damage is to the buildings. And, once you know what you're up for, you could organise a fundraiser.'

'You sound like you know what you're talking about.'

I laughed, thinking of all the school fetes, cake stalls, fun runs, golf days, quiz nights and even a ball I'd been involved in organising. Although I occasionally complained about always being roped in, I mostly enjoyed the experiences, which gave a thrill when successful. 'I've organised a few.'

'Don't suppose you'd want to help with this one?' He gave me a pleading smile. His mouth was lovely even when he wasn't smiling, but when he did ... My insides twisted and I chastised myself, quickly banishing that thought from my mind.

'Don't get me wrong,' he added, 'the members of the IPA are great but most of us are doers, not planners.'

I found myself tempted to say yes but couldn't commit to something I wouldn't be able to follow through on. Good fundraisers took months to organise and my trips to Ragged Point would soon come to an end. That thought made me sadder than I'd ever have imagined, but my family were my priority. Having us all back together would more than make up for missing my morning beach walks and my time spent with Jedda.

'I'm sorry, but I ... I think I might be getting back together with my husband soon, and then I won't be coming up here anymore.'

'Oh, I see.' Dan shoved his hands into his pockets. 'Never mind. I'm sure we'll work something out. Come on, I'll show you the rest and then we'd better be heading back.'

The rest included another hut, which he called the church—'Bill was quite a religious man and had a great faith'—and a little memorial site where the town had put up a white cross and a special sign for him that had miraculously survived the storm.

'We had a special celebration for him out here,' Dan said. 'Practically the whole town came over for it.'

'Where's Bill buried?' I asked.

'Nowhere.' Dan sighed and shoved his hands into his pockets. 'Because they can't identify him the police have never been able to find his next of kin, so he's still in a mortuary in Perth. If he just didn't have family, we could give him a burial in Ragged Point, but the law states a person must be identified before they can be buried.'

'It's so sad that no one's ever come forward. Surely someone knows something about him.'

'You'd think,' Dan said with a slightly bitter chuckle. 'Forensics did the usual taking of samples and running of tests when he first died, but his DNA didn't come up in any of the national databases.'

I took a few more photos of the damage and forced myself to ask questions related to the cyclone damage, as that's what my article was supposed to be about, and then we finally started heading back to the boat.

On our way, Dan stilled, then reached out and touched my shoulder. 'Look.' He nodded ahead, and I sucked in a breath at the sight of three sea lions frolicking in the shallows just off the shore.

'Oh my goodness, they're adorable,' I gushed, grinning as a little head poked up out of the clear green water and looked at us like we were exhibits in a zoo.

'Yep,' was all Dan said.

As we headed back to shore, he remained almost silent. I had more than enough information and photos for the article, but there was one more question I wanted to ask. Not for the paper but to satisfy my own curiosity.

'I agree the island and the castle are pretty special, but why do *you* care so much about saving all of it?'

Dan took his time replying, then when we were almost back to the shore, he said, 'Because I cared about Bill, and sometimes I feel like he was the only person who ever really cared about me.'

33

Perth

It had been a busy week in Ragged Point. Thankfully Payton's soccer team had a bye, which meant I'd been able to stay the whole weekend to finish my article and help Jedda put together the cyclone edition of the *Reporter*. Come Thursday, the town had been swimming with insurance assessors, among them one who Wei had taken out a policy with when he and Meili inherited the shack. Turned out he was smart as well as good-looking—no wonder Hayley was smitten.

The assessor declared the ceiling replacement straightforward and was happy for the team already booked in to go ahead. I'd left the key with Jedda, who promised to let them in, and now I was heading back to the city, ready for a rest.

I couldn't wait to see Payton and Saxon and to show them and Hayley my article. Maybe I'd even show Adrian when we went to our counselling session on Wednesday. It had turned out pretty well, even if I do say so myself; once I'd started typing, my fingers had flown over the keyboard and I couldn't get the words out fast enough. The thrill of writing something of my own—not for the clinic or school—for the first time since I'd been at university had been unlike anything I'd experienced in a long while and had given me the confidence to try and write something else.

I was still thinking about the blog Hayley had suggested and also the possibility of contacting small online publications to pitch some ideas when I arrived back at the house. Charlie bounded ahead of me to the front door and jumped up against it, making it difficult for me to unlock and open it. 'Calm down, boy,' I said as I pushed it open.

He raced ahead down the hallway and I followed him into the kitchen. I grabbed a pod for the machine, and then drank my coffee while I made a shopping list so I could get the groceries on the way to pick up Payton. When I'd finished, I opened the dishwasher to put my mug inside, only to discover it was still full. Struck by the warm smell of clean but not aired dishes, I started to unload it, trying not to feel too aggrieved at the fact Adrian hadn't done the job. Maybe they were in a rush that morning—at least he'd turned it on.

I was almost done when I noticed a stain on the rim of a wineglass. Frowning, I peered closer at the glass—was that *lipstick*? A cold dread washed over me, but I told myself maybe Payton had been experimenting with my makeup. Then again, if she'd been doing that *and* using a wineglass to boot, she'd have been much cleverer about covering it up. She ran rings around her father in that department.

My heart squeezed. Surely Adrian wouldn't have been so disrespectful to bring a woman home? And if he had, did he think I wouldn't notice the evidence? Even without the lipstick stain, the wineglass would have been a dead giveaway because Adrian hardly ever drank wine. He was a beer man through and through.

The magnanimous thoughts I'd been feeling towards him moments earlier evaporating, I raced outside. Sure enough, when

I checked the bottom of our council rubbish bin, I found all the confirmation I needed.

Tears sprang to my eyes at the sight of a half empty bottle of expensive wine unsuccessfully hidden under two garbage bags from the kitchen bin.

Trying to regulate my breathing, I retreated inside, sniffing the air like some kind of hound dog tracking prey as I searched for more clues. I ventured into our bedroom and froze.

Was that sweet and sickly lingering smell perfume? Or was I simply being paranoid now? I yanked a pillow from the bed and buried my nose in it. But Adrian had changed the bedding as per our agreement, so it smelled like freshly washed linen. As I dumped the pillow back on the bed, my gaze flickered to the open door of our ensuite, landing on something white, visible through the holes in our black, imitation wicker bathroom bin.

A tissue!

Actually, on closer inspection, two tissues—one with a bright-red lipstick print that matched the colour on the glass and the other streaked with mascara, as if someone had used it to blot the wand.

Oh Lord. Whoever she was had been in our bedroom. Did that mean Adrian's 'friend' had stayed the whole night? I doubled over, pain shooting to my stomach as if someone had punched me in the gut. How could he do this to us? To *me*?

I longed to interrogate the children when they came home from school. Had they seen or heard (shudder) anyone in the house after they'd gone to bed? Surely Adrian wouldn't have been stupid enough to bring home his date when they were awake. Then again, he hadn't been smart enough to cover his tracks.

I snatched up the makeup-stained tissues and flushed them down the toilet, wishing it was that simple to erase the knowledge there'd been another woman in my house.

In my bed. My husband between her legs.

One glance at our bed and I could visualise it all too well. How many times had they done the deed there? Had she been on top? Adrian loved it went I rode him cowgirl style, or at least he used to. Had she given him a blowjob? Or worse, had he put his mouth to her?

I shuddered. Was she the first he'd brought home or was she one of many?

Did she … *mean* anything to him?

Did I even want to know the answer?

While in theory I knew that our trial separation meant Adrian would fuck other women—hell, he'd blatantly told me that to my face—the reality hit me much harder than I'd imagined.

I started to cry—big, ugly sobs that had water pouring down my cheeks and snot gushing out of my nose, but I couldn't bring myself to take a tissue from the same box she had. Instead, I wiped my eyes with the sleeve of my jumper, picked up the box, hurled it out the window and screamed until I went numb.

What the hell was I supposed to do now?

34

Just before midday on Wednesday, I parked my car on the side of the road in Subiaco and rested my head on the steering wheel. Two days since I'd discovered the wineglass and the tissues, and I still didn't know what my next move should be.

Should I go in or was I fighting a losing battle? Did our marriage really have any chance of survival now, even with Megan's professional help? And did I still *want* to save it?

The last two days at home had been like being stuck in a bad movie—I longed to be in Ragged Point where I wasn't faced with memories from our marriage like I was at home. I hadn't been able to bring myself to sleep in our bed, so had been spending broken nights on the couch. I'd been living on autopilot since Monday afternoon. Talking to the kids, making their lunches, cooking their dinners, washing their clothes, walking Charlie and cleaning the house, but inside I was a zombie, completely numb.

Twisting my wedding ring on my finger, I climbed out of my car and took a deep breath as I beeped it shut and headed towards

Megan's office. I shivered as I stepped up onto the porch, unsure whether it was the wind or my nerves that were making me cold. Pulling my cardigan tightly around me, I wondered whether to ring the bell or wait for Adrian to arrive.

Hell, maybe he wouldn't even turn up. That would seal the deal. Like the toss of a coin, if he didn't show, my marriage was over, but if he did, I owed it to my children to at least follow through on this one session. I owed it to *myself* to get all the answers I could.

Barely after this thought had entered my head, I heard footsteps behind me and turned to see Adrian walking up the garden path.

I'd always been a peaceful person—avoiding conflict at all costs—but rage reared up inside me at the sight of him and I fought the urge to grab hold of his tie and tighten it until his face turned blue. All I could think about was that nameless woman's hands sliding all over his body. A body that according to our wedding vows was supposed to be for my pleasure only.

'Hey Ash,' he said, clearly oblivious to my rage as he stepped onto the front porch and leaned forward to kiss me on the cheek.

I jumped back out of his way, almost knocking over the massive pot plant that stood on one side of Megan's door. I couldn't bear to have his lips on me—who *knew* where they'd been.

'Ash?' He frowned as he reached out a hand to try and help me. 'What's wrong?'

Wrong? How could he act so damn normal?

I narrowed my eyes at him. 'I know what you did.'

When he still looked blank, I added, 'How dare you bring some woman into our home and fuck her in our bed during the week you're supposed to be in charge of our children! Couldn't you keep it in your pants a few more nights?'

Even then, when I'd been confronted with all the evidence at home, I still hoped he'd give me some kind of reasonable explanation. Ever since Monday I'd been stewing on this, trying to come up with rational reasons, but I hadn't been able to think of any, and now Adrian offered me no such excuses.

'She came after the kids went to bed and she was gone before they woke up.'

His words winded me.

'I don't care,' I yelled a second later. 'That's against the rules. We were clear when we set up the boundaries—no lovers at the house.'

He looked at me like *I* was being a hysterical little woman. 'Sax and Payton had no idea—there's no harm done.'

'No harm?!' My nails curled into my palm—yet if I was honest, it wasn't really the kids I was worried about. My heart ached at his blatant disregard for my feelings and I could honest to God have murdered him in that moment, but the door opened, and the arrival of the perpetually serene Megan saved his life. For now.

'Hello, Ashling,' she said, not exactly smiling as she glanced between us, clearly trying to read the situation. She offered her hand to my husband. 'You must be Adrian? I'm glad you decided to see me. Come inside.'

As she held the door open, Adrian—ever the gentleman—gestured for me to go in ahead of him. Megan led us into her therapy room, yet even though I'd been there before I felt no comfort in the familiar as I sat down in one of her plush leather armchairs.

She offered us drinks and Adrian requested a flat white with extra milk as if we were in a cafe, then crossed his legs and leaned back in his chair. Every little thing he did infuriated me.

'No thanks,' I said, not sure I could trust myself with a hot drink. It was liable to end up all over my husband's pale blue shirt. 'I'm good.'

I death-stared at Adrian while Megan retreated to make his coffee. *How could you?*

'Calm down, Ash. Take a chill pill.'

'Don't tell me to calm down,' I spat. 'And a *chill pill*? What are you? An adolescent? You've certainly been acting like a teenager lately, you self-centred arsehole.'

He blinked, clearly shocked by my outburst, but Megan appeared carrying a tray before he found the words to respond.

'I understand emotions are wrought,' she said, putting the tray down on the coffee table between us, 'but yelling at each other isn't going to get you anywhere. Let's all take a deep breath and try and have a rational conversation.'

Adrian picked up his mug and took a sip of his coffee. 'Good idea.'

'I want to talk about why Adrian broke our rules and slept with someone in our house,' I said, my arms folded so tightly they could cut off my circulation.

Adrian put down his mug again and sighed loudly. 'I don't know why you're getting so crazy. You knew I planned on sleeping with other women; it shouldn't come as a surprise that I did.'

'Everything about the last few months has been a surprise, but it's not so much the fact you slept with someone but that you didn't follow our nest-parenting agreement.'

Adrian opened his mouth, but Megan got in first. 'Are you sure that's the part you're most upset about, Ashling? I imagine that knowing Adrian has been with another woman is fairly upsetting, no matter where it happened.'

I felt like someone had poked a pin into me—everything inside me deflated as I nodded. She was right. I wanted to ask him why I wasn't enough, but I wasn't sure I could handle the answer.

'So,' Megan said, her voice still annoyingly calm, 'let's try to talk about the root of the problem. Sex is clearly a contentious issue between both of you right now, but as I mentioned to Ashling, there has to have been other issues for you to get to this point. I want you both to try and respect each other as we go back a bit and talk about the early days of your marriage.'

'Okay.' We spoke in unison, both sounding like petulant children.

'I want to get to know you both, find out who you are as individuals, but also the things that you like and dislike about each other. Adrian, how about you start? What first attracted you to Ashling?'

'Um …' He ran a hand through his hair and his forehead creased as if he was having to dig deep.

'Is it really that hard a question?' I asked, trying to hold on to my anger because right now it felt safer than the other emotions plaguing me.

'Ashling, please let him answer,' Megan reprimanded.

Adrian cleared his throat. 'Well, she was smarter than a lot of the girls at school, but still … you know, attractive. I guess she also felt familiar—she already spent a lot of time at my house because she was friends with my sister. I liked that she was straightforward and not high maintenance like some other girls.'

'Great.' Megan smiled encouragingly at him.

'She also had a wicked sense of humour.'

I couldn't help noticing his use of the past tense—hey, I could still be funny! However, although I desperately wanted to say something that would prove this point, my mind refused to cooperate. It was trying too hard not to let me cry.

'Ashling is a great mother—she's a very organised person and never puts herself first. She created a warm, comfortable home for us all and I really appreciated that.'

I felt myself losing the battle of the tears at his words.

'And what about you, Ashling?' Megan asked before I could hit him with a question of my own: *If I'm so wonderful, why are we even here?*

'Well ...' I swallowed. 'Much of the same, I guess. Adrian is very passionate about whatever he gives his heart to—at school that was sport and his studies and me. He made me feel like I was the only girl in the world, and I liked that we could talk about anything.' I suddenly realised I'd also slipped into past tense. 'He's a great dad and a wonderful podiatrist and boss. He really cares about his patients and his employees ... which is why I don't understand why he no longer cares about me.'

'I do care about you, Ash. You're the mother of my children, I'll always care.'

I snorted. 'You sure have a funny way of showing it!'

'If I didn't care about hurting you, I wouldn't have been so honest. I would have had an affair. I was trying to do the right thing and make this as easy as it could be on all of us.'

'Adrian,' Megan said sharply, 'let's take a look at your desire to sleep with other women. When did you start having these feelings?'

Part of me wanted to shove my fingers in my ears but the other part of me needed to hear the answer to this question. Just how long had I been living a lie?

'I don't know exactly ... I guess ... maybe since before we got married.'

'What?' I barely heard the word as it slipped from my mouth.

'Oh,' Megan said. His admission seemed to have taken her by surprise as well. She recovered quickly. 'If you had doubts back then, what made you go through with the wedding?'

Adrian refused to look at me as he spoke. 'Ashling and I got engaged because she got pregnant, then when she lost the baby ... well, she changed.'

'I didn't lose Leo,' I whispered, no longer trying to fight my tears. '*We* lost him.' And none of this made any sense because I'd always thought our shared heartbreak had brought us even closer together.

Adrian had taken such good care of me during that time. I didn't know if I'd have got through the loss without him.

'I know we did,' he said, blinking, as if he too was close to tears now. 'But we were so young, and then life suddenly got serious so fast.'

'You know, if you were having doubts, you didn't have to marry me.'

'I could hardly break things off after Leo, you were a mess—the wedding was the only thing keeping you going. I'd have looked like a bastard!'

'Okay, Adrian and Ashling, let's calm things again. Why don't we talk about that time—when you lost your baby. How many months pregnant were you?'

I ignored Megan's question—I didn't *want* to talk about my son—and tossed another one at Adrian. 'Did you *ever* love me? Or did you just feel sorry for me? Did you just feel obligated?'

'I'm not even sure I knew what love was back then,' Adrian said regretfully.

I recoiled as if he'd slapped me. His words wounded me beyond repair. I could no longer ignore what was happening to my marriage or cling to a dim hope that I could fix it. The day Adrian had asked me about nest parenting had just been a bad nightmare; *this* was the real betrayal.

I felt despair in every part of my body—from my leaking eyes to the feet that were encased in bloody ugly, podiatry-grade shoes. Suddenly feeling as if I knew Megan better than the man I'd lived with for over twenty years, I shot up from my seat, yanked off my shoes and threw them at my husband.

The first got him right in the mouth and the second one narrowly missed him as he ducked, but I didn't hang around to hear his reaction or to find out if Megan had any words of wisdom. Needing to escape, I grabbed my handbag and stormed out.

How could I have been so stupid to believe Adrian had any intention of working on our marriage? Was he just humouring me when he'd agreed to attend counselling? And why had *I* followed through after what he'd done?

This thought bore more rage—but this time at myself.

I couldn't believe I'd even entertained the idea of taking him back after his shenanigans of the past couple of months. I'd been so desperate not to put my children through any of the anguish or upheaval I'd suffered in my childhood that I'd been prepared to sacrifice my own self-respect and happiness.

But no more. Now that the truth was out, I was done.

35

As I climbed into my car, I tugged off my wedding ring and shoved it in the glovebox. Then, my breathing ragged, I drove as fast as I could to the most expensive shoe shop in town—a beautiful boutique in Claremont—and phoned Hayley.

She answered on the second ring. 'Hey babe, what's up?'

'You know that divorce lawyer you mentioned?'

'Yes.' She sounded wary.

'Is she really that good?'

'Yep. Absolute best. Better than the best.'

'Excellent.' I didn't plan on making this easy for Adrian. I'd wasted decades of my life with him and he was going to compensate me accordingly. 'Can you give me her number?'

'Does this mean what I think it does?'

'Damn straight it does.' I briefly told her what I'd come home to and the disaster that our session with Megan had been.

'I'm so sorry,' she said, 'but I'm proud of you. I'm not flying today; do you want me to come over? You probably shouldn't be alone right now.'

'I'm fine, really,' I lied. 'Text me the lawyer's number and I'll talk to you soon.'

I hung up before she had the chance to say anything else, but I was too shell-shocked, too angry, to feel bad. I wasn't in the mood to listen to Hayley wax lyrical about the wonderfulness of Wei. And she might be my best friend, but she was also Adrian's sister, and everyone knew that in the end, blood trumped water. I wished I could see Jedda instead, but as much as I wanted to, I couldn't drive back to Ragged Point right now. I had to pick up Payton in a couple of hours so shopping therapy it would have to be.

Fifteen minutes later I walked into a shop I'd only ever fantasised about visiting.

'Well, hello,' said Erica, the shop assistant, a woman I recognised as the mother of one of Saxon's band mates. 'Long time no see. How's things?'

'Oh, you know ...' *Just dandy. My husband has been fucking other women in our bed and I'm about to file for divorce.* Thankfully, I still had enough self-control not to say this out loud; the last thing I needed was Sax hearing about it from someone else. 'Just the usual.'

'And how's Saxon?'

I frowned, momentarily nonplussed. It was Erica and her husband's garage that the boys used every Sunday afternoon to rehearse. Saxon loved going there. Not only had they set up the garage specifically for the band, but apparently Erica always baked delicious goodies for the boys to eat while they were there.

'I've missed seeing the boys lately, but when Saxon quit, the others lost interest as well.'

It took every cell in my body to hide my shock, but I didn't want to admit that this was the first I'd heard about it.

I managed a shrug. 'Yes, well, he still loves his music, but his academic studies are his priority right now.'

Erica sighed. 'You're lucky. I wish Jacob had the same dedication. Anyway, how can I help you?'

'I need new shoes. As you can see.' I gestured down to my bare feet, knowing Erica had already noticed but was too polite to say anything. 'I want the prettiest, most expensive and most impractical shoes you have. And I want lots of them.'

Erica's eyes widened. 'Any specific occasion?' she asked, clearly trying to narrow down my options.

'All of them. Casual shoes. Dressy shoes. Boots. Heels. Sandals. Do you have slippers?' Adrian hated them almost as much as he hated thongs.

She turned up her nose a little. 'Slippers aren't really our clients' go-to footwear.'

'Okay,' I said as my gaze landed on a pair of sparkly silver thongs. 'How much are they?'

Erica named an outrageous price for what was essentially two bits of spray-painted rubber. 'But they're fifty per cent off because it's the end of the season.'

Even with the discount they were almost as much as I spent on groceries each week. 'I'll take them. And have you got any other colours?'

'What size are you?'

'Eight.'

She nodded. 'I think we've still got some in gold, pink and white.'

'Grab me a pair of each. And I'll try on those as well,' I said, pointing to a pair of knee-high black boots with heels so big I wasn't even sure I'd be able to walk in them.

'Are you okay?' Erica asked about fifteen minutes later when I had a tower of shoe boxes piled up on the counter and still hadn't finished.

I pointed my foot in front of me, admiring the shiny pink satin of fancy high heels I'd probably never have cause to wear. I didn't even like pink that much, but that was beside the point. It would kill Adrian when he read our joint credit card statement and saw how much money I'd spent at a shoe shop that didn't have the tick of approval from him.

And, right now, a dead husband appealed far greater than the one I had.

'I will be,' I told her, just as the door opened and another customer came in.

Only it wasn't another customer.

'What are you doing here? How did you know …?'

Hayley held up her mobile phone. 'You forget we have the Find My Friends app. What the hell are you doing?'

'What does it look like?' I snapped, gesturing to the tower of boxes.

She and Erica exchanged a look, then Hayley said, 'Do you mind if I have a private word with Ashling?'

Erica looked relieved to get away and made herself scarce at the other side of the boutique.

Hayley sat down beside me and wrapped her arm around my shoulder.

'Don't,' I whispered, tears threatening again.

'You're allowed to be upset,' she said, ignoring me as she drew me into a hug.

Within seconds I was bawling, too upset to even care that Erica was bearing witness to my meltdown.

'What am I going to do, Hayls? I know it's over, but how on earth am I going to survive on my own? What about the kids? This will probably mess them up and they'll end up blaming and hating me. And now I definitely need to get a proper job. But who will hire me? I don't even know how I'm going to pay for the lawyer.'

I didn't know how Hayley managed to understand my words through my sobs and hyperventilating, but she squeezed my hand, stroked back my hair, and looked me in the eyes.

'It's going to be okay, Ashling. I know it might not feel like it now, but it is. The kids will be okay. You'll be okay. And we'll manage the lawyer. Don't stress about money right now. Just focus on what you need to do to protect yourself and the kids going forward.'

'I feel like such a failure.'

'A twenty-year marriage and two beautiful kids is hardly a failure,' Hayley said firmly. 'Last I heard the average marriage in Australia was only about twelve years; in my book that makes you an over achiever.'

I sniffed, almost smiling at that.

She dug a tissue out of her handbag and handed it to me. Of course, it reminded me of the tissue I'd found in the bathroom and I squeezed my eyes shut, trying not to start crying all over again.

Would I never be able to use a tissue again without thinking of *Adrian's betrayal*?

Once Hayley gave her the okay, Erica brought me a glass of water and asked if there was anything she could do to help. I guess, despite trying to make herself scarce, she'd got the gist of our conversation.

'No thanks.' I forced a smile and took a sip. 'You've been helpful enough already.'

In the end, I only bought one pair of the outrageously expensive thongs, a pair of boots that I *could* walk in, some sneakers that were so pretty they couldn't really have been intended for exercise, and the pink heels, because Hayley liked them and we had the same shoe size. All up they came to almost fifteen-hundred dollars and I didn't feel one iota of guilt.

'Good luck,' Erica said as Hayley ushered me out of the store.

A teenage girl in a private school uniform walked past and my hand rushed to my mouth. 'Shit. I almost forgot about Payton. I need to pick her up but I'm a mess. I can't let her see me like this.'

'It's all right,' Hayley said, taking my arm and leading me over to my car. 'Go home. Go to bed and I'll pick Payton up. I'll tell the kids you have a migraine.'

'What about dinner?'

'I'll sort it,' she promised. 'Now go.'

'Thank you,' I whispered as I threw the bags in the back of my car.

Hours later I woke in my dark bedroom at the sound of the door opening.

'You awake?' came Hayley's voice as she closed the door behind her.

'Uh-huh. Just.' I switched on the bedside light and winced at the brightness. 'How are the kids?'

'They're fine,' Hayley said as she proffered a plate of Vegemite toast and a cup of tea. 'Thought you might be hungry.'

'A little. What did you guys have for dinner?'

She smiled. 'Wei brought over some pizza.'

'Sax and Payton are probably wishing I had a migraine every night.'

'No, they were both worried about you.' Hayley sat and swung her legs up beside me. 'I've just read Payton a story and put her to bed, and Saxon retreated to his room an hour ago. I've packed their school lunches for tomorrow and thrown a load of washing in the machine. I'll get it out and put it in the dryer before I leave. Is there anything else you need?'

'Wow. Look at you being all domestic. Next you'll be telling me you're moving in with Wei and starting a family.'

She gave me a look of horror. 'Let's not get ahead of ourselves. I'm quite happy as an aunty, thank you very much.'

'But you and Wei seem to be ...'

She held a finger to her lips. 'Shh ... don't say it. I'm freaking myself out enough as it is. Now, I'm going home, but call me if you need anything.'

'Thanks, I will.'

As Hayley kissed me goodbye, I couldn't help shaking my head at the irony. In all the years we'd been grown-up friends, I'd fantasised about her having a serious enough relationship that we could go out to dinner as couples and, now that it looked like she might actually have that, I was all alone.

36

Sunday morning, my heart lurched as Adrian approached me on the sidelines at soccer. We hadn't spoken at all since Wednesday afternoon when I'd stormed out of marriage counselling.

'Morning, Ash,' he said, nodding towards the coffee cup in her hand. 'Didn't think to get me one?'

'Nope. Sorry.' I wasn't sorry at all and didn't sound it either. I was proud of my sass. He'd given up any right to expect anything from me when he'd made the decision to break our vows.

'Never mind. By the way, I paid for the counselling after you left and booked another session, same time, same day when you're next in Perth.'

He'd done what? Was he for *real*?

I laughed so loudly that one of the other mums gave me a weird look and stepped even further away from us.

'What's so funny?'

My husband might be the doctor among us—or so he liked to say, but come on, *podiatrist*?—but I felt qualified enough to give him an official diagnosis. 'You. Are. Insane.'

'What?' Adrian sounded genuinely confused and his ears twitched as they always did when he was irritated.

I shook my head. 'You can't think I still want to try and make things right after what you did in our bed? What you said at therapy! Forget about marriage counselling. I suggest you get yourself a lawyer, because I've just hired one of the best.'

'You're filing for divorce?'

'In ten months, one week and two days I will be.'

The most disappointing part of my meeting with lawyer extraordinaire, Alexandria Honeymen, had been the discovery we had to have been separated for twelve months before either of us could file for an actual divorce. Twelve whole months. The agony!

Now that I'd made the decision, I didn't want to wait twelve days, never mind twelve months. I couldn't bear to be married to him a second longer. I'd already discarded my ring—well, put it away in a box in case Payton ever wanted it—and had begun the process of changing my name back to Murphy.

'But although we have to wait to make this official,' I added, 'we can get started sorting out everything else.'

'Everything else?'

'Yes.' I sighed loudly, watching our daughter run about on the pitch rather than look at him. 'We need to formalise our custody arrangements for the children. I think we should continue with our nest-parenting set-up as the kids are used to it. We don't want to unsettle them any more than necessary.'

'Right … I see.'

'So that means we'll have to keep the house somehow—we should probably see a financial planner together to work out how we're going to divide all our assets. Apparently, we don't need to wait for the divorce before finalising this stuff either. I was thinking maybe you keep the business, but I get the house and you pay rent during the weeks you're there with the kids.'

'*Me* pay *you* rent?'

'Either that or we keep the house in joint ownership until Payton is finished school and you buy me out of the business. I'm going to get a job, but it's unlikely I'll be earning as much as you, so there'll be child support to work out as well.'

'Are you sure about all this, Ashling? This is all moving pretty fast. I thought you wanted to try and work things out?'

And *I'd* thought he'd be relieved to receive this Get Out Of Marriage Counselling Free card, but he didn't sound it. Probably because I was the one making decisions when he'd always been used to calling the shots.

'Not anymore. And anyway, isn't this what you wanted all along?'

'Well, I think so, but ...'

'I'm sorry, Adrian, this isn't the place to discuss this and I don't really want to say much more to you without consulting my lawyer.'

His mouth gaped open, but I didn't wait around to see if he had anything to say.

My heart beat wildly as I turned away from the man who would soon be my ex-husband and walked over to join Tonia, Manish and some of the other parents. I might have sounded all bravado, but inside I felt anything but. I'd been a mess since Monday and if it wasn't for my kids, I'd probably still be lying in bed. If Hayley hadn't been flying today, I'd have begged her to take Payton to soccer for me.

'Are you okay?' Tonia whispered to me as I came up beside her.

I swallowed. 'I will be.'

In reality I felt completely overwhelmed by everything that lay ahead.

37

Ragged Point

Slipping off my fancy thongs and thinking I should probably buy a less extravagant pair now I'd made the decision to live half my life by the beach, I carried them as Charlie raced ahead of me to the water. He couldn't be happier to be here once more and while I loved being in the Point as well, my previous stays had felt a little surreal—almost like a hiatus from my real life—but this time was different. This time I was here without any hope of rebuilding my marriage and that thought brought with it a darkness that tainted the beauty of the ocean.

My solution? Keeping very busy to try and stop from sinking into the gloom. I didn't want heartbreak to take over my life. Whenever I started to feel too sad, I reminded myself that this pain was nothing compared to losing Leo and somehow I'd found the strength to survive that, so I would survive this too.

Two weeks after the cyclone the beach was clear again, except for the usual bits of washed-up seaweed, and the town had almost returned to normal as well. According to Jedda lots of people were still waiting for repairs to their properties, so I felt lucky that the ceiling replacement had gone ahead as planned last week while I was in Perth.

I didn't want any part of the shack unliveable when the kids came to stay next week. Saxon hadn't been enthused when I'd told them, but Payton was excited to be actually going away for some of the holidays. It had been a few years since we'd had a proper vacation as Adrian always resisted taking more than a few days away from the clinic. Ever since I'd told them about the trip, Payton had been asking me all sorts of questions about Ragged Point and had already packed her bag even though they were spending the first week of the holidays with Adrian.

Although Easter Sunday had landed on the last day of my week with the kids, Adrian had asked if he could take them to his mum's place for the usual egg hunt and extended family lunch. His short message had been like a blow to my head *and* my gut—a king hit and a sucker punch at once. Easter, Christmas, birthdays ... these would be changed forever. How would we decide who'd have the children when? Maybe Adrian would get Easter, but I'd get Christmas, and the following year we'd swap. Or would it be better if they spent the morning with one of us and the afternoon with the other?

Easter was bad enough, but I *loved* Christmas and the thought of not waking up with my kids, spending the whole day with them, didn't bear thinking about.

As I'd stared down at his message, I'd wanted nothing more than to reply with a simple 'No' or, better still, not reply at all. Petty or not, I'd wanted to punish him, to show him that he couldn't have his chocolate eggs and eat them too—but that would also be punishing my kids. Saxon pretended to be too old for the Easter Egg hunt, but he secretly loved it as much as his little sister. It was a tradition that began when he could barely walk and, as hard as it would be for me to spend Easter alone, I couldn't begrudge my babies this special activity—their lives were changing, and they were losing enough already.

Five minutes after I'd reluctantly agreed to Adrian's request, I'd received an awkward phone call from my mother-in-law, reminding me that I was still part of the family and more than welcome to 'tag along' to Easter lunch as well. I don't think she'd meant anything by her choice of words. Glennis and I got along well; she'd called me her 'other daughter' as Hayley and I were growing up, and she and Paul had joked at our wedding that Adrian had finally made that official. But her 'invitation' had felt like being asked to the wedding of an ex-boyfriend.

I'd rather pull my own toenails out than suffer through a family Easter with everyone knowing Adrian and I were over, all of them speculating about the ins and outs of our separation.

For this reason, I'd politely declined, suggesting I hand over the house and the kids to Adrian a day early, which also meant I could drive up to the Point earlier than usual. This wasn't something I planned on making a habit of, but now that I'd made arrangements with Wei and Meili to make my stay in the shack temporarily permanent, I couldn't wait to get there and start making the place feel like home—for when the kids came to stay, but also for myself. The only thing about the house in Perth that felt like home anymore was the kids and Charlie; everywhere I looked there were memories of a life that hadn't been what I'd imagined it to be. Being there made me feel like a fool and a failure.

'Ashling!'

Lost in my thoughts of the past, present and what the future might hold, I jumped out of my skin at the sound of my name, then glanced up to see Dan on the balcony of his big glass monstrosity.

'Stay there,' he shouted and then disappeared inside.

Less than thirty seconds later, he reappeared round the side of the house and headed towards me. He wore black shorts, a blue Lobster Factory polo shirt, no shoes, and his damp hair suggested he'd either been for an early morning swim or just come from the shower. The shadow of dark stubble on his jawline only added to his casual attractiveness.

Not used to thinking about strange men naked in showers, guilt swamped me. *But hang on!* I was a free woman. I could think illicit thoughts about whoever I wanted. Whenever I wanted. Hell, I could even sleep with them if the opportunity arose. My insides tingled as I contemplated what it might be like to sleep with Daniel Emerson, but I almost instantly berated myself. Sex, especially of the rebound variety, should be the last thing on my mind right now.

I wouldn't even know how to go about it!

Quite aside from being ill-prepared mentally to fall into bed with another man, such an occasion would require intense physical preparation. Like leg waxing, fancy underwear purchasing—my current bras and knickers were suitable for married eyes only—toenail painting, exfoliating, and, most vital of all, bikini waxing. I'd been hugely lax in that department. No one aside from Adrian and the doctor who performed my bi-annual pap smear had been anywhere near my nether regions in the last few years, never mind anyone with hot wax.

Eek. I'd probably have to go the full shebang and get a Brazilian—wasn't that what men expected these days?

I shuddered. How could I even think about getting naked in front of Dan (or anyone) with my podgy mummy-tummy and droopy, baby-feeding breasts? Maybe it was time I started actually remembering to do my pelvic floor exercises.

Or ... maybe I should stop thinking about the possibility of ever sleeping with anyone else again and focus on more important things—like keeping my kids as happy as possible and working out how I was going to provide for us all going forward. I'd been a *little* all over the place (okay, I'd been losing the plot) ever since I'd made my decision to file for divorce. The shoe-buying frenzy had been the first in a long line of weird and wacky behaviours.

Now I could add pondering preparing myself for sex to the list.

'Hey gorgeous.'

My heart jumped as Dan dropped to the sand and rubbed Charlie's neck. Of course, he was talking about the dog. While he cooed over Charlie, I tried to collect myself, sucking a steadying breath in and out of my lungs.

Finally, Dan turned his attentions on me, or rather my bare feet. I dug my toes into the sand, wishing I'd bothered to give myself a pedicure, and squirmed a little as his gaze travelled up and landed on the thongs still in my hand.

'I thought thongs were bad for your feet?'

I dropped *my* gaze to the sand, staring at our feet, which were less than a foot apart. I could simply say I'd changed my mind, but from the expression on his face and the tone of his question, I knew he recalled our first conversation about my husband being a podiatrist. I didn't think the significance was lost on him.

'That was my soon-to-be ex-husband's opinion, however I'm becoming quite a fan.' I sounded more flippant than I felt.

'*Soon* to be ex-husband?' Dan's eyes widened as his eyes sought my ring finger. There was still a pale band across it where my wedding ring had been until only a few days ago. 'I thought you said you were probably getting back together?'

'Isn't it a woman's prerogative to change her mind?' I said lightly, not wanting to get into the nitty-gritty details of my sudden volte-face.

'So I've heard.' Dan gestured to my thongs. 'I didn't know they made thongs as stunning as those.'

Even though the compliment was for my footwear, I blushed. 'Me either, but I bought them as a reward for making the scary decision to leave my husband for good.'

'Welcome to the club.'

'What club?'

He quirked an eyebrow and pushed his hair up off his forehead. 'The divorce club.'

Divorce. I flinched. I'd always feared that word more than any other. It sounded so final and, even though that's exactly where Adrian and I were headed, I still struggled to say the word out loud.

'No offence, but it's not a club I ever wanted to join,' I said with a sigh.

'No one does.' He offered a sympathetic smile. 'And, while I won't pretend it's anything like Scouts or Brownies—it's totally shit in fact—there is light at the end of the tunnel.'

'Is there?'

His existence didn't seem very bright, living in a big house all by himself.

'Yes. It's better to be alone than in an unhappy marriage.'

'What if I didn't think my marriage *was* unhappy?' I asked, wriggling my toes in the sand.

'As I said, it's tough, give yourself time to grieve, but then try and look upon this as an opportunity rather than a conclusion. Treat it as the end of an act, rather than the finale.'

'Now I'm not sure whether you're sounding like a marriage therapist or a musical theatre director,' I derided.

He chuckled and shoved his hands in his pockets. 'Sorry. And feel free to tell me to bugger off, but if you ever need someone to talk to, I'm a good listener. I work weird and wonderful hours, but you know where I live. Just give me a shout if you ever need an ear.'

'Thank you,' I said, although I had no intention of accepting his offer. I had Hayley, and now Jedda, if I needed to vent or cry or solicit advice, and at least being around them didn't give me a funny feeling in my stomach.

'No worries. By the way, I wanted to thank you for your article about the island. It was fantastic. I mean obviously the subject wasn't great, but you provided the facts with a lot of heart and the writing was awesome.'

My heart swelled. 'Oh, that's great. I was so nervous, but I also really enjoyed it and it looks like there might be more of my articles to come.'

'Really?'

I nodded, certainly hoping so—writing had given me a new purpose and felt like a lifeline all of a sudden.

'I'm going to be here every second week at least until I finish renovating the shack, so I've offered to help Jedda with writing, editing and producing the paper.'

'That's great. You and Jedda will make a great team, I'm sure. She's lucky to have you.'

'I actually think it's the other way around,' I said with a smile.

Truthfully, I didn't know where I'd be right now if I didn't have the shack, Jedda and the Point to distract me from the breakdown of my marriage and the fact I now went days at a time without seeing my kids. And, not only had she been an emotional support, but she'd also offered to throw me a few shifts at Brewed Awakening during the weeks I was in town, starting tomorrow. It wasn't going to make my fortune, and neither was working on a community newspaper, but both would bring some variety to my resume.

'Maybe you're both lucky to have each other,' Dan said. 'Now, as much as I'd rather hang here and talk to you all day, duty calls. But don't forget my offer; I'm only a few houses away if you need anything.'

As he turned to go, I realised I hadn't asked him how things were on the island. 'By the way,' I called. 'How's the island clean-up going?'

He stopped and looked back. 'I've done a bit when I can get away from work, but everyone's been pretty busy with their own properties and insurance claims. However, I loved your idea for an official busy bee, so that's scheduled for this Saturday. I've spread the word around town so we should manage to clear enough to see what structural damage we're going to have to deal with before moving forward.'

'That's great. How will everyone get to the island?'

'Lots of people have their own boats and others will catch a lift with people that do. Why?'

'I was wondering if there was any way I could get over there?'

'You want to write another article about the clean-up mission?'

I rubbed my lips together. 'Well, maybe—I'd have to run that idea by Jedda ... but I was actually thinking of coming along to help. That's if I wouldn't be in the way,' I added quickly.

'Not at all. You'd be most welcome. More hands make less work and all that. You can come out with me. Bring Charlie if you want, rather than leave him locked up in the shack all day.'

Charlie's impressive ears must have heard his name, for he ran back from where he'd been chasing seagulls in the water, shaking himself vigorously as he landed beside us.

'Yuck,' I squealed as salty dog water splattered all over us.

Dan jumped back and we both laughed.

'I think Charlie would love that,' I said. 'What time should we meet you on Saturday morning?'

'Is eight am too early?'

I shook my head. 'We'll be ready and waiting. See you then.'

Dan nodded. 'I'm looking forward to it.' Then he swaggered off towards his mansion.

38

'Having fun yet?' Dan asked, as he lowered himself down next to where I sat on the beach with Charlie, eating a piece of delicious hedgehog slice from Jedda's cafe. Unable to help with the busy bee due to her fear of water, she'd generously supplied morning and afternoon tea for the troops, which Gail and her husband had transported in their boat.

'If by "fun" you mean muscles I didn't even know I had aching, and calluses forming on my hands, then I'm having the time of my life.'

He chuckled. 'You have been working pretty hard. Thanks for helping out.'

'The pleasure is all mine. It's been a great opportunity to get to know everyone better.'

Sitting in small groups around us now were all the other volunteers, and there were plenty of them. This might have been the brainchild of Dan and me, but it felt like the whole town had got on board in some capacity. I'd discovered that many locals, like Dan, had also had a personal connection to Bill and were there as much for him as for the potential attention his castle could bring to Ragged Point.

Almost everyone had a story to tell, either because they'd worked with Bill on the boats, because they'd helped him find supplies for the castle or because they'd been frequent visitors to the island when he was alive. For some it was all three. I learned he had a great sense of humour, was a wonderful cook and grew much of his produce right here on the island, and that he loved animals. Apparently, Lion wasn't his only pet; he'd also had some chickens and a goat who'd provided him with milk until not long before he died, when the goat passed away.

Not everyone appeared to be as fond of the cat as Dan was, however. One guy kept making underhanded comments about the wildlife—every time a lizard scuttled past or a bird landed nearby, he'd say something about being glad the feral feline had been banished.

Although I was one of the few who hadn't known Bill when he was alive, not once had I been made to feel like an outsider.

'Are you pleased with how it's all going?' I asked Dan now.

'Couldn't be happier. We're clearing things a lot faster than I thought we could.'

'What's the next stage of your project, then?'

'I've been talking to a construction company that are going to assess the damage and see how much we need to spend on strengthening the walls before we allow the public out here. But whether we can do that, or indeed when, will depend on how much it costs and if we can cobble together the funding.'

'You know,' I said, not realising what I was going to say until I heard the words come out my mouth, 'now that I'm going to be here every second week, maybe I could help with some kind of fundraiser?'

'Really?' Dan grinned. 'That would be great. I'm not bad at manual labour and fixing things up, but organisation and planning are not my strong points.'

'I don't know …' I gestured around us. 'You seem to have done a great job getting everyone organised today.'

Upon arrival at the island, Dan had broken the volunteers into groups—there were clearing and repairing teams in each hut, another couple of people on the toilet building, a few groups clearing the big debris across the island, and a number of us in the castle, removing all the rubbish and salvaging what we could of Bill's displays and collectibles.

We talked for another few minutes about the future of Bill's island before Dan announced it was time to get back to work.

'Slave driver,' I teased as I pushed myself to my feet.

'You better believe it,' he said and then went off to get everyone else moving again.

The first half of the day our main focus had been clearing the debris from the castle, being careful not to lift anything that might sacrifice the stability of the rocky walls, and we'd made significant progress, which meant we were now beginning to uncover some of Bill's collectibles. With the aim to salvage anything we could, I felt like some kind of archaeologist. By midafternoon we'd amassed quite a pile.

Charlie was having fun playing excavator, but most of what he'd found so far had been bones of what looked to be small animals. When I heard his paw scrape against something in the detritus at my feet, I glanced down, expecting him to have uncovered another one, yet when he almost immediately lost interest, I stooped to investigate myself. My fingers brushed against something cool and hard beneath a pile of palm leaves. Pushing them aside revealed an old, rectangular-shaped, slightly rusty tin.

It must have been buried longer than the storm, because it took some effort for me to loosen it. I brushed off some dirt to expose the crackly image of the famous Arnott's parrot pecking at a Nice biscuit and smiled with nostalgia. The box was so light I expected it to be empty, but tried opening it anyway. After a few attempts, the stiff lid finally budged, and I discovered dozens and dozens of handwritten letters on terribly thin, lined paper.

Without thinking, I lifted the top one and, resting the tin back down on the ground, unfolded it. It took only a few seconds to realise they were love letters.

'What have you got there?'

I startled at the sound of Dan's voice. 'You shouldn't creep up on people like that.'

He grinned. 'Sorry.' He peered over my shoulder at the page, his warm breath dusting my neck. I shivered involuntarily and silence followed as we both read.

My darling, Bill—last night I snuck out of the house and sat on the sand for over three hours looking out to sea, wondering what you were doing and wishing I was with you. My whole body hurts when we're apart and I would give anything for us to be together, but I just don't see any way for it to work.

'Geez,' Dan said.

'You didn't know Bill had a lady friend?'

He shook his head. 'He never mentioned anyone to me. Where'd you find this?'

My gaze dropped to the ground and I nudged the tin with my foot. 'There's a whole bunch of them in there.'

Dan bent to pick it up. '*This* tin?'

'Oi! You two,' shouted one of the other volunteers good-naturedly before I could reply. 'Stop slacking off on the job.'

'Shut up and mind your own business, Chuck,' Dan replied in the same amiable tone. He looked to me and held out his hand for the letter. 'Here, let's put that back in here for safe-keeping. They're obviously private. Perhaps we shouldn't even be reading them?'

I nodded as I gave him the letter and watched him shove it back in the box and replace the lid. It felt thrilling to have discovered a bunch of love letters. Adrian might have let me down, but I still wanted to believe in romance, and part of me wanted to argue the point about us not reading them. Obviously, they were from long ago, what harm would there be? But we were here to work, and Chuck would call me out for slacking off again if I took a break to read.

Over the next couple of hours, we made excellent progress and I forgot about the letters, once again getting caught up in the job and the community spirit. By late afternoon, the volunteers began to drop like flies, downing tools and climbing into boats to retreat back to the Point. My muscles ached so badly they were starting to seize, but I felt proud to have been a part of something so special.

Even Charlie was exhausted and slumped down on the floor of the boat when Dan finally called it a day.

'What are you doing for dinner?' he asked as he directed the boat towards the mainland.

Dinner? The only thing on my mind at that moment was a long soak in a warm bath and then bed. 'I'll probably make myself beans on toast.'

He screwed up his nose. 'Beans on toast isn't enough after all the hard work you've done today. Why don't you come over to my place and I'll cook for us both?'

My stomach tensed and the boat suddenly felt tiny. Was Dan asking me on a date?

'How can *you* feel like cooking after all the hard work *you've* done today?' I asked, delaying a decision.

He shrugged. 'Cooking helps me unwind, and I also like to eat but rarely get the pleasure of cooking for other people. So, what do you say? Care to join me for a meal?'

'Um ...' I liked him ... as a friend ... but wasn't sure about spending an evening alone with him. I didn't want to give him the wrong impression. Being near him in a group was one thing, but when we were alone, my body started to get ideas. Ideas I wasn't sure I could trust. Maybe I was feeling attracted to him simply because he was the first guy that I'd had anything to do with post-Adrian.

My fingers drifted to Charlie's warm fur for comfort.

'I have no ulterior motives, if that's what you're worried about,' Dan said, and I wondered if he could read my mind or was simply responding to my hesitation. 'I'm not trying to get into your pants—although I'm sure the experience would be pleasurable ...' He said it in a way that made my insides tumble. 'I know you've been through a rough trot lately and I'd never take advantage of that. I just thought it would be nice to debrief with someone after today, maybe even start discussing the fundraiser. But if you'd rather eat your *beans* alone, that's your prerogative.'

The way he said beans made me smile, and someone else cooking for me sounded much better than whatever I'd make myself.

'Okay,' I said, finding the courage deep within. 'I'll come. When you put it like that ... how can I resist?'

39

As Payton told me about her day—she and Adrian and an apparently reluctant Saxon had been to the Maritime Museum—I glanced out the window at the sun sinking over the ocean.

'I'm so glad you had fun, sweetheart ... but I'm going to have to go.'

'Go? Where?'

I could just visualise the confusion on her face—my kids were not used to me having a life outside of them. *I* was not used to having a life outside of them.

'Um ...' I couldn't bring myself to admit I'd be spending the evening alone with a man. 'I'm just going to a friend's for dinner.'

'Oh, okay.' Thankfully, Payton didn't question which friend. Although I wouldn't mind Adrian knowing about my evening plans, I didn't want to confuse or upset her any more than she'd already been by our separation. 'I miss you, Mum.'

My heart felt as if someone was wrapping their hands around it and squeezing tightly. Maybe I should cancel on Dan and spend longer on the phone with her. Shouldn't my daughter be my priority right now? Part of me relished the excuse—I'd been nauseous ever since I'd agreed to going over there—but how would I let Dan know? I didn't even have his phone number. It would be rude to simply not turn up.

Making a concerted effort to ignore both the cyclone in my stomach and my mother-guilt, I said, 'I know, sweetheart, I miss you too. But only two more sleeps until I see you. What are you guys up to this evening?'

'Dad and I might watch a movie.'

As long as Adrian didn't break our rules and have some woman over to watch the movie as well ... 'That sounds great,' I said, not wanting to hurry a goodbye but at the same time needing to get going before I really did chicken out. 'You have fun. I'll talk to you in the morning, okay?'

'Okay, Mum. Love you.'

'Love you, too.'

I took Charlie out for a quick pee, then gave him his dinner. After a big day in the fresh sea air, digging and running around on the island, he was knackered and would likely sleep until my return, which shouldn't be long anyway. Once Dan and I had exhausted the fundraising topic, we'd likely be scraping the barrel looking for other things to talk about.

While Charlie munched loudly on his favourite dog biscuits, I went to grab the bottle of sav blanc I had chilling in the fridge, but hesitated.

Maybe I shouldn't take it?

Although Dan had said I didn't need to bring anything, I couldn't turn up empty-handed. But two people sharing wine would definitely feel like a date.

Oh Lord. I glanced around the kitchen looking for something—*anything*—else to take. Once again, I silently cursed Adrian for putting me in this predicament. The day I said 'I do' I'd assumed I'd never have to contemplate dinner with a man that wasn't my husband. Yet, here I was.

Finally, deciding to heed Dan's words and take nothing, I slammed the fridge shut and slipped on my jacket.

Grow up! said my inner critic with a roll of her eyes as I headed for the door. *What are you? Twelve?*

And she was right. If I was going to Jedda's I wouldn't be thinking twice about taking wine. Resolving to stop overthinking everything, I went back and grabbed the bottle. As it was getting dark, I walked along the road rather than the beach, waving to Mrs Fine who was sitting out on her porch. She frowned at the bottle in my hand, but I hurried on, not wanting to risk a lecture.

Less than two minutes later, I stood at Dan's glass front door, about to ring the bell when panic set in. Going out to the island to research my article and help with the clean-up had been one thing, but *this* felt on a different level. If anyone had told me three months ago that I'd be going to a strange man's house for dinner, I'd have laughed in their face. My life was changing too fast and I wasn't ready to step out of my comfort zone.

'Sorry,' I silently apologised to the sassy voice in my head, 'but I can't do this.'

As I turned to flee, a shadow appeared, the door peeled back and there was Dan, standing in front of me in faded jeans that hugged his hips and a pale blue shirt, the top few buttons undone and sleeves pushed up to his elbows. Soft jazz music drifted from somewhere inside.

'You came!' He appeared almost as surprised as me.

'I said I would.'

'I know. I'm sorry, I just lost track of time. I was ...' He glanced back into the house, then shook his head and reached out to grab my free hand, drawing me inside. 'Never mind. Come in, come in.'

40

As the door closed behind us with a loud thump, I followed Dan through the entrance hallway into the depths of the house and looked around in awe. The glass mansion was just as massive as it looked from the outside, but it was warmer and cosier than I'd imagined. I'd pictured a cavernous space with a minimalist look, bare walls and surfaces, except maybe for a few bits of abstract art and a couple of pieces of feature furniture. The reality was far from that. It wasn't messy, and nowhere near as cluttered as Xiang's shack had been, but it was clear the owner had many varied interests and cared more about them than he did about maintaining a show house.

Large bright colourful paintings hung on the walls—mostly landscapes, a lot including water—and some framed puzzles were also in the mix. There were very healthy-looking houseplants scattered throughout (which I admired because indoor plants were one thing I'd never managed to keep alive), mismatched but quirky floor lamps spilling soft light from the corners, and in the living room a fire crackled away happily, adding to the relaxed ambience.

'It's the first time I've had a fire this year, but it felt like the night for it,' Dan said, noticing the direction of my gaze.

'I've been looking forward to it getting colder so I can try the one in the shack,' I replied. 'There's something special about a warm fire on a cold winter night.'

'I couldn't agree more.'

Two well-loved leather couches were angled to form an L-shape in front of the fireplace, and aside from the space where a large TV screen hung, the walls were lined with bookshelves. All of them jam-packed.

I marvelled at Dan's collection, which appeared to include everything from classics to sci-fi and fantasy. I even noticed a copy of my favourite book—*The Thorn Birds*.

'This is some library you have here.'

'Do you read much?' he asked.

'I haven't in the last few years, but it's something I used to love. I joined the library a few weeks back because I thought I might have some more time up here, although I reckon you might have more books than they do,' I said, referring to the tiny town library attached to the primary school.

He laughed. 'My ex-wife called it my addiction, but I always told her there were worse ones.' There was a moment of silence and I almost asked him about his wife, but the moment passed before I got the guts up. 'Anyway, you're welcome to borrow them any time you like,' he said.

'Thank you.' It was the first time Dan had referred directly to his past relationship and I desperately wanted to know more, but it seemed like a conversation we should work up to. Instead, I pointed towards the coffee table that held a half-completed jigsaw puzzle, a pair of black-rimmed glasses beside it. 'And you like puzzles as well?'

He gave me a sheepish grin. 'See, now you *know* I'm not trying to impress you. If this was a date, I'd definitely have done my best to hide my nerdy tendencies, but as it's not, I may as well tell you that I also have a whole room full of Meccano models and I only finished the last one a few weeks ago.'

I laughed—it was impossible not to relax at his words. 'My son loves Meccano and I don't mind the odd puzzle myself.'

'Well, feel free to have a go at it while I make dinner,' Dan said. 'This one is proving to be a real doozy. Or if you'd rather you can come sit at the breakfast bar while I cook?'

Both choices were appealing in different ways. 'What are you making?'

'A creamy lobster linguine. It's my specialty and it'll go perfectly with your wine,' he said, nodding towards the wine bottle I'd almost forgotten in my hand.

Lobster? It was all I could do not to screw up my nose. Why hadn't I considered that a man who lived, breathed and worked the ocean would favour seafood as well? Too late to tell him I didn't. I'd just have to swallow it down with wine and hope he followed it up with something more appetising for dessert.

Dammit, that's what I should have brought. Dessert would have been safe!

'Sounds delicious,' I said.

Dan took the wine and I followed him to the kitchen. Although tempting, hiding behind a puzzle would be cowardly and we were going to have to talk eventually. He reached up to a cupboard to grab two glasses, his shirt inching up to reveal a strip of tanned, taut skin. Maybe now I lived by the beach, I'd manage to boast a similar tan next summer. Along with the fab body I planned to acquire to make Adrian live in eternal regret for letting me go.

Dan handed me a glass of sav blanc and clinked his against mine. 'Cheers.'

'Here's to our successful clean-up day,' I said, before taking a much-needed sip.

He drank, then put his glass down beside the stovetop. 'That's a good drop.'

'I bought it from the pub—Jedda got me onto the brand,' I said as he filled a saucepan with water.

'You've become good friends with Jedda, haven't you?'

'Yes. She's great.'

'I admire her—she does a lot for this town. Her Jack was a good bloke, even if a bit of a daredevil.'

'You knew him?'

'Yeah, he worked for us and we were good mates growing up. Dad doesn't like to talk about it as he's the only employee we've ever lost on the boats. We weren't found at fault, but Dad felt terrible about losing a guy on his watch. He gave Jedda a good payout and there was insurance on top of that. Still doesn't feel enough, but Jack would be happy to know she's doing okay.'

'To be honest, I think she struggles a little with everything on her plate but keeping busy also keeps her going.' Thinking I'd probably already betrayed her confidence, I changed the subject. 'Is there anything I can do to help with dinner?'

'Nah, you relax. I've got all this under control. You're my guest tonight.'

I wasn't used to watching other people cook, but relaxing was exactly how I found it. Dan sliced through onions like an expert and then tossed them into a frying pan with a few spices, the oil sizzling as he did. He was clearly a competent chef—it wasn't long before delicious aromas of butter, garlic and chilli filled the room—and we chatted easily about my time so far in the Point.

'How's the renovation of the shack going after the cyclone?'

'Not too bad. The ceiling has been replaced and already it makes the place look ten times better. I've got big plans, but there's no real rush,' I said. Now that I wasn't going to be reuniting with Adrian, my only concern was making sure I got the work done in a fair time for Wei and his sister. 'The owners want it ready for the summer if possible. I've almost finished painting the bedrooms, the living room will be next, and I have tradies booked in after the school holidays to start on the kitchen and bathroom renovations. While they're doing their thing, my next step will be stripping back the carpets and starting to revamp the original floorboards.'

'You're gunna do all that yourself?'

I nodded. 'I'm actually a bit of a renovation junkie—self-taught over the years. When I was pregnant with Saxon, I stripped back all the old paint in his nursery and played with different paint effects.' I didn't mention this was because I'd been so paranoid and anxious after losing my first baby that I'd needed to do something to distract myself—that felt far too personal to share with a man I barely knew. 'I made shelves and took up the carpet and polished the old floorboards. I enjoyed it so much that gradually I did the same with the rest of the house.'

'Wow—that's impressive.'

'Not really,' I said, a blush creeping up my neck. 'You'll be amazed what you can learn from magazines, and more recently DIY home reno videos on YouTube. It's not only soccer skills, lip-synching videos and famous teen vloggers offering life wisdom on YouTube, you know. Initially I thought we were going to have to replace the window frames in the bedrooms, but I managed to bring them back to life myself.'

Dan smiled. 'I stand by what I said—impressive. But how are you managing to fit everything in while also working at Brewed and on the newspaper?'

'I'm just doing what I can when I can. Most of my writing and newspaper work I do at night, the cafe shifts were always during the day, and this week I've been getting up early and fitting in a few hours' painting before doing anything else. It's therapeutic. I'd actually been thinking it was time to redecorate my house again, but now ... well, I'm not sure exactly what we'll do with that in the long run, so this is the perfect outlet. Wei and Meili have basically given me free rein and it's fun to be able to make decisions about paint colours and tiles, et cetera, without having to consult anyone else.'

'There are indeed perks to being single,' Dan said.

He tossed lobster meat into the skillet, then followed soon after with the cooked linguine. I tried not to gag at the sight of the lobster; eating it would be just another new adventure in my new life, alongside leaving my marriage, dipping my toes back into employment and making friends outside my kids and my husband. I mean *ex*-husband—it was going to take a while to get the hang of calling Adrian that. Was it even the correct term until we'd officially divorced?

Pushing Adrian out of my head, I focused on watching Dan instead, which I had to admit was much more enjoyable. When the sauce had thickened and the pasta was coated, he spooned it into two bowls and then topped up our wineglasses. We took our dinner and drinks into the living room and sat down at opposite ends of the couch. I wasn't sure if this felt more or less intimate than if we'd sat at the dining table.

'Wow. This is ...' I was lost for words after tentatively tasting my first mouthful.

Dan looked at me expectantly as he wrapped linguine skilfully round his fork.

I bit my lip on a smile. 'Is this where I confess I hate seafood?'

'What?!' The fork froze midway to his mouth and his eyes widened. 'Why didn't you say something?'

'I didn't want to offend you.'

'You shouldn't do things simply to make other people happy.'

His words rattled because that's exactly what I'd been doing most of my life, certainly the years since I'd been a wife and a mother. But wasn't that what having kids was all about?

'I'm sorry.' He reached for my plate. 'I'll whip up something else.'

'No,' I all but shrieked as I swatted his hand away. 'Don't you dare. I'm glad I didn't say anything because while I agree we shouldn't do things only to please others, we also sometimes need to be open to new experiences. If it wasn't for you, I'd never have tried seafood again and discovered that maybe I like it. Or at least I like this.'

'Really?' Dan quirked an eyebrow. 'You're not just saying that?'

I shook my head. 'I promise.'

He relaxed back into the couch and smiled. 'Well, I'm glad to hear it. You've obviously never had it cooked properly before, but I do know how to make a good linguine, even if I do say so myself.'

I laughed.

'And,' he continued, 'if you like this, then I promise there are all sorts of other seafood dishes you'd enjoy as well. Next time I'll make you my famous fish pie.'

This time I did screw up my nose. 'Let's not get carried away—I'm not sure fish and pie should *ever* be combined. And won't it be *my* turn to cook for you?'

Part of me couldn't believe we were even talking about *next time*.

He winked. 'If you insist, I won't object.'

I shouldn't have been worried about the evening being weird or not having anything to chat about because there wasn't one moment of awkwardness. The conversation flowed as we talked about everything under the sun. Normal things like favourite music and movies—Dan favoured jazz whereas I was a bit of an eighties tragic, and he preferred horror movies and I didn't think anything could beat a good romantic comedy—and much more personal things, such as our relationships and failed marriages.

'Why'd you guys break up?' Dan asked, after we'd shared stories of how we'd met our spouses. Dan's wife Tessa was the younger sister of one of his mates from boarding school.

I took a sip of wine and sighed. 'Adrian told me he didn't find me attractive anymore, that he wanted to play the field.'

'He sounds like a dick,' Dan said. 'And a stupid one at that. The man must be blind.'

A warmth flushed through me and I couldn't help smiling. 'Thank you. That's kind of you to say, but it doesn't stop me feeling like a failure. And I feel stupid too, because everything I thought about our marriage was clearly a lie. You think you know someone ... It was a big shock to discover I was living with a stranger.'

'Tell me about it.' Dan topped up my wine.

Maybe it was the alcohol making us both loose-lipped or maybe it was simply talking to someone who had been through a separation, but in that moment, I felt as if I could tell him anything.

Maybe Dan could be my divorce guru!

'What about you?' I asked finally. 'Why did your marriage end?'

He confessed that Tessa had left him after five failed IVF attempts.

'We wanted a big family—it's why we built this place—and she decided if my sperm couldn't fertilise her eggs, then rather than consider a donor, she'd find someone whose could. She already has two kids with her new husband. The perfect pigeon pair,' he joked, but I could hear the raw pain in his voice as he spoke about how fraught things had grown between them in their last year of marriage. 'When Tessa and I found out I couldn't have kids, she totally changed. She quickly grew to resent me, and at a time when we should have been supporting each other, we started to argue over tiny things. Although if our relationship wasn't strong enough to survive infertility, then maybe it was for the best.'

'That's true,' I agreed, wondering what would have become of me and Adrian if we hadn't been able to have children. It was all very well judging Tessa's actions as callous, but would I have stayed with Adrian if he'd been unable to give me the family I'd always wanted?

Dan took our empty plates into the kitchen and then refilled our glasses. 'Sorry, I'm jabbering on about my ex. More proof I'm not trying to crack onto you, because from what I hear, the first rule of first dates is never mention the ex.'

I smiled. 'Don't apologise, I asked you. But speaking of dates, have you been on many since your divorce?'

I was curious about how long it might be until I felt ready to consider putting myself back out there, if ever. Then again, as Dan and Jedda both said, there were perks to being single. Just because I was accustomed to being in a relationship, didn't mean I needed to be.

'Nah. I'm not really the type to join a dating site or download an app, and there aren't often new women in town, except on holiday, but then they're usually here with their husbands and kids.'

'You've never thought about moving away?'

'Why would I do that?' He gestured to the darkness out the windows like some model on a TV game show presenting all the prizes. 'Have you looked outside lately? The Point, the coast ... it's in my blood. Working with my family might have knobs on it—they drive me insane much of the time—but I love the business and I truly couldn't imagine wanting to live anywhere else.'

'I can understand why. I might only have been here on and off for a few months, but I already love it too.' The people of Ragged Point had snuck under my skin and into my heart. I liked the fact it felt as if everyone knew everyone else, and I'd never seen anything like the way locals had come together to help each other recover from the cyclone.

'So now that you and your ex are officially separating, will you continue to alternate living in the house with your kids? What did you call that again?'

'Nest parenting,' I said, and nodded. 'I never thought I'd agree to having one full week away from Saxon and Payton, but I have to think of what's best for them. Part of that is them not having to move from somewhere Adrian lives to somewhere I do whenever we switch custody, but it's also still spending as much time as possible with each of us.' I swallowed and took another sip of wine. 'However I feel about Adrian right now, I wouldn't want our break-up to jeopardise his relationship with the kids any more than I want it to hurt mine. This is the fairest situation on everyone, and although I don't relish the idea of having to maintain a civil relationship with him, I'll do whatever I can for my children.'

'That's very admirable,' Dan said.

I shook my head. 'Not really. My parents had a super messy divorce, but even before that I can only remember them hating each other. I used to hide under my bed when they had screaming matches in the kitchen.'

'Was there abuse?' Dan's forehead creased.

'No, not physical, but definitely verbal and emotional, and I never wanted that for my children. I still don't. What about you? What was your childhood like?'

'Not idyllic. My mum died when I was five. She suffered an aneurysm at my party.'

'Oh my God.' I felt like an idiot—here I'd been hoping for something happy to lift the mood, but I'd totally forgotten about his mother. And while I'd already heard this from Gail, I didn't know how or *when* it had happened. Hearing the words uttered from Dan's mouth only made it more tragic. My heart ached. Poor Dan, sharing his actual birthday with the anniversary of his mum's death.

'It was a pretty crap birthday,' he said with a shrug, 'but I was young, so I don't remember much about her. Dad worked a lot and hired a lot of nannies to look after Gemma, Ben and me, but as we got older, we just kinda looked after each other. They remember our mother, they try to share memories of her with me, but it's not the same.' He took a long sip of wine. 'Her death lingered in our house growing up though—Dad wasn't around much. I think he worked to escape his grief. My brother and sister are closer to him, because they had his attention before Mum died.'

'When did he remarry?' I asked.

'Only recently.' He thought a moment. 'I think it's coming up to two years. Gemma's worried she's only after Dad's money, but Ben says as long as he's happy again, he doesn't care.'

'And you?'

He shrugged. 'Money's not really important to me and I know it's harsh, but Dad and I aren't close, so what he does with his personal life doesn't affect me. Guess 'cos I also don't have kids I'm not so worried about leaving an inheritance, but Gem and Ben do care about all that and, well, I care about them.'

'Fair enough,' I said.

Despite the differences in our upbringings, neither of us had felt particularly cherished or happy in our home situations and had longed to create better ones as adults. I felt sad that Dan hadn't ever had the family he clearly craved.

'I'm sorry you couldn't have children,' I found myself saying. 'I think you'd have made a great dad. I can't imagine how I'd have felt if I wasn't able to have my three.'

Dan frowned. 'I thought you only had two?'

Whoops. I swallowed and then told him something I rarely told anyone I didn't know at the time because talking about how I lost my little boy always ripped me apart. I hadn't even told Jedda.

'I had a son five years before Saxon.' My voice cracked as I spoke. 'Leo was born sleeping at twenty-eight weeks.'

'Oh, Ashling.' That's all Dan said but his voice was full of warmth and understanding as he reached out and covered my hand with his, squeezing it gently. A tear slipped down my cheek, but I suddenly didn't know whether I was crying because of my first born or because without him I might not be in the predicament I was now.

'Adrian all but told me recently he only proposed because I was pregnant.'

'I'm beginning to think "dick" isn't a strong enough term.' Dan leaned across the coffee table and grabbed a packet of tissues. 'Here.'

'Thanks.' I put my glass down, then sniffed as I took a tissue and swiped at my eyes. 'Sorry, I think exhaustion has made me overly emotional.'

'You have nothing to apologise for,' he said.

I opened my mouth to thank him again when a large ginger ball of fur sprang up from behind the couch and landed between us.

'Oh my God!' My hand rushed to my chest.

'Ashling meet Lion.' Dan chuckled, reaching out to run his large hand over the scruffy orange cat. It was the biggest one I'd ever seen and did look rather feral as the volunteer on the island had inferred, but once my heart stopped racing and I stretched my hand tentatively towards it, I discovered he was really quite affectionate.

'He's adorable,' I said as Lion purred loudly under my touch. He was exactly the kind of medicine I needed. 'How's he settling in?'

'He has moments where he tries to escape, but I haven't let him out yet because I don't want him to try and head back to the island.'

'Are you going to keep him here?'

Dan nodded. 'I think so. He's getting old and might get stressed when people start coming and going to assess the structural integrity of the buildings and then, if we can afford them, to do the works. Anyway, he's good company.'

I could see he would be, I thought, as I rubbed him under his chin. I'd always wanted a cat but never had one because Adrian was allergic, or so he said. I suspect he just didn't like them. Over the last couple of months, I'd started to realise there were a number of things I'd avoided because Adrian didn't like or approve of them.

I chuckled as I added getting a kitten to the list I'd been drafting in my head for one of my blog posts: 'Top Ten Things to Celebrate Being Single Again'.

I'd already ticked number one off the list—replacing my old shoe wardrobe with shoes entirely impractical and pretty that I chose myself—and was rapidly adding to it. In fact, the way I was going I might make it a Top 100 list!

'What's so funny?' Dan asked.

'Sorry.' I took a breath, deliberating for a moment whether to tell him about my blog or come up with some other excuse for why I was grinning like an idiot. In the end, I told him the truth, explaining that I was hoping the regular blogging combined with the writing I was doing for Jedda would get me back into the habit and give me the confidence to pursue journalism again once my divorce was finalised.

'Why wait until your divorce is through?'

'I don't want to overwhelm myself just yet. Right now, I'm taking things one step at a time. My priority has to be making sure the kids are okay.'

'Fair enough.'

'But if my blog can help anyone in a similar situation to me, then I'll be happy.'

'I think it's a great idea. What's the address?'

I frowned. 'The address?'

He flashed me his shiny white teeth in a bemused smile. 'Of your blog.'

'Oh, right.' I flushed a little but gave it to him and then drained the last dregs of my wine. He was probably being polite. It was unlikely he'd actually read my first two very long-winded posts.

'You want a top-up?' Dan nodded towards my empty glass. 'We've finished your bottle, but I've got another, or maybe you'd prefer something else. Beer, whisky, a coffee?'

I glanced at my watch, unable to believe how fast the last few hours had gone. So much for being tired and needing an early night.

'Thanks, but I'd better make a move. The kids are coming up on Monday and I still have a few things I want to get in order in the shack before they arrive.'

'No worries.' He pushed to a stand.

'But let me help you clean up before I go.'

'Don't be silly, you're my guest.'

I held up my hand. 'I'm not taking no for an answer. Don't you know the rule about the person who cooks not having to clean up?'

Dan tried to put up a fight, but I marched into the kitchen and got stuck in, leaving him no choice but to follow me. Lion rubbed himself against my legs while I rinsed and Dan stacked the dishwasher. It felt so normal chatting and working alongside him, but I pushed that thought quickly out of my head. Despite the fact Dan and I got on well and he was certainly easy on the eye, I didn't plan on falling head-first into another relationship. I needed time to help my children through my divorce and also to focus on me.

We'd almost finished when I noticed a tin right at the far end of the bench, almost hidden behind the microwave.

'Is that the tin we found this afternoon?'

Dan hesitated and his cheeks flushed before he nodded. 'I know I said maybe we shouldn't be reading them, but I thought they might give some insight into Bill. Maybe there'd even be something that might help the police work out who he was?'

'So you're going to read them to look for clues?'

His blush grew darker. 'I already have.'

'I see.' I couldn't quite work out the expression on his face—was there something else he wasn't telling me? 'And? Did you learn anything about Bill?'

'Not really, but I'm pretty damn sure I know who wrote these letters.'

'Really? Who was it?'

Dan dumped his tea towel on the bench, then leaned back against it. 'My mum.'

I was still trying to wrap my head around what he'd just said when he continued, 'She collected tins exactly like these. They're all on display at Gemma's house in a special cabinet. She continued collecting after Mum died and still buys every new Arnott's tin that comes out. A few years ago, she realised there was one missing—one that was released when Mum was alive—so she hunted on eBay until she found a replacement. I can't help wondering if this is the missing one.'

It took a moment for me to realise what he was getting at. A chill spread over my skin leaving goosebumps in its wake. 'You think *your* mother wrote those letters?'

He nodded. 'She must have given Bill the tin as a gift and that's why he kept her letters in them.'

That was a bit of a jump. It sounded like Dan was clutching at straws, wanting to find more connection between himself and Bill, who'd clearly been more of a role model to him than his own father.

'You know,' I said tentatively, 'those tins were pretty common. My granny had one almost exactly the same that contained what she called her "rainy day fund". She kept it in a "safe" spot under her bed—a safe spot that *everyone* knew about.'

Dan's lips quirked, but then he let out a long heavy breath. 'Anyway, whoever sent those letters to Bill was definitely married, that's clear, but they had more than just a love affair. They also had a baby together.'

41

'What?' I blinked. 'How do you know?'

Dan turned and reached for the tin, opening it and pulling out the very top letter. 'It's all in there.'

I took the paper and read the writer's confession that they were pregnant with the recipient's child.

'The next few letters—if I've managed to order them correctly—she's pondering what she's going to do. She talks about being scared of her husband and how he might react if he finds out the baby isn't his. I wish I could see Bill's replies as well; I wish I knew how he felt about the baby and whether or not he wanted her to leave her husband so they could raise it together. But in the end, it looks like she decided she couldn't choose love over her older children, so she stayed in what sounds like a loveless relationship.'

I frowned as I dried my hands on a tea towel, thinking of my own situation. Was that what I'd been prepared to do for my children?

'You know, just 'cos the letters are in a tin like the ones your mum collected, doesn't mean they're hers. Arnott's produced thousands of tins exactly like that, probably more. Maybe someone else gave it to Bill? Or maybe he bought it himself?'

'Maybe. But it's not just the tin.' Dan pulled a postcard-size card out of his pocket and handed it to me. 'This was also in there. At the very bottom. I shoved it in my pocket when I heard you at the door.'

I glanced down at the most startling painting I'd ever seen. The colours were magical. It was almost a cross between abstract art and traditional portraiture. It took my breath away and I couldn't draw my eyes from the man in the image. He was incredibly good-looking in a rugged kind of way, with sandy, scruffy hair, olive skin and a smile that was neither happy nor sad. I'd only ever seen him before in photos, but I felt I knew him. Although he looked totally smitten with whoever was painting him, the expression on his face also hid deep pain.

Goosebumps skittered across my skin.

Dan remained silent while I soaked it all in, only speaking when I looked back up into his eyes. 'That's Bill,' he said, unnecessarily.

'And your mum painted this?' I whispered, thinking of Gail and Cassie's conversation at the trivia night and already knowing it to be true.

He nodded. 'It's her style all over. Come look.'

I followed him out of the kitchen and back to the entrance hall, where he pointed to a painting of a toddler done in exactly the same style as the postcard one. I'd been so nervous when I'd arrived, I'd not registered it among all the other paintings on the wall.

'Mum did that when I was two,' Dan said. 'There's a couple more of me at Dad's place, along with loads more of him, Gemma and Benjamin. Half the town have portraits she did hanging on their walls.'

'She was very talented,' I said, and he looked at me like I was crazy—Bonnie's talent wasn't what was up for debate. 'Okay, I'll admit, there's no chance anyone else did that, but it still doesn't mean ... Maybe she simply painted him. You said yourself she painted half the locals.'

'Yes, but all those paintings were much bigger, and people were proud of them—they hang them in pride of place in their homes and show them off. You'd think if Bill didn't have anything to hide, he'd have framed this painting and hung it on his wall of fame.'

I nodded. 'So, you think your mum had an affair with Bill and that the baby she writes about is either your brother, your sister or you.'

'It's gotta be me—she writes about her two older children in the letters. And this would explain a lot about my childhood.'

I frowned. 'What do you mean?'

Dan ran a hand through his thick hair and sighed. 'I told you Dad and I aren't close? Well, it's more than that. He definitely favours Gemma and Ben over me. They've got an idea for the business, he listens. They need a boost up for something, he gives it to them. The only time I ever got a handout was when he gave me and Tessa a deposit for this place for our wedding, whereas he's always throwing extra cash at Gemma and Ben. And it's always been this way, even as a kid—the baby of a family is supposed to be spoilt and favoured, but not me. If Gem or Ben did well at school, Dad showered them with praise and rewarded them somehow, but if I did well, he barely even noticed, never mind made a fuss.'

Although it was a grown man standing before me, I couldn't help seeing the little boy he'd been, and my heart felt heavy that any child could be made to feel that way.

'Gemma and Ben reckon it's because he associates me with Mum's death. And while I thought maybe that was true, there's always been something else I couldn't quite put my finger on. It's like when he looks at me, the first feeling I see is loathing and then he quickly covers it up. I've always felt like a disappointment to him.' Dan sighed. 'Ben's more of a man's man, like Stephen. They're always the life of the party. They love getting drunk, belching and yelling at the TV over football and car-racing, whereas I've always preferred being outdoors or, if I have to be inside, watching nature programs. Told you I was a nerd,' he added.

I gave him the briefest smile—whatever he kept saying, there was nothing nerdy about him.

'I always just assumed I was more like my mum, but maybe there's more to it than that? Maybe I'm not anything like Stephen because he's not actually my father.'

I pondered this possibility. Now that I thought about it, Dan didn't bear much resemblance to Stephen, Gemma or Ben at all.

'It would certainly explain his apathy towards me,' Dan said.

'But that would mean he knew. You think your father has suspicions you're not his biological child?'

'Maybe.' He shrugged. 'Bill always spoke fondly of my mother. Stupidly, I never questioned *how* he knew her. I guess I just took it at face value that they were friends and she visited the island like others did, but now that I think about it, he was the one who instigated our friendship. I spent a lot of time on the beach as a teenager and he started talking to me on his trips across for supplies. Eventually, he invited me over to the island. We had lots of great times together until Stephen found out what I was up to and hit the roof. He forbade me from seeing Bill but, when I became an adult, I reconnected. Stephen couldn't control my friendships then.'

'So, you think there was more to his opposition than the fact that a grown man hanging around a child who wasn't related to him is pretty suspicious?' I raised an eyebrow. 'I can tell you, if a middle-aged man started befriending one of my kids, I'd probably call the cops!'

'Yeah, but things were different back then, especially in a small town. Everyone else trusted Bill. Dad's animosity towards him never made sense, but if he knew about the affair, or worse, about the baby ...'

I nodded as Dan's voice drifted off. 'That would probably do it.'

'And it would also make perfect sense why he refuses to even entertain the idea of helping with funds for the island. But what I don't get is, if Stephen knew, why didn't he say anything? All these years, he's never once come out and said anything about me possibly not being his son.'

'Maybe he doesn't know, maybe you're right that you're not close because of your mother's death and he just felt guilty at you spending time with Bill when he wasn't making the effort,' I suggested. 'Or maybe it's a pride thing?'

'What do you mean?'

'Maybe he doesn't want his friends and employees to know that he couldn't satisfy his own wife? That she betrayed him.'

Dan snorted. 'That does sound very Stephen-like—he likes being the big man about town, everyone looking up to him. But I don't get why Bill didn't say anything. I guess I understand why he didn't tell me when I was a kid, but surely when I was an adult ... I mean, Mum was long gone, so he didn't need to worry about her.'

I wished I had the answers Dan clearly wanted, but all either of us had were questions. Without Bill's side of the story, we couldn't be certain of any of our theories.

'If you are Bill's son, maybe he thought Stephen could offer you more than he could?' A successful local businessman as opposed to someone who was essentially a squatter.

'Maybe. But there's more to life than material possessions.'

I couldn't argue with that. My parents had been fairly well-off, and while I'd never wanted for clothes or toys, it was peace and stability I craved.

'So, what are you going to do about your suspicions? What do you *want* to do?'

'I don't know.' Dan's sigh was heavy with defeat as he ran one hand through his shaggy hair. 'Part of me wants to know the truth, but then maybe knowing it would only bring more questions. More hurt. At least I know who Stephen is. If Bill's my dad, it'll only be more frustrating that I never really knew who he was. I'm not sure how I'd feel about him or the island anymore if I found out he was my father. I've been working my butt off to preserve his legacy, but he couldn't bring himself to tell me the truth. Or didn't have the guts to.'

'Maybe he promised your mum he wouldn't? Maybe he just didn't want to upset you? Maybe he was protecting you from something we know nothing about?'

Maybe we were completely barking up the wrong tree?

When Dan didn't say anything, I added, 'Assuming the writer *is* your mother, I wonder how she knew the baby was definitely Bill's. I mean, surely she and Stephen were intimate as well.'

'I dunno.' A slight blush crept up Dan's neck—I guess no one liked thinking about their parents doing the deed, even at our age. 'Dammit, all these letters have created is one bloody question after another.'

I startled as he slammed his fist down on the counter.

'Sorry.' He flashed me a sad smile. Despite all the wine we'd drunk, Dan looked like he could do with a stiff drink.

'It's fine,' I said, stifling a yawn because I wanted to be here for him, but it had been a long, physically exhausting and now emotionally draining day.

'What about blood types?' I suddenly thought. 'Maybe you could find out the blood types of your dad and siblings and compare them with yours. See if the equation fits?'

'All that might prove is that I'm not his, but how will I ever prove I'm Bill's?'

'Maybe the coroner will agree to have your DNA cross-matched?'

'Maybe.' He smiled sadly. 'Sorry, I really didn't mean to dump all this on you. Hope it hasn't ruined your night.'

I touched his arm. 'I had a lovely evening. And I'm more than happy to be a sounding board if you need someone to talk all this through with. That's what friends are for, right?'

He nodded and then closed the distance between us. For a moment I thought he might kiss me, but he simply drew me into a hug. My body stilled and then relaxed in his warm, comforting embrace. I couldn't remember the last time someone held me like this, and it felt so good. Not awkward. Not suggestive. Just really, really good.

When Dan pulled back, the smile he gave me no longer held so much anguish. 'Come on ... I'll walk you home.'

'You don't have to. It's not like Ragged Point's the crime capital of the world or the shack is far.'

He cocked his head to the side. 'Do you want me to have any more of a sleepless night than I already will?'

'Of course not.'

'Then stop objecting and let's get walking. Charlie will be wondering where you are.'

'Okay.' Seeing I wasn't going to win this battle, and secretly quite happy for his company, I gave Lion a quick pat goodbye and then Dan and I stepped out into the night.

After all the words we'd exchanged over the last few hours, our walk was strangely silent but not at all uncomfortable. The night breeze had a chill to it, but I didn't feel cold next to Dan, and when we arrived at the shack, I couldn't help feeling disappointed the evening had come to an end. We paused at the bottom of the porch steps and I had a ridiculous urge to ask him in for coffee.

'Thanks for walking me home,' I said, looking up into his face, only partially visible due to a sliver of moonlight.

He smiled down at me. 'You're absolutely welcome. Thanks for a great night.'

And then, he stooped and kissed me chastely on the cheek, before turning and striding back along the sand towards his place. Heat spread from that one spot right through my body and I palmed my hand against my cheek as I watched his dark silhouette grow smaller.

How different the evening could have ended if I was another kind of person. Just because I didn't think getting into a relationship with someone new was a good idea right now didn't mean I couldn't have fun. Did it? Someone like Hayley, or maybe even Jedda, would have dragged Dan into the shack and had their wicked way. I shivered at the thought but told myself it was safer this way.

I wasn't a coward, I was sensible. Sex complicated things.

Only as I was giving Charlie hello cuddles did I realise we hadn't spoken about the fundraiser at all. *Whoops.*

42

'I thought you said this place was nice,' Saxon said the moment he stepped inside the shack. 'Looks like a total dump to me.'

My heart sank. While it might not be The Ritz and still needed a lot of improvement, I'd worked hard to make the place feel warm and welcoming.

'Can we go for a swim?' Payton asked, thankfully less concerned about her accommodation, as she and Charlie rolled around on the floor reuniting.

'What's the wi-fi password?' Sax had already dropped onto the sofa and was opening up his laptop.

'I don't have internet yet, but there's plenty to do up here. A few days disconnected from devices won't kill you.'

'Are you *fucking* kidding me? What kind of backwater place has no wi-fi?'

'Excuse me?' I felt my cheeks heat as I glanced in embarrassment at Hayley and Wei who had delivered my delightful children only five minutes ago.

He shrugged. 'What?'

'I won't have you speaking that way in my house. You're not too old for me to wash your mouth out with soap.'

'Sorry,' he said, in that tone kids use when they don't actually mean it. Where was my beautiful, *polite* son?

I took a deep breath as Hayley and Wei retreated down the short hallway to take a look around, no doubt trying to make themselves scarce.

'Sax says the f-word all the time now,' Payton tattled. 'He thinks it makes him cool. Dad doesn't tell him off, but I guess that would be the pot calling the kettle black because he swears more than a pilot.'

'I think you mean pir—' I went to correct her, but Saxon shouted over the top of me.

'What would you know? No one even says *cool* anymore!'

'They do so,' she shouted back. 'Cool! Cool! Cool! Cool! Cool!'

A sharp pain shot through my head. I raised my eyebrows, my hand *and* my voice all at once. 'That's quite enough you two!'

Due to their different genders and almost five-year age gap, they'd never been what you'd call close, but they didn't fight much either. I didn't like this development any more than I liked Saxon's new vocabulary and I planned to nip them both in the bud.

'I've missed you guys like crazy and I want us to have a good week, so enough with the mean stuff, okay? Yes, we can go swimming, Payton, but first we're going to have a nice lunch with Aunty Hayley and Wei, then go for a walk so I can show you all round the Point before they have to drive home.'

Saxon rolled his eyes, snapped his laptop shut and flopped back against the couch as if his life was over.

'But when can we go swimming?' This from Payton, obviously.

'Why don't you get changed into your bathers now? Then you'll be ready after lunch and a walk. I'll show you to our room.' I nodded to the door that led to the two small bedrooms, and then looked to Saxon. 'You coming?'

He reluctantly followed us into the first bedroom, the one I'd been using and that Payton would share with me. Wei and Hayley were already in there, looking out the window and admiring the view of the beach.

'Wow,' Hayley said. 'This place looks ...'

'Boring?' Saxon glowered from where he'd stopped in the doorway. 'I can't believe we have to stay here for a whole week. How lame!'

I opened my mouth to ask him exactly what his problem was, but Hayley got in first.

'Stop being such a grump,' she reprimanded, then turned back to me, her eyes sparkling with encouragement. 'I can't believe how much you've done in such a short time—the transformation from those first photos you sent us is amazing. You are a superwoman.'

While I smiled proudly, Wei nodded his agreement and pointed to the walls, newly painted in duck-egg blue. 'I love the colour scheme.'

'Thanks.'

I'd wanted something bright, fresh and calming to match the seaside location so, in consultation with Wei and his sister, had decided on a Hamptons-style look throughout. The windows and doorframes were all painted white, and I was having fun hunting for inexpensive or second-hand furniture and decorative pieces to complete the look in the bedroom, including some rugs I'd earmarked online for when the floorboards were finished throughout. 'There's still a lot to do, but it's starting to feel like home.'

When Hayley's eyes widened and then sparkled, I realised my faux pas.

'Well, not *home*-home obviously. It can't be home without the kids here ...' I pulled Payton into a hug, not stupid enough to risk that with Saxon in his current mood. 'But it's starting to feel like my space. I love waking up on the beach and I'm enjoying meeting people and being part of the community.'

'It certainly looks a lot nicer than I remember as a kid,' Wei added. 'Never underestimate a woman's touch, that's what I say.'

The way Hayley grinned at him was really quite nauseating. Perhaps I should offer *them* a room?

'When did you say the kitchen renos were starting?' she asked.

'Not till next week. I didn't want to have tradespeople here while the kids were staying. I'm actually thinking that I might attempt the bathroom overhaul myself.' I looked to Wei. 'That's if you trust me.'

He nodded. 'Go to town.'

'Can you guys get out so I can put on my bathers?' Payton asked, shooing us with her hands. 'There's a beach outside with my name on it.'

We all laughed, well, everyone except Sax.

'I hope it's not too cold,' I said as she shut the door.

The rest of us headed into the other bedroom. Saxon dumped his laptop and bag on the bed, then told us he was tired and needed a lie-down.

'Are you okay?' I asked, reaching out to feel his forehead.

He shrugged me off. 'Fine. Just want to rest.'

I tried not to feel hurt—we used to be so close—and told myself that he'd had a busy first term at school and was likely exhausted. Hopefully this week by the sea would be the break he clearly needed and also give us a chance to reconnect.

'Okay. But do you want some lunch first? I've made pumpkin soup and some fresh home-baked rolls.'

'Not hungry.' Sax climbed into bed. 'Maybe I'll have something later.'

I wanted to object, to say he should eat with us—he might feel better after he'd had a good meal—but I didn't want to risk another confrontation in front of Wei. 'All right. Let me know if you need anything and maybe you can come for a walk with us later?'

He made a non-committal noise and rolled over, pulling the doona on top of him.

Hayley and I exchanged a look as we left his room. I closed the door, waited until we were in the kitchen and then said in a hushed voice, 'Was he all right in the car? He seems a little off.'

'He was fine,' Hayley said, lifting the lid on the saucepan of soup and leaning close to sniff it. 'Yum.'

'He was on his phone most of the time,' Wei added, 'but I think that's pretty normal for a teenager, isn't it?'

You'd know, you're not much older than one yourself.

Thankfully, I had enough restraint and sense not to voice my narky thought. Hayley and Wei had done me a favour driving the kids up, but already nothing else felt as if it was going as planned.

Hayley squeezed my shoulder. 'Try not to stress. He's a good kid.'

'Did you hear the way he was talking to us? And that language?'

She actually smiled. 'I'm sure I said much worse to my parents.'

I couldn't believe that—she forgot I knew her parents and I reckon Glennis would have washed Hayley's mouth out with soap if she'd dared to try anything like Saxon just did.

'Saxon's behaviour is totally normal,' she added. 'He loves you, but he's got all these adolescent hormones wreaking havoc on his emotions and of course he's going to take that out on those closest to him.'

I sighed. 'I guess. That, on top of the fact we've just dumped news of the divorce on him. You're right. Maybe I need to be more patient, more understanding.'

'Good idea. But first food. I'm starving.'

I laughed and turned to retrieve the rolls that had been warming in the oven. At the smell of fresh bread, Payton emerged from the bedroom, wearing nothing but her one-piece bathers, goggles and flippers.

'Where'd you get them?'

'Wei gave them to me.' She pushed the goggles up onto her forehead and smiled at him as she flapped loudly to the table.

While we ate, we talked a little bit about my plans for the shack going forward.

'You sure you won't get lonely up here all by yourself?' Hayley asked, before popping another spoonful of soup into her mouth.

'Lonely?' I snorted. 'I've had more of a social life here in the last couple of months than I've had in Perth the last few years, and I'm enjoying actually working again too.'

She'd already heard about the trivia night, but I caught her up on the last week—getting to know locals during my shifts in the cafe; attending an evening meeting of the CWA so I could write an article about their drive to attract more younger women; another couple of nights at Jedda's place drinking wine as we worked on the *Reporter*; and, of course, about yesterday's busy bee out on the island.

'I thought you had more colour in your cheeks than usual. The fresh air and sun clearly agree with you.'

'I'm going to help the Island Progress Association with some fundraising,' I finished, not mentioning Dan or our dinner because I didn't want Hayley to jump to conclusions.

She rolled her eyes. 'You just can't help yourself can you—if there's a committee or something to be organised, you've got to be in it.'

'I've actually resigned from the P&F and the school fundraising committee, so now I'm on fewer committees than I was before.'

'That's something. Anyway, this island and castle thing sounds fascinating. Can we have a look?'

'Sorry, it's not open to the public yet and you need to have a boat to get out there.' Dan might take them, but even if he wasn't working, I wouldn't ask him. I didn't want to push our newfound friendship.

'What are you smiling for?' Hayley's question caught me unawares, but luckily Payton asked another before I could answer it.

'Can I go swimming yet?'

'Okay.' We'd kept her waiting long enough. 'Why don't you have a piece of caramel slice and I'll go get Sax?'

I found him sitting in bed, his laptop on his knees and headphones in his ears.

'I thought you were having a nap!'

He blinked at the sound of my raised voice and yanked out one earbud. 'Huh?'

'I thought you said you were tired.'

'I am, but there's stuff I need to do. Just give me a bit more time and I'll come do whatever lame family stuff you want.'

He put the earbud back in his ear, dismissing me.

'Saxon isn't coming,' I told the others as I entered the kitchen. 'He's on his computer, studying.'

Payton laughed through her mouthful of caramel slice.

'What is it?' I asked.

'You guys think he's so perfect, but you're just blind. He's not doing *homework* on his computer. He only brought it for *The Tournament*.'

'What tournament?' It took a few minutes for my brain to click and when it did, I frowned. 'You mean that video game?'

She nodded. 'He's obsessed with it. Plays it night and day—I reckon he'd play in the shower if he could.'

'But he hasn't got internet here?' Payton had a tendency to over-dramatise things, not to mention the fact her brother's never been that kind of kid. Sure he played a bit of Xbox with his friends, but he'd always been more interested in his music.

She rolled her eyes. 'He'll be using his phone internet. Once he's used up all his data, he'll ask for yours. Anyway, can we *please* go swimming?'

'I ...' I was torn between putting on my bathers and telling her to wait while I confronted her brother.

Hayley clearly read my mind. 'How about Wei and I take Payton to the water and you can join us soon?'

'Thank you,' I mouthed.

Saxon scowled as I entered his bedroom again, not even bothering to remove his earbuds this time. 'What do you want now?'

I went over to the bed and peered down at the laptop screen. Sure enough, my eyes were met with a gruesome image of blood and gore, little characters with massive guns shooting at other little characters.

'Since when do you play games like that?' I asked, my stomach turning over at such graphic violence.

Sax exhaled loudly, pressed a button on the screen and finally took out his earbuds. 'A while now. I know how much you hate violence, but it's not as bad as it looks. There's a real strategy to winning and I'm pretty good at it.'

'I see.' My jaw clenched. 'And what about your schoolwork?'

'Mum,' he groaned, 'it's the holidays. Most of the time you're telling me I study too much and that I need to take a break, now that I've taken your advice, you want me to study instead?' He slammed the lid of the laptop down and hurled it across the bed. 'I can't win with you!'

I caught the computer before it fell onto the floor. 'That's not true. Of course I want you to relax and have fun, but I have concerns about this type of game.'

'You'd rather I play chess with Payton?'

Well, yes, but I wasn't stupid enough to say that. 'I'd rather you read a book.'

He made a face. 'I read enough books at school. Holidays are supposed to be fun and this way I can chat to my friends while we play. *Tournament* isn't some evil cult, you know? All the guys are doing it.'

I pursed my lips and nodded. I thought his music was his 'fun' but he hadn't even brought his guitar with him. 'Fine,' I said, pushing to a stand. 'Play your stupid game. Hayley, Wei, Payton and I are going for a nice walk.'

In the past, reverse psychology had almost always worked wonders with Saxon. A people pleaser, he never liked letting me down. I fully expected him to climb out of bed and come with us, but instead he said, 'Thanks. I will. And can I use your hotspot? I've almost run out of data.'

We did have a 'nice' walk. Wei ran into a few people he vaguely remembered from childhood and Payton splashed in the sea for what felt like hours. When we finally returned, I prayed Saxon had miraculously improved both his attitude and his mood.

'Mum, what's this?' Payton shouted from the front porch where she'd run ahead of us.

'I don't know,' I replied, squinting as I tried to make out what on earth the brown globe hanging from the porch gutter was. 'I've never seen it before.'

'Looks like some kind of animal home,' Wei said as we approached the steps.

'There's a note attached,' Payton shrieked with excitement, already ripping open the envelope.

'Give that here.' I snatched it from her just in time and was aware of three pairs of eyes on me as I opened it.

Thanks for the other night. It was good to be able to talk it all through with someone. I wasn't sure how to show my appreciation, so I made this for you. Hopefully it keeps your possum cosy and it stops bothering you inside. Dan.

'Who's Dan?' Hayley asked, reading the note over my shoulder.

I snapped it to my chest and couldn't help blushing, although I had absolutely nothing to hide. 'Just um ... just a neighbour. You know the article I wrote about the cyclone damage on the island?'

She nodded.

'It's him. I was just helping him with some ideas for a fundraiser and he wanted to say thanks.'

Hayley frowned up at the possum home. 'Hasn't he ever heard of a box of chocolates?'

The others had already lost interest and headed into the shack. I laughed, but the truth was, this sweet gift felt more special than a box of chocolates ever could.

43

You know when you look forward to something so much, like a movie or book that everyone has raved about, and then you actually experience it and it's not as fantastic as you imagined? That's exactly how my week in Ragged Point with the kids was going. They simply didn't have the same affection for the place I did.

Payton loved the beach, but it was too cold to stay in the water all day now, and if she wasn't kept active, she got bored. The one TV in the shack didn't have Netflix, Stan, Apple or any of the bells and whistles the kids were used to in Perth and they didn't want to watch any of my DVDs. I tried to get Payton into some baking, but the only times outside the ocean that she seemed to enjoy herself was when we went to Brewed Awakening or kidnapped Bindi for a couple of hours and took her to the park or the beach. The two girls adored each other. Payton would have made an awesome big sister, but that possibility had flown years ago, so she loved it when Jedda said she could be Bindi's surrogate sister.

'What's a surrogate?' she asked, sparking a massive in-depth conversation about all the different ways to have a baby. Now Payton had decided that when she grew up, she was going to 'choose sperm' like Jedda and have a baby without a man.

'I think men are more trouble than they're worth,' she told me and Jedda, as if she was a middle-aged woman who'd been married for decades.

We'd both stifled smiles. Although in my current predicament—with neither a husband nor a son in my good books—I had to agree, I didn't want Payton to catch my bitterness towards the opposite sex. Surely there were *some* good men out there.

Saxon only emerged from his room grudgingly to eat and pee, although he wasn't eating as much as usual and I feared his showering habits were getting slack, but when I tried to talk to him about both these things, he'd yelled at me to stop being intrusive. Yelling, it appeared, had become part of who he was. He yelled at Payton if she so much as dared to breathe near him, which was one of the reasons I'd ended up letting him hibernate in his bedroom more than I thought healthy. I was trying to be calm and patient as Hayley had advised, but there was only so much any of us could take.

Saxon was waiting on the back porch when Payton, Charlie and I returned from our morning walk along the beach. The sight surprised me because it was earlier than he usually surfaced of late.

'Hi Sax.' I felt a lift in my heart at the sight of him. 'Would you like me to cook up some bacon and eggs for breakfast?'

'Yum!' said Payton.

'I need more data,' Saxon said. 'Yours has run out.'

'And a very good morning to you too.' The flutter of maternal affection vanished, and I marched up the stairs and past him into the shack.

'Good morning,' he said snottily as he followed quickly on my heels. '*Now* can I have your credit card so I can top up my phone? I tried to ring Dad but he's not answering.'

He was probably bonking someone! I pushed that irritating thought aside and focused on our son.

'If you've used up your data *and* mine, then maybe you've used enough. We're going to have a nice breakfast and then we're going for a drive.'

He crossed his arms over his chest. 'I'm not going anywhere until you refresh the data.'

I narrowed my eyes. 'And I will not be blackmailed by you, so I suggest you change your tune.'

'*Whatever*. I wouldn't be even having this problem if you'd let me stay in Perth with Dad.'

'As if your father would have wanted you there cramping his style on his kid-free week. And right now, I'm not sure I want you here either!'

Saxon recoiled, Payton started to cry, and Charlie growled in a way I'd never heard before. My heart was beating so fast it hurt. I'd never said anything like that to either of my kids, but I simply couldn't control my anger.

'You should be thankful to be able to stay in such a lovely place, Saxon. And if you don't pick up your act and come out with Payton and me, and at least pretend to have fun ...' See, my bar wasn't aimed too high. 'Then not only will I cancel your phone plan altogether, but I'll throw it and your laptop into the sea.'

'You wouldn't dare,' he seethed. 'I need them both for school.'

My hands on my hips, I leaned into his face. 'Just try me.'

So much for reconnecting this trip.

After breakfast, Saxon—still grumpy—climbed into the back of my car and glowered all the way to the Pinnacles. I contemplated apologising for some of what I'd said, but in the end decided it might be better to *show* him rather than tell him that I loved him and just wanted us all to have a good time together.

The national park was riddled with other families taking in the impressive mounds of limestone that poked out of the earth. I couldn't believe we'd never bothered to drive up here before. It wasn't as if it was too far from Perth, but it was like nothing else I'd ever seen. The butter-yellow sand contrasted with the dark green shrubbery and the clear cobalt-blue sky made me feel like we were in an exotic postcard. And the weather was simply perfect—not too hot, not too cold.

'It looks like something out of a movie,' Payton marvelled, as her hair blew into her face.

Sax opened his mouth as if he was about to say something derogatory to his sister but took one look at me and smartly shut it again.

Although our surrounds were beautiful and I was trying to enjoy time with my children, I couldn't help noticing the two-parent families all around us. Everywhere I looked I saw a happy family, admiring the rocks, kids running in between them, laughing and squealing with delight, and parents watching as they smiled tenderly at each other. I knew I wasn't the only single mum in the world, but it felt like it out here, and the thought brought a lump to my throat. This was not the life I'd wanted for myself or my children.

Damn Adrian, for ruining everything.

Determined to salvage the day, I pushed my soon-to-be ex-husband to the back of my mind and adopted the chirpiest, most enthusiastic voice I could muster. 'Let's explore,' I said as I set off on foot from where we'd parked, digging my phone out of my pocket to take photos. Payton skipped ahead of me, running in and out of the mounds.

'This would be an awesome place for hide-and-seek,' she shouted back.

I snapped a pic of her peeking round a rock twice her height and nodded.

'How long do we have to stay here?' Saxon grumbled.

I chose not to answer. 'Go stand with your sister so I can take a photo.'

Remarkably, he did as he was told—no doubt thinking about his phone and laptop at the bottom of the ocean—and I got some lovely snaps for my post-Adrian family album.

'Can you take a photo of me at the top?' Payton asked, one foot already on the bottom of a pinnacle ready to launch.

'No,' I shrieked. 'Climbing is forbidden. Get down!'

'But …' Payton pointed all around her. 'Everyone else is doing it!'

'Not quite everyone,' I said, although there were indeed quite a few people blatantly disregarding the rules. Couldn't they read? Hadn't they heard what the park ranger had said as we paid to come in?

'What's the point if you can't climb them?' Sax said, not attempting to hide a yawn. 'Can I go sit in the car?'

'No. Come on.' I flashed him an encouraging smile. 'I think there's a lookout in that direction. Let's take a look.'

Payton rushed ahead again and as Saxon and I followed at a more leisurely pace, I tried talking to him. I asked him about his friends, about school, what he'd got up to in the first week of the holidays, but it was like trying to draw blood from a stone.

I sighed as we reached the lookout and began climbing the stairs. I'd been determined to have a good week with my kids but three days of trying to communicate with this one and I was exhausted. Half an hour of wandering around the Pinnacles and it was clear Saxon felt as if I'd brought him to hell. It saddened me that he couldn't (or rather wouldn't) appreciate such an iconic part of Western Australia, but then again, he was a teenage boy—maybe I was expecting too much?

When Payton started to lose interest as well, I suggested we go have lunch at The Lobster Factory.

'Yuck.' She scrunched up her face and stuck out her tongue. 'I don't want to eat lobster.'

'I thought you didn't like seafood, Mum?' It was the longest non-argumentative sentence Saxon had said all week.

'As it happens, I've discovered it's not so bad.' When neither kid looked convinced, I added, 'Don't worry, I'm sure they'll have other stuff like burgers and chicken nuggets on the menu, and there's also a museum and a factory tour.'

Payton groused at the mention of the M-word, but I bribed her with the promise of seeing if we could steal Bindi for a couple of hours after her nap.

I was surprised by the size of The Lobster Factory and the number of cars in the car park, but it was school holidays and although we weren't huge fans of marine life, plenty of people were.

'See how popular it is,' I said, as the three of us climbed out of the car. 'It'll be great to learn a bit about the lobster industry and local history.'

Neither Payton nor Saxon responded as they walked ape-like towards the buildings. 'Apparently we can take a tour through the actual processing plant to see what happens to the lobster when it gets off the boats. Jedda said there's a really fascinating display about all the ships that have been wrecked off the coast.'

I was aware I was rambling; I didn't know who I was trying to convince—myself or the kids.

'Ugh, it stinks in here.' Payton used her fingers to peg her nose as we stepped inside.

'Shush,' I said as a young woman in a bright blue Lobster Factory shirt approached us.

'Welcome to The Lobster Factory.' She tipped her head, then clicked her fingers and exclaimed, 'You work at Brewed Awakening, right?'

I nodded. 'I'm Ashling.'

'Bronte,' she said, smiling back as she gestured to her badge. 'Are these your kids?'

'Yes. This is Saxon and this is Payton.'

'Welcome.' Bronte beamed but they barely managed to summon one smile between them. Somehow, I resisted the urge to kick them both. 'Since you're local, you get a discount. Are you guys here for lunch, the factory tour, or both?'

'Both, please, but lunch first.'

'Excellent and are you after a casual lunch or our fine dining experience?'

'Casual, please.' Fine dining and my children in their current moods would not a joyous lunch make.

Bronte led us to a table outside on the verandah that had an almost Californian beach feel to it. The tables and chairs were a rustic wood, each of them under a bright red umbrella, and we had a perfect view of the beach. Adjacent to the restaurant stood the processing plant and museum and right in front of us, a private jetty.

'Can I get you some drinks to start with?' Bronte asked.

We ordered three soft drinks—hey, it was school holidays and if Adrian could treat the kids, why shouldn't I? Two could play at the bribery game—and then Bronte left us to peruse the menu.

'You said there'd be nuggets,' Payton exclaimed loudly.

'And burgers,' Saxon added, for once aligning with his sister.

'I said there probably would be,' I replied, dismayed as I glanced down to notice there was only seafood on the menu. The closest thing to a nugget was a fish finger! 'Look, there's a vegetarian pasta. You could both have that.'

Saxon made a face, but Payton was too busy exclaiming over the large fish tank on display, in which a number of lobsters were ambling around. 'Oh my God! Are they alive? Are those what they feed people here? *Ew*. Why would anyone eat something that has been swimming only a few minutes earlier?'

'People like it fresh, stupid,' Saxon said, then immediately looked to me. 'Sorry. I'm sorry, Mum.'

Clearly their moment of alliance had passed. 'It's your sister you should be saying sorry to.'

He looked to Payton—'I'm sorry'—then back to me. 'But I actually meant I'm sorry for earlier. I know it wasn't your choice to separate or to come here and that you're just trying to do your best.'

I swallowed, not wanting to cry in public, but his words blindsided me. 'Thank you,' I whispered, reaching across and squeezing his hand just as Bronte returned to the table with our drinks. 'Ready to order yet?'

'I'm just having chips,' Payton declared.

'Me too.' Saxon pulled his phone out of his pocket, leaned back in his seat and began to play with it.

I swallowed and smiled at Bronte. 'Two servings of chips please and … I'll have the lobster linguine.'

When she retreated, I yanked the phone out of Saxon's hand.

'Hey!' He looked at me like I'd cut off his hand—so much for our reconciliation.

'No phones at the table,' I reminded him, dumping it in my handbag.

'Dad lets me,' he spat, crossing his arms over his chest.

'Is that right?'

'He only lets you because you refuse to come out of your room for dinner if he doesn't,' Payton said.

It sounded like my household was going to hell in a handbasket. What else was Adrian letting them get away with? 'Well, that's too bad because we're going to talk to each other, not text people who aren't even here.'

'I don't *text* my friends,' Sax said, his tone scathing.

'He uses Snapchat or TikTok ...' Payton said, adding a whole host of other things I assumed were social media apps.

'No, I don't. I talk to other gamers through *Tournament*.'

Thankfully, our lunches arrived before the kids could get into an all-out brawl but, despite my desire for conversation, we ate in near silence. Why was this so hard?

Knowing I was probably flogging a dead horse, once we'd finished eating, I insisted on heading into the processing plant to do the self-guided tour and look at the local history displays. I took solace in the fact Saxon showed a slight interest in the shipwrecks display, but we didn't last in the actual plant two minutes because Payton couldn't bear the smell.

'Can we *please* go back to the shack?' they both begged.

'Fine,' I snapped. 'Let's go.'

I left feeling even more disheartened than I had that morning. I hadn't even caught a glimpse of Dan, which if I was honest, I'd been hoping for. Now that he didn't need to go out to the island daily to feed Lion, I missed running into him on my morning walks and I hadn't yet had a chance to thank him for the possum house.

Back at the shack, I left Saxon to his own devices, while Payton and I took a walk along the beach to Jedda's cafe. Pity she didn't serve anything stronger than coffee.

We were almost there when we met Dan coming out of the post office.

'Well, isn't this a pleasant surprise?' Although he smiled, he didn't look his usual perky self.

Still, it was nice to talk to someone who wasn't glowering or whining at me. 'Hi,' I said, smiling back. 'I'd like you to meet my daughter, Payton.'

'Hi there.'

'Hello.' She looked at him suspiciously as he offered his hand but shook it nonetheless. 'How do you know my mum?'

'We're neighbours,' Dan replied, nonplussed.

She nodded then yanked my hand. 'Come on, let's go see Bindi.'

'You go ahead. I'll be there in a minute. Thank you so much for the gift,' I said to Dan as Payton skipped the few metres to the cafe.

'You're welcome. Hopefully your possum friend won't try to get back into the roof now.'

'I think it's working. I haven't heard a noise since you hung it up.'

Silence reigned a few minutes as we smiled awkwardly at each other.

'How are you feeling about ... you know? Have you made any decision about if you want to try and find out the truth?'

He let out a heavy breath. 'Funny you ask,' he said, then glanced around before lowering his voice. 'I confronted Stephen about it this morning. I didn't know I was going to until I did, but I told him again why I thought opening the island to the public was a good move for the town and would only draw more tourists to the area, not take away from the Factory, and asked again if he'd consider helping with funding.'

'I'm guessing his answer was no.'

'Yep. He flat out refused to even consider it, so I outright asked him if the reason he was so opposed was because Mum had an affair with Bill. If I was the result of that affair.'

He paused and I realised I'd been holding my breath. 'And?'

'And he flew into a rage. Said he'd always known he wasn't my father but that he never told Mum he knew because he wasn't going to let Bill win; he didn't plan on letting her go and leaving him with two little kids to look after. However, he said he couldn't be sure Bill was my father either, because my mother was a floozy, who as far as he knew would drop her pants for anyone when he wasn't around to keep her under control.'

'Wow.' I rested my hand on his arm in a show of comfort; I didn't believe anything of the sort about Dan's mum, but the fact his supposed father could say those things clearly hurt him. So much for Stephen Emerson being the good guy around town.

'What happened next?' The footpath was not the place for such a big conversation, and I didn't really have the time, but as I was the only other person besides Stephen and Dan that knew what was going on, I felt compelled to be there for him.

'We had words. Turns out you were right, Stephen doesn't want anyone to know the truth—nothing about doing what was right for me, all about saving face for him. He doesn't want to look like a laughing-stock for raising another man's child.'

'Plenty would think taking on a child that isn't biologically your own is a noble thing to do,' I said.

'Not the way he did it. Anyway, he told me if I pursued the issue, he'd cut me out of his will and sack me from the Factory.'

I honestly didn't know what to say.

'However, if I keep my mouth shut, not only will I keep my share of my inheritance, he'll also give the IPA whatever money we need to stabilise the castle and help me get the rest of the shire on side with any legalities.'

'He cares about his reputation that much?'

Dan nodded. 'Crazy, huh?'

'So, have you made a decision?' I reckoned a man as proud and horrible as Stephen Emerson clearly couldn't be trusted to keep such a promise after he died. What if Dan did as he asked and then he left him nothing anyway?

'Mum, hurry up!'

I glanced over to see Payton sticking her head out of the cafe.

I sighed and looked back to Dan, hating to leave him in the middle of such a big conversation. 'Sorry, I'm going to have to go. I've got my kids for another three days but then maybe we can catch up and talk more about this?'

'That would be awesome. Thanks. Good to see you're having fun with your family.'

I snorted in a most unladylike manner.

'You're not having a good time?'

'Not really.' I told him about the kids being bored, me trying to get us to do stuff together and our less-than-successful trip to the Pinnacles and The Lobster Factory. 'Saxon and I aren't getting along. I'm thinking maybe I should take them home early.'

Dan considered all this a moment. 'Do you think they'd like to come and have a bonfire on the island? I was thinking it would be a good way to get rid of some of the fallen tree branches and stuff.'

'What? At night?'

His lips quirked. 'That's generally the best time for bonfires.'

'Just the four of us?' I asked, wondering if that would be weird. How would the kids feel spending the evening with a man who wasn't their dad? Even if nothing was going on between me and Dan, it still might be too soon.

'We could ask the rest of the committee if they'd like to come out, bring their children as well? Max and Shanae have a girl about your son's age.'

'That'd be great. Maybe if they knew some other kids their own age here, they wouldn't hate the Point so much.'

'They *hate* the Point? That's tragic.' Dan placed a hand theatrically against his heart. 'Bonfire it is then. I'm not taking no for an answer—I'm going to make it my mission to convert Saxon and Payton before they leave.'

I loved that even though Dan was going through some pretty heavy stuff himself, he could still joke. Maybe the bonfire would also help distract him from his own woes.

We made arrangements to meet on the beach tomorrow afternoon and then I headed into the cafe. It was empty except for a couple of older women sitting at one of the tables, nattering over scones and tea.

'Who was that man?' Payton asked me accusingly. She was sitting in the playpen in the corner with Bindi. 'Is he your *boyfriend*?'

'What? No!' I felt my cheeks flare and turned my attention to Bindi, who giggled as she knocked over Payton's block tower. 'Hello, my sweet, fancy a paddle in the sea?'

Jedda groaned from where she was wiping down the counter and I abandoned the girls and went across to say hello. 'Busy day?'

She shrugged. 'Not too bad for a Tuesday. Are you still okay to work next Wednesday and Thursday?'

'Of course,' I said, knowing she was taking Bindi to Perth for an appointment.

Jedda smiled. 'Great, thanks. Can I get you a coffee?'

'Yes, please. I'm not sure I've ever needed one more.'

'Tough day, hey?' she said as she started working the coffee machine.

'You have no idea.' And I was quite prepared to tell her—Lord knew I needed to vent and perhaps get some unemotional advice about how to deal with Saxon going forward—but she lowered her voice and asked another question instead.

'Who did Payton think your boyfriend was?'

'Just Dan.'

Jedda's eyebrows crept upwards.

'What?'

'Rumour has it you've been spending quite a bit of time with dear Daniel.'

'I ... I ... what?'

'Apparently you went to his place last Saturday night with a bottle of wine. No one saw you return to the shack.'

At the expression on my face, Jedda laughed—it was more like a cackle. 'Oh girlfriend, haven't you learnt that nothing goes unnoticed in a small town.'

'Mrs Fine,' I said with a sigh.

Jedda nodded. 'Never mind about that old busybody, I'm more concerned about the fact you didn't mention this date to me. I thought we were friends.'

'We are. And it wasn't a date. I *returned*, but Audrey was probably in bed by the time I did. There isn't anything to tell. We got together to plan a fundraiser for the island, that's all.'

Jedda passed me my coffee. 'So, what did you decide?'

'Um ...' I swallowed. 'We didn't actually get around to talking about that.'

She gave me a look. 'What exactly *did* you get up to?'

'We just talked. It was nice. He's been through a divorce—he understands how I'm feeling. We're just friends.'

'Whatever you say. But you know, you could do a lot worse than Dan Emerson. I'm not a fan of his family as a whole, but he seems a good sort.'

'I agree,' I said, 'but I'm not interested in a new relationship. Not yet. Maybe not ever. You do fine on your own, don't you?'

44

While Dan didn't exactly make Ragged Point converts of Payton and Saxon, he did help make their last couple of days bearable, starting with the bonfire. Payton made friends with two boys and a girl who were of similar age, and Saxon seemed to get on well with Max and Shanae's daughter, Jana. Aside from while they were munching on sausages and later roasting marshmallows over the bonfire, we barely saw the children. They were given clear instructions to stay away from the castle and the other collapsed buildings, but the island was big enough that they had plenty of other areas to explore.

I must admit to feeling nervous at first—especially about the four younger kids wandering off on their own where there was easy access to water and who knows what other dangerous but inviting elements of nature. However, the other parents assured me they'd be fine and after a while I began to relax and enjoy the adult conversation. Before the bonfire, we spoke mostly about island business. In addition to getting the buildings up to scratch and having a display of Bill's memorabilia, the committee had plans to set up barbeques and build a proper toilet block so people could come over and spend the day here. Ideas were bandied around about a possible fundraiser, most of them dismissed as unoriginal or not having the potential to raise enough funds.

'What about an island-themed ball?' I suggested. It probably wasn't very original either, but the alcohol in my veins gave me courage to put it forward.

Everyone was silent a moment and then exploded at once with enthusiasm.

'That's a great idea,' said a woman called Davina. 'I saw this gorgeous gown online the other day and that would give me the perfect excuse to buy it.'

Her partner groaned. 'Does a ball mean we'll have to dress up in suits?'

'Come on, Gav,' Dan teased. 'I reckon you'd scrub up quite well.'

I couldn't help thinking Dan would as well.

'And,' he added, 'we know how excited everyone around here gets about dressing up.'

'I love it.' Sophie clapped her hands together. 'We need to set a date and find a venue. If we're going to do it this year, we need to get a move on.'

'Town hall?' suggested Gav.

'Music?' Sophie added.

'What about your band?' Davina said.

Sophie grinned. 'If you guys would have us, I'm sure the others would come on board. And I reckon I can twist their arms to do it for free since it's such a good cause. What about food?'

The next half hour was spent throwing ideas around and when the kids returned, demanding it was time for the marshmallows, we were all mega excited and had even set a tentative date for the ball in the spring.

Once the marshmallows had all been scoffed, the kids and teens wandered down to the shore, leaving the adults alone. Dan sat next to me on the ground and while those around us grew louder the more they drank, we sipped our beers more slowly and talked in whispered voices.

He surprised me when he said he'd been reading my blog. 'It's really good. Even though you're writing about a female experience and I don't have kids, I can relate to a lot of what you feel, but it also made me laugh. I like your self-deprecating tone.'

'I can't believe you read it!' My cheeks burned and it wasn't because I was close to the fire.

'I didn't only read it, I subscribed. I can't wait to read what you publish next.'

'Oh my God—you're BeachBoy77?'

He gave me a sheepish smile. 'Pretty unoriginal username—I thought you might have guessed.'

I laughed, unable to believe that while I'd been lying in bed late at night pondering the letters and the mystery of his possible father, he'd been thinking about me. I'd noticed one new subscriber—bringing the grand total to three, including Hayley and Jedda—and had been stoked to have caught the interest of someone who didn't know me. Turns out I hadn't, but that didn't stop the buzz that came with Dan's admission.

'Now I'm going to second-guess everything I write.'

'Don't,' he said. 'Keep doing exactly what you're doing.'

I wanted desperately to ask him about the whole Bill-Stephen thing again, but didn't want to risk anyone else overhearing, however when Dan suggested we go for a walk to check on the kids, I couldn't resist.

We took our sweet time walking down to the ocean and occasionally Dan's hand swinging by my side would brush against mine and send a shiver of something pleasurable but also terrifying through my body. I had this ridiculous urge to grab hold of it, but if Dan had similar thoughts, he didn't act on them. Perhaps it was because we weren't entirely alone or maybe he meant it when he said he simply wanted to be friends; either way I wasn't sure if I was disappointed or relieved.

No matter how much my head said now wasn't the right time to get entangled with another man, especially not one with the kind of baggage Dan was currently dealing with, my attraction grew every time we were together. And I found my mind drifting to him often even when we weren't and every time it did, something deep inside me tingled. Of course, I wondered if this was simply because I hadn't felt the touch of *any* man in months. The last couple of years, I'd barely been able to raise any enthusiasm for sex and now suddenly I was thinking about it as much as a teenage boy—perhaps it was a case of wanting what you couldn't have.

To try and divert my unsettling thoughts, I apologised for the interruption of our conversation yesterday and added, 'I guess since you're letting everyone get excited about fundraising, it means you haven't decided to accept Stephen's deal?'

'Hell no.' He shook his head. 'I refuse to be bought or bribed. His stupid ultimatum has only made me more determined. Not only am I going to do whatever I can to find out if Bill was my father, I'm going to keep pursuing public access to the island and I'm also going to run for shire president at the end of the year, try and wrench control of this town off Stephen. I can't be the only one tired of him calling all the shots.'

'That's great.' With his passion for Ragged Point and its people he'd make a great president. 'I'm not sure I can vote, not being an official resident or anything, but you've got my support in any other way I can help.'

'Thanks. That means a lot.' Dan reached out, took my hand, gave it a quick squeeze and dropped it so fast again that I almost thought I imagined it.

'If he'd been a good father,' he continued, 'maybe I'd feel like I owe something to him, but the only person I feel like I owe anything to is me ... and I'm curious. I'm going to contact the police and see what they can do about cross-testing me and Bill. I doubt I'll ever be able to find out who he really was, but at least if I can prove I'm his son, maybe they'll release him to me and let me give him a proper funeral.'

I nodded, hoping this was the case, but unsure what would happen since Bill's identity would still be a mystery.

'I've been thinking about this a bit,' I began. 'Maybe you could do a DNA test?'

'What do you mean? Isn't that what the police will do?'

'No, I'm not talking about a test to find out if Bill is your father, but one to try and find out where he came from. Who he was.'

Dan blinked. 'I'm not following.'

'Surely you've heard of amateur genealogists testing their DNA to research their family trees.'

'Yeah, sure. The ads are always flashing up on Facebook when I'm trying to update the Factory's social media.'

'It could be a long shot, but maybe if you do one of those tests, you might find someone who is related to Bill?'

His eyes gaped at the possibility. 'You think?'

'Yes. One of Payton's friend's mums who was adopted as a baby found her biological family that way.'

'You're a fucking genius.' He grinned at me. 'I'm going online to order a kit tonight.'

I smiled at his enthusiasm, only hoping I hadn't got his hopes up.

Sadly, eventually the evening came to an end, but even Sax had to admit he'd had a good time, although perhaps that was as much to do with the fact that Dan had offered his wi-fi anytime he wanted it over his last couple of days in the Point.

Everyone packed up their things, made sure the bonfire was thoroughly extinguished and then piled into the boats. The look on Payton's face when Dan let her have a turn steering back to the shore made my heart swell.

Two days later I drove my children back to Perth feeling far more affectionate towards them than I had midweek. Yet I had to admit that things had changed. The thought of returning to the Point and not seeing them for another week didn't bring quite the same pang to my heart it originally had.

For the first time I could remember, I had somewhere else that had also begun to feel like home.

45

Perth

A week later, after another busy, productive and very enjoyable stint in Ragged Point, I left early, arriving in Perth just after 10 am. Despite the fact the weather had cooled over the last couple of weeks, I didn't want to leave Charlie in the car while I did a grocery shop, so I swung by the house to drop him off first.

Dragging my suitcase behind me, I unlocked the front door and let him rush ahead to reacquaint himself with the lay of the land.

'What the hell!' I exclaimed as I stepped into the house behind him. I almost tripped over Payton's sports bag in the hallway and that was only the beginning of the wreckage. I'd always prided myself on keeping a neat home, but this place was barely recognisable as anywhere I'd ever lived. There was mess everywhere—shoes and what looked to be dirty clothes strewn on the hallway floor, soft drink cans and empty water bottles, and when I went into the kitchen there were plates stacked in the sink and a carton of milk left open on the bench. Bits of cereal and other near unidentifiable foods were scattered across the benchtop. I lifted the milk to my nose and sniffed—ugh—then immediately went to throw it in the rubbish bin. I opened the cupboard, only to find the bin already overflowing with takeaway containers—I guess Adrian's resolve to feed everyone properly had crumbled.

I slammed the door shut before Charlie could start on it, then stalked through the rest of the house.

The kids' rooms both looked like they'd exploded. I couldn't see the floor in either of them and the stench emanating from Saxon's bed had me suspecting the sheets hadn't been changed in weeks. Their bathroom smelled horrendous and it looked like they'd been using paper towels to wipe their butts. Although Adrian had stripped our 'marital' bed of his sheets, he hadn't remade them with mine, which was our deal, and there were two empty beer bottles on his bedside table—so much for not drinking during his weeks. I felt my blood rise to boiling temperature as I went into the ensuite to find toothpaste stains and whiskers in the sink. *Ugh.* The toilet looked as if it hadn't been wiped down in the three weeks I'd been away. At least I knew there was no way Adrian could have brought a woman here—no female in their right mind would put up with this—but what the hell had happened to his cleaner?

Whereas a couple of months ago I'd have been smug about the fact that Adrian was clearly struggling to maintain our agreed upon standards and hopeful it would help him see the error of his ways, now it only put me in a mood. Our nest-parenting arrangement wouldn't work unless we both kept up with our side of the agreement. He couldn't have women on the side but still expect me to keep house. That was *not* part of our deal.

But what was I supposed to do? If anyone dropped by and saw how the kids had been living, they were liable to call child services. The way I saw it, I had two options—I could either call Adrian and demand he come and make the house presentable or I could do it myself. Neither speaking to him nor seeing him appealed and I'd always found cleaning relaxing, but I had better things to do with my days now. In addition to spending quality time with my kids, I had blog posts to write and also planned on starting to solicit sponsors for the ball.

A third option popped into my head—I could do the absolute bare minimum to make the house liveable for me and the children but leave it almost as bad as I found it.

I shuddered at the thought—no way could I live in this pigsty—as a fourth option struck and a smile sprung on my lips. I could hire a cleaner myself and send Adrian the bill. That'd teach him. It was bad enough doing the lion's share of the housework when you were married to someone, but no way was I going to pick up after him now!

After scouring the internet for a cleaner who could come at such short notice, I did what all women with regular help do. I'd always laughed at my friends who tidied for the cleaner, but there was no way I could expect anyone to attack this mess without at least picking up the rubbish. With Charlie following behind me, I filled three massive bin bags with debris from the kids' bedrooms, my bedroom and living areas, then started on the kitchen. I had déjà vu from when I'd first started clearing out the shack.

By the time I picked Payton up from school, I swear steam was shooting from my ears. So far, I'd written about fifty sarcastic notes to leave for Adrian when I went back to the Point next week. The one for the kitchen bin was my favourite: *If you can't fit anything else in me, it's time to take me outside.*

I was too late to wait in the Kiss and Drive, so I had to park and go into the grounds, something I'd been avoiding for months because I couldn't stand the pity or nosiness of the other mums.

'Ashling,' a few of them shrieked in unison as I approached the classroom. Hugs were exchanged as they made gushing noises about how lovely it was to see me again.

'Looks like single life is treating you well,' pondered Liza, a mother of twin boys—joint class clowns—who always looked like she could do with a good night's sleep. 'You look fantastic.'

'Thanks,' I said, thinking my cheeks were probably still pink from my Adrian-directed rage.

'Or have you lost weight because you're stressed?' Melissa Diamond threw me a synthetic smile—she was one of those people who simply couldn't bring herself to compliment others, but I was not going to give her the joy of making me feel bad about myself.

'*Stressed?* I haven't felt this good in years.'

And this was true, in most ways. With each day that passed—and each moment I spent in Ragged Point—I felt less emotional, less of a failure and more positive about myself and the future. That had a lot to do with the friendships I'd made. People I hadn't even known last year had now become my lifelines, and my new lifestyle was also healthier. Last week I'd gone to Pilates at the town hall twice with Jedda and Gail, and every morning I rose early and welcomed the sun with Charlie as we walked along the beach. There was something about starting the day with sand running through my toes, fresh air pumping through my lungs and the backdrop of the shimmering ocean that never failed to put a smile on my face. More than once Dan had joined us, and the days he didn't Charlie missed him, drooping his tail and glancing longingly up at the glass mansion when we passed by.

I won't lie—my dog wasn't the only one who enjoyed Dan's company. We got along so well it felt like we'd known each other much longer and conversation was effortless. Talking about our family issues meant we had plenty to discuss, even if we hadn't had the island fundraiser to plan as well. The DNA test kit that he'd ordered had arrived last Monday. He'd spat into the tube, sent it back almost immediately, and was now waiting impatiently for the results. I only hoped they would give him some kind of answer.

'Oh really?' Melissa didn't sound convinced about my stress levels.

Understandably everyone was curious about how I'd been coping and desperate for gossip about how things were between Adrian and me. Some of them seemed disappointed to hear how well the nest-parenting arrangement was working—there was no excitement in success and good news.

'Isn't it weird living in a house with your ex-husband?'

It was the first time I didn't flinch at the term 'ex', which definitely counted as progress. 'We don't *live* in the same house together—we take turns and there are strict rules we're following.'

Obviously, I didn't mention the mess I'd come home to, the beers on the bedside table or the major rule Adrian had broken when he'd had sex with someone else in our bed. Overall the nest arrangement *was* working better than I'd imagined.

My mum friends had many other questions. How were the kids coping? Were either of us seeing other people yet? What were we going to do if one of us got into another serious relationship? Would the nest-parenting situation be a permanent thing?

'We're taking things day by day and week by week at the moment, but the prime focus for both of us is making sure Saxon and Payton's lives are disrupted as little as possible.'

Although Adrian was clearly seeing other women, jumping into any kind of commitment would cramp his new-found freedom, so I didn't think worrying about how such a thing would affect our custody arrangement was something I needed to concern myself with just yet.

'What are you doing with yourself on the weeks you're not with the kids?' asked Liza, her tone slightly accusatory.

'I'm keeping busy. I've got a casual job in a cafe and I'm also working on a newspaper. I'm loving it. I'd forgotten how good it feels to be doing something for *me*.'

'You sound like a new woman,' Liza said wistfully as the siren sounded.

I smiled as the classroom door opened and children spilled out, putting an end to the interrogation. Facing the other mums hadn't actually been as bad as I'd imagined.

I opened my arms wide so Payton could run into them, but she barely gave me a hug before pulling away. 'I'm starving. What's for afternoon tea?'

And I missed you too, I thought, trying not to show my hurt that she seemed more interested in food than seeing me.

'I was thinking of making pumpkin scones,' I said with a smile.

Payton hesitated a moment as if considering whether this was to her satisfaction and then shrugged. 'Okay.'

As we started to the car, I asked her how her day had been and was relieved when her mouth ran off like normal. 'We have to do a personal learning project and I'm going to write a biography of Sam Kerr. Dad said you'd be able to find the photo he took of us when she signed my T-shirt at the game last year?'

'Of course, and that sounds like your perfect project.'

I wondered why Adrian, who probably still had the photo on his phone, couldn't find it himself, but then again, in the past he'd never had to because I'd always managed this kind of thing. I certainly wouldn't make that mistake again if I ever entered into another relationship.

Payton talked all the way home, barely even pausing when eating her afternoon tea. She did however admit that, no matter how much she enjoyed the processed snacks Adrian provided, my fresh-out-the-oven scones were far superior to anything he could buy.

Call me petty, but I couldn't help but glow at the praise.

Sadly, however, my smugness was short-lived and within hours of being back with my kids, I was reminded that single parenting was *not* for the faint-hearted.

46

Friday evening, when Saxon had retreated to his room and Payton was watching replays of the last World Cup on YouTube, the doorbell rang. I was delighted to find Hayley standing on the front porch. Between my weeks in the Point and her relationship with Wei, I hadn't seen her as much as I usually did.

'Hello,' I shrieked, dragging her into the house, happy for some adult company. 'Long time no see.'

'I know. I've missed you,' she said, holding up a bottle of sav blanc and then giving me a quick hug. 'We're long overdue for a drink.'

I eyed the wine in her hand with lustful yearning—nothing appealed to me more than alcohol right now. 'I'm not supposed to be drinking during my week at home.'

The expression on Hayley's face told me exactly what she thought of that. 'It's Friday night. What Adrian doesn't know won't hurt him and surely one glass won't do any harm?'

I thought of the beer bottles I'd found on Adrian's bedside table—why should he be the one having all the fun? Besides, it was unlikely Saxon would emerge from his bedroom again and Payton was so glued to the soccer she wouldn't notice if the house caught fire. Not to mention the fact that unlike my ex, I'd be sure to cover my tracks.

Arm well and truly twisted, I led Hayley into the kitchen, grabbed two glasses from the cupboard and together we sat perched on stools at the breakfast bar.

'So, how's things?' she asked, twisting the stem of her wineglass between her fingers.

I took a sip from mine and almost moaned in satisfaction. It felt like years since the last glass of wine I'd had with Jedda on Sunday night.

'Exhausting,' I admitted. 'I'd been so looking forward to coming home but arrived to an absolute mess and I've spent all week nagging the kids to do homework, eat their vegetables and stop bickering. Not to mention the words I had with Adrian.'

'What do you mean? I thought with this arrangement you guys barely spoke.'

'Emails and the odd text message have sufficed the last few weeks, but he called me the other day because I took "unapproved" money out of the podiatry account for a cleaner to tidy up his mess.'

Since my splurge for shoes on our joint credit card—and hadn't *that* been a fun conversation—we'd started to divide our finances and no longer shared any accounts, except the clinic ones, which because they were part of a family trust business would take longer to settle. The money I was earning at Brewed went into my brand-spanking new personal savings account. No way I was spending any of it on *his* mess.

'Ooh.' Hayley's eyes sparkled. 'What did my brother dearest have to say about that?'

I relayed our phone conversation to her word for word:

'Who is Handy House Inc and what on earth have you paid them three hundred dollars for?'

'They're a cleaning company I had come over to annihilate the mess you left me.'

'You can't just take money from the work account for household bills.'

'Fine. Then next time don't leave the house in such a state that I have no other choice. That wasn't part of our deal.'

I'd braced myself for an argument but got a surprising apology instead. Adrian sounded super stressed. 'I promise I'll do better next time. My cleaner fell through and I haven't had a chance to get another one.'

'Okay,' I said, wondering if she'd quit because Adrian didn't know the rule about cleaning for the cleaner. 'Good. And while we're talking, you need to make sure the kids' clothes are washed properly too. Saxon stunk when he came home from school on Monday. He's a teenage boy—sometimes you need to remind him to take a shower. And also, how many nights did you feed them takeaway? The whole thing about two fruit and five veg isn't just a catchy phrase, you know.'

'Calm down,' he interrupted. 'I had a busy couple of weeks and things got on top of me. It's okay for you, you're not trying to hold down a full-time job as well as look after the house and children. Taking care of them—cleaning, cooking, washing, trying to help with homework—is a full-time job.'

By this stage, Hayley was laughing uncontrollably. 'He said that? As if it was news to you?'

I nodded and smiled too; it was easy to find the humour in hindsight. 'A full-time job he never showed any appreciation for me doing!'

'How did you respond?'

'I told him he didn't need to do it all by himself, that Saxon and Payton are old enough to take on some household responsibility themselves and that we *both* need to encourage them to do so.'

Hayley was disappointed I hadn't totally given her brother what for, but I'd reined myself in, thinking of the kids. My lawyer had warned me how often separations became acrimonious—as if I didn't remember firsthand—and getting into a war with Adrian wouldn't be good for anyone. If we wanted this to succeed, we needed to work together while being apart.

'So, do you think …' Hayley began, 'now that your separation is definitely permanent, you'll continue with the current custody arrangement?'

I took another gulp of wine. 'We're still settling into the situation—Adrian, me, the kids, we all have some adjusting to do—but, as much as I hate to agree with him, I do believe this is the least disruptive for Sax and Payton long term.'

Not to mention the fact I'd come to love my weeks in Ragged Point.

Although a couple of months ago I'd wanted to chop off my own hands at the thought of spending every second week without my kids, I'd discovered that being a single parent wasn't a walk in the park, no matter whether you had another full-time job or not, and I relished the break between shifts. For the first time in as long as I could remember I had me-time.

Pushing this selfish thought aside, I added, 'I never wanted my children to have to deal with a divorce, so the least I can do is make their experience better than mine was. I hated moving from house to house.'

Hayley gave me a sympathetic smile. 'Anyway, what's the latest on the shack? Got any more photos?'

I showed her some and she was impressed by my progress.

'I've just started gutting the kitchen so the new cabinets can be installed.'

'Your eyes light up when you talk about Ragged Point.'

I shrugged. 'It's a special place.' I went to take another sip of my wine only to discover it was empty. Grabbing the bottle, I was about to top Hayley's glass up and frowned. I'd guzzled a whole glass but she hadn't even touched hers. 'Are you okay?' I asked, suddenly worried.

She glanced around and then replied in a near whisper. 'I'm pregnant.'

I blinked, not sure if I'd heard properly. 'Did you just say you're pregnant?'

Hayley nodded.

'Oh my God!' My hand rushed to my mouth. 'Why did you bring over the wine then?'

'Habit.'

I took a deep breath and refilled my glass. It might not be very kind to drink in front of someone who couldn't, but I was in shock and now it looked like I was solely responsible for not letting good grog go to waste.

'Wow,' I said after a pregnant—no pun intended—pause. Hayley had always been a fabulous aunt but she'd never ever made any murmurings about the ticking of her own biological clock. In fact, she'd always professed she didn't want children. 'Are you keeping it?'

She nodded slowly. 'I think so. I know it's not environmentally friendly to add another mouth to the planet, and ...' She placed a hand on her stomach and her eyes grew shiny. 'I thought if I tested positive I'd be devastated, but I found myself anything but. It's a shock to me as much as it is to you, but I want this baby, more than I've ever wanted anything. It feels like it's meant to be.'

Thanks to her heartfelt words, she wasn't the only one with misty eyes. I reached across the table and squeezed her hand. 'Congratulations. I'm so happy for you guys. I bet Wei's excited.'

'Um …' A shadow fell over her expression. 'I haven't exactly told him yet.'

'I see.' I paused a moment, still taking it all in. 'Are you worried he might not share your desire to have it? Or …' It suddenly all made perfect sense. 'You were ready to dump him but now because of the baby, you'll be linked with him forever?'

'What? No.' She shook her head furiously. 'That's definitely not it. I've never felt about anyone the way I do about Wei—we have so much fun together and we talk too. It's not just about sex like it's always been with everyone else. He's the longest relationship I've ever had, but ever since our second week together, I've been living in terrible fear that he'll get bored and dump *me*.'

'What?' I couldn't believe this—oh how the tables had turned. I'd never heard Hayley sound so vulnerable and her confession sparked guilt in my heart. I'd been so hung up on my own woes I'd had no idea she'd been feeling this way. 'How could anyone ever get bored of you?'

Although I absolutely meant this, Hayley shrugged. 'I'm shit-scared that when I tell him about the baby, he'll tell me he's not ready and then I'll lose him. That thought is unbearable, and not just because I know how hard being a single mum would be.'

I could hardly argue that point when I'd just spent the past half hour unloading on her about my shitty week of parenting alone—why oh why hadn't she come right out and told me her news straightaway? I was about to remind her that no matter how difficult they could be Saxon and Payton were still the best things in my life, when she added, 'But that's not the worst possibility.'

'Oh?'

'My biggest fear is that once I tell Wei he'll feel obliged to stay with me because of the baby. As much as I don't relish the idea of raising a child alone, even worse would be for him to feel trapped. Look what ...'

Hayley snapped her mouth shut but I knew immediately what she'd been about to say. Babies changed things—getting pregnant had meant Adrian and I were linked forever and look how that had ended. But Hayley was my age; if she wanted to have children, she couldn't afford to let this opportunity go.

'You're not stupid, Hayls,' I said, 'but you can't try and guess how Wei will feel about this. You need to talk to him and be totally honest. When you tell him you're pregnant, his initial reaction will tell you exactly how he feels.'

'But what if I don't like what I see?'

I swallowed. 'Then you'll come straight back here, and we'll commiserate over choc-mint ice-cream.' (Her favourite.) 'But if you don't tell him, you'll drive yourself crazy and sooner or later, he'll work it out for himself.'

'You're right. I guess there's no time like the present.' Hayley pushed to a stand. 'Thanks, Ash, I don't know what I'd do without you.'

'The feeling's mutual,' I told her as I walked her to the front door, hugged her tightly and then watched her drive off into the night.

I'm pleased to report I didn't see my sister-in-law again that night.

47

Ragged Point

'Fancy meeting you here.'

I jumped at the sound of Dan's voice and whirled around to find him standing almost immediately behind me in the aisle of the general store. 'You almost gave me a heart attack.'

He winked. 'Lucky I know mouth-to-mouth.'

I felt a jolt inside my stomach at his words. Was he flirting with me? I could never quite tell where Dan was concerned, and I didn't know how I'd feel if he was. My body said one thing and my brain said another. My heart had no idea how it felt.

'Haha.' I tried not to sound affected at all. 'Shouldn't you be at work?'

'I'm on my lunch break. Lion wasn't great this morning, he's off his food again, so I came to buy something different.' He gestured to the basket in his hand that held lots of little tins—looked to be one of every variety the general store stocked.

'Oh, no,' I said. 'Do you think you should take him to the vet?'

'We went on Friday, and she couldn't find anything physically wrong. She said she thinks he's just getting old and probably feeling unsettled not being on the island. Maybe I should take him back?' Dan shrugged. 'Anyway, how was your week in Perth?'

'Not bad.' I wasn't about to unload my problems with Adrian and the battles I'd had with the kids. 'I got some exciting news though. My sister-in-law's pregnant.'

The moment the words were out I thought maybe they were insensitive considering his inability to have children, but he seemed genuine in his reply. 'Wow, that's fantastic. Congratulations.'

'Oh no.' I slapped my hand over my mouth. 'I don't think I'm supposed to be telling anyone yet.'

Dan pretended to zip his lips. 'It's okay, your secret's safe with me. I'm like a vault. And I'm also quite partial to farfalle.'

'Huh?'

He gestured behind me to what happened to be the pasta section. 'The bow-shaped variety. I figured since you owed me dinner, you might like to know my tastes.'

'I owe you dinner?'

'Sure do. After you inhaled my very delicious linguine, you said it was your turn to cook next. Then again, I'll be happy with anything. Doesn't have to be pasta.'

'We might have to take a raincheck,' I said, genuinely disappointed. 'My kitchen isn't really set up for making fancy meals at the moment. It's smack-bang in the middle of major renovations.'

'It doesn't have to be fancy.'

I chuckled. 'I don't even have an oven. Everything has been ripped out ready for the new cupboards. I'll be living off microwave meals for the next while.'

'Ugh.' Dan made a face as if I'd just announced mud pies for dinner. 'You could always use my kitchen.'

'You have an answer for everything, don't you?'

'You didn't think I was going to let you off the hook? And it just so happens I'm free this evening. What time should I expect you and your culinary skills?'

'I can't tonight. I'm helping Jedda with the layout of the next edition of the *Reporter*.'

'Dammit.' He clicked his fingers. 'If I wasn't such a self-assured, cocky kinda guy, I'd think you didn't want to have dinner with me.'

As he spoke, a lock of sun-kissed hair fell across his face. I resisted the urge to reach up and tuck it behind his ear. If he were Saxon, I'd have told him he needed to get a haircut, but I had to admit, the scruffy, slightly too long style suited him. In fact, he really was a lot better looking than I'd initially given him credit for.

'What about tomorrow?' I asked, before I could think better of it. There was no need to stress about dinner between friends. And it would be the perfect opportunity to catch him up on all the sponsors I'd already managed to secure for the ball, before our committee meeting Thursday night.

He pretended to consider my offer a few moments. 'I do believe I have a vacancy in my busy social calendar.'

I laughed. 'Isn't that lucky.'

'What time should I expect you?'

'How's six o'clock?'

'Perfect. See you then.' And with that, he turned and sauntered down the aisle towards the checkout, leaving me standing there trying to work out what the hell I was going to cook.

Seven hours later I sat in Jedda's office helping her collate the *Reporter* and was still no closer to making a decision.

'What about chicken curry? Or maybe stir-fry?'

'For someone who alleges this is only dinner between friends, practically a business meeting, you seem to be worrying an awful lot about tomorrow night.'

Her teasing tone almost made me regret asking her opinion. 'I want to cook something nice, but I don't want to go too over-the-top in case I give Dan the wrong idea.'

'And what idea would that be? That you'd like to bonk his brains out?'

'Jedda! Don't be ridiculous.' But my temperature soared. I'd be lying if I said the idea hadn't crossed my mind. Dan was hot, but this was all so new to me and we were both neck-deep in drama. 'I'll admit I enjoy his company, but I'm not planning on rushing into another relationship.'

'Who said anything about a relationship?' Jedda said. 'But you don't have to become a nun. Dan's not stupid, I'm sure he'd understand you wouldn't want to rush into anything serious so soon after your marriage ended. Stop stressing so much and just have fun.'

Fun? This was all too weird. I couldn't believe this was my life we were discussing. It was almost as if I'd stepped into a parallel reality. Maybe in the real world I was still happily married to Adrian. Maybe I was in a coma and this was all a dream.

'Okay. You're right.' I nodded, inhaling what I hoped would be a calming breath. 'And anyway, I could be worrying over nothing. Who says he wants to sleep with me? We've spent a fair bit of time together since the cyclone and, so far, he's been the perfect gentleman.'

Jedda snorted at this. 'Oh, he wants to sleep with you all right. I've seen the way he looks at you when he comes to buy his coffee.'

Something inside me glowed at her words, yet at the same time, I squirmed. 'Do you think it's too late to go to Jurien and get a bikini wax?'

Once again, Jedda howled with laughter.

When she finally calmed down, she said, 'Personally, I'm against grooming for anyone but myself, but I don't think you need to worry anyway. If you let Dan inside your knickers, the last thing he'll care about is if you're a little overgrown. Trust me. Now, what about risotto?'

48

Carrying ingredients for a portobello mushroom risotto, I knocked on Dan's door just before six. I was starting to think he wasn't home when the door finally opened.

'Oh shit.' He glanced down at the bags and then back up to meet my gaze. 'I'm sorry. I totally forgot you were coming.'

Geez, way to make a girl feel good. This thought had barely entered my head when I noticed he didn't look himself. His eyes were bloodshot, the skin around them puffy and he sounded blocked up.

He was either sick or something awful had happened. As far as I knew he'd only spoken to Stephen about his suspicions, but maybe he'd confided today in Gemma and Ben and it hadn't gone well. 'What's wrong?'

He sniffed—was he fighting emotion or a cold? 'It's Lion. He's gone.'

'You mean he's run away? Or did you take him back to the island?' Yet, even as these questions spilled from my lips, reality dawned. 'Oh my God. No.'

'He hadn't eaten and had been sleeping all day, so I've been watching him closely ... He passed away about ten minutes ago.'

I dropped the bags to the floor, stepped into the house and wrapped my arms around him. 'I'm so sorry.'

I knew how much the cat meant to Dan. He was his last link to Bill. We stood there for what felt like forever, holding each other.

Finally, he pulled back. 'Thanks. Look, I know I badgered you into dinner, but ...' He frowned and ran a hand through his hair. 'I don't think I'm going to be very good company and I need to ... I need to deal with Lion. Do you mind if we reschedule?'

'Are you going to bury him tonight?'

'Yeah. I'm gunna take him across to the island.'

'Shouldn't you wait until morning?'

'No. I want to put him next to Bill's memorial; I won't be able to rest until I do.'

There was no logic in grief and no point arguing with him, but no way was I letting him bury Bill's cat alone. 'Then I'm coming with you.'

'You don't have to do that.'

'I *want* to.'

'Thank you,' Dan said. 'Lion's this way,' he added, nodding towards the living room. He picked up the bags at our feet, carried them into the kitchen and shoved everything into the fridge.

I followed him to where Lion lay peacefully on the couch. If I didn't know any better, I'd think he was asleep. Emotion clogged in my throat.

'He just slipped away. It took me a while to realise he was actually gone.' Dan let out a choked chuckle and I looked up to see tears in his eyes. 'Damn animal. He's turned me into a sook.'

I squeezed his arm. 'Losing a pet is like losing family or a very close friend. It's okay to be sad. I'll be a mess when Charlie goes.'

'Yeah, but Lion wasn't even my cat.' He smiled sadly. 'Come on, if you're sure, let's do this.'

Dan fetched us both heavy waterproof jackets—I briefly wondered if mine had belonged to Tessa—before wrapping Lion's lifeless body tenderly in a blanket. We sat in the boat in solemn but not uncomfortable silence, me holding the lifeless bundle close to my chest, as we shot across to the island.

I'd visited Bill's island three times now and tonight was the first time it felt eerie. Except for the gentle wash of waves on the sand and the wind whispering through the remaining trees, it was silent, but I didn't feel scared or unsafe. Not with Dan.

I couldn't believe we'd only known each other a matter of months. Perhaps we'd met before in another life. I'd never believed in reincarnation, but I'd also never felt such an intense connection to someone in such a short amount of time. An intense connection that only grew stronger each time we were together.

Shining a torch ahead, Dan led us inland to fetch a shovel from Bill's supplies, then we made our way to the memorial site.

'They'll be glad to finally be together again,' he said with a sigh as he started to dig.

Thanks to the moonlight and the torch I aimed in his direction, I had a great view of Dan shovelling dirt and found myself admiring his impressive masculine form.

What the hell are you doing?

I snapped my eyes away, chastising myself. The man was digging a grave!

When he finished, Dan dropped the shovel to the dirt and turned towards me. Our hands brushed against each other as I passed the cat to him and our gazes met with such intensity that, for a second, I thought he might kiss me. Everything inside me stilled, but of course I was the only one thinking such ridiculous thoughts at a time like this.

The moment broken, Dan stooped to lower Lion into the ground and I exhaled deeply. He reached out and stroked his hand over the cat's now cold fur. 'Goodbye little guy, say hi to Bill for me.' Then he covered Lion with the blanket before reaching once again for the shovel.

'Do you want to say a few words?' I asked, when he finished smoothing out the dirt.

He looked at me like I was crazy.

'It might help to talk about him.'

Dan managed a slight smile and cleared his throat. 'Lion, you were a good cat and you had a good innings. Thanks for keeping me company since Bill died. I hope there's lots of good fish in the afterlife. Rest in peace, you mad feline.'

I stepped up next to him. 'Yes, rest in peace, Lion.'

We stood in silence, both of us gazing down at the makeshift grave, the moonlight flickering above us. Dan slipped his hand into mine and my heart hitched a beat.

'Thank you for coming with me,' he said after a few moments. 'For being here.'

'I'm glad I am,' I whispered.

Another extended silence followed and then, 'Do you want a drink?'

'Here?'

He nodded and snuck his free hand inside his jacket, pulling out a small bottle. 'That's if you're not in a rush. Maybe you're hungry?'

'Let's have a drink. I'd like that.'

He kept a hold of my hand as we walked down to the beach and sat on the sand, not far from where the boat was moored. Dan unscrewed the lid and handed me the flask and I took a sip, making a face as the whisky burned the back of my throat.

He chuckled, took it from me and swigged. 'So, what were you going to cook for me this evening?'

'Risotto. If it's not too late, I can still make it when we go back.'

'Sounds good.' He shifted a little closer and once again offered me the bottle.

As we drank, we talked. About everything. The island—Bill's dreams and Dan's. My writing and work on the shack. The local shipwrecks that Dan found fascinating. Saxon and Payton. The ball. We swung from the general to the personal and back again.

'How's things with your family?' I asked.

'Okay. Apart from work stuff, I haven't really spoken to Stephen since I last confronted him. And I haven't told Gemma or Ben about the police yet.'

'So you've contacted them?'

He nodded. 'Yes, and I sent off a sample, but they couldn't give me an idea of how long a result would take. You'd think they'd want to close cases and get dead bodies off their hands, but they didn't seem that enthused. Anyway, I figure, no point worrying anyone else until I know.'

'Do you think Stephen will follow through on his threat to fire you when the truth comes out?' I asked.

He shrugged. 'He's not one to change his mind, but maybe I'll quit first.'

'Really? What will you do for work?'

'I've got plenty of options. Stephen might own one of the biggest lobster operations in these parts, but he's not the only one. With my experience I could easily get work on boats, or maybe I'll start my own business offering charters from the island. No one talks about the shipwrecks much in tours, so that could be my unique selling point. I was thinking of combining sea lion watching with a little local maritime history. The world's my oyster.'

He paused a moment. 'Can I ask you a question, Ashling?'

I nodded. The way I felt right now I'd tell him anything.

A serious expression fell across his face. 'I was wondering if you'll be my date for the island ball?'

I sucked in a breath, my stomach somersaulting. 'Date, as in just going together because we're friends and organisers, or date as in ...'

'*Date*,' Dan finished the sentence for me. If this one word wasn't potent enough, he added, 'I'm not going to lie, my preference is definitely for the latter, but I'll go with whatever makes you comfortable.'

Whether it was courage from the whisky, or the fact Dan had pretty much just admitted he liked me in the same way I liked him, something spurred me on to lean right in close.

'Maybe I'm sick of being comfortable,' I whispered.

Time stood still as Dan's fingers slid up into my hair as he drew my mouth to his. One minute we were talking, the next we were kissing like our lives depended on it, and seconds later we were tearing at each other's clothes.

Our heavy jackets were yanked open and tossed aside, our lips parting only long enough for us to tug each other's jumpers over our heads. Dan's hand slid around my back, snapping open my bra and I heard a guttural groan from somewhere deep inside his throat as my breasts spilled out. The cool evening air barely had a chance to touch them before he rolled me onto my back, straddled me and covered each one with a large warm hand. The heat shot from my nipples right down to my core as he moved his already rock-hard groin against my pelvis. Need swelled within me. Dan had barely touched me and already I couldn't stand the barrier of our jeans.

Two words—pleasure and torment—came to mind as he teased his thumbs over my nipples. My skin came alive from head to toe, tingling and burning as his hungry gaze swept over my bare chest, then moved lower, his hands following its path. I sucked in a breath when his fingers dipped inside the waistband of my jeans and then groaned when, moments later, he teasingly pulled them out again.

But my disappointment didn't last long.

Dan lowered his face, so our lips were almost but not quite touching. 'I want to explore every inch of you,' he whispered, before unbuckling my jeans and slowly peeling them down my legs. Once they were off, he took my left foot in his hand and ran his thumb under the arch, before replacing it with his mouth and kissing all the way up to my inner thigh.

Sprawled on the sand, I was helpless but to enjoy as he knelt between my legs and spread my thighs wide. Dan gave me one big grin, and I didn't have time to feel embarrassed by the fact I hadn't managed to get that bikini wax, before he pushed his tongue inside me and rendered me incapable of thought.

A few minutes later when Dan hit me with a smug smile, my body felt thoroughly sated, yet I still desperately wanted to have him properly. My hands reached urgently for the button on *his* jeans. 'You let that out and ...' He sounded choked.

'And we'll have sex?' A ripple of anticipation shot through my body. 'Don't you want to?'

'More than anything.'

Relief flooded through me. 'Then what are you waiting for?'

And that was all the go-ahead he needed.

Moments later, with all clothing between us gone, Dan surged into me, filling me so wonderfully and completely that I screamed in pure ecstasy.

'What even *was* that?' I asked when I finally caught my breath. In twenty-two years with Adrian, I couldn't remember ever having sex that good. It had taken years before he'd ever managed to get me to orgasm at the same time as him. But what we'd just had ... *that* was the stuff I used to read about in romance novels!

Dan pushed up onto his arms and looked down at me. 'I'm so sorry that was over so quickly. That wasn't the way I intended our first time to be.'

'Don't apologise, that was *amazing*,' I said, squirming as I felt sand in places it really shouldn't be. 'If anyone should be saying sorry it's me—I may have been a little eager, but it's been a few months between rodeos.'

And much longer since I'd experienced such desperate need and the kind of desire Dan invoked within me.

He dropped a kiss on my nose. 'You were more than perfect. I'm surprised I managed to hold out that long myself. It's been years since I last had sex.'

'*Years?*' What were all the single women in Ragged Point thinking?

He laughed at my shock.

'So was Tessa your last?' I asked.

'No. After Tessa left, I tried to fix the pain by sleeping with one girl after another, but after a while I realised how meaningless it was and the thrill of getting my rocks off with just anyone lost its shine. I decided to wait for someone special.'

The way he was gazing down at me made me *feel* special. A feeling I now realised had been absent in my life for a long time.

'So, Dan ...' I walked my fingers up his bare chest, smiling mischievously. 'How long exactly have you been thinking about our first time?'

'From that first moment I saw you on the beach.'

'And how did you imagine our first time to be?'

'Well ...' He cuddled me close and stroked my hair off my face, as he whispered exactly what he'd envisioned in every minute detail.

Oh. My God!

49

Perth

I never imagined I'd fall so hard and fast for anyone after Adrian, but, from that first time we slept together, every cell in my body obsessed over Dan. I wanted to live and breathe him. Now that he didn't have Lion to go home to, the nights I was in the Point he stayed over at the shack and we had sex at the rate of teenagers but with much more depth. During the days, when I wasn't working at Brewed or on the paper, Dan would sometimes sneak away from The Lobster Factory, allegedly to help me with some heavy lifting at the shack. However, although he had helped me a little with the revival of the old floorboards, more often than not we ended up between the sheets instead.

Sometimes we didn't even make it to the bedroom.

With Dan I felt like a new person. We made love on the floor in the kitchen surrounded by half-built cabinets, in the shower, on his boat, and once in the town hall after the rest of the committee had left following a meeting.

Phone sex was another whole new world Dan had opened me up to. On my nights in Perth, when the kids were safely asleep, we'd FaceTime. I missed him like crazy, but technology helped bridge the gap—I could see why Generation Z were so addicted to it! Thanks to him, a smile had become a permanent fixture on my face, and no mess Adrian left in the house or argument I had with Saxon and Payton could erase it.

Hayley noticed the first time she saw me in person post-sex. We were chatting on the sidelines at Payton's soccer game when she frowned. 'You look different. Have you changed your hair? No, that's not it. New outfit? *Oh my God.*' She gasped. 'You've had sex!'

'Shhh,' I hissed, thrusting my finger against my lips. Thankfully, the kids were all occupied with the game and Adrian was doing linesman duty on the other side of the pitch.

Not that I cared if he found out—my body and what I did with it was no longer any of his business.

'You have though, haven't you?' Hayley asked, her hand still resting against her chest.

Her eyes widened as I grinned my reply, but this time she had the good sense to lower her voice. 'Where'd you meet him? Tinder?'

'Don't be ridiculous.'

'Well?' she prompted.

'His name's Dan and—'

'Your neighbour!' Hayley clapped her hands together and danced a little on the spot like an excited schoolgirl. 'Tell me *everything*.'

I started to explain that he was the third child—well, possibly—of a prominent local businessman, that he was married years ago but didn't have kids, that he was a very good cook.

'Not *those* kinds of details,' she said, waving her hand in dismissal. 'I don't care how good he is in the kitchen, I want to know about his prowess in the bedroom. Is he better than my brother?'

'*Hayley!*' One topic we'd always managed to steer clear of was mine and Adrian's sex life. She shared plenty with me about her sexual escapades, but I listened (and if I'm honest sometimes felt a twinge of jealousy) rather than participated.

'What?'

'Have you noticed where we are?' I gestured to the kids running around madly on the field. 'Besides, I don't kiss and tell.'

'Spoilsport.' Hayley poked out her tongue.

'Okay, I will tell you that being with Dan is … amazing. I thought it would be awkward sleeping with someone else—Adrian and I had been together so long we knew what each other liked and didn't like, or so I thought. But it wasn't clumsy or embarrassing at all. Dan is a very generous lover and he makes me want to be generous right back. I feel alive in a way I now realise I hadn't for years.'

'I'm so happy for you,' she said, grinning. 'When can Wei and I meet him?'

'Meet him?' I gulped. Meeting the family would feel like serious business and I wasn't sure Dan and I were at that point yet. We were having fantastic sex and a lot of fun, but neither of us had mentioned commitment or thought about the future. Yet at the same time, I'd love Hayley and Wei to come up to Ragged Point again and see how the shack was taking shape. I'd love her and Jedda to have the chance to get to know each other. If they happened to meet Dan as well, so be it.

'Come whenever you want.' Then a thought struck. 'Why don't you guys come up for the island ball?'

'A ball doesn't sound much fun when I won't be able to drink. By then I'll be almost ready to pop.'

I glanced down at her still flat stomach. Hayley had always had a gorgeous figure and you could just tell pregnancy was going to make her look even better. Wei had been over the moon when she told him she was carrying his baby, but due to Hayley's age—the doctor called her a 'geriatric' mum; *I know!*—they hadn't announced their news yet.

Hayley liked to party and usually for her that included a drink, but I knew how to twist her arm. 'But just think of the opportunity for a new frock?'

She sighed but her eyes glistened. 'Okay, it's going to be hard to accommodate my bump, but I do like a fashion challenge, so ... it's a date. When shall we go shopping?'

I laughed and it was decided. Our excursion was scheduled for next time I was in Perth, and Hayley and Wei would make sure they were rostered off the weekend of the ball, which thankfully also coincided with one of Adrian's weeks with the kids. Knowing I was going to have my oldest and best friend there for the evening as well as my newest ones only added to my excitement.

Adrian came up beside us, a slightly uncomfortable expression on his face. 'What are you grinning at?'

Sundays at soccer were the only times we saw each other now—all our other communication occurred via email, text messages or passive-aggressive post-it notes left around the house, but we tried to be courteous in person for the children. Hayley and I had been so lost in conversation we hadn't even noticed the game had finished and I really hoped no one asked me the score.

'Secret women's business,' Hayley told him as Payton joined us. She leant down to give her a hug. 'Hey sweetheart. You were a superstar out there.'

'Thanks, Aunty Hayley.' Payton turned her attention on me. 'Can I go to Prosecco's? Her mum said she can drop me home just before dinner.'

While I felt slightly saddened that Payton would rather spend our last day together at a friend's house than with me, I knew she'd only sulk all afternoon if I said no. And although I definitely harboured concerns about anyone who'd name their child after an alcoholic drink, Prosecco's parents were nothing but nice and always worrying about whether she had enough sunscreen on, so I was okay with the request. 'Sure. I'll come talk to Jane and Tim now.'

Maybe having plain names themselves had led them to be creative with their daughter's.

'Does Dad get a hug before you go?' Adrian asked, leaning down. As Payton slipped into his arms, he glanced at my shoes and it looked as if he was about to have a conniption. 'What on earth are you wearing?'

Call me childish, but I couldn't help smirking as I stuck out my foot like some kind of model, admiring my star-speckled silver ankle boots with their high heels and pointy toes. 'Aren't they gorgeous?'

He visibly shuddered. 'They're death for your toes, that's what they are. You should *know* better.'

If Adrian felt this strongly about my footwear, I wondered how he'd feel if he knew that shoes weren't the only new thing I'd been trying on for size. While I could have been petty and told him *all* about Dan in an aim to make him jealous, it was freeing to discover I no longer cared. And more importantly, I didn't want to cheapen Dan by using him as a pawn in a game I didn't want to play, so I offered my ex-husband a saccharine smile instead.

'Lucky my toes are no concern of yours anymore,' I said, then took hold of Payton's hand. 'Come on, let's go see Prosecco's mum.'

I arrived home half an hour later to a silent house, but the pantry doors were wide open, telling me Saxon had risen from his deep adolescent slumber and been foraging for food. I wandered down the hallway to his bedroom to find him glued to his laptop, Charlie asleep at his feet and half a dozen empty muesli bar wrappers on his desk.

I tapped him on the shoulder and he jumped.

'What the hell, Mum? You trying to scare me half to death?'

I ignored that and gestured to the wrappers. 'Just because there's oats in those, doesn't make them a good breakfast. And are you still playing that game?'

'Yeah?' He shrugged. 'So what?'

'How much homework have you got this weekend?'

Saxon groaned. 'Not much. Can you stop being such a nag?'

'Fine,' I said through gritted teeth. 'But I want you to get some fresh air soon and walk Charlie, okay?'

He smiled and my heart flipped over—it had been a while. 'All right. Just let me finish up this game.'

I wasn't quite sure how long that would take, but I nodded, kissed him on the head and left him in peace.

Once upon a time an afternoon to myself was a rarity that I'd have filled with cleaning, cooking, washing or pulling up the weeds that were trying to take over the back lawn, but now I had better things to do. Unable to even recall the last time I'd bothered ironing, I made myself a coffee and sat down at my laptop to finish the article I was writing about nest parenting.

I'd made a deal with Dan that I'd submit it to an online magazine this week and I couldn't wait for his 'reward' when I told him that I had.

50

Ragged Point

Following the lunch rush on Wednesday afternoon, I was wiping down the counter at Jedda's cafe when the little bell above the door jingled and I looked up to see Dan.

I smiled as he walked towards me. 'Well, isn't this a pleasant surprise.'

He leant across the counter, grabbed hold of my face and planted a deliciously sloppy kiss right on my lips. 'Hello, gorgeous.'

Cheers erupted from Jedda and the other customers and I felt my cheeks turn a colour that'd give Rudolph's nose a run for its money, but my smile only grew broader.

'What can I get you?' I asked once the fanfare had died down.

'I don't think what I really want from you is on the menu,' Dan whispered with a wiggle of his eyebrows, 'but I'll take a coffee for now. What time do you get off?'

'About half an hour.'

'In that case, I'll have my coffee here and a slice of that—' Dan pointed to Jedda's famous salted caramel carrot cake in the display cabinet, 'while I wait.'

Exactly thirty minutes later, I hung up my apron and he took my hand as we headed to his ute. 'I've got something to show you. Your place or mine?'

I assumed show-and-tell was in his pants and didn't have any objections, but I knew that once we fell into bed it could be hours before we came up for air. 'Let's go to the shack. I don't like leaving Charlie too long on his own.'

Said dog greeted us enthusiastically the moment we stepped inside. Once he'd calmed down and was contently chewing on an empty toilet roll, I gazed up at Dan with my best bedroom eyes. 'What was it you wanted to show me?'

He pulled his phone out of his pocket. 'I got an email from the DNA people today.'

Still lost in my bubble of desire, it took a moment for me to understand what he was saying, and then my heart clenched. 'Oh my goodness! And? Anything useful?'

'*And* I haven't opened it yet.' His Adam's apple moved slowly up and down as he swallowed. 'I wanted to do it with you.'

'Okay.' I knew he was nervous, but couldn't help feeling chuffed. 'Go on then.'

We sat on the sofa and I squeezed Dan's knee as he opened the email on his phone and clicked on the report. It was divided into two main sections: DNA Story (which gave an ethnicity estimate) and DNA Matches (showing anyone in the register who shared some of his DNA).

Dan's DNA was split almost equally between the UK and Southern USA. He told me his mother was born in Northern England and immigrated to Australia when she was a teenager, but he knew of no one in her family or Stephen's who came from America. While this merely confirmed what we already suspected, it was the matches we were more interested in, especially because there was one listed as 'close family' and a number of others listed as 'first cousins'.

I could barely contain my excitement. This was exactly what we'd been hoping for. 'Do you recognise any of those names?'

'Not one.'

A little online research informed us that persons listed as close family could be parents or siblings.

'Fuck,' Dan breathed, and I noticed his hand was shaking. 'Do you think this Stacy Wilson is my sister? What should I do now?'

I put my hand on his. 'What do you want to do? I guess you could start by messaging her. Tell her who you are, who you think your parents are, and that you're trying to work out how you guys are related.'

'But what if she doesn't reply?'

I smiled encouragingly. 'You won't know unless you try.'

'True, but what if she's a racist, or a drug addict or a bigot or something.'

'Or, maybe she's a serial killer and in jail!' I gave him a look, trying to remember that while this was an exciting mystery for me, it was actually his life. No wonder he felt anxious and emotional.

'Seriously though,' I said, 'you don't have to rush into this. You can sit on the information as long as you want, but this woman is obviously open to being contacted or she wouldn't have made her profile public. Same goes for the other matches.'

'You're a very wise woman, you know that?' Dan pressed his lips against mine, then leant back into the sofa with a sigh.

'This wise woman has another idea too. Why don't we search for Stacy online and see what we can find out about her and some of your "first cousin" matches?'

Dan thought this a sensible suggestion, so I went to get my laptop and we made a deep dive into the cyber life of Stacy Wilson. She was older than him by eight years and lived in San Francisco with her wife. She worked in IT and posted a lot of photos of two clearly spoiled dachshunds.

'She looks normal, doesn't she?' Dan said, his voice a little higher than usual. 'People who love dogs are generally trustworthy.'

I smiled at his logic. 'Looks can be deceiving but yes, she looks very nice. Do you want a drink?'

'Yeah, that'd be good.'

'Let me fix us up something to eat too,' I said, realising it was getting on towards dinner time.

'Want some help?'

I shook my head. 'I'm just reheating the pasta I made yesterday, but can you take Charlie out for a quick pee?'

His head shot up from where he'd been slumbering on the rug at our feet.

'Sure thing,' Dan said. 'Come on, boy.'

Ten minutes later we reconvened on the couch, this time with bottles of beer, bowls of pasta and a wood fire crackling in front of us. I couldn't remember feeling quite as content for a long time. When we finished eating, Dan put his bowl down on the coffee table and picked up my laptop.

'Okay. I'm gunna message them,' he said. 'What do you think I should say?'

I took a sip of my beer while pondering. 'Start general,' I suggested. 'Say you did a DNA test to try and find relatives who might be able to help you find answers about the man you suspect was your father.'

Dan began to type furiously. I read the message over his shoulder and my stomach dipped as he pushed send.

He put the laptop back on the coffee table. 'Thanks for doing this with me. I'm not sure I'd have had the guts to follow through on my own. I doubt I'll be able to think about anything else until she replies. That's *if* she replies.'

'I think I might have a way to distract you,' I said, putting my drink down before climbing onto his lap.

Seconds later, his hands found their way under my jumper and, at least for a little while, we succeeded in forgetting all about Stacy Wilson and how she might be related to Dan or Bill.

51

Perth

Almost a week later, we were losing hope that Dan was ever going to hear from his possible sister when he woke one morning to a reply. He rang me immediately and his voice was shaking so badly he could barely get the words out as he read me the message.

Dear Daniel

Sorry for taking so long to answer your message. My wife and I were camping, and I didn't receive your message until we returned. I must admit I'm both surprised and very curious to have heard from you. The DNA results indicate that we are either siblings or first cousins, and as my father William Jackson ...

'William?' I interrupted. 'As in the long form of Bill?'

'Oh geez, you're right. I hadn't even thought about that.'

Silence followed a few seconds as we both digested this.

'Anyway, what else does the message say?'

'That although my profile picture bears a strong resemblance to William, I'm much more likely to be a cousin than a half-sibling, because her father died in an explosion while fighting in Vietnam, when her mother was pregnant with her. He didn't even know he was going to be a father, and that was eight full years before I was born.'

'An explosion?' Goosebumps rose on my arms. 'Wow. That doesn't sound like something anyone would survive, but the timing is interesting. Stacy's father, presumed dead, never returns home and then a man turns up in Ragged Point a couple of years later with a very similar name. If they are one and the same, what was Bill doing in those in-between years? What brought him to Australia and how did he get here?'

'Who knows,' Dan said, clearly as baffled as me. 'And, if he survived the explosion, why didn't he return to his wife? This makes it look like he used it as an opportunity to fake his own death, but that sounds like some kind of crazy film plot.'

'It sure does. Have you replied to Stacy?'

'Not yet. I have no idea what to say. She thinks her father died, but if we find out we're siblings, then that will confirm that Bill is my dad and therefore hers did not die in the war like a hero as she'd always believed.' Dan sighed long and loud. 'And if that's the case, the knowledge that he may have willingly abandoned her mother might be upsetting. I don't want to cause any more hurt to Stacy or her mum.'

I loved that he cared about two people he'd never even met, but was about to say he'd already opened Pandora's box when Payton burst into my bedroom, her hair standing up at all angles.

'I can't find my sports T-shirt!'

I held the phone against my chest. 'I'm sure there's one in your wardrobe. All the washing's been put away.'

She narrowed her eyes at my phone. 'Who are you talking to?'

'Jedda,' I lied, not ready to confess my relationship with Dan. 'I'll come look in a moment. Go brush your hair while you're waiting.'

As she flounced off, I lifted the phone back to my ear. 'Sorry,' I whispered, 'I've got to go, but try not to stress too much. It's been a long time since William apparently died in the war. It might hurt Stacy, but if it is him, she might be interested to hear about his life in Australia.'

'That's true.' Dan sighed again. 'The police would at least be happy to be able to close his case.'

'Yes.' Although I cared much less about this than I did about how the mystery was affecting him. 'But you've got to do what feels right for you. I've got to get the kids off to school and then I'm meeting Hayley, but I'll call you later and we can talk more if you want.'

'Thanks.'

My mind buzzed with Dan's exciting breakthrough as I climbed out of bed and went down the hallway to hunt for Payton's T-shirt. As suspected, I found it immediately and while she got ready, I went into Saxon's room. Gone were the days when he rose before everyone else; now getting my son up in the morning was like trying to rouse the dead and I never knew how he was going to respond.

'Rise and shine, sleeping beauty,' I said as I went over to the bed and gently shook his shoulder. 'Time to get ready for school.'

'Five more minutes. I'm stuffed,' he groaned, his words barely distinguishable through his yawns.

'Go have a shower to wake yourself up, and I'll cook you some bacon and eggs.'

The next hour passed in the usual whirlwind of morning crazy, making lunches while also making sure everyone was fed, clothed and scrubbed—not necessarily in that order—before hustling them out the door. Payton was ready early enough that she had time to kick the soccer ball around the backyard, but Saxon dragged his feet and missed the bus.

'It's okay,' I told him. 'I'm meeting Hayley in the city to go shopping, so I'll drop you off on the way, but don't make this a habit.'

'Why are you going shopping?' Payton—ever curious—asked.

'I'm looking for a dress to wear to the ball.'

'What ball?'

I managed to smile rather than shake my head in frustration. I'd definitely told her about the ball, but kids only seemed to listen when it affected them. 'It's to fundraise for the island, remember?'

'Oh right.' She hitched her backpack on her shoulder as we all headed out to the car. 'Isn't that ages away?'

'Yes, but it takes time to find the perfect dress.'

Payton nodded. 'Can I skip school and come with you?'

'Ah, let's see? No.' I tapped her playfully on the bum. 'To the car, missy.'

After a brief squabble about who was going to sit in the front, we were on our way. Half an hour later, both kids delivered, I met Hayley in front of Myer.

'Nothing too expensive,' I warned her as we headed inside. 'Now I'm a single mum I need to watch my pennies.'

'Whatever.' Hayley marched into the women's formal wear section and immediately began flicking through the racks. 'I'm thinking a silver or blue would suit your skin tone. How's this?'

I grimaced at the dress she held out—that's if you could even call it a dress. There appeared to be a gaping hole in the midriff area. 'Hayley, I've had two kids. I need twice as much material to cover up my war wounds.'

She sighed, hung it back on the rack and continued her mission. Although she declared me impossible to please and looking for herself a waste of time as anything she tried would be too tight by the ball, we managed to find a couple of dresses each to take into the fitting rooms.

I immediately fell in love with a shimmery silver V-neck gown that pinched in at the waist and then rippled right down to the floor. Sequins and diamantes covered the bodice but grew sparser on the skirt until there was only a scattering around the hem. Although the back was bare, the V-neck lower than I'd usually be comfortable in, and the price higher than I'd been hoping to spend, I felt like I was wearing the twinkling night sky.

'But is it a bit too much?' I asked, twirling slowly in front of Hayley.

'Not at all. It's a ball. It's supposed to be too much!' She wolf-whistled loudly enough that everyone in the whole shop probably heard. 'Dan is going to lose his shit when he sees you wearing it. He won't be able to think of anything all night except taking it off.'

Her declaration sealed the deal. 'I guess this is it then,' I said with a grin.

'Great choice.' The sales lady smiled as I paid for my dress. 'I've been eyeing this one myself.'

'Come on. I'll buy you an early lunch,' Hayley said as I shoved my purse back into my handbag.

We'd barely left the counter when my phone started ringing.

'Maybe it's lover boy,' she teased. I'd updated her on Dan's family saga, and she was as intrigued about the whole mystery as I was.

'Maybe.' My heart skipping a beat, I scooped my mobile out of the bag, but my excitement vanished when I saw the number of Saxon's high school on the screen.

A phone call from school rarely delivered good news. I thought of how pale Sax had looked that morning. What if it wasn't down to a lack of sleep? What if he was actually sick and, too consumed with thoughts of Dan's predicament, I hadn't been on my mother game?

I swallowed and accepted the call. 'Hello, Ashling speaking.'

'Mrs Wood? This is Vera Diapolos, the principal at Perth Selective. I have to speak with you and your husband—'

'*Ex*-husband,' I corrected, the term now easily rolling off my tongue. 'And I'm actually Ashling Murphy now.'

'Ms Murphy,' she said, her tone impatient. 'I need you and your *ex*-husband to come into school as soon as possible.'

'Has something happened?'

'I'm afraid it has. Saxon was in an altercation with another student at recess.'

My heart leapt to my throat. 'Oh my God. Is he okay?'

'Apart from sore knuckles, Saxon is fine, however we cannot condone this type of behaviour.'

'I'm sorry ... What are you ... I don't quite ... Are you saying Saxon *hurt* someone?'

Another irritated sigh from Mrs Diapolos. 'I'd really rather discuss this in person, Ms Murphy—with you, your ex-husband and Saxon, who is waiting in my office. Considering your circumstances, would you like me to call Mr Wood, or ...?'

'No. I'll do it. We'll be there as soon as we can.'

'Thank you. That would be appreciated,' she said, in a tone that made me feel as if I'd committed the misdemeanour.

The moment she disconnected, I called the clinic and demanded Kristen put me through to Adrian immediately.

He picked up less than thirty seconds later. 'Ashling, I've told you—'

'This *is* an emergency, Adrian. I need you to meet me at Saxon's school asap. Apparently, he punched someone and we've both been summoned by the principal.'

'He what?' His voice echoed my own shock. 'That doesn't sound like Sax. He must have been provoked. Have they asked him why he did it? Do we need to get a lawyer?'

'Adrian,' I yelled. 'I don't know any more than what I've told you. The principal wants to talk to both of us, but I think we hold off on the lawyer; this isn't America. Do whatever you need to do so you can meet me at the school asap.'

I disconnected before he had the chance to object. Saxon was more important than any discomfort either of us might feel.

I left Hayley at the shops. My gut churned as I drove through the city to the school. I couldn't believe that Sax had hit someone. On one level it didn't make any sense, but I had to concede he hadn't been himself for months. I'd just assumed he was entering that normal stage of teenage rebellion—possibly aided and abetted by the disruption at home—but had that been naive?

Was there something deeper going on? And if I'd missed it, what did that say about me as a mother?

52

Exactly an hour later, Adrian and I found ourselves in the school principal's office—Saxon sitting between us, his arms crossed, a sullen expression on his face and what looked to be drops of blood staining his white shirt. That and the fact he refused to even meet our gaze didn't help my desperation to believe that this was some kind of mistake.

I wasn't sure whether I wanted to wrap my arms around him or scream and shout.

Thanks to Payton's short fuse, we'd been in this situation a number of times with her, but in all his years of schooling, never once had Saxon received a reprimand that required our attendance at school. Talk about not doing things by halves!

'Thank you for coming in,' Mrs Diapolos said from across her desk. 'As I mentioned on the phone, Saxon got into a fight at recess, which resulted in another student getting a bloody nose. Do you want to tell your parents what happened?'

Saxon mumbled something so softly I couldn't tell what he'd said, but at a guess I'd say, 'Not really.'

'Saxon,' I said sharply. 'Now is not the time for games. Is this true? Did you hit someone?'

He nodded, still not looking up.

Even though I was sitting, I felt as if the ground had been swept from under me. 'Why?' I pleaded, desperate for him to give us some kind of explanation.

'Whatever the reason,' said Mrs Diapolos, 'I think you'll understand that we cannot tolerate violence in any shape or form and—'

'Of course we understand that,' Adrian interrupted, his arms folded exactly like our son's, 'but I'd still like to hear Saxon's side of the story.'

The principal nodded. 'So would I, but so far, Saxon has refused to give any explanation.'

'*Sax*. Tell us,' I urged. '*Please*.'

Didn't he understand how serious this was? It was a privilege to go to Perth Selective and I was afraid they'd expel him if he didn't have a good reason. I was also afraid what a random act of violence said about him. And us.

'Fine. James was having a go at me—he wouldn't let up—and I just lost it.'

'Okay.' I nodded. 'What was he taunting you about?'

His shoulders slumped as if he'd lost a battle. 'We were arguing about *Tournament*. James, me and a couple of other guys have a team in the game and James wants me out because he reckons a two-year-old can play better than I do. I asked him if he reckoned a two-year-old could do this, and then I hit him.'

I gasped, unsure whether I was shocked about the fact Saxon had punched someone or the lack of remorse in his voice.

'You were fighting over a video game?' Adrian sounded as flummoxed as I was.

'You wouldn't understand,' Sax said at the same time Mrs Diapolos let out a disapproving sigh.

'*The Tournament*?' She shook her head. 'I've heard of this game causing issues at other schools, and studies have linked games like this with an increase in violence among kids, but this is the first time we've had this kind of issue at PS. Gaming isn't always a problem, however *The Tournament* is particularly violent and not all children have the cognitive development to know the difference between fantasy and real life. That's why it's rated R.'

I couldn't believe my ears. Her words might not be aiming blame at us, but her tone definitely was—as if we'd been remiss in allowing him to play.

'Online games have far more traps than the types of computer games available when we were younger,' she continued. 'In fact, the World Health Organization has recently recognised gaming disorder as an actual disease. A gaming addiction is no joke and can lead to other serious addiction problems, not to mention social ones. Now, I'm not saying Saxon has this disorder, but spending too much time online gaming could also account for his—'

I'd heard enough. So Saxon was in the wrong, and perhaps thanks to our separation had spent more time online than he should, but the school needed to accept *some* responsibility.

'If you know of these dangers,' I interrupted, hearing the venom in my own voice, 'then can you please explain to me the school's reasoning in handing out an assignment that required students to actually play and analyse an R-rated game? Until Saxon had to do this for media, he'd never shown the slightest interest in *The Tournament*.'

The principal's eyes widened as she looked uncertainly at Sax, then back to me. 'I'm not sure I know what you're talking about. As far as I know Year 9 media focuses on short film, music videos and advertising, but I'll certainly check in with the teacher about that.'

The penny dropped. My face burned as I slowly turned to look at Saxon. 'You lied about the assignment?'

'You've always been such a screen Nazi you wouldn't have let me play if I told you the truth. And everyone's playing it!'

My heart squeezed at the resentment in his tone. What had happened to my sweet little boy?

Adrian shook his head at Sax and then turned his most charming smile on the principal. 'I'm sorry, Vera, this situation has clearly gotten out of hand, but I can assure you that now Ashling and I know what's going on, this *Tournament* thing will no longer be an issue.'

'That's good to hear,' she replied. 'I'm sure you'll both understand the need to suspend Saxon for a week over this, but his violent outburst isn't the only reason I wanted to speak to you. What's come to light today, however, might explain a few other things as well.'

What on earth was she talking about? Did all teachers speak so cryptically? Reining in my anger and irritation—and the need to blame someone other than myself—I asked, 'I'm sorry, what other things?'

'Saxon's decline in grades and his less than enthusiastic attitude towards his schooling. A number of his teachers have raised concerns with me recently that his homework isn't always completed and his grades are no longer what they should be.'

'What?' I felt as if I'd been the one punched. 'How bad are they?'

'Some of his classes he's barely passing.'

'I don't understand,' Adrian said, raking a hand through his hair, his ears twitching.

I turned on Sax. 'I thought you quit the band to focus on your studies? Don't tell me it was because you wanted more time to play *The Tournament*?'

Adrian answered instead of Sax. 'You quit the *band*?'

Saxon stared into his lap, refusing to meet my gaze. What a mess—if I wasn't so worried about him, I'd be embarrassed about Mrs Diapolos bearing witness to how little communication was clearly going on in our family.

Then another thought struck. 'Hang on, if things are that bad, why are we only hearing about it now? If today's incident hadn't happened, when would you have let us know?'

'Various teachers have reported trying to contact you both numerous times via email, which is always our first point of call,' she said calmly. 'They were all going to bring it up at teacher-parent interviews the week after next.'

'I haven't received any emails!' I turned to Adrian as I yanked my phone out of my handbag to prove it. 'Have you?'

'Well, yeah,' he said, sounding uncertain, 'but we agreed that you'd continue dealing with all school communication, so I just deleted them.'

Oh my God! If I'd felt embarrassed before, now my cheeks were so hot I could probably fry an egg on them. Silence descended upon the room as I glanced down to check my junk folder. Sure enough, there was a number of emails from various teachers.

'I changed my email a couple of weeks ago when I decided to change my name,' I tried to explain. 'I gave the new email to the office, but it looks like the new address sent the school ones to spam.'

'That's unfortunate,' said Mrs Diapolos, 'but what's important is moving forward.'

'Exactly.' Adrian nodded his agreement, refusing to meet my gaze. 'There's no point either of us laying blame. In future we'd expect a phone call if Saxon is struggling with his work, and we'll make sure he stays on top of his schoolwork.'

'Thank you,' she said. 'I'm glad to hear we're on the same page regarding this situation and hopefully Saxon's suspension will give him time to think about his behaviour and also spend some time trying to catch up. Considering today's incident, his possible addiction to gaming and your current home situation, I think it would also be a good idea to have our school counsellor do a few sessions with him. We understand parental separation is tough and perhaps his inner turmoil has exacerbated this situation, but there are only so many allowances we can make.'

Despite his views on therapy, Adrian agreed to this and we were all dismissed.

While Saxon retreated to his locker to collect his things, Adrian and I waited in the car park. He might have put on a united front in the presence of the principal, but his true colours returned the moment we were out of earshot.

'Why didn't you tell me Saxon had left the band?'

'Because you and I are separated, in case you hadn't noticed!' Maybe he was right and this was something we should have discussed, but I was feeling enough guilt of my own without him trying to put even more blame on me.

He tossed his car keys in his hand. 'No need for sarcasm, Ash, it never suits you.'

'What suits *me* or not is no concern of yours,' I said through gritted teeth. 'What *is* our mutual concern is what we're going to do about Saxon and getting him back on track, before it's too late.'

'Hmm.' Adrian shoved his hands in his pockets. 'I've been thinking lately, and today confirms it. Perhaps this nest-parenting arrangement isn't working after all. Maybe I should just have the kids on the weekends—or even every second weekend—and you should be with them during the week.'

I couldn't believe what I was hearing.

While this was exactly what I'd wanted a few months ago—if I couldn't have all four of us back together—now the thought of leaving Ragged Point, of leaving Jedda, the cafe, the paper, the island, and of course Dan, filled me with despair.

I shook my head and held up my hand. 'No!'

Adrian wasn't getting out of his parenting responsibilities that easily—whether we liked it or not, we were in this parenting gig together. I wasn't going to let him continue to live the high life and renege on his obligations while I sacrificed my own needs and desires once again.

'No?' He blinked, anger flashing through his eyes. 'What do you mean *no*?'

'Exactly that.' I smiled sweetly at him. '*You* were the one who did this to our family. *You* decided the grass was greener elsewhere and that nest parenting was the best for the kids. We've had a few hiccups—I stuffed up not noticing the lack of emails from the school and *both* of us should have been paying more attention to what Saxon was getting up to in his room—but that doesn't mean we have to change a situation that's working fine in every other way.'

'Fine' might be an exaggeration, but I'd rather put up with the odd domestic grievance than give up everything else now. It was time for Adrian to step up.

'I thought you'd be thrilled with this suggestion!'

'Well, you thought wrong. I don't think you spending less time with the kids, especially Saxon, is the answer to the problems we're having with him. Teenage boys need their fathers—maybe the answer is you actually spending *more* time with him. You could take him out on one of your rides.'

'Yeah, like he'd appreciate that. I can barely get him out of his bedroom for dinner, never mind outdoors.'

'Well, clearly that's an issue we both have to address. From now on we both need to be more diligent about our screen rules. No more *Tournament* or any other online games, not after school, not even on weekends. Not until his dedication to schoolwork, his grades and his attitude picks up again. And no phones or computers in bedrooms either. Suspension is one thing, but we need to show him how disappointed we are as well.'

'And how the hell am I going to police this after school while I'm still at work? I can't exactly expect Topaz to babysit Sax as well, she's only a few years older than him.'

As Adrian raised his eyebrows at me, I bit my lip—there had to be a way.

'I know,' I said after a few moments, 'Saxon can go to the clinic straight after school and do his homework there until he can regain our trust. Or, you could rearrange your appointments. You're the boss, remember? Schedule shorter hours the weeks you're with the kids and work longer hours when you're not. I don't care how you do it, just find a way to make it work.'

He snorted, clearly unimpressed. 'It's okay for you. You're a lady of leisure, while I'm the one working hard to pay for our family.'

'Lady of leisure?! Do you listen to anything I say? You know I've got a job now too. I'm working in a cafe and—'

'Is that why you're resisting this situation—because you have a few shifts in some small town cafe? Why not look for a job here? It's only waitressing—surely you can find something closer to home?'

Only waitressing? My fingernails dug into my palms. I could tell him that Ragged Point offered me so much more than a few shifts in some cafe; I could remind him I was also getting paid for renovating the shack, and that I was pursuing a writing career again—but he was so self-centred, it wouldn't make an iota of difference.

Besides, his opinion of me didn't matter anymore. I certainly didn't care for it.

Before I could work out how exactly to respond, Saxon came up behind us. Digging my keys out of my handbag, I said, 'I'm sorry, I don't have time for this right now, Adrian. I need to take Sax home, but *our* situation stays the way it is. Have a nice day.'

Before he could object, I turned and strode towards my car. Saxon, clearly not wanting to get in any further trouble, hurried after me.

My heart thundered as I slammed the door shut. I'd never liked conflict and realised now that because of this, Adrian had always got whatever he wanted in our marriage. Well, no more. However terrifying standing up for myself was, it was also empowering, and I was so damn proud of the woman I was becoming.

53

Ragged Point

Leaving my children again after the drama we'd had with Saxon wasn't easy. I got into a routine, checking in with Sax morning and night—making him offer me more than his standard one-word answers—and I also called Adrian for a daily update on our son's progress as well. He wasn't very forthcoming, clearly trying to punish me for my decision, but I refused to cave to his desires and tried to ease my anxiety about what was going on at home by keeping busy.

While I enjoyed my shifts at Brewed Awakening and putting more of my own mark on the *Reporter*, it was continuing to renovate the shack and working on the ball that I found the most rewarding. These were things I could visibly see taking shape and it gave me a buzz in the same way breathing fresh air into my lungs while walking on the beach did.

After asking Jedda's thoughts on food for the ball, she'd talked to her friend, the president of the local CWA, and they'd offered to take on the catering. The menu they'd proposed made my mouth water—no one cooked better than country women—but I wanted Jedda to enjoy the night as well.

'How will you be able to dance and have fun while you're in the kitchen?' I'd asked.

'Are you kidding? I can't think of anything worse than having to get all glammed up to sit at a table and make polite conversation.'

'But you loved dressing up for trivia night—you were the life of the party.'

'Silly costumes and fancy ballgowns are two very different things. I'm glad to help but I'm no Cinderella.'

In addition to the menu, the band was locked in, the local Year 6 class had been given the task of making the decorations as part of their community project, the prizes and items for the silent auction were piling up, and the tickets had just gone on sale.

Of course, the best part about being part of the IPA was working alongside Dan, not that we needed an excuse anymore. Any time he wasn't at The Lobster Factory he spent with me—turned out he wasn't only good in bed but pretty handy with a hammer as well. While we alternated between working on the shack and working on each other, we also talked. Much of our conversation revolved around the mystery of Bill and I felt almost as invested in his story as Dan.

Since the first email from Stacy, he'd exchanged many more with her, coming completely clean about his suspicions they shared the same father. She was shocked at first, but then he'd emailed the picture his mum had painted of Bill and some of the photos from the wall of fame. Although Stacy had never met her father, the few photos she had in her possession left no uncertainty that it was him. She sent Dan photos of Bill's dad and brother, and the likeness between these strangers and Dan was what my grandmother would have called uncanny.

Even without the confirmation from the police, these images and the close DNA match between him and Stacy all but confirmed that Bill had fathered them both. Sadly, the report couldn't offer the new-found siblings answers to all the questions that had arisen.

'It'd be virtually impossible these days to disappear or fake your own death—what with all the newfangled technology,' Dan had said.

I agreed. 'Facial recognition photography, digital imprints and Mark Zuckerberg have a lot to answer for.'

His lips had quirked a little at that. 'But it would have been different in the seventies. Especially in a war zone.'

We'd come up with a number of possible ways Bill might have done it and subsequently come to Australia, our favourite being that he'd hitched a ride on one of the many refugee boats that came to our shores during that time. But it wasn't the logistics that truly bothered Dan.

So many times he'd pause while we were talking and drop his head into his hands. 'But why? I just don't understand. It's bad enough being a deserter ... but to leave your pregnant wife.'

'Remember, he didn't know she was pregnant,' I said, 'and although we might never understand, I'm sure he had his reasons. Maybe he was dealing with something we'll never know, like he'd done something and was scared for his wife's safety? It could have been his way to protect her.'

'You mean like a witness protection kind of thing?'

'Maybe not exactly that, but maybe something along those lines. War changes people. Or maybe he suffered PTSD or other mental health issues that led him to make certain decisions. Maybe he became someone else because it was the only way to escape pain. We can't ever completely understand what's going on in someone else's head.' Adrian had certainly taught me that. 'You'll probably never know for certain Bill's reasons for what he did, but do you really want to let that ruin the good memories you have of him? Of the times you spent together?'

Dan took his time replying but then solemnly shook his head. 'No.'

'Then focus on what you've found,' I'd encouraged. 'A sister who sounds like a great person and is very keen to get to know you better.'

Despite his misgivings, Dan couldn't help wanting to hear about the man Bill was before arriving in Ragged Point and Stacy was curious to hear more about her long-lost father's 'life after death'. As she had never known her father, I think she felt less betrayed than Dan—you don't miss what you don't know—but she told him that her family and Bill's friends had described him as a happy-go-lucky kinda guy, hugely resistant to the idea of fighting in a war. When he was drafted, he said he'd rather be thrown into jail than go, but Stacy's mother came from a renowned military family and it became a point of contention between them and his in-laws.

In the end, he'd done his duty and gone, and William's wife, Adele, had never got over the guilt of what she saw as her role in his death. Although still alive, she lived in residential care due to advanced Alzheimer's. Stacy had decided it best not to burden her mother with their discovery—she likely wouldn't understand anyway.

However, she and Dan were now in discussions about meeting and I couldn't have been more excited on his behalf.

54

'What do you think, Charlie? Time for a break?'

He lifted his head from where he'd been supervising—read slumbering—on the floor, while I was tiling the new splashback in the kitchen. Although only half finished, it looked amazing, even if I did say so myself. Grinning, I downed tools and went to fill the kettle.

I washed my hands while it boiled, then made a coffee and took it and my phone outside onto the back porch. Charlie made a beeline for the water—he didn't care that it was now freezing—as I sat down on the back step and watched him frolic. It'd be hard to say which one of us was more in love with Ragged Point and having the beach on our back doorstep. I still couldn't understand how the kids didn't share my passion, but I guess their lives and friends were in the city.

No longer worried about Charlie running away, I picked up my phone to check Facebook and saw a notification for an email. A slight chill filled my heart as I silently prayed it wasn't bad news from the school. Saxon had been resentful when we'd banned him from screens, but after a few days' detox from *The Tournament*, by the time I'd left for Ragged Point I could already see early signs of the child I knew and loved slowly returning to us.

I sucked in a breath as I opened my mail app, but almost fell off the step as I registered the sender of the email.

Not Perth Selective after all, but *FamilySpot* magazine.

My fingers shook as I opened it, not wanting to get my hopes up. It had been almost two weeks since I'd submitted the article—they were probably finally getting around to rejecting it.

'Oh my God,' I shrieked, jumping up and knocking over my coffee mug as I read the words on the screen.

Dear Ashling

Thank you for submitting 'The Family Nest' to FamilySpot*—it was both enlightening and a joy to read and we would love to publish it on our website. We can offer you a payment of $250. Please sign the attached document and send it back to us if you would like to go ahead.*

Kind regards

Loretta—Features Editor

'Oh my God!' It appeared I'd lost the ability to formulate any other words. But could this day get any better? It might only be one article, but it was a very encouraging start.

At my shrieking, Charlie dashed back up the beach to see what was wrong. Laughing as he stepped into the spilled coffee, I dropped back down onto the step and ruffled the wet fur around his neck. 'I'm going to be published! My work is going to be in print!'

Unable to stop beaming, I took a screenshot and immediately messaged it to Dan and Jedda. *Thank you both for giving me the confidence and encouragement to do this. Come over for dinner to celebrate. xx*

Jedda's reply came within seconds and consisted of about fifteen emojis, mostly streamers and champagne bottles.

Hell yeah, I replied as I headed back inside to the kitchen to work out what I might need to create an amazing celebratory dinner and came face to face with the mess of my tiling. *Whoops*, in my excitement I'd totally forgotten about the state of the kitchen.

I tapped out another message to Dan: *Change of plans. Can I cook dinner at your house again instead?*

Half an hour later, Dan still hadn't replied, but I knew he wouldn't mind, so after a phone call to tell Hayley my news, I was writing my shopping list when I heard the front door open.

Seconds later the man himself appeared holding a bottle of expensive champagne in one hand and a bunch of slightly droopy orange flowers in the other.

'You're a few hours early,' I said, leaping to my feet and kissing him hello. 'Not that I'm complaining.'

'I knocked off work the moment I got your message. News of your awesomeness required congratulations in person.' He thrust the bouquet towards me. 'Sorry. They were all the general store had, but I promise where the flowers lack, I more than made up for with this.'

Before I could tell him that this was the most perfect bunch of flowers anyone had ever given me, he popped the cork on the bubbles.

Charlie growled and I raised an eyebrow. 'Shouldn't we wait for Jedda?'

'I'm sure she'll bring her own bottle. Now, where are your glasses?'

'I still haven't got any,' I said, producing two coffee mugs. 'Will these do?'

Dan nodded. 'But remind me to buy you some as a shack-warming gift,' he said, filling both mugs to the brim.

'Hey,' I objected. 'If I drink all that I might not have the wherewithal to make dinner.'

'Let's worry about that later,' he said, before stooping and capturing my mouth with his.

Pretty soon the mugs were discarded, and we were making our way to my bedroom, bits of clothing strewn across the floor in our wake.

'You know how us Yanks celebrate success?' he asked as we tumbled onto the bed. He'd been emailing lots with his new-found sister and jokingly practising his American accent.

'No.' I laughed, but I had a feeling I was about to find out.

'Is that *really* how the Americans celebrate?' I asked Dan half an hour later, my body thoroughly played.

'I think it's how *everyone* should celebrate,' he replied with a wink, just as my phone started ringing from somewhere in the kitchen.

I groaned.

'Don't answer it,' Dan said, sliding his hand between my legs.

I squeezed them together in an aim to resist, but I was a lost cause. Where Dan was concerned my libido had no end. I closed my eyes as I lay back on the pillow and gave myself over to the feeling as the phone grew silent.

Seconds later it began again, and Charlie started barking—my ringtone always drove him bonkers.

With a sigh, I flung back the bedcovers. 'I'll go deal with that and be right back.'

'I'll be waiting,' Dan promised as I padded out of the room completely naked.

The phone stopped ringing the moment I reached it, but I barely had time to register it was Adrian before it started up again. Although tempted to ignore him, I decided to be the bigger person, just in case it was something to do with Sax.

'Hello, Adrian?' I said in a tone I hoped didn't give away the fact I'd just been laid.

He didn't waste time with greetings. 'It's Payton. She's been hit by a car.'

55

Perth

Sharp pain stabbed at my chest and my phone fell from my grasp, clattering across the floorboards as I sank to the ground.

Dan appeared in the doorway, glancing from me to my phone. He stooped to pick it up. 'What's the matter?'

'I … It's …' My words came in sharp, jagged breaths. 'It's Payton. Oh my God.' Tears sprouted in my eyes. 'She's been hit by a car.'

His face went pale. 'Fuck. Is she …?'

'I don't know,' I whispered, staring at the phone in his hand as if it were a bomb.

'Ashling! Ashling! Are you there?' Adrian's shrill voice shot out of it.

Dan pressed the phone against his chest. 'Do you want me to talk to him?' he asked softly, his voice full of concern.

I shook my head and held out my hand, my heart frozen as I lifted the phone back to my ear. 'Is she—'

'She's shaken up, but aside from a few cuts and bruises she doesn't seem too bad. However the doctors are currently checking for internal injuries and she did hit her head, so they want to keep her overnight for observation, in case of concussion.'

'Internal injuries.' I sagged against a cupboard. 'How the hell did this happen?'

'She was walking home from school—'

'What was she doing walking home?' It was a good ten-minute drive. 'And what was she doing walking *alone*?!'

'Calm down, Ash. She's going to be okay.'

'*Calm down?*' I shrieked. 'What happened? You were supposed to be looking after her.'

'I'm sorry. Topaz was running late and Payton got sick of waiting so she decided to walk home herself. It wasn't her fault. She was crossing at traffic lights and some loser ran a red. The police have taken him into custody. Topaz is beside herself, but we should be grateful it wasn't a lot worse.'

'Don't tell me how I should feel!' But the blame and fury I felt wasn't for Topaz, the guy who'd hit her, or even for Adrian.

It was for me.

If I'd been in Perth this afternoon, *home* instead of bonking Dan's brains out, my little girl wouldn't be lying in the hospital with possible internal injuries. Worst Mother of the Year didn't even come close.

'She wants you, Ash.'

'Huh?' Lost in self-loathing, I didn't even hear what Adrian said.

'Payton. She wants you here.'

'Of course.' I nodded even though he couldn't see me. 'I'm on my way. I'll be there as soon as I can.'

'I'll drive you,' Dan offered the moment I hung up.

'You don't have to.'

'No way am I letting you drive all the way to Perth after the shock you've just had. Come on,' he said, helping me off the floor. 'Let's get dressed and we'll be on our way.'

I couldn't say what Dan and I talked about during what felt like a longer than ever drive to Perth, or if we talked at all—I was incapable of thinking about anything except Payton. We arrived at Perth Children's Hospital just before 6 pm and I leapt from the car before Dan had even parked. Following the directions Adrian had given me, I ran through the hospital corridors and was almost at Payton's room when Topaz appeared out of nowhere.

'Mrs Wood?' She rushed towards me and held me by the arms. 'I'm so sorry. I don't expect you to ever forgive me or let me look after Payton again. I should have called the school to let them know I'd be late, but I thought she'd just wait.'

Tears streamed down her face, blending with her heavy eye makeup to give her puffy panda eyes. My motherly instincts kicked in. This girl was barely more than a child herself; she should never have been given the responsibility of taking care of mine.

'It's okay. This isn't your fault. It's just one of those horrible things,' I told her, even though I didn't believe that at all. This was someone's fault—*mine*. 'Go home and try not to worry. I need to see Payton now.'

Topaz nodded, relief filling her eyes. I turned for Payton's room, took a deep breath, and stepped inside, barely registering Adrian, Saxon, Hayley and Glennis as my gaze snapped straight to Payton sitting up in bed, a sour expression on her face and a big black moon boot on her foot.

'Ash.' Adrian cut me off as I headed for our daughter and yanked me into his arms. 'Thank God you're here.'

Stunned, I automatically burrowed my head in his shoulder and then recoiled at his now unfamiliar scent. 'I thought you said she didn't break anything?'

'I said they were still checking her over,' Adrian said. 'She's got a small fracture in her ankle.'

'Mum-my,' whined Payton and then promptly burst into tears.

Shaking free of Adrian, I launched myself at my daughter and enveloped her in my arms. 'Oh *baby*, look at you.'

As I held her, she tried to speak through sobs. 'I'm not going to be able to play soccer for months. I'll be out for the finals—that's if we even make them now. Without me they might not have a chance and what am I going to *do* with myself? I wish I'd died.'

'Don't even say that,' I scolded, my heart shuddering. That could so easily have been the outcome. We'd been damn lucky. 'I know this feels like hell, but you'll recover, and you will play soccer again. Right now, your priority needs to be getting better.'

'You're not going to leave me, are you? I don't want to stay here alone tonight, and I know it's Daddy's week, but I want you.'

'It's all right, baby, I'm staying.' Guilt ate at me—I *should* have been here all along.

'Good.' Her tears started to subside, and she looked like she was about to smile but changed her mind at the last moment. 'What's *he* doing here?'

All of us looked over to see Dan at the door.

'Hey.' He lifted his hand in a clearly nervous wave.

'Dan drove me to Perth,' I said. Now was definitely not the moment to introduce him as my lover, but I tossed him a grateful smile. 'Come in.'

'How are you doing, Payton?' he asked as he entered.

She glowered back at him. 'Terrible.'

Adrian offered Dan his hand. 'Thanks for driving Ash, mate. I'm Adrian. Her husband.'

Husband? I met Dan's gaze—both of us clearly thinking the same thing. Adrian must have sensed there was something going on between us and his use of the term was both funny and annoying.

A bemused expression on his face, Dan shook Adrian's hand, then also acknowledged Saxon—'Hi mate'—and introduced himself to my mother-in-law, Glennis, and then Hayley.

'I've heard a lot about you,' he said.

'Me too. And all very, *very* good,' Hayley teased. 'These weren't the circumstances I was hoping to meet you under though.'

'No,' Dan agreed.

'So, how exactly do you know Ashling?' asked Glennis, her tone cool.

'Um …' He cleared his throat. 'We're … neighbours.'

'*And*,' Hayley added, 'they've been working *very* closely on a fundraiser, I hear.'

I glared at her. Now was not the time or place to antagonise anyone.

Thankfully a nurse entered, putting a stop to conversation. 'Now, sweetheart,' he said, making a beeline for Payton. 'How's your pain levels?'

'Unbearable,' she groaned.

The nurse smiled sympathetically. 'I can imagine. Look, I'm going to give you something that will help but also might make you a little drowsy.' He glanced around the room at the rest of us. 'And I'm sorry to say, visiting hours are over. Mum and Dad, will one of you be staying tonight?'

'Me,' I replied and then realised I'd have to get a change of clothes from the Perth house. We'd left in such a hurry I hadn't brought anything with me except Charlie.

Shit, Charlie. I'd almost completely forgotten about him.

'What did you do with Charlie?' I asked Dan, as the nurse went off to get Payton's medicine.

'He's in the car. I left the windows down slightly. What do you want me to do with him now?'

'I'll take him,' Adrian announced as if Dan was stupid to ask such a question.

I turned to Adrian. 'Could you bring me a change of clothes from the house?'

He nodded. 'Of course. And do you want me to stay here tonight as well?'

'No,' I said, perhaps a little firmly, but the thought of spending the night in his company no longer appealed in the slightest. 'Someone needs to stay with Saxon.'

'I can grab some clothes from your place and then drop them back on my way to the airport,' Hayley offered, glancing at her watch. 'I'm doing the midnight horror tonight.'

'Thanks.' I smiled at her. 'That would be great.'

'Okay then, time's up,' announced the nurse as he returned to the room. 'Everyone except Mum and patient need to leave.' Although his words were stern, his tone was anything but, and he gave us time to say goodbye.

'Can you bring my iPad too, Aunty Hayley?' Payton asked hopefully.

Adrian and I exchanged a look.

'I can download some books on it,' I said, not wanting Saxon to think we were giving his sister special treatment. This was clearly not what she had in mind, but she didn't push it.

I hugged Hayley and Saxon hard, exchanged an awkward embrace with my mother-in-law, gave Adrian an equally awkward wave and then squeezed Dan's hand as I kissed his cheek. 'Thanks for everything.'

'You're welcome. Call me if you need anything else.'

I stood by the door as they all filed out, Hayley last. 'He's smoking!' she whispered as she leaned close. 'Well done, girlfriend.'

My cheeks heated as I shooed her out.

56

Despite her ordeal and the painkillers she'd been given, Payton was showing no signs of sleepiness. We were watching *My Kitchen Rules* on the TV hanging on her wall when Adrian entered the room.

'Where's Hayley?' I asked as I took the bag he held out.

At the same time Payton demanded, 'Did you bring the iPad?'

He nodded towards the other bag he'd just put on the bed. 'It's in there.' He looked back at me. 'I asked her to stay with Saxon for half an hour. I wanted to kiss my girl goodnight.'

His words sounded sweet, but I'd known him long enough to suspect that wasn't his only reason.

'Please can I watch some soccer videos?' Payton glared up at the television. 'This is bor-ing.'

I was about to say that it was time to get into her nightie, brush her teeth and settle down, but Adrian got in first. 'Okay, but not for long. I need to talk to your mother anyway.'

Not wanting to argue in front of her, I let him give her the iPad and then followed him out into the corridor.

He took my elbow and started to walk me away.

I stopped, pulling my arm back to my side. 'I'm not leaving her. Whatever you need to say you can tell me right here, where we can hear her if she needs us.'

'Okay.' Adrian nodded, showing rare acquiescence, but stood silently beside me.

I crossed my arms over my chest and tapped my foot. 'Cat got your tongue?'

He cleared his throat, then, 'Is Dan your boyfriend?'

'What?' I wasn't sure I'd heard him correctly because his voice was hushed; clearly he didn't want Payton to hear.

'That bloke. Dan,' he clarified. 'There's something going on between you, isn't there?'

I blinked. 'So, what if there is? Jealous?'

'I ... I'm a little surprised.'

'What did you expect?' I hissed, trying not to raise my voice. 'That I'd join a convent? You're not the only one with needs, Adrian. Or are you *surprised* that somebody else wants me when my own husband no longer does?'

'I'm not surprised anyone would want you, Ash. You're amazing. I've been a bloody fool.'

'Excuse me?' I seriously couldn't believe my ears. These were the last words I'd expected to come out of his mouth.

'I don't know what happened to me,' he went on. 'I haven't been feeling myself the last couple of years. I can't really explain it, but ever since Dad died ... I've felt different. Empty or something. Maybe I realised how short life was or something and it made me start questioning not only the relationship I had with Dad but the others in my life too.'

'I wish you'd told me how you were feeling earlier,' I said.

'I probably should have talked to someone—talked to you—but ...' He shrugged. 'Talking about stuff like that has never come easily to me, so instead, I think I started to resent you. I thought having sex with other people might numb the pain, the emptiness I feel, but it hasn't. I've been drinking more as well, but that's not working either. These months apart and then Payton frightening us today has made me realise how stupid I've been.'

I raised my eyebrows—he wasn't going to get any arguments here.

'I'm sorry for causing you and the kids such pain.' Adrian paused, took my hands in his and held them as if they were the most precious things in the world. 'I'd do anything to be able to take these last few months back, but do you think you could find it in your heart to forgive me?'

Forgiveness was one thing, but something in his voice told me that wasn't all he wanted. 'What exactly are you asking?'

'I miss you, Ash. I want you back. I want to put our family back together.'

'What?' I tore my hands from his, unable to believe my ears and his about-face. 'This is because of Dan, isn't it? Now that somebody else is interested in me, you want me back?'

'No.' He shook his head and ran a hand through his hair. 'It's not *just* because of that. I fucked up. Made the biggest mistake possible. And because of my mistake, our daughter almost died.'

Wow, I couldn't believe him capable of making such a connection, never mind admitting it, but I wasn't going to argue the point. If he hadn't left me, I'd never have been in Ragged Point and our daughter would never have needed to even consider walking home alone.

Adrian went on. 'The shock of getting that phone call and seeing Payton in emergency made me realise what's really important in life. It's the kids. It's you and me. It's family.'

'What about what you said to Megan? You told her you weren't sure if you ever really loved me. That if it weren't for Leo—'

'That was wrong of me. I can't pretend to know what life might have been like if you didn't get pregnant or Leo had lived, and I meant it when I said I wasn't sure what love was back then, but I know now. It's you and me and the kids. It's us. I'm sorry I lost the plot for a while, but I promise you I'll make it up to you.'

We stood there in silence a few moments as my thoughts tried to catch up with what was happening. His declaration had been my mantra the last twenty-two years, especially since Saxon was born—nothing meant more to me than my little family. But it was too late.

'I seriously think this is just a reaction to what's happened today,' I said finally, 'and you probably won't feel this way tomorrow but—'

'I will,' Adrian gushed, reaching for me again. 'I promise I will.'

I held up my hand, warding him off. 'Well, even if you do, I won't. I'm sorry, but you ruined us, Adrian, and I hated you for it at first, but now I'm thankful for your wake-up call. You weren't the only one at sea, I was losing myself too. I had no idea who I was outside of motherhood and marriage; you forced me to find out and I like what I discovered. You're right, we're different people than we were when we first got together, but even more importantly, I'm a different person than I was at the beginning of the year. There's no going back now.'

'Please, Ash, don't say that. At least give it some thought, some time.'

I'd never heard him sound so desperate; I don't think I'd ever even heard him beg before.

'I'm glad you're feeling better about yourself,' he added, 'but you don't need to lose *you* to save *us*. I'll be a better husband, I promise. You can get a job if that's what you still want, we'll share the housework more evenly, I'll support whatever you want to do. We can go to more counselling. We can work on reconnecting, spicing up our love life. I'll do whatever it takes. I know we can make this work—we can make *us* work again.'

'I don't think so,' I whispered, a lump swelling in my throat. This time I wasn't going to let guilt and obligation sway me. 'I don't want to have to work hard at a relationship.'

I wanted it to come easily, I wanted it to be fun like it was with Dan. Maybe it was only that way because it was new and fresh, maybe it wouldn't last, but if I couldn't have that, I'd rather be single.

Despite knowing this was the right thing for all of us, tears pooled at the corners of my eyes. Things might not have been great these last few years, but we'd made two amazing kids together and there had been plenty of good times.

'Are you sure?' Adrian blinked and it looked like he too was close to tears.

I nodded. 'Sometimes the secret to winning is knowing when to admit defeat. But you should get some help for how you've been feeling—you should go to counselling to help you with your grief and to try and find yourself again too. For your sake and that of our kids, I hope you work through your issues, but you and me, Adrian? We're done.'

His face fell but not before I saw a flash of anger there. 'I can't believe you're choosing that Dan guy over me, over our children, our *family*!'

'I'm not.' I swallowed the lump in my throat, lifted my chin high and looked him dead in the eye. 'I'm choosing *me*.'

57

Although Adrian and I had broken up months ago, my heart felt heavy as I returned to the room. I might not love him anymore, but we had kids together and I would always care about him, so I really hoped he would get the help he clearly needed.

'Aw.' Payton groaned as I prised the iPad off her long enough to help her into her nightie and brush her teeth, but then I gave it back and climbed up beside her on the bed, snuggling in as best I could, considering the moon boot. Soccer videos weren't usually my viewing of choice, but tonight I was just thankful she was okay, and I could be with her. I never wanted to let her out of my sight again.

When she finally fell asleep, after more soccer videos than I should have allowed, I was spent. Physically *and* emotionally. What a day! This whole year so far had been one drama after another.

But it hasn't been all bad.

My heart swelled at the thought of Dan. I had no idea where he was, whether he'd gone back to the Point or found somewhere to stay the night in Perth. But either way, I needed to thank him for looking after me today.

Careful not to disturb Payton, I slid my arm out from under her neck, climbed out of bed and retrieved my mobile from my bag on the floor. There were tons of messages; many from mums of Payton's classmates who must have heard about her accident and wanted to send us their thoughts, love and prayers. The sentiment warmed my heart, but I couldn't face replying to any of them right now. There was only one person I wanted to talk to and there also happened to be a number of messages from him:

I'm here if you need me. x

Hope Payton isn't in too much pain and gets a good night's sleep. x

I love you. xx

'Oh.' I gasped and pressed the phone against my chest. It was the first time either of us had used the L-word and although warm fuzziness flooded my entire body, it felt incredibly soon to be saying such things.

Did I love him?

I liked him a lot, I enjoyed spending time with him, and he'd definitely changed the way I felt about sex. Before Dan, if someone had asked me if I'd rather give up sex or chocolate, there'd have been no contest. He'd shown me that sex could be as good as it was in romance novels and yes, even better than chocolate. He always made sure I had a good time; in fact, he made it all about me—about my satisfaction, my pleasure, putting my needs before his time and time again. I hadn't even known that type of man existed.

But did I *love* him?

Maybe I did ... Maybe I *could*. Maybe it wasn't something I should worry about tonight. Not waiting a second longer, I called him.

He answered barely before the ringing began. 'Hey. How's things? How's Payton? How are *you*?'

It was *so* good to hear his voice. 'She's good, considering. She's sleeping. I'm better than I thought I'd be. Thankful she's okay. Where are you?'

'In the waiting room at the end of the corridor.'

'What? *This* corridor?' I asked, already on my way to the door. Had he overheard my conversation with Adrian?

'Uh-huh.'

I glanced at Payton—she was definitely asleep—hurried out the room and down the corridor to find Dan sitting on a plastic chair, a TV playing some Disney movie on low volume in the corner, a bag of Smiths chips on his lap.

He put the chips and his phone down on the seat beside him and stood. 'Hello.'

I ran right into his arms. 'I can't believe you stayed.'

'I wanted to be close in case you needed anything.'

'You are the sweetest man in the world, you know that?' Before he could answer, I grabbed hold of his face and kissed him hard. He tasted of barbeque chips and coffee and I couldn't think of a sweeter combo.

'You're pretty sweet yourself,' he said when I finally broke our lip-lock.

Still holding each other, we sank down on the plastic seats and my head fell against his shoulder. 'Sorry about having to deal with Charlie and Adrian. Was it awkward between you?'

I felt Dan shrug his shoulder. 'Wasn't too bad. Saxon was there, so we didn't really say much to each other. I got the impression he didn't like me much though.'

'Saxon?'

'No, silly. Adrian.'

'Ah, right. Well, that could be because he's decided he wants us to get back together and sees you as an obstacle to achieving that. Adrian is used to calling the shots and getting what he wants.'

'Hang on ...' Dan turned to meet my gaze. 'He wants you back? You didn't say yes, did you?'

I gave him a look. 'Now who's the silly one? I pretty much told him to go to hell. The countdown till our divorce is officially still on.'

'Thank fuck for that.'

I laughed and pressed my finger against his lips. 'Shh ... I don't think you're supposed to swear in a children's hospital. Can I have some of your chips?'

'Of course.' He grabbed the bag and offered it to me. 'Have you had any proper dinner?'

'No. You?'

'I'm fine. I've been stress-eating; this is my third bag of chips and I've had two bars of chocolate.' He patted his six-pack stomach. 'But do you want me to go get you some takeaway and bring it back?'

I shook my head. 'Thanks. Another packet of these will do just fine.' And it would mean him being here with me a little longer.

Dan went to the vending machine and got not one, but three different flavours. Hungrier than I realised, I devoured them all.

'Do you have somewhere you can stay tonight?' I asked, my appetite finally sated. 'I don't want you driving home in the dark.'

'Will Payton be getting out of here tomorrow?'

'I think so.'

'Well, I'll find a hotel room, then once she's settled back at home, I can drive you and Charlie back to the Point.'

His words were like an icicle stabbing right into my heart, bringing with it a reality I hadn't contemplated until that moment.

I couldn't leave Payton tomorrow. I couldn't leave her next week. I wasn't even sure I could leave her and Saxon ever again.

Trying to quash the gnawing ache in my heart, I squeezed Dan's hand. 'I'm not going back to Ragged Point.'

'What do you mean? Isn't this still Adrian's week with the kids?'

'Yes, but I can't leave Payton now.'

'Of course. She'll probably want her mum around a bit after today's trauma and ...' His voice trailed off when he registered the expression on my face. 'You're not talking about temporarily are you? You're not coming back at *all*?'

I shook my head, once again fighting tears. 'If I'd been here then Payton wouldn't be lying in there. Missing the rest of the soccer season is going to break her heart and it's all my fault.'

'That's bullshit,' Dan said. 'You can't blame yourself for this. You can't let one incident shape the rest of your life.'

'You can't understand because you don't have your own kids.'

He flinched and I immediately regretted my words.

'I'm sorry,' I rushed, 'that was uncalled for, but I wouldn't be able to relax there anymore. It was torture being so far away after hearing about Payton's accident. All I could think about was the worst—how I'd cope if she'd ...' I couldn't bring myself to finish the sentence. I'd lost one child and I never wanted to lose another. 'But it's not just Payton. Saxon needs me too and Adrian's not in the best shape mentally at the moment. I think he's got depression and maybe even addiction issues, so I need to be close and available for the kids.'

I expected Dan to say something about me not being able to wrap my children up in cotton wool, to tell me I was overreacting and being ridiculous, but instead he nodded. 'I understand, and I respect you for being such a good mum, but what about your job at the cafe and the shack?'

He didn't mention himself or the ball, but I knew he was thinking it.

'I'll miss everything about Ragged Point,' I told him. 'I've had the best time there these last couple of months, but it was only ever a stop-gap until I finished renovating the shack. Hopefully Wei and Meili will understand I can't continue now, that my family has to come first.'

He nodded. 'So the nest parenting thing is finished? You're going for full custody?'

'Yep. I guess I am.' Decision made as I said it. 'I'll move back into the house full-time and the kids will probably go to Adrian on weekends or something. We'll have to negotiate the exact details.'

'You know, there is an alternative,' Dan said after a long moment's silence. 'You could *all* come live in Ragged Point instead.'

'What?'

'You love living in the Point—you've got friends there, a job in the cafe, you enjoy working on the *Reporter* and you can continue to pursue your freelance writing from anywhere, so why not move Saxon and Payton up there? It could be the fresh start you all need.'

I let out a sigh. Although the idea appealed on a number of levels, it was also ridiculous. 'Don't you remember how much my kids hated Ragged Point? They found it dull enough for a holiday, but full-time? They'd never forgive me.'

'Can't say I don't wish otherwise,' Dan said as he pulled me into his arms, 'but I get it. I do.'

Tears prickled my eyes as I clung to him. 'So, I guess that's it then?'

He lurched back. 'What do you mean?'

'Well, my life's in Perth, yours is in Ragged Point …' It felt like a serious case of right feelings, right person, wrong time.

'Is that what you want? For us to be over?'

'Of course not. But I don't see any alternative. Saxon and Payton have to be my priority.'

'And I wouldn't expect otherwise but that doesn't mean I want to give up on us.' A slow smile formed on his face. 'Just because you have to be in Perth for now, doesn't mean we have to be over. I thought after Tessa that I was done with relationships. I didn't think I'd ever feel the same away about anyone ever again. And the thing is, I don't. What you and I have feels so much bigger than what I had in my marriage and I don't want to throw that away. Plenty of people have long-distance relationships. That's if you can even call a mere two-hundred kilometres a long distance. We can make it work.'

And there was that four-letter word—the one I didn't think belonged in a relationship.

Could I be wrong? Maybe I felt that way about a relationship with Adrian because deep down I knew my marriage had long passed its use-by date.

'While I'd love to believe that,' I said, 'I'm not sure how often I'll be able to come visit. Even on the weekends Adrian has the kids, Payton has her soccer games and I have to support—'

Dan pressed his finger to my lips. 'It's okay—I like driving, I'll come to you as often as I can, but we can worry about the logistics later. Right now, all I need to know is that you want this. That you want me.'

'I do.' My chest ached with how much I wanted him. Even if I thought Dan deserved a woman who could give her everything to him, I couldn't give him up. I couldn't give up on *us*.

'Thank fuck,' he said again, his relief clear in his grin. 'But right now, you should probably be getting back to Payton and trying to get some rest.'

Holding my hand, Dan walked me back to the room, then kissed me long and hard. The kind of kiss that didn't only curl my toes and warm my heart, but also held a promise of much more to come.

'I love you, Ashling,' he said.

'I love you too,' I whispered, suddenly knowing it to be true.

58

The following day, the hospital discharged Payton and Adrian drove us home. I can't deny things were tense between us, but although we hadn't discussed the change in custody arrangements yet and it was technically still his week with the kids, he was quite happy to leave me to take care of Payton. He asked if there was anything we needed, then promised to stop by tomorrow before going to stay with Brad.

Charlie was super concerned about Payton's moon boot and refused to leave her side when I set her up on the couch in front of the TV before microwaving some popcorn. I'd decided on a movie marathon and takeaway for dinner when Sax came home from school so we could rest and recover from yesterday's ordeal. We started with *Bend It Like Beckham* and I couldn't believe we'd never thought to show it to her before. She liked the main characters well enough but found the idea of arranged marriages horrifying.

'Does that still happen?' she asked, as if the movie was set in some long-forgotten era, not less than twenty years ago.

'In some cultures, yes,' I said, not adding that quite often these 'arranged' marriages were just as successful if not more so than the ones people chose themselves—not that I'd have ever trusted my parents to make such a choice for me. Sure, I might not have made the best match myself, but perhaps Adrian *was* right for me at that stage of my life. Maybe I was even right for him.

'That sucks,' Payton said.

I nodded. 'But we've come a long way since this movie was made. I'd like to think people aren't as racist and we're working hard for gender equality, but we can't forget where we've come from. These girls had lots more hurdles to jump through to try and play professional soccer than you and your friends do.'

It never hurt for kids to be reminded how lucky they were.

'If you or Dad tried to make me stop playing soccer like Jules' mum, I'd …' Her voice rose but I cut her off before she could finish.

'We *wouldn't*,' I said, immediately thinking of the few seconds last night when I'd contemplated moving us all to Ragged Point.

'Good.'

Payton's attention returned to the screen, but my mind stayed firmly wedged in the Point, along with my car, my clothes and my Thermomix. When on earth was I going to get them all back?

I was pondering this issue when the doorbell rang. Charlie looked torn between coming to investigate and staying to watch over Payton. In the end, his curiosity won out and he bounded ahead of me down the hallway.

It took a moment for me to collect my thoughts when I opened the door to Jedda balancing Bindi on her hip. 'What are you doing here?'

'And it's lovely to see you too,' she replied as Charlie launched himself excitedly at both of them.

I looked past her to see my wagon in the driveway.

'You drove my car down?'

She nodded as Bindi squirmed to be let down. 'And most of your stuff. You had quite a lot of it, but I couldn't fit anything else in due to this one's car seat.'

'Mum! Who is it?'

Payton's voice jolted me into action. 'Thank you. It's so good to see you.' I pulled both Jedda and Bindi into a hug and yanked them inside. 'Come see the patient.'

I closed the door and Jedda followed me into the living room.

'Surprise!'

Payton's eyes lit up and her mouth formed a large O. 'Bindi!'

Jedda laughed and let her daughter down onto the floor. She toddled over to Payton and climbed up on the couch beside her. The movie was immediately forgotten as the two of them got reacquainted.

I turned to Jedda. 'Can I get you a coffee?'

'That would be good. And, I've got cake to go with it in the car.'

While I made the drinks, Jedda went outside to retrieve the 'cake' and returned with her arms loaded up with containers.

'That looks like more than a cake,' I said.

She shrugged as she put them on the counter. 'When I heard what had happened, I thought you might be a little busy to cook. These meals and snacks should get you through a few days.'

'Hang on …' A thought struck as I handed her a mug. 'It's Friday. Who's looking after the cafe?'

'I closed it for the day. Priorities, girlfriend. Friends in need trump work every time.'

'How'd you get into the shack?'

'Security is pretty dismal without Charlie there, but don't worry, I have tricks that meant I didn't have to break a window or anything.'

I almost spat out my mouthful of coffee. 'Of course you do. But how did you know I needed my car and all my stuff?'

'Your spunky hunk of a man.' Jedda wriggled her eyebrows. 'He called me yesterday afternoon to let me know dinner was cancelled and—'

'I'm sorry,' I said, having completely forgotten. Yesterday was such a blur I couldn't even remember if I knew Dan had called her. 'I should have rung you myself.'

'Don't be ridiculous. You were concentrating on your daughter, which is what you should have been doing. But Dan kept me updated, and this morning he asked if I'd mind bringing your car down. He's going to drive us back, but said to call when we're done as he wasn't sure if your ex would be here and he didn't want to cause problems.'

'He thought about all *that*?' My heart swelled.

'Yep. I have to concede he's not a bad sort; not surprising he's not really an Emerson.'

'He told you that too?'

'Yup, we had quite the chat. I reckon you should bottle him.'

'What?'

'You know …' She cocked her head to one side as she leant back against the kitchen counter. 'Stuff him into a jar, seal the lid, then pop him onto a shelf so you can preserve and admire him. That way he won't go off with someone else or die on you! All the best men seem to do one or the other.'

I snorted. 'I'm going to miss your crazy outlook on life.'

'So, is it true you're not coming back to the Point?'

I nodded glumly, blinking back more tears as emotion welled in my throat. 'I'm sorry to desert you in the cafe and on the *Reporter*. I'll miss working for you.'

'Perhaps you don't have to give up everything.'

'What do you mean?'

'Well, working off site in the cafe would be impossible, of course,' Jedda said, 'but I'd love it if you continued to help me with the paper. I could send you articles to edit and you can do some of the layout and then send it back. That's if you want to. No pressure, but I thought it also might help fill out your resume.'

'Thank you.' I put down my coffee and threw my arms around her. 'I'd absolutely love that.'

I might have chosen to leave Ragged Point because of the kids, but that didn't mean everything was going to go back to normal. I'd keep helping Dan and the IPA as much as I could, and I'd rather spend time helping Jedda than join any school committees again. At least until I could get a proper job.

She chuckled. 'Ah, don't go getting all emotional on me. This situation is as much for my benefit as it is yours.'

'Whatever you say.'

Both smiling, we took our drinks in to join the girls and talked for another hour before Jedda called Dan to come collect them. I snuck out to see him while she and Bindi were still inside with Payton.

'Thank you so much for organising my car and everything,' I said, sliding my hands around his back and pulling him close. 'What did I do to deserve you?'

'Absolutely nothing.' He winked, then added, 'Except be your amazing self.'

I swatted him on the arm and then we kissed goodbye with the promise of phone calls and sexting to keep us busy until we saw each other again.

Who knew? For Dan, I might even be prepared to take a naked selfie.

Epilogue

Ragged Point

'You did it,' I said as I stood next to Dan in front of Bill's castle in all its restored glory. In addition to this pièce de résistance the island now boasted self-cleaning toilet blocks, numerous picnic tables (thanks to the local Men's Shed) and coin-operated barbeques. A new jetty was in the pipeline, but we didn't quite have the funds for that yet, so today the shore all around us was dotted with boats of all shapes and sizes.

Smiling down at me, Dan squeezed my hand. '*We* did it.'

He took a couple of steps towards a microphone to address the crowd gathered for the official opening of what was now a registered picnic spot. He was right, what we'd achieved here had been a team effort, one that included many in Ragged Point and beyond. The island ball had been a massive success, raising the money we needed for the structural assessment of the castle, and we'd managed to secure some grants, generous donations and people-power to achieve the actual reconstruction.

Hence there were too many people here to count—some old friends, many new and lots of faces I didn't even recognise—but all the important ones had made the short boat ride across to celebrate what had been almost two years in the making. Well, that's if you counted from the cyclone, but maybe we should be counting from the day Bill first visited the island, or the day he started on the castle, or even the day he disappeared in Vietnam.

Who knew where anyone's story really began or where it would end—it was the journey that mattered and although mine had taken a few surprising turns over the past couple of years, I didn't regret any of them.

Saying that, I still couldn't cut oranges without thinking of the day Adrian asked me about nest parenting. At the time, it felt like the end of my world, but it was simply the beginning of a new one. Since then I'd done so many things I'd never have even considered possible back then. I'd conquered life as a single mum, started a new business, had my faith restored in love and, most importantly, I'd become my *own* person again.

Dan began his speech with an acknowledgement of country, introducing and recognising the traditional custodians of Bill's island, before a little spiel about the restoration project. He thanked everyone involved individually and then all present for coming across to commemorate Bill, his amazing creation, and to celebrate the opening of a unique tourist attraction for Ragged Point.

Gesturing to the impressive structure behind him, he added, 'Coffs Harbour may have the Big Banana, and Rottnest its cute little quokkas, but not many Aussie towns can boast a castle!'

The crowd erupted into whoops and applause. When the din died down, Dan cleared his throat. 'And, speaking of the rest of the world, I want to thank Bill's daughter, my recently discovered *sister*, for making the longest journey of all to get here. Your presence means a lot to me.'

I followed Dan's gaze to two women standing in the front row. Stacy and her wife, Roxanne, had flown in especially to be part of today's proceedings. It was the first time either of them had been to Australia, but it wasn't the first time we'd met. A year ago, Dan and I had flown to San Francisco. It was my first overseas trip without my children, my first *Christmas* without them. I'd been terrified about leaving, but it had been Adrian's turn to have them anyway and they'd promised they'd manage without me if I brought back plenty of presents.

Which I did, and they were right, we'd *all* survived just fine.

I had the time of my life with Dan in San Fran and really got along well with his sister. Stacy was a lot like him—quietly funny, not materialistic, with a very nurturing nature. Over the past year or so, I'd also come to know Gemma and Ben quite well. When the truth about Dan's parentage had come out and Stephen Emerson had threatened to disown him, Gemma and Ben had shown their true colours.

And it turned out those colours weren't bad at all. They'd basically threatened their father right back, telling him that if he cut Dan off from the family business, he'd lose them both as well. I'd thought it a risky bluff, but it worked. At least in that Dan hadn't had to choose between the job he loved and the island he adored. Not that Stephen and Apinya had come to show their support today. They had to be the only locals of Ragged Point not here—even Jedda had braved the seas to come—but perhaps I couldn't blame Stephen for that. If Adrian had had an affair while we were married, I probably wouldn't want to celebrate his mistress or her achievements either.

Speaking of my *ex*-husband (yes, now well and truly official), I'm pleased to report he's doing well. He started counselling just after Payton's accident, gave up the grog and was spending quality time with his children once again. He'd even bought a second-hand road bike for Sax and the two of them now went on regular rides. Of course, he'd hoped all these things would make me change my mind about us getting back together, but once he finally accepted this wasn't going to happen, he moved out of Brad's and into a small three-bedroom duplex not too far from our family home.

Theoretically—according to our custody arrangement—the kids now stayed there every second weekend and went for dinner Wednesday nights, but they also dropped round whenever they felt like hanging out with their father.

And, instead of pining for my babies as I once might have, I'd made the most of those weekends, escaping to Ragged Point to finish what I'd started on the shack, which was where Stacy and Roxanne were currently staying. We'd wanted them to have their own space and privacy, but also because me, the kids, Hayley, Wei and their adorable baby, Alby, were staying in the glass monstrosity with Dan.

Our American visitors had gushed when they'd first seen the shack and I had glowed accordingly. The end result was even better than I'd imagined. Meili and Wei had been over the moon, the shack had been fully booked since registering it on Airbnb and had almost all 5-star ratings. I'd written an article about the transformation and it had been published in an actual print magazine. The cheeky local possum had not only featured in my story but also become the resident pet, living between the trees out the front and in the special nest Dan had made. Guests were informed of its presence and encouraged to leave pieces of cut-up fruit on the porch rail.

Payton loved the possum so much she wanted me to create an Instagram account for it. I hadn't admitted it to her yet, but I was seriously giving it some thought! That's if I could find the time in my busier-than-ever life. Because, you see, although the print by-line had given me a massive thrill, the real reward had been the transformation of the shack itself.

It had reminded me how much I loved home renovation.

Even more than I did tinkering with words on a keyboard. The moment I realised this, I decided to make my passion my livelihood. This had been a massive leap of faith, but with the encouragement of family and friends it was paying off.

Now, although I still helped Jedda with the *Reporter* and had sold a few more freelance articles in the early days to help pay the bills—including a big feature about Bill and the island—I'd all but given up writing and earned a reasonable living helping people renovate and redecorate instead. Dan and I were about to buy another rundown old house in Ragged Point to do up and sell. Apparently, this was called flipping houses, but whatever you called it, I absolutely couldn't wait.

Of course, this was going to require me spending more time up here than every second weekend, so Adrian and I had decided to give the whole nest-parenting thing another go and this time I felt confident in our ability to succeed.

We'd worked hard, not only on ourselves over the last two years, but also together, to make sure our interactions were as amicable as possible for our children. And looking at Payton and Saxon today, I was thankful and relieved that it appeared to have worked. Sure, we still had the odd hiccup, but mostly they'd come out the other side of our divorce relatively unscathed.

Sax's grades had improved again and now that he was just about to start Year 11 he was stoked he'd no longer have to move his stuff between two houses. My eyes drifted to where he stood a few feet away taking photos with Jedda's camera. He'd developed a keen interest in photography on his trips to the Point this past year, and thus had been charged with taking photos for the *Reporter*, a job he took very seriously.

I was so proud of the man he was growing into, and Payton had really matured as well. Right now, she was trying to entertain Alby so that Hayley and Wei could listen to Dan's speech, but that wasn't a hardship for her at all. Although still passionate about soccer, she'd become obsessed with babies. She was way too clucky for a twelve-year-old, always going on about how she wanted to be a mum. It had started with Bindi, who she still couldn't get enough of, and then she'd fallen head over heels the moment Alby was born.

Honestly, who could blame her? Born with a shock of jet-black hair like his dad's and Hayley's mischievous grin, he truly was the cutest little thing you'd ever seen, but also already a handful.

'Alby, no!' Payton hissed, as he tried to shove a handful of sand into his mouth.

Wei caught me smiling and grinned back. Now that he was part of the family—even if there wasn't a simple word for my ex-husband's sister's-boyfriend, our kids were cousins—I'd got to know him a lot better and I couldn't be more thrilled for Hayley. I'd been wrong to judge them on him being so much younger than her—they were absolutely perfect together.

And, they weren't the only ones.

Once again, my eyes drifted to Dan who stood proudly at the front, almost coming to the end of his speech, which I knew by heart myself because I'd already heard him rehearse it numerous times. As if he sensed me looking, his gaze met mine and I gave him a thumbs up.

He smiled back and I knew I'd made the right decision.

Some relationships were definitely worth doing whatever it took to make them 'work'.

Acknowledgements

As always thanks to everyone at Harlequin Australia for everything you do to bring my books to life, with special mentions to the following: Sue Brockhoff, for having faith that I can turn the seed of an idea into something worth reading. My editing power team, Annabel Blay, Dianne Blacklock and Julia Knapman for bringing out the best in *Flying the Nest*. Adam Van Rooijen and Natika Palka for working so enthusiastically on the publicity campaign. Darren Kelly and the wonderful sales team across Australia and New Zealand. And last but by no means least, to Christine Armstrong for her stunning cover design and to Alice Lindstrom for the artwork.

Thanks also to my wonderful agent, Helen Breitwieser, for being a great reader, listener and supporter—I love our chats and your insight into my books.

To all my wonderful writing friends—you know who you are—who keep me sane, help me brainstorm ideas, talk through plot problems, celebrate when the occasion requires and commiserate if necessary, as well. I wouldn't be without any of you. Extra special thanks to Beck Nicholas, Anthea Hodgson and Brooke Testa, all who read and provided feedback on early drafts of this book.

Lots of love and gratitude to my family—to Mum, Craig, Hamish, Lachlan and Archie—for being my biggest champions through the highs and lows of this crazy life. I'm sorry I get grumpy sometimes when the books don't feel like they're working but thanks for always believing that they will.

To my readers Sonja Altmann for letting me borrow your gorgeous dog for the character of Charlie in this book and to Lisa Mansfield for suggesting the name Brewed Awakening for Jedda's cafe.

And finally, thanks to you guys for buying my books, reading them, reviewing them, raving about them to your friends and messaging me to let me know my stories have touched your heart in some way. It's knowing you're holding out for my next book that keeps me writing.

talk about it

Let's talk about books.

Join the conversation:

facebook.com/harlequinaustralia

@harlequinaus

@harlequinaus

harpercollins.com.au/hq

If you love reading and want to know about our authors and titles, then let's talk about it.